Published in the United States by Clay Urn Publishing LLC,
2501 Chatham Rd. Suite R, Springfield, IL, 62704
www.clayurnpublishing.com

Second Edition, 2026
ISBN 979-8-9905036-1-8 - Hardcover
ISBN 979-8-9905036-0-1 - Paperback

Cover Art: Adrian Baxter: www.facebook.com/adrianbaxterillustration

THE
CHIMERA
SNARE

FRAGMENTS

S & E BLACK

Content Transparency

Alchohol Use, Smoking, Profanity, Violence, Gore, Body Horror,
Death, Sexual Situations, Sexual Abuse & Implied Sexual Abuse

No part of this story was produced with the use of generative AI.
We hold firm in our belief that to truly heed the call of creative
will is to commit to a journey that involves passion, vision, and
human inspiration—all traits that a soulless machine cannot
replicate.

Stay human.

Enjoy the process.

Keep art alive.

Music is one of the most important facets of our lives. It kept us going when nothing else could, and fueled our journey with inspiration and energy. Our series is dedicated in part to the people who have inspired us on our creative journey and fueled our passion. Hails and eternal thanks to the following bands/artists, in alphabetical order:

Abigail Williams, Agalloch, Ahab, Alcest, Altar of Plagues, Amenra, Asbestoscape, Bell Witch, Bella Morte, Bongripper, Caspian, Clouds, Cult Of Luna, Diary of Dreams, Emperor, Enslaved, Esoteric, Evoken, Eye of Solitude, Fen, Frostmoon Eclipse, Funeral, God Is An Astronaut, God Module, Hammock, Heilung, Herbst9, Katatonia, Krohm, Krzysztof Drabikowski's Batushka, Les Discrets, Leviathan (USA), Light Field Reverie, Lights Out Asia, Lords of the Manor, Lycia, Mephorash, Mogwai, Mono (Japan), Moonlit Sailor, Morgion, Mournful Congregation, My Dying Bride, Nhor, Nine Inch Nails, Orgy, Pelican, Rapture (Finland), Russian Circles, Schammasch, Shape of Despair, Signal Hill, Swallow the Sun, Sylvaine, The Howling Void, This Will Destroy You, Towards Darkness, Un, Unto Ashes, Wolvennest, Wolves in the Throne Room, Wumpscut, Velvet Acid Christ, Zeraphine, Zeromancer.

We would like to send special thanks to our panel of beta readers in alphabetical order:

Aimee Cozza
Donna Reidhaar
Green Neen
Jeanna Snell
Killy Flux
Klara Pelcl
Lady Alchemy
Lauren Barkell
Lauren Lujo @thereaderandthebeast
Lynn Sweetman-Cochran
Sabia
Suzy B
Tara Porphy
Tory Keith

Your feedback has been crucial in the final stages of development and we greatly appreciate the time you spent providing your honest thoughts.

A special thank you Genevieve Baker for your insight and lending help with the blurb.

We would like to express our deepest appreciation to the following folks who supported our Kickstarter project and made it a success. Thank you for believing in the project and in us. Without you, we couldn't have launched "Fragments" the way we envisioned.

Our backers (in chronological order):

Maša Absec
Amanda Eschmeyer
Bobbi Iszler
The Creative Fund
Trish Schneider
Alexandra Corrsin
Henry Partida
StacieDee
Max & Dayja W.
Tom & Virginia Steuber
Fam
Justise B.
Life Schneider
Stacey Encinas
Lola Badmus
Chris & Sondra Hutson
Scott Bryant
Rachel Luangphonh
Christina Raiburn
Michael Bower
unpr3d1ctab13
Bianca-Tatjana
Lydia & Shawn
Tracy Dale
Raymond Howard
Amy Hubert
Debbie Sultemeier /
Fredericksburg Essentials

Greg Jenkins
Gilberto Vargas
Susie Bryant
Christina Pfaff
Parsley42
PyeLokie4ever
Studio Moonfall
The Petty's
Courtney Vida
Carly Rios
Stephanie Neitzel
DiMari
Kathy Matysek
Jerald Wegehenkel
Allison Stroud
D. Cesna
Lily G.
Liam Victor Sherlock
Pam Billeci
Sharon G. Harris
Jojo & Jeff
Michael Johnson
Jen & Gus
Dennis Bärtschi
Emily
Lani Jenkins

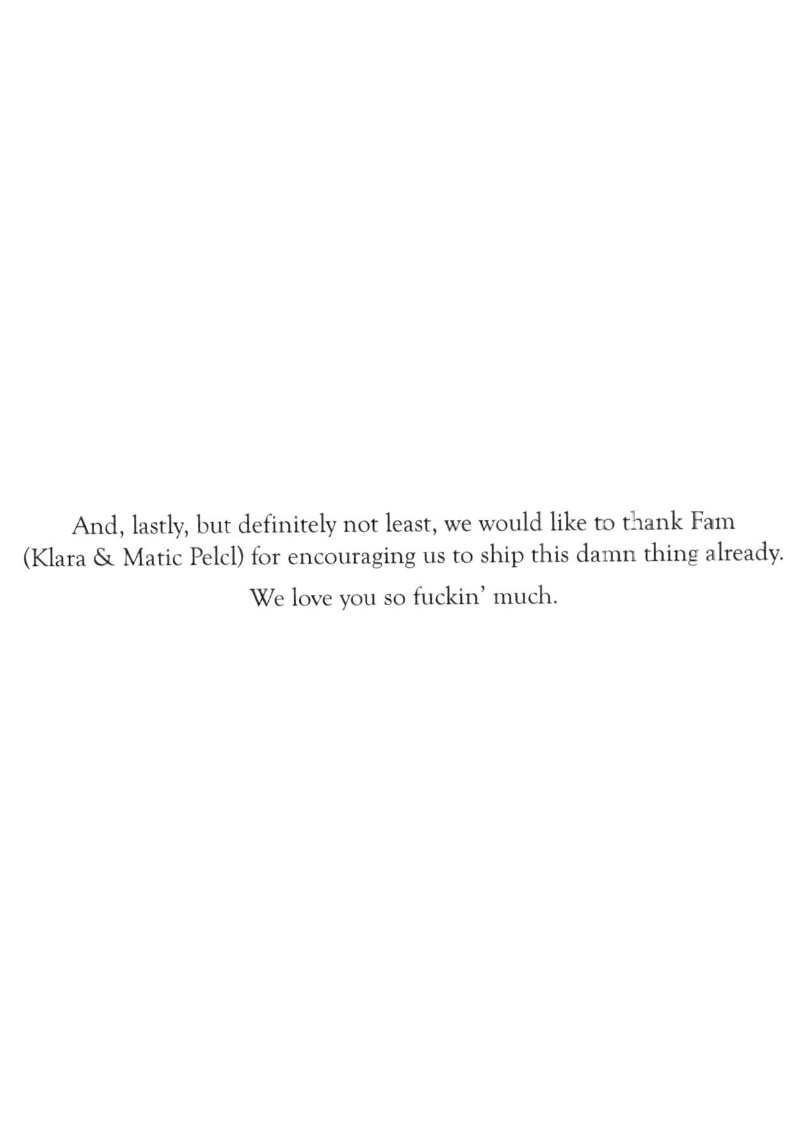

And, lastly, but definitely not least, we would like to thank Fam
(Klara & Matic Pelcl) for encouraging us to ship this damn thing already.

We love you so fuckin' much.

Chimera noun

chi·me·ra

/kīˈmirə,kəˈmirə/

The term chimera has come to describe any mythical or fictional creature with parts taken from various animals or to describe anything composed of very disparate parts or perceived as wildly imaginative, implausible, or dazzling.

The sight of a chimera is perceived as an omen of disaster.

CHAPTERS

PROLOGUE

THE WAY OF LAYLANAILEE

Shiny strands of long black hair whipped over Von's face as he settled into his dreamwalk. With anxious, dashing eyes, he scanned the bleak landscape surrounding him until the silhouette of a woman in a flowing white nightgown slipped out from behind a thicket of knotted deadwood. Navaryn, whose essence he had relentlessly tracked, clutched the sides of her arms and watched the dense fog roll through petrified tree branches.

As she traipsed ahead, perplexed by the encompassing desolation, Von released a tense, warm breath into the air. Though so close, she felt just as far away as she did since the fateful day she was banished from Celestine. No matter how helpless an endeavor it seemed, he always returned to her side, determined to free her from the cursed diablerie that bound her.

Von eased his rigid posture and set out toward her, pondering a new approach that might trigger the awakening of her memories. His rugged boots crunched over the uneven terrain and filled the air with eager disharmony as he descended a low-rolling hill.

Startled, Navaryn turned towards the racket of tumbling rubble behind her. "Who are you?" she sternly uttered. "And where am I?"

Her inquiries felt like a sword to the gut, even though he knew she wasn't to blame for her predicament. The gentle smile he wore failed to mask the depth of heartache that bled through his eyes. Strength wasn't something he typically battled with, but his waning patience and self-doubt persistently tested his fortitude.

Once through the maze of deadwood, he replied, "This is what controls you."

Confused, she uttered, "This wretched emptiness?"

"Yes. You've shown me this very place."

"Do I ... know you?"

Von nodded. Though it was typically difficult to interact with her inside the dreamwalk, their conversation prompted him with an idea of how to part the veil over her memories. He lifted his hand towards the sky and evoked the shimmery apparition of a crimson-tinged moon.

"This is Hirunae," he revealed as her eyes widened. "The triad's crown. Don't you remember?"

"I-I wish I could. It's beautiful."

As she gazed at the looming satellite, Von hoped to find the familiar longing in her eyes. Yet, no matter how lovingly she watched Hirunae trail above her, emptiness sat within her distant, hazel irises.

"It feels like ages since I last watched you admire it. I've missed that."

Embarrassed by his confession, Navaryn looked at him and said, "How do you know me? Tell me who you are."

Von hesitated. He had answered the same questions in various ways, yet she never remembered.

"Tell me," she pressed. "Please?"

Frustrated and yearning for an outcome different than all the times before, he took her by the shoulders and proclaimed, "My name is Von. I *need* you to remember me and what's surrounding us."

"How?! I don't even know who I am."

Von's gaze hardened. "You're Navaryn! You're a warrior and guardian of Celestine! Come on. You're stronger than this! You have to fight to remember what happened," he urged. "It's the only way I can bring you back."

His passionate declaration only sowed further confusion. "Bring me back to what?!" she shouted as she tried to wriggle out of his grip.

"To Celestine. To your home!"

"This doesn't make any sense!"

Von pulled her in close. "You *have* to remember. I won't stop until you do. *Everything* depends on that." As he revealed more details of her forgotten past, his red irises began to glow.

Fearful at first, Navaryn found herself fixated on the strange comfort she felt while looking into his eyes. Her expression relaxed as a soothing, weightless sensation overtook her, a feeling that had eluded her since it all began. Time slowed to a crawl, and Von's voice dampened until it became inaudible, as if she were submerged underwater. She continued to study his face through his sentimental testimonial, placing her hands on his cheeks.

Her unexpected gesture, a gentle smile which parted her lips, stopped him in his tracks. As she motioned to speak the thoughts that filled her heart, a vibrant light ignited inside her throat. Glowing, golden pink orbs wisped from her mouth in place of words, blotting out Von's bewildered face. Suddenly, her feet gave out from under her.

The apparition of Hirunae quickly dissolved as Von shifted to catch Navaryn. In a near instant, a moment before he took her into his arms, the ground between their feet broke open. A powerful force pulled her through the rift, and hungry, white light devoured everything in its wake.

Von dropped to his knees at the escarpment's crumbling edge, then yelled, "Take my hand!"

Navaryn reached out for him, but she was already out of range. With no way to reverse their distance, she succumbed to her heaving breaths. Tears pooled in her eyes and left her purblind in a coffin of cementing light.

Despite Von's earnest attempt for a different outcome, the thieving light prevailed yet again. As she continued to float away into the void, he pulled back and slammed his fists into the dirt. While belting a barrage of obscenities, he tried earnestly to preserve the thread of hope that kept him stitched together. But the unbearable idea of hope coaxed him to seek comfort in the blissful fever of rage.

Von pulled his abraded hands out of the dirt and bellowed. From fingertip to forearm, his skin blackened with fragments of flashing ebon shards, and thick, ridged claws emerged from his nailbeds. Without hesitation, he tore ribbons through the obsidian-like formations into flesh and vein, pelting Navaryn with blood as she fell away.

Von's belting energy continued to surface. Thick and smoky bone broke through the vertebrae along his arched back, spiking high before it coiled towards his ripping, transforming flesh. As he roared, his jaw dislocated and morphed into a new structure that split his lips. Massive clumps of muscle exploded over his frame, and razor-sharp teeth pierced through his gums in both directions. Beads of sweat gathered atop the pulsing veins rising beneath his skin, and four broad, unevenly twisted horns slid out of his head, completing his hideous transformation.

Amidst the ruins of Von's perceived failure, Navaryn studied his menacing form, kneeling at the cliff above. Focused upon his hauntingly familiar crimson gaze, a disorienting vision overtook her.

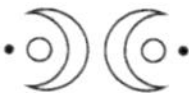

Navaryn sauntered down a stone hallway drenched in an amber glow from the rows of tapers that lit the way. She carried a bottle of wine she had picked up before her visit and was smiling at the label, almost entranced by her delight.

"You will never guess what I found at Teagan's—"

Upon finding the obliterated wooden door to Benson's study, her jovial gait suddenly stopped. Fragments of broken viridian glass scattered across the stone floor after the bottle fell from her hand. The sweet yet pungent aroma of wine snaked up to her nostrils, but did nothing to break her senses from the terrifying sight before her. Standing askew with her mentor's throat in his grasp was a tall, misshapen beast with crooked horns atop its head, clothed in garments bursting at the seams.

Navaryn took hold of the dagger strapped to her thigh. As she swiftly unsheathed it, the sound of metal slipping past the scabbard caught the beast's attention. Strands of bubbling saliva dribbled off his long, razor-sharp teeth as he turned his head. Benson's body went limp under the eerie glow of his red eyes.

Enraged, she charged the beast with her dagger gripped tightly.

Anticipating a clumsy, lumbering response was a mistake, as he effortlessly maneuvered through her advances, then backhanded her into the rafters of the three-story library. Winded but still alert, she desperately reached for anything that could break her fall to no avail. Unable to reorient herself for a proper landing, she crashed atop the stone floor with her dagger clanking just outside of her reach. The beast watched her wince and squirm while she collected herself, then gave Benson one last glance before tossing him to the side.

As the beast bolted her way, Navaryn snapped to her senses and scrambled to retrieve her dagger. With clenched teeth and trembling muscles, she darted toward him with a wrenching grimace, swung her blade against his impending fist, and then rolled beneath the remainder of his follow-through. A spray of red flicked onto the floor as she quickly hopped to her feet. While he recoiled, she leaped onto his back and plunged her dagger into his shoulder. The beast blustered and flailed until she eventually lost her footing, yet she refused to dismount until she reclaimed her blade. Before she found the proper leverage on a large clump of writhing muscle at her shins, he reached behind his back and sank his claws into her thigh, then hurled her into the bookshelf at the far end of the room.

Navaryn readied herself in a defensive stance while Benson struggled to his feet. Grateful he was still alive, she urged him to flee as the beast prepared to charge her once again. The dagger, pointed at the creature in her line of sight, glinted over a jagged edge where his blood had crystallized. The peculiar characteristic fascinated Navaryn, though she broke away from her bewilderment in time to catch his approach.

Focused and determined to prevail, she conjured a ball of fire within her palm, then lobbed the augmenting current into his face. As he howled and stumbled backward, Navaryn clasped her dagger above her head and lunged for the pulsing rope-like artery on his neck. Though distracted, he was keen to her intent and swiftly thwarted her downward stab. The pair battled against each other's leverage and will until Navaryn's knees buckled under his weight. While pinned to the ground, he tore away her dagger and then pummeled her with his fist and elbow until her welted, bloody face no longer cried out.

Dazed and on the verge of losing consciousness, Navaryn cleared her bloody airways with forceful coughing. Before she could manage a restorative breath, the beast snatched her by the hair and reeled her face into his. Acrid vapor rushed through his teeth and made her puffy, swollen face twist. Relishing her distress, his putrid grin stretched and peeled his blistery cheeks open. Certain that he aimed to claim her life, Navaryn's vision quaked with white as she struggled to break free.

Beneath the ominous silence that befell the room, the beast suddenly released his grip. Puzzled by his unexpected yield but not intending to waste the opportunity, she wriggled out from underneath him and reclaimed her dagger. The overwhelmingly dark, frenzied energy within him soon calmed, and as the uncertain moments passed, the haunting glow retracted back into his irises.

While Navaryn remained locked in thought, a strange, glowing blue smoke slithered along the ground, coiled around the creature's limbs, and robbed him of control before he could react. As soon as his menacing energy resurfaced, his glowing red eyes reignited.

Navaryn traced the flow of the glowing smoke to find its source, aghast to discover it was pouring out of Benson's outstretched palms. The conjuration continued to wrap around the rest of the creature's body, constricting his misshapen limbs and strangling his breath. Panicked, he tried to break free with such feverish exertion that it appeared the veins on his neck would burst. Not long after his glowing eyes found Navaryn again, he gave up the fight and succumbed to his restraints. Immediately, the smoke surged into his body and turned his flesh transparent.

The room quaked as a series of indiscernible markings fell from the ceiling. Brilliant sparks quivered and formed a sizable double circle of light on the ground surrounding the creature. As shadows whipped across the room, Benson called for Navaryn's retreat. Four ropes of light emerged from the symbol and took hold of the beast's fading limbs, quartering him to the ground. Following a blinding flash, he was gone. As the glowing smoke dissipated, Navaryn inspected the scorched sigil on the ground left behind by the Snare.

Silence overtook the study again, and Benson ambled over to

his desk to rest himself after his demanding conjuration. Navaryn approached him but was quickly reminded of the deep gashes on her thigh as she stumbled. Although the steady flow of blood was concerning, she could not pull her eyes away from the thick crimson that drenched her leg. Entranced by the metallic stench wafting in the air, she pressed into her wound and then slid her slick fingers together, detecting sharp particles of the beast's crystallized blood.

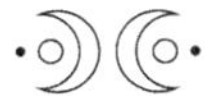

The brilliance of a red halo retracted alongside Navaryn's turbulent memory. Suspended in weightless white light, she watched the creature's despondent glowing eyes fade. Inside her radiant durance, Navaryn unlocked her fingers to find her hands bespattered in sparkling red shards. As she gazed upon them, the seed of a deep and painful longing sprouted in its rightful place within her heart. She could feel the incalculable distance between them, and though the task seemed nearly impossible, she knew Von would stop at nothing to reach her once again.

1

THE KNOWN

Beep, beep, beep, beep …

Rayshell squished a pillow over her head, but the muffled sound seeped through.

Beep, beep, beep, beep …

Grumbling, she turned off the alarm and rolled onto her side. The somniferous warmth trapped within her blankets coerced her eyes to close again.

"Ray!" yelled her younger brother as he pounded on her bedroom door. "Wake up!"

She mumbled to herself inside her dark room and reluctantly opened her eyes. The alarm clock's glowing red numbers were blurry and unreadable, but she could tell she had overslept.

"I'm coming in," he warned just before he turned the doorknob.

Rayshell pulled the blankets over her head and proceeded to groan once Jakobe drew the curtains. Her naked feet dangled off the bed and met the chill of the late autumn air.

"Get up, Ray. We're gonna miss the bus. You know Mom will be pissed if we're not gone before she gets home."

Rayshell squirmed, then finally rose. Her wild, ashy brown locks were just as bent and crooked as her scowl. She promptly gathered an outfit from her messy drawers, then walked down the hall and into the bathroom.

"You'd better wait until tonight to take a shower! There's no time."

Rayshell flicked on the light. "*Fine*," she griped, turning to her mascara-smudged reflection in the mirror.

She shut the door, then turned on the faucet, and just as she reached for the soap, a small spot of red under her eye caught her attention. In a hot breath, she paused, recalling the beast from her dream, and leaned towards her reflection with bent eyebrows.

Jakobe looked through the living room window just as their bus passed by. "Hurry up, Ray! Now we're gonna have to walk to the next bus stop so Mom doesn't know we're late."

The way his voice trailed in and out gave Rayshell the impression he was turning about the living room, gathering her scattered school books to pack into her backpack.

"Did you hear me?!"

Ray jolted away from her reflection, then quickly lathered the soap.

"Ugh, I shouldn't have let you sleep this long."

"No one said to wait for me," she hissed back, then proceeded to rinse and then dry her face.

Goosebumps flocked her arms and legs as she disrobed. Shivering, she fumbled with her clothes and quickly dressed. As she fastened her bra, she discovered a barrage of tiny, shimmering red droplets.

"No fucking way. It *can't* be ...." Rayshell whispered while she ran her fingers over the oddly sharp textures. She slid her fingernails underneath one and peeled it off her skin. Under the bathroom light, the thin scraping sparkled brilliantly. Holding her breath, she scratched the rest off until they became invisible among the dust and hair strands on the floor. As she looked at her reflection, a warm and prickly sensation expanded in her chest. Moments later, she was seized by a vision.

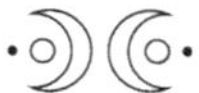

The final rays of daylight cut through waving, distant tree branches. Navaryn stood in the middle of a clearing studded with various shredded targets and markers, and a ruby-hilted sword jabbed in the dirt by her feet. Her arms trembled as she brought a pack of water to her lips for a drink. Off in the shadows by her side was an older man on his knees, assembling a large piece of equipment. While he toiled, Navaryn reset herself and then walked through a set of fearsome maneuvers and offensive strikes until she ran out of breath again. Out of the corner of her eye, she watched the man come her way.

"All finished over there, Fallon?"

After a gratifying exhale, he announced, "Just finished settin' it up."

"Great! That means you're free. How's about a sparrin' match real quick before callin' it a night?"

Fallon, nearly defeated, stood with his hands on his hips. "But, you've been here all day, Navaryn. Surely a young lady such as yourself has something more interesting to do this evening other than train."

Navaryn sheathed her sword, her expression contorted. They looked at one another as a symphony of crickets sounded, and soon lost themselves in laughter.

"Good one. You almost had me fooled there."

Fallon's chuckle waned as he collected a few chunks of splintered wood from the ground and tossed them into one of the nearby fire pits.

"So, how about it?" asked Navaryn as she watched him call the pit to flame with a graceful dance of his hand.

"Oh, well, I didn't think you were actually serious." Fallon sighed as Navaryn's smile grew. "Not tonight, Nav. I'm still plenty spent from our session this morning." He anticipated the same pleading eyes she looked at him with, so he added, "Why don't you test out my new piece of equipment? I was hoping to break it in tomorrow, but you can have the honors."

"Really?!" Navaryn clamored excitedly.

"Yeah, sure. This one is for practicing close-quarters combat."

"Ah, like the wooden dummies you used to have?"

"Eh, kinda. This is a new design of mine, built to handle much more impact. And there are a couple of new features those dummies never had. But I'll let you try to unlock them on your own if you're able."

"Consider your challenge accepted," she chimed with a grin.

The peachy sky above them slowly settled into a deep cobalt blue. Fallon lit an array of fire pits surrounding the training yard while Navaryn quickly cleared the grounds of the rest of her wreckage, whistling an upbeat tune.

"I'm thinking about fixin' something to eat. You interested?"

Navaryn nodded as she threw a bundle of hacked wood into the fire pit at her side. "Sure! I'm starving."

"Great. I'll come get you when it's ready," said Fallon. He headed for the front entrance of his shop but stopped after a few paces. "Oh, and uh, go a bit easy on it, just in case. I don't want you to wreck it before I get a chance to try it out."

Excitedly, Navaryn shuffled to the dark piece of equipment while Fallon continued through the threshold. There were several pivot points and precariously positioned protrusions encompassing it. She stepped into one of the modest openings and studied each element in the firelight before making her first move. With a focused mind and curious eyes, Navaryn knocked one of the wooden arms to the side. The piece of equipment rotated at its corresponding joint, triggering a series of reactions. In addition to the components that spun her way from the opposite side, a hinge was unlatched, releasing an extension by her shins. Navaryn yipped as the protrusion belted her with a zing of energy. She quickly gathered her concentration and deflected the series of rotating arms that came her way.

"What the hell is this thing?" she barked to herself as she stepped into her next defensive stance.

Another hinge unlatched, and soon Navaryn was swarmed by even more dashing arms. She quickly realized that the energy cracked more potently the harder she hit them. After working through her initial clumsiness, her defensive strikes transitioned into steady and postured offensive attacks. The variety of wooden arms slapped against the fluid movements of her tight limbs. As she studied the pivoting sectors, a glowing white haze veiled over her eyes, and her vision shook. An eager and almost menacing smile quickly cut across her face. She tightened her muscles and braced herself with heightened intensity. Her nerves surged with pain, yet she didn't let the sensation overtake her. After a few more rotations, she discovered the point in the equipment's complex pattern where the extensions reset on their hinges. One by one, she knocked them up and over as the tiny gaps emerged.

Sweating and winded, Navaryn stepped away from the trainer. The flickering white in her eyes receded, but her prominent smile remained. She raised her trembling arms, clenched her hands into fists, and reveled in her short-lived triumph.

The sound of a timid footstep cut through the quiet air, and every one of her hairs stood on end. She instinctively dropped to the ground and then swept her leg behind her. Wasting no time, she rushed atop the intruder and mounted him.

"Geez, Navaryn!" clamored a young man after he dodged her crashing fist.

"Kumiko!?"

Firelight reflected off his discontented lavender eyes. "Did you *not* see my Parafall?!"

Navaryn frowned back at him and hissed, "No."

"Seems I need to finally just accept this type of greeting from you," he grumbled and wriggled out from underneath her.

"How many times have I told you *not* to sneak up on me?"

As Kumiko dusted off his backside, he answered, "And how many times have I reassured you that you don't need to be on such high alert?"

Navaryn's face fell flat as she motioned to the piece of equipment.

"Oh, come on, Nav. You know as well as I do that you do this to me more than just when you're training." He followed after her dragging footsteps, listing the instances. "You do this to me in your garden, in your sunroom, at Teagan's ...."

Navaryn couldn't help but snicker.

"Why can't you just relax?"

"I've told you before. Maintaining an upper hand is important."

"Yeah, in battle. Not in the middle of a book. Or a pint."

Navaryn sat on the stone border of the largest fire pit. "I can't help my instincts."

Kumiko sat beside her and took her by the hand. The way their fingers intertwined felt dreadfully awkward and uncomfortable. He scratched the back of his head and listened to the choir of crickets and crackling embers.

"It's getting late," said Kumiko as he looked at the first stars in the early evening sky. "And I bet you're famished after all your training. I can cook you dinner."

Navaryn ran her boot over chunks of rubble as she responded, "Actually, Fallon is already making something for me."

Kumiko tried to hide his disappointment as he replied, "I see."

"And I still want to beat on that piece of equipment for a while if he'll let me. That thing is amazing. Hey, maybe he'll let you have a turn. He just set it up today."

"Eh, I'm not really in the mood for more training. I was hoping we could have a nice dinner together and relax for a change."

"We can do dinner tomorrow."

Kumiko gently pulled his hand away and muttered, "I guess we'll just have to see."

"What do you mean by that?" she asked as he stood.

Kumiko shook his head and replied, "Never mind. I'll see you tomorrow."

Navaryn crossed her arms and watched Kumiko walk toward the forest line in the same direction where the sun had set. A strange feeling of relief came over her as he gradually disappeared into the shadows.

·◐)(◑·

Suddenly, the front door to the apartment flew open, and an irritated voice cut through the quiet air. "There'd better be a good reason why you two are still here."

"Hi, Mom," Jakobe said as she entered the living room. As a kind gesture, he walked outside and locked her bike to the metal railing in front of the door. "How was work?"

Ignoring her son's feeble attempt to divert the conversation, she continued, "I see you have your backpack on, so why aren't you on your way to school?"

"Well, I was waiting for Rayshell, but she wouldn't wake up."

Her voice wasn't any less irritated as she asked, "What do you mean? Is she okay?"

"I think so. She's getting ready now."

The commotion coming from the living room pulled Rayshell out of the vision. She turned on the faucet, wet a rag, and quickly worked to remove the last remnants of red from her neck and chest.

Elizabeth grabbed a bottle of water and sat in the armchair closest to the front door. Just as she did every morning, she lit a cigarette and closed her weary eyes.

"Any luck with the search?" Jakobe asked, referring to the list of rentals she had been combing through.

Elizabeth tilted her head back as she exhaled. "It's been rough. But I've got an appointment this Saturday for a house downtown. It seems like it's in a pretty good neighborhood." She opened the bottle of water and took a long drink.

Dressed in her favorite black and red plaid outfit, Rayshell opened the bathroom door down the hall from where her mother sat, still brushing her teeth. Once they made eye contact, Elizabeth shook her head.

"Why do you have to do this?"

Rayshell spat in the sink and continued brushing. "Do what?" she asked over the rotating bristles.

"Being late for school. This is the one thing I count on you both to do while I'm out busting my ass. The last thing I need is the school on my back again because you can't be responsible."

"I didn't do it on purpose."

Elizabeth grumbled. "You are always late, Rayshell. So get your ass to the bus stop."

"Rushing ain't gonna help anything now," she replied while tilting her head back, fighting with the foam in her mouth. "We still got like fifteen minutes 'til another bus comes." She spit into the sink again and rinsed her mouth out.

Elizabeth snuffed her cigarette. "I don't care if it's five minutes or fifty. Get to the damn bus stop, *please*."

Jakobe leaned against the cold wooden door jamb and stared bitterly at Rayshell while she grabbed her backpack. After hastily throwing it over her shoulder, she reached into the front pouch and pulled out her pack of Lights.

"Crap," she whispered, then closed the lid.

"Are you ready yet?" Jakobe asked impatiently.

Rayshell looked at him with accusing eyes and shouted, "Oh, shut up! You only act like this when Mom's here."

"*Both* of you, *knock it off!*" their mother roared, taking turns staring at her kids with fierce eyes. She paused and took a breath. "I'm exhausted, and I don't need to hear this. Just get to school. I need to get some sleep."

Both Rayshell and Jakobe reset their attitudes with wide eyes, recognizing that, for some odd reason, their mother's presence seemed to incite their argument.

"Sorry," said Rayshell as she bent down to kiss her cheek. "I love you, Mom."

With an aggravated look still affixed, Elizabeth closed her eyes and replied, "I love you, too."

"I'm running low on cigarettes. Can I have one of yours?"

"Geez, Rayshell! Really?"

Rayshell grinned as she opened the lid to her mother's pack of menthols. She took out two, then closed the lid.

Jakobe rolled his eyes and walked out the door. "I love you, Mom."

"Love you too, Jakobe. Get to school safe—the both of you. I'll call and let them know you'll be late."

Rayshell shut the door behind her and shuffled to catch up to her brother. "What's your problem?" she asked as he shook his head.

"You're impossible," he grumbled as he turned his attention to the upcoming flight of rickety stairs.

"Am not," she said, teasing his words with a slight chuckle. "Just a little unbearable, is all."

The morning sky was gray with thick clouds standing adamant against the rising sun. Dead brown leaves fluttered in the parking lot, still damp from last night's rain. Rayshell and Jakobe carefully descended the slippery stairs and past the row of apartments, following the awning and dilapidated rain gutter.

"Mom's gonna be checking out another place this weekend," Jakobe muttered.

"You don't sound happy, though."

"I'm just tired of getting my hopes up," he languished while stepping through a puddle. "It seems like we'll never move out of this shit-sty. I miss our old home."

"Well, no sense in being sad over shit you can't control. Things are changing out here big time. Hell, I can't blame the landlords for selling. That shitty little house went for a few thousand shy of a million."

"But it was our shitty little house. I loved that place. I'm sick of being stuck out here in this shoddy apartment where the roof leaks every time it rains."

"At least there is a roof. Some people aren't lucky enough to have even that."

"That's not the point I'm trying to make. I miss feeling safe. I miss our friends. I even miss that old lady at the corner store who always yelled at the kids who came in wearing their backpacks after school."

Rayshell chuckled. "I remember her. She was a nutcase."

The pair rounded the short, crumbling stone wall that lined the entrance to their apartment complex, then headed to their bus stop. In the brief moment of silence that bloomed, they each recounted some of their cherished memories of their old neighborhood, which always brought them comfort during their displacement. It had been nearly three and a half years since Rayshell, Jakobe, and their mother were evicted from their old home. With the housing market as drastically inflated as it was, the only thing their mother could afford on her own was an apartment in a complex webbed within the dying remains of a commercial area on the edge of town. Whereas Rayshell understood their situation and tried to accept things as they were, Jakobe refused to. Not only were their amenities lacking, but the neighborhood felt treacherous and unforgiving. The abrupt change caught everyone off guard, but they all tried to cope as best they could.

"I know Mom keeps looking, but I don't understand why it's taking so long."

"I do." As Rayshell locked onto the curious eyes of her brother, she continued, "We don't have anything. People like us are getting left behind. Every year, it gets harder, and things keep getting more expensive. You know why?"

Jakobe nodded.

"There's just too many people." Rayshell leaned against the cold metal bus stop pole and asked, "You know what happened to our old house, right?"

"Yeah," Jakobe confessed. "I went back there in the summer."

"Fuckin' luxury condos. The whole block."

"It's sad."

"It's sadder for Mom. It's just not fair. And that's why I say to be patient."

When their bus finally approached, Rayshell crammed her fingers into her ears to ease the shrill sound of squealing brakes.

Jakobe walked past her with a grin, dismissing her contorted expression. "You're so dramatic. Come on," he said before hopping aboard.

Rayshell rummaged for her monthly pass but then froze at the door.

"Ya gonna get in 'r not?" groaned the irate bus driver.

Hesitantly, she stepped aboard and watched his eyes follow her as she passed by. Jakobe was in the back of the bus, waving her down as if she were in a gigantic crowd. Embarrassed, she continued to the window seat he had saved for her.

The bus rolled to a halt at the next stoplight, pushing everyone into their seats simultaneously. Rayshell's eyes trailed over the frigid-looking passengers, then fell onto the large rear-view mirror hanging crookedly from the windshield. The driver's bulging emerald-green eyes were painted right into it, piercing straight through her. A few unbearable moments passed, and neither of them blinked. Prominent wrinkles beneath his eyes squished and creased, giving Rayshell the impression he was smiling. Once the surrounding cars pressed forward, the driver's eyes panned back to the road.

"What's wrong?" Jakobe asked as his sister let out a tight breath.

Confused and a bit uncomfortable, she whispered, "The driver. He was staring at me."

"So?"

"Look. I'm not tryin' to be hella dramatic or anything, but this whole morning has been weird as fuck. And I don't want to add in some creepy-ass dude starin' me down."

"Well, why don't you just sleep for the rest of the way like you always do? I'll make sure the '*big bad bus driver*' doesn't get you," Jakobe teased.

Rayshell smiled, but it faded as she recalled her haunting dream and the invasive vision from earlier. "I don't even wanna sleep," she answered, then turned away.

"That doesn't sound like you. Are you sure you're my sister?" asked Jakobe as he picked up a tress of her frizzy, ashy brown hair. "Not gonna find any antennas hiding under here, am I?"

"I'm not an alien, okay."

"Gills, maybe?"

Rayshell shook her head and hugged her backpack. "No gills. I wouldn't be able to—ugh, never mind. The only thing you'll find is a fist ready to punch you the next time you grab my hair," she warned playfully, then sighed. "Promise you won't let him get me?"

"Well, at this point, if he pays me enough, I might reconsider," jested Jakobe as his sister rested her head against the window.

"You better not."

The sound of wind and passing cars droned in Rayshell's ear through the thick plastic-like windows. As her mind relaxed, so did the strain in the back of her eyes. Without a way to listen to music since her phone was broken, the everyday sounds that accompanied her commute had to suffice.

Jakobe looked into the crooked mirror and watched the driver's bloodshot eyes scan the road. After clearing five stops free of invasive glances, Jakobe slipped in his headphones and watched the passing buildings. Stringy raindrops spattered the windows, foreshadowing that their trip would take longer than usual. After a disappointed sigh, Jakobe tapped away at the blue plastic armrest on the seat before him, mimicking the drum beats to the track he was listening to. Rayshell typically would have smacked him, but the numbness in her head subdued her. Slowly, the busy sounds around her converged, gifting her the perfect moment to drift away into another dream.

"I told you to be careful, Navaryn," a polite but subtly frustrated voice called out.

"But they're all dead, Aalrija."

"Not quite. Here, let me show you again." Aalrija knelt beside Navaryn and grabbed the remains of an excavated raspberry bramble she had placed atop her pile. She pushed aside a clump of dirt, revealing a row of vibrant shoots growing along the side. "These plants spawn under the ground," she continued. "You want to clip the dead shoots down instead of ripping them out of the ground."

"But it's more work that way," Navaryn whined. "We can just plant more."

"Not only is it less work to prune them, but it's also the best practice."

"Why?"

Aalrija passed the bramble into Navaryn's small hands, then handed her a pair of shears to cut down the dead growth. Through a sigh, she reluctantly prepared herself to explain the fundamentals of maintaining her garden yet again.

"If the plant is still producing, you let it continue until it has run its course, which is the natural way of things. Plants like berries will continue to spawn for many seasons. It means less work for you, fewer resources you will need to use, and less time to wait for produce." She looked at Navaryn's quizzical expression as she ran her finger over the soft pink and green protrusions. "You are killing your plants for no reason when you just rip them out carelessly."

Navaryn gripped the large shears awkwardly, then cut where Aalrija instructed.

"Now, we must give this a fighting chance to survive since you've torn it from the mother root. I want you to dig a shallow hole in the area you cleared, then fill it with a little bit of compost."

"Eww. The stuff that smells bad?"

"Yes, Navaryn. And once you're done with that, put the pruned segment on top and cover it with dirt," instructed Aalrija as she stood and fetched her a trowel. "The shoots can be covered, just not very deep, so be careful."

While Navaryn did as instructed, Aalrija resumed her examination of the other excavated items.

"Remember what I told you about friendly plants?" called Aalrija as she plucked a few things from the pile.

"Kinda. Why?"

"Because, again, you removed the mint. Berries like mint because they protect their base." She walked over to a few rooted coils of mint and directed, "Here. Dig these guys a new home, too. Mint is incredibly resilient. They should do fine without the compost nest."

As Navaryn reached for the coils, a meaty brown and yellow spider slid down on a line of its silk. Instantly, she recoiled her hand with a shriek.

"What is it?"

Navaryn backed away and yipped, "A spider!"

Aalrija rolled her eyes as she lifted her hand to get a good look at the arachnid. "My, what a beauty. You know, Navaryn, this weaver is more scared of you than you are of it."

Navaryn cinched her lip as she watched Aalrija pluck the spider by its silvery web. Carefully, she set it into a flowering balm cluster bordering their first manicured box.

"The next time you see a spider, think of it as your little warrior friend. They fight off the bad bugs that hurt your garden. This beauty will go on to build a new home in the balm where it will continue looking after things in its perimeter."

Navaryn reluctantly took the mint coils from Aalrija's outstretched hand and replanted them. Just as she was finishing up, a swift energy wave cracked the air in front of her castle. She stood and wiped her sweaty brow, then spotted Demelza and Lowenna walking around the bend.

"Good Afternoon, Aalrija."

"Demelza, Lowenna. What a nice surprise. How is everything?"

Lowenna, holding canvas bags in both hands, looked up at Demelza and waited for her to answer.

"Just fine. Lowenna and I finished early and came to deliver you both some harvest."

Navaryn looked at Demelza's subtle smile with narrow eyes, nervous that her kind comments would eventually twist into condescension.

"I see you still have help," said Demelza, referring to the trio of attendants working the outermost garden beds. "Tasked to pick up the slack, I see. You know, for Navaryn being almost eleven, she should be more than capable of doing this on her own now."

"She is. A little bit of help now and then is okay."

"That's what you're for."

"Don't you think I know that?" replied Aalrija, opening her soiled palms. "I'm not just sitting pretty."

"Maybe if you did a better job instilling the fact that the garden was her primary source of food, she'd be further along. Lowenna has been doing everything on her own for the past year."

Aalrija sighed. "She knows how important it is."

Demelza walked to the freshly weeded box of greens and pea shoots. "Are you not giving them a boost?"

"We're starting off doing things naturally."

"You're making it harder."

"Are you going to fight me on every little thing?!"

Wincing at their elevating voices, Navaryn and Lowenna locked eyes with one another and slowly inched away from their guardians.

"I'm just saying that you could make it easier for her with Material Displacement. Like this ...."

Demelza swooshed her deep, sparkling fingertips. As golden orbs fell, the plants immediately began to mature. Navaryn watched in awe as the pea plants sprouted thick, twisting tendrils that latched onto the center trellis and coiled upwards. Delicate white and violet blossoms

slipped out of the expanded formation. The waves of bordering kale and chard bobbed and feathered open as they shot upright.

"What did I just say?! I didn't want to introduce Shahiri techniques like this to her garden. Not yet."

"Oh, lighten up, will you? I don't understand your hesitation. You know as well as I do that Material Displacement simply uses the natural energy of what's surrounding us."

"Because. I want to do things my way. Not yours."

Once side-by-side, Navaryn reached for two of the canvas bags to free up Lowenna's hand. In a sneaky and stealthy sprint, Navaryn led their escape into the orchard as the women continued to bicker. Giggling, they stopped next to a row of freshly planted peach saplings.

"What did you bring me this time?" asked Navaryn excitedly, then dropped to her knees.

"Lots," Lowenna answered and sat in the clover beside Navaryn as she rummaged through the bags. "Confetti beets, a whole bunch of carrots, onions, and greens. I think Demelza had me put some of our new sweet potatoes in there, too."

"Eww, gross. You know I hate those things."

"I know," Lowenna said with a chuckle. "Demelza wanted me to give you some anyway. She says you should keep trying to eat them because they're really good for you. I don't mind them, to be honest."

"They're terrible!"

"These ones are purple if that changes anything." Lowenna looked up just in time to catch Navaryn miming a retch.

"What else ya got?"

"Um," she said mid-thought, "I think there are a few different kinds of—"

"Apples!"

"... apples," Lowenna concurred as Navaryn bit into one feverishly. "Have you eaten today?"

With a full mouth, she replied, "A little. But working in the garden always makes me hungry."

"Same here, I guess," Lowenna answered, unable to dissolve the mild revulsion from her face before Navaryn looked her way. "I, um, also brought you this." She dug through another bag and handed her a pack of cells with tiny shoots, each a few centimeters tall.

"What are these?" she said, taking the tray.

"The butterfly vines you like so much. You know, the one with the flowers you can use for tea?"

"Oh yeah! I know which ones you're talking about."

"I gathered some of the seeds and started them for you. That way, you can grow your own." She then sarcastically coughed and continued, "Instead of taking all of mine."

"Thanks, Lowenna. I think I know just the spot for them," she said, turning to Demelza and Aalrija, who were still bickering. "Right over there, at the corner bend of the castle. I want to make an archway with them."

After Navaryn mowed through another apple, Lowenna shyly stated, "Demelza has been teaching me some Shahiri techniques, like the one she just demonstrated."

"That stuff is weird. I don't really like it," said Navaryn as she rested back in the grass.

"I know. You've told me before. But, if you learned the principles, I'm sure you'd begin to appreciate it."

Navaryn's expression smoothed over, indicating she was uninterested in hearing anymore, so Lowenna took another approach. She put the cell tray between them and held out her hands.

"Don't turn them into thistles or tumbleweeds."

"Very funny."

After a few concentrated moments, tiny glittery golden orbs flocked to her small fingertips. Navaryn would never deny the beauty of the technique, nor the whimsical feeling it evoked whenever she observed it, but there was something about it she didn't trust. She watched the golden orbs slowly descend upon the shoots, narrowing her eyes. Similar to Demelza's demonstration, though less intense, the sprouts absorbed the energy and swiftly augmented, their spiral leaves unfurling into a shimmery emerald expanse.

Slightly winded, Lowenna announced, "Now they are ready for transplant."

Navaryn rolled forward and plucked off one of the newly formed leaves. Under the swaying rays of sunlight that cut through the juvenile trees, she carefully inspected it. Within the clear aqueous bead that formed at the base of the leaf, a swirl of glittery fragments collided and then slowly disappeared. No matter how beautiful the peculiar method was, the simplicity implied over such a delicate balance kept Navaryn skeptical and wary of looming repercussions.

"Come on, sleepyhead," Jakobe chimed to Rayshell while he shook her shoulder. "It's our stop."

The bus hummed beside the sidewalk as the pair shuffled to the crosswalk. After a few dashes, they rounded the first corner to escape the main street traffic. Rayshell waited until they passed a few houses before lighting a cigarette.

"Feel better?"

She nodded after a lengthy exhale.

"Well, it's been an interesting morning, that's for sure."

Rayshell's steps contracted in the midst of recalling Von and his brilliant red eyes. "Yeah? You don't even know the half of it."

Jakobe simply shrugged away her ambiguous confession and turned his attention ahead of him.

The back streets they meandered through weaved under statuesque elm trees. Charms of finches dashed through the intertwined branches, calling out to one another in delight above the rows of quaint houses.

"Oh, damn it," Rayshell griped as her brother laughed. "Why didn't you say anything?"

"Too late to turn back now."

"I bet you didn't say anything on purpose, huh?"

Bright green and overly decorated, the house on the corner of Smith and Taylor stuck out like a sore thumb among the otherwise neutral neighborhood. But it wasn't the house's color that irked Rayshell; it was the abundance of creepy little garden gnomes in the front yard. They lined the fence, and each carefully manicured bush, and their beady eyes seemed to follow after passersby. Rayshell didn't realize until two houses down that she had grabbed hold of Jakobe's arm.

"Fuck," he hissed and pulled away. "Throw your cigarette, Ray."

The front bumper of a police car poked out from the shrubbery at the corner ahead. Resisting one last drag, Rayshell casually slid her hand behind her and flicked it into the yard beside her. The police car quickly approached and then abruptly stopped beside the curb. A familiar voice greeted them sternly through the passenger-side window.

"Hello, Officer Allen," Rayshell blandly replied as she peered inside the car.

He removed his aviator sunglasses. "You guys aren't ditching school, are you?" he asked, furrowing his thick black eyebrows.

"No. We're just late. Our mom should have called in for us."

"You guys want a lift to school?"

"No thanks," answered Rayshell anxiously. She put her hand on the passenger door and patted it. "We're fine walking."

"I shouldn't have said it like you had a choice. Get in the car."

Rayshell stared blankly at the windshield, wishing she had hidden behind a car before he turned the corner.

The door locks clunked open. Jakobe rounded the car's rear end and got in without saying a word, while Rayshell pleaded with herself to keep her sour face from showing as she sat down. Officer Allen jerked the car out of park and spun a U-turn toward campus.

"I've already brought you to campus six times, Ray," he uttered and rubbed his wiry mustache. "And we're barely, what, three months into the school year? You also smell like cigarettes. Again."

"My mom smokes."

"Does she use tobacco-scented laundry detergent, too?"

"Mm-hmm, *and* fabric softener."

Officer Allen grunted at the traded smart remark. "You know when I was your age …."

Here we go again, Rayshell thought, resisting the urge to roll her eyes.

"… I got into trouble, too. Heck, I myself used to smoke on account of my friends …."

Rayshell nodded with feigned attention.

"... they made me cut classes with them, I gave attitude to my teachers, and eventually, my bad habits influenced my younger brother. I didn't want him to make the same mistakes I did, so I cut that shit out. I admit it wasn't fun, but I knew I had to set a better example.

"I know both of you are going through a hard time with your displacement. I went through something similar when I was about Jakobe's age. But you have to be strong and take school more seriously. Your future is shaped by the decisions you make today. And once you're in the adult world, your mistakes will cost you so much more than they do now."

"I know," answered Rayshell disingenuously.

The car was silent for the last two blocks until the passing bell sounded ahead of them. Following the final left turn, their school came into view through the surrounding trees. The morning's cool drizzle kept students from lingering in the bus circle. Officer Allen parked his patrol car, then opened the rear passenger door. After bidding him a brief farewell, Rayshell slid her backpack over her shoulder and started toward the glass entry doors.

"Hey. We need to get our passes," Jakobe called as the second-period bell rang.

Frustrated, Rayshell clomped ahead of her brother toward the administrative offices, housed in temporary portables while the new campus expansion was under construction. As she ascended the small steps, the door suddenly swung open.

"Ew, did you see his post last night? I thought they broke up." Stephanie blurted as she and her friend ambled out from behind the door.

Rayshell scowled as she hissed, "You wanna watch where you're going?" though she knew she'd receive no apology.

As Stephanie and Rayshell threw daggers at one another, Amanda stepped through their line of sight and blew a bubble with her gum.

Officer Allen called out as they started to bicker, "Hey, Ladies!" When he finally got their attention, he directed the students with his stiff finger. "Amanda. Stephanie. Get to class. Now. Rayshell. In the office."

Rayshell disconnected from Stephanie's arrowed gaze, flung open the Administrative Office door, and stormed inside. The Attendance Secretary slid her thick gold-framed glasses onto the bridge of her nose as Jakobe followed behind Officer Allen with his eyes to the ground.

"Ah, Officer Allen. How are you doing this morning?"

"Fantastic. Just escorting these two to your office before I make my rounds."

She smiled as she walked to her aide. "Can you find the call slip for Jakobe and Rayshell Stone and make two copies, please?"

Principal Roxard stepped out of his office and locked eyes with Rayshell down the narrow hall as she and her brother walked to the row of old chairs that lined the office wall. "What do we have here?" he called in a laugh, causing his plump belly to roll over his belt buckle. "Brought us a little present, I see."

"Yep. Just gave these guys a lift from down the street," confirmed Officer Allen while he adjusted his utility belt.

"Here you are," the aide called out to Rayshell with a snotty stare. "One copy for each of you. Authorized by *father*."

"It should be *mother*," muttered Rayshell as she walked to the counter.

"Well, she sounds rather man-ish," teased the aide discreetly.

The snide remark was no surprise since she was another of Stephanie's friends. Rayshell snatched a copy of the call slip and crumpled it in her hands.

"Well, it's off to class then," Roxard announced proudly. "Have a great day, and stay out of trouble."

"Hey, Rayshell, remember what I said, okay?" Allen asked with pleading eyes.

She let her half-assed smile be her reply as she exited with Jakobe in tow.

Once inside the main hall, Rayshell paused and rummaged through her backpack. "I need to trade out some books from my locker, so I guess I'll see you at home."

Jakobe hugged her and then continued down the hall toward the restrooms.

"Sorry about today," she called, to which he threw a thumbs-up.

Rayshell smiled, staring at the seemingly endless rows of taupe lockers lining the wing, then sighed. Luckily, her locker was just a few classrooms down.

·)(·

Jakobe made a quick pit stop at the restroom before heading to class. After he dried his hands with a brown paper towel, he bumped into a taller boy who was entering.

"Sorry," he muttered and continued to walk away with his eyes on the ground.

"Long time no see, Jakobe," Shawn taunted as he took notice of the passing face.

Though his voice wasn't immediately familiar, his signature flip-flop sandals confirmed who he was dealing with. Jakobe turned to him with a frown.

"Been wondering when I'd run into you," Shawn continued with his hands on his hips. His smile forced the freckles on his cheeks to crowd together. "I've been dying to settle the score between you and me, and your bitch of a sister."

"There's nothing to settle, Shawn. Just fuck off and leave me alone."

Irritated that his attempt to intimidate Jakobe had failed, Shawn pushed him into a nearby locker. When the crash sounded around the corner, Rayshell had just finished loading her backpack. Curious, she tiptoed toward the main hall and peeked around the bend. She caught an earful of the berating voice and instantly recognized the antagonist.

Just as Jakobe dropped his backpack to retaliate, Rayshell barked, "Get your hands off my brother."

Smirking, Shawn turned toward Rayshell as she advanced, then shoved Jakobe away.

"You should get to class now, bro."

Jakobe frowned as he fixed his shirt, wishing she had never interfered. "But, Ray ...."

"It's okay. I'll be fine."

Shawn continued badgering Jakobe after he turned and walked away.

"Stay away from Jakobe," Rayshell demanded. "This is between you and me."

Shawn looked side-to-side to make sure they were still alone. "You know, things wouldn't be this way if you hadn't embarrassed me in front of all my friends like the little slut you are."

Rayshell's veins swelled. "Just returning the favor."

"What does that even mean?"

His impression of innocence made her want to hurl. "Don't play fucking *idiot*. The night before we met at the park, you decided to play 'tossing tongues' with Stephanie. You didn't think I knew, did you?"

Shawn's baby blue eyes dashed back and forth as he thought of a way to reply.

"And before you start giving me more bullshit like 'it wasn't me,' no one wears the same ugly-ass shorts and sandals like you do!"

"Come on, quiet down."

"I watched you make out with her for way longer than I should have. You broke my heart, you cheating asshole! Why couldn't you just—"

"*Shut up*," he interrupted, taking her by the shoulders.

The heat of his body felt like tiny insects crawling under her skin. As Rayshell prepared to shove him away, the sound of footsteps caught her ear.

"Hey, lovebirds. Break it up and get to class," called a stern voice from the side.

Shawn and Rayshell, wide-eyed, turned their heads toward the voice. A campus security guard stood with folded arms and her left foot tapping impatiently on the ground. The walkie-talkie at her waist crackled with indiscernible chatter.

"You're lucky I'm not taking you straight to Roxard's office. Now, get a move on."

Rayshell shoved Shawn's hands away, then started down the hall to her class. After she rounded the corner and fetched her call slip from her backpack, she glanced behind her to ensure Shawn wasn't following.

The door to Rayshell's classroom was closed by the time she arrived. She peered through the small center window in the door and found her teacher, Ms. Briggs, pacing while pointing toward the overhead projector screen. All eyes fell onto Rayshell as she meekly entered the room. Ms. Briggs carried on with her lecture as Rayshell tossed the crumpled call slip atop her desk, then took her seat.

"What happened to you?" Sheila whispered.

"Don't get me started," Rayshell whispered back and locked to her teacher, pretending to be listening in. She unzipped her backpack and took out her binder and history book.

"I would be rich if I had a dollar for every time you were late to one of your classes."

Ms. Briggs quickly turned to the pair, causing Sheila to straighten her smile.

"Now, if everyone could open their textbook to chapter six, lesson two on page one-hundred and twenty-seven, we can begin talking about The American Revolution."

"Now there's a topic that could put me out," Rayshell muttered as she turned to the requested page.

As Ms. Briggs began the lesson, Rayshell dwelt on her confrontation with Shawn. She scribbled some lines in her notebook to distract herself, yet it lent no relief to her buzzing mind. Once she ran out of doodles to keep her occupied, she began to tap her pencil on the paper. After a few pages of her history book forcefully turned, her gaze wandered through the window to a wing of playful birds whizzing about. Once situated within a reverie of Von, her eyes drifted past the trees and into the sky. What she experienced in her early morning dream felt so real, from the cold touch of his hands to the swarm of emotions she felt as she looked into his red eyes, deep like thick blood encased in a glassy reflection. Recalling the sincerity within his gaze, even while in his beast form, made her blush.

"Alright, Rayshell. Please read the second paragraph below the illustration," Ms. Briggs called out once another student had finished reading aloud.

When Rayshell didn't oblige, Ms. Briggs folded her arms and waited to see how long it would take for her to realize that class had stopped. Sheila, however, felt compelled to intervene. The class stirred with whispers as she tried clearing her throat to get Rayshell's attention. Moments away from succumbing to her anxiety, she called her name until Rayshell's daydream shattered into a million pieces.

"*What?*" she hissed.

With a worried expression, Sheila pointed to the front of the class. Rayshell rolled her eyes, then looked to where she had instructed. Everyone, including the teacher, was leering at her. Immediately, Rayshell's face caught fire. She scanned the silent room and wondered what she had done.

One of the students in the corner blurted out, "Has our space cadet finally come down for landing?"

As the entire class burst into laughter, Ms. Briggs closed her eyes and sent her index finger flying horizontally into the air to demand silence. She tucked her pen behind her ear and asked, "Rayshell, since you stepped in here, have you honestly heard one thing I've said?"

Rayshell felt as if she were moments away from dying of embarrassment. She glanced at the doodles on her binder paper, then answered, "No. Not really."

"Well, I suggest you start paying attention now unless you don't plan on graduating this year."

The class clamored at the teacher's ominous statement.

"Yes, Ms. Briggs," she answered as the passing period bell rang.

"Don't forget!" she called as the students simultaneously packed up. "Everyone needs to do their study unit for chapter six, lessons two and three. There will be a quiz tomorrow."

The class wailed in disapproval.

"Sorry about that," Sheila said softly. "I didn't know what else to do."

"Don't worry about it," she answered, quickly grabbing her belongings. "I'm out before Briggs decides to talk to me."

After a hug, Rayshell dashed out the door and then disappeared into the flood of passing students.

·)(·

Trish waited down the hall by the last row of lockers with her headphones on. Enjoying one of her favorite songs, she swayed her head with closed eyes. Once Rayshell spotted her through a break in passing students, she ran to her side with a beaming grin.

"Trish!" she called, hugging her tightly.

Her blue eyes bulged as Rayshell, full of merriment, spun her around. Following a yip, she pulled her headphones down. "Geez, Ray! You scared the hell out of me! At least I'm awake now."

"Next best thing to caffeine?"

"Sure, I guess," she replied and snatched her backpack from the floor.

Rayshell turned to the small glass doors at the end of the hall. "Come on. Let's blow this joint."

Rayshell and Trish's eager steps slowly cut through the teacher's parking lot to the shrubbery at the corner. To their relief, the streets were empty, and no security guards were in sight. Their anxious eyes glistened at one another, agreeing that it was safe to proceed to the apartments across the street.

"One," Rayshell chimed lightly.

"Two," Trish followed.

"*Three!*"

Together, they darted across the small two-lane street and through the carport.

"Finally, a breath of fresh air," chimed Rayshell as she slung her backpack into her hand.

"Not for long," teased Trish as Rayshell pulled out a cigarette.

Trish opened the small metal gate to an untidy playground and headed for an old wooden picnic table under the shelter of a thick and twisted tree. An uneasy smile tightened Rayshell's cheeks as she took a seat.

"What is it?" Trish asked as she crammed her hands into the pockets of her thick black jacket.

"I ran into the inevitable."

"The inevitable? You mean, Shawn?"

Rayshell nodded and took a long drag. "That jerk. I found him picking on Jakobe during second-period today. We were late as usual, and I went to grab some things from my locker, thinking he was just going to class." She paused and shuddered at the thought of Shawn's gelled and frosted light brown hair. "I guess they ran into each other, and Shawn had pushed him into a locker."

"Geez. Shawn is such a bully."

"Yeah, but I know Jakobe could have put up a really good fight. I didn't want to see it come to that again, so I had no choice but to intervene."

"Again? I don't understand. What did Jakobe do to piss him off in the first place?" Trish asked.

"Well, you know that Shawn and I broke up during summer, right?"

"Yeah, you mentioned it. But you never wanted to talk about it, remember? You basically left me to figure things out on my own. The only thing I could really do was read his and his friends' shitty posts."

"Well, this morning, I feel like storytelling."

"Finally," said Trish while she dug out her oversized knit beanie from her backpack. "I'm surprised it's taken you more than four months to say anything about it in the first place."

"So, the day after Shawn and I broke up, he came over to start more shit. Jakobe saw us fighting in the parking lot and stepped in just to calm things down. Instead, things just got worse. He ended up socking Shawn."

"I wish I could have seen that."

"It was awesome. It felt good to have him stand up for me, being that he is younger and all."

"You're his sister. Of course, he would try to protect you." Trish picked at her nails, then continued, "What was the real reason you and Shawn broke up? There's all this talk about you cheating on him in the park with one of his friends."

Rayshell threw her cigarette into the damp tanbark and lit another while recounting the deceitful night to her friend, which was the catalyst for her upcoming actions.

"What a fucking jerk, man."

"... and I knew right away that it wasn't his older brother. Aside from the fact they were leaning on his stupid car, no one else would be caught dead in those ridiculous palm tree shorts. I think he's dating Stephanie now. At least, that's what I remember reading before i threw my phone out the window.

"Whatever, though. I knew Shawn was going to meet some of his friends around noonish the next day, so I decided to beat him to it. I looked for Tobias. Long story short, I ended up kissing him."

Trish cinched her lip. "You shouldn't have done that. Even if you didn't want to confront Shawn, you should have just broken up with him."

"I know."

"So I take it Shawn flipped his shit when he got there, huh?" Trish asked and tore open the brightly colored wrapper of a meal bar.

"Oh yeah, he went ballistic! The two of them started yelling at each other, then at me. I tried to get some words in, but I don't think either of them heard me. With how Shawn acted, I thought maybe I saw things wrong the other night."

"You don't need to fool yourself like that."

"I know," she whispered. "I know what I saw."

Rayshell finished her recount of the incident, which concluded with her throwing a brick through the windshield of Shawn's car. Shortly after, the warning bell sounded in the distance. She groaned, then flicked her cigarette next to her previous one.

"Well," Trish began and playfully smacked Rayshell's back. "I'm glad you shared that with me."

"Sorry I took so long," she said, then doused herself with melon-scented body spray. "Just do me a favor. Don't tell anyone. I am almost certain that Shawn made a pact with Ryo and Vic never to speak of it. Maybe even paid them off for all I know."

After Trish gave her word, the pair sprinted across the street and through the teacher's parking lot, where they started in separate directions. Rayshell walked through the glass doors and dragged her feet down the hall. Even though biology was one of the more tolerable subjects, she still dreaded it. Having to endure the judgmental eyes of her classmates while the teacher droned on about topics she couldn't care less about made her want to escape to a place where she could be alone.

2

THE UNKNOWN

Before Rayshell knew it, the lunch bell blared. She typically had her things packed up preemptively, which always annoyed her teacher, but she had found herself in the wake of another shattered daydream. After cramming her backpack with her belongings, she jogged out of the empty classroom.

The bustling hallways made Rayshell's maneuvers difficult. On her way to the music room, she dodged through herds of cackling girls, smiling and ranting with their friends, and packs of boys parading around with outlandish gestures to their comrades. Rayshell pushed through a set of glass doors that split open to the quad. Expertly, she continued to dodge through the slower-moving groups of students and the ambling stragglers. Just around the corner of the cafeteria was a side entrance that led to her destination. One hall later, she arrived at a small set of windowed doors and peered inside to find Trish situated at the grand piano.

Quietly, she slipped inside and then sat on one of the hard blue plastic chairs lining the wall of windows. Her fingers danced inside one of the hidden compartments in her front pouch, reaching for a bag of cut carrots and other colorful veggies, nuts, and cheese she had prepped and packed the night before.

Once Trish finished tinkering with the new segment she had been working on, she took her fingers off the keys and said, "Almost got it down."

"It's sounding great," Rayshell complimented as Trish made a few revisions to her manuscript. "Pretty cool that you have double the practice since music is your next class."

Trish giggled and poked at the middle C key. "You didn't see Shawn again, did you?"

"Nah," she said through a mouthful of carrot and bell pepper, "Lucky for me, I don't have any of the same classes he does."

The large clock on the wall caught Rayshell's eye and confirmed there were only eleven minutes left until it was her turn to play. She smiled and watched the shadows of the passersby slide past the stretch of tinted windows. Her heavy sigh prompted Trish to look her way.

"What's wrong?" she asked while replaying the segment again.

"Besides all this crap going on with Shawn, something else has been getting to me. I've had some of the weirdest and most vivid dreams this morning."

Trish's fingers fumbled over the keys after her statement. She looked at her friend suspiciously and asked, "What about?"

"I don't know where to begin," Rayshell confessed, then shoveled more veggies and cheese into her mouth.

Anxious to hear what it was she had to say, she encouraged, "Give it a try."

"Well, first, I was standing with this black-haired guy in this creepy, dark place that somehow felt just as familiar as he did. He said he was gonna bring me back and help me remember who I am. He even brought me the moon." Rayshell looked to Trish and continued earnestly, "The feeling I got from looking at him hasn't left the entire day."

Trish stopped playing and then beckoned for the bag of veggies.

"He was determined, and the sadness in his eyes was intense," she continued, taking a few more carrot chunks out of the bag before throwing it to Trish. "Afterwards, I don't know. I fell away from him. Then he transformed into this demonic creature. Fuckin' scares the shit out of me to think about it outside of the dream. But when I was there, all I could think about was how much I longed for him. I just can't get over his eyes. The color of them intensified as he transformed. They were beautiful, glowing—"

"Red," they confirmed in unison.

"Wait. What? How did you know they were red?"

"I, um … guessed?" Trish answered back. Truthfully, she didn't mean to speak the word out loud.

"Good guess." Rayshell shook away the odd feeling and continued, "When I woke up, I had another dream as I was getting dressed in the bathroom. But it felt more like a memory than anything."

"A memory, huh? Was it about the same demon creature?"

"No. This time I was with someone different. I was with an older man for a moment as I did some target practice with this bad-ass sword. It had three ruby spheres on the hilt, each just a little smaller than the one before. Then, when he left, someone else showed up. Someone with these odd yet gorgeous purple eyes."

"Interesting."

"You're telling me," she said as she ran her fingers through her hair. "Then, on the bus, I had another one that was more of a child's gardening lesson than anything. These dreams were just … different. Different than any I've ever had. And all of the people kept calling me by some weird-ass name. N-Navaryn, or something like that."

Trish slowly crunched down on a chunk of celery. She didn't notice how wide her eyes were until Rayshell narrowed.

"What?" she called out.

"Nothing," Trish replied as calmly as she could manage, then turned to the clock on the wall. "Oh, hey. It's your turn."

Rayshell sauntered over with folded arms as Trish rose from the bench. She maintained her suspicious gaze, though she didn't know what to be wary of.

With the bag of lukewarm veggies and sweaty cheese, Trish walked to the window and peered toward the football field while Rayshell began playing. Since the earlier part of the summer, she, too, had suffered from oddly vivid dreams. Due to their potent effects, she chose to keep them to herself until she understood what was happening. However, the instances only intensified as the months passed, leaving her with more unanswered questions. Trish was shocked to learn that her best friend had suffered the same affliction.

The pleasing keystrokes that filled the air soothed Trish's mind for a few moments, but her friend's usual melody transitioned to a simple yet beautiful tune she became familiar with through her strange dreams. Trish slowly turned to Rayshell, gently swaying with her eyes closed as she played. Her jaw slowly fell as a vision veiled over her eyes.

Dressed in shimmering wine-colored fabric with a slit high up her right thigh, Navaryn sat next to Lowenna at a white, grand piano. Strapped to her leg with a purple ribbon was a deftly crafted dagger adorned with three gleaming red spheres. Their echoing words bounded over the pleasant keystrokes of a simple melody. Though the tune was winsome and peaceful, Navaryn's face was full of sadness. Tears fell from her eyes as she played until she eventually succumbed to her seizing breaths.

"I miss him, Lowenna," she uttered as she lowered her face into her arms over the corner of the keyslip.

"I know, Nav."

The sound of her weeping rose. "This isn't fair."

"We'll figure a way to make this right. I promise. Just hang in there, okay?"

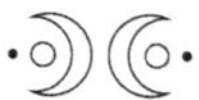

Trish slipped from the vision as the melody Rayshell played transitioned to a series of her usual notes. Once the elements around her hardened back into view, she dropped the bag of eats to the ground and frantically dashed to Rayshell's side.

"Play that again!"

Rayshell's heart nearly left her chest upon hearing Trish's abrupt request. "For fuck's sake, Trish!"

"Play what you were just playing before this."

"What the hell are you talking about?"

"That melody ...."

"What melody?"

"*Oh my god*," Trish groaned, "the one you were *just playing*."

Rayshell looked at her while crafting something on a whim to appease her.

"You weren't even playing that!"

Rayshell stood from the bench and belted, "What the *hell* is wrong with you?! You've been acting batty this whole lunch break."

"I have not."

Following a sloppy putter of her lips, Rayshell replied, "You better quit messin' around and just tell me what the hell is going—" The warning bell for class interrupted her demand. "You lucky fucker," she hissed, irritated by the exquisite timing.

Trish shrugged as Rayshell walked to retrieve her backpack and the bag of veggies lying on the ground.

"Don't let this victory go to your head. School will be over soon enough, and I want you to tell me what's got you acting all weird."

Trish hugged her and teased, "Try not to pass out in algebra like you always do. I hate waiting around for you to get out of detention."

"Ha-ha," Rayshell said with her eyes on the ceiling. Before she left the room, she turned to Trish one last time with a squinty, suspicious grimace. "See you after school. You'd better not try to ditch me."

"Bye, Ray," she replied, wiggling her fingers until her friend's clomping steps passed through the door frame.

A portion of students remained in the quad conversing with their friends, unhurried to get to class. Rayshell gripped the straps of her backpack and sighed as she glanced at them from under the cafeteria's awning. Just then, it started to sprinkle, and all she could wish was for the day to end.

"Pass it *long!*" a freshman boy called out as he dashed away from his group of friends.

Across the quad, a tall boy with long black hair launched a football high into the air. Rayshell watched a subtle smile cut his face as he cleared the hair from his eyes. Her steps contracted as their distant eyes locked. For a moment, she could have sworn he was Von. Lost in thought, Rayshell came to a standstill and failed to recognize why his smile faded as it did.

"Got it!" the boy yelled, jumped into the air, and then collided with Rayshell on his way down.

The furious gait of his friends and other bystanders ended around the toppled pair as they slowly untangled their limbs.

"Are you okay?" he asked Rayshell as he helped her to her feet.

Wincing, Rayshell answered, "I think so," and pressed against a sore spot on the back of her head.

It wasn't long before two security guards arrived to assess the pair's condition. Rayshell stayed quiet and hoped they would be distracted long enough for her to sneak off to class, though the opportunity never came. Instead, she and the freshman were reluctantly ushered to the nurse's office for evaluation.

·)(·

"Oh my god, Ray!" Trish shouted as she burst into the resting room nestled inside the nurse's office. "Are you okay?"

Startled by her abrupt entry, Rayshell jerked backward, then answered, "I'm fine, except for the part of my arm I tore off on this stupid vinyl daybed thing."

Trish chuckled as she hugged her.

"How did you know I was here?"

"Savannah. She saw the whole thing. When I went to meet you after your math class, she told me what happened. Showed me the video someone took, too."

"Great. With my luck, it'll probably go viral," she mumbled with a frown.

Trish pulled out her phone and teased, "You're probably right. Wanna see?"

Rayshell feigned a threatening look as she held up her middle finger.

Snickering, she grabbed Rayshell's backpack as the school nurse entered the room.

After setting down a stack of paperwork, she moved her straggly mahogany hair to the side. "How are you feeling? Still doing okay?"

"Yeah, I'm fine. Better than earlier, that's for sure," she replied and took her backpack from Trish while fighting away a small dizzy spell.

"Remember to continue icing it when you get home, okay?"

"Will do. Thank you for letting me hang out here and for, ah, fixing me up," Rayshell concluded and pushed on Trish's back to jumpstart her gait.

"Bye, ladies," she called out as the girls quickly shuffled out of the room.

The pair used the side exit to avoid further questions or comments from the remaining staff and quickly crossed the street before the stoplight turned green for oncoming traffic. Since Rayshell had eight periods, there were considerably fewer students on or around campus, so the assigned officers had already departed. She took out a cigarette and lit it quickly.

Trish groaned as the acrid smoke sailed by. "So, Ray. About earlier, when we were in the music room ...."

Though Trish welcomed the thought of avoiding her explanation, she knew she'd find no relief. She looked to the passing sidewalk lines for close to a half-block before she found the words to begin.

"Ever since the start of summer break, I've been having these strange dreams." She met Rayshell's curious eyes for a moment, then disconnected. "I didn't think much of them at first, but they continued to get worse."

"What do you mean, worse?"

"More vivid and more frequent. Sometimes I have them when I'm awake."

Rayshell clenched her teeth, noting the incident in the bathroom earlier in the morning. "When you say, 'have,' you mean you still get them?"

Trish nodded.

"Why didn't you tell me this sooner?"

After a heavy breath passed through her lips, she answered, "Well, a few reasons, I guess. I mean, you had your own stuff going on during the summer. Plus, you broke your cell."

Rayshell puttered her lips. "Well, yeah. But there's still the house phone."

"Those things still exist?" After a shared chuckle, she continued, "Look. I was scared, okay? I thought it would be better to keep it to myself until I could figure out what was happening. Turns out I still don't have any answers." Trish looked at her hand while she balled it into a fist.

"So, it wasn't just a guess."

"What wasn't?"

"When you said that the demon's eyes were red." Rayshell watched her friend's eyes harden. "It wasn't just a guess, was it? You've had dreams of him before, haven't you?"

Trish's expression was difficult to read. It looked as if she were flipping back through chapters of instances to pull the recollection. "Yes, I have. But differently, I guess you can say."

"How so?"

"Ugh, this is all so hard for me to explain."

"It wouldn't be this way if you had told me sooner."

Trish rolled her eyes, though she more or less understood it was true. "Okay. Promise you're not gonna freak out?"

"I promise. Now out with it already."

"The demon. The one in your dream. He's not really a demon, exactly. His name is Von."

In the middle of her last drag, Rayshell paused with wide eyes.

"You said you weren't gonna freak out."

"How in the fuck did you know that? I never mentioned his name to you," she fired, then squished her cigarette butt with her heel.

"He's one of the people I've had dreams of, so when you described him, I instantly knew who you were talking about."

Rayshell folded her arms. "What about the song?"

"The one you played in the music room?" Following Rayshell's eager nodding, Trish continued, "I've heard that in my dreams, too. It's a song someone would play. Someone whom I've come to know is called Navaryn. Just like you mentioned."

Rayshell's face contorted with disbelief.

"Von had taught the tune to Navaryn, and she played it often, especially when she was sad."

"You sound like these are people you know, which sounds–"

"Crazy?" Trish answered in her place. "I know."

The pair had stepped onto the main street about a half-block away from Rayshell's bus stop, but neither of them walked in its direction.

"Do you have to go home right now?" Rayshell asked.

"Eh, I got about an hour. Wanna maybe grab a coffee?"

"Did you mean froyo?"

"It's cold, though, Ray."

"It's never too cold for froyo. Come on. I'll treat."

Rayshell's statement was correct. Though the shop shortened its hours as winter approached, it was just as busy as ever. They studied the patrons as they filled their cups and realized most were fellow students. Desiring privacy, Trish led them to the pavilion's fountain after paying. Rayshell was nearly halfway through her creation when they sat down.

Trish picked at the colorful toppings with her spoon and debated how much she should divulge. Discovering her best friend was part of the puzzle put her at ease; however, she was skeptical of her ability to take the matter seriously. Once again, Trish looked at her fist as she balled it. It was prickly hot with a strange, unrelenting surge that she grew accustomed to embracing. Unbeknownst to her, Rayshell was studying the apprehension and concern painted so vividly upon her face.

Interrupting the silence with a full mouth, Rayshell inquired, "So, do you have dreams of this Von person a lot?"

"I do. But honestly, there are others that I dream of more frequently."

"Like who?"

"Well," Trish began after sliding a scoop of mango tart over her tongue, "I guess there are two people in particular. One is a woman named Demelza."

Rayshell squinted at the sound of her peculiar-sounding name. "Demelza?" she repeated, then quickly recalled the vision with Aalrija from earlier in the day.

"She's a brilliant teacher. One of my first dreams of her was in this magnificent library packed with books, charts, and a bunch of other things I don't know how to describe. And just like you mentioned, how you were being called a weird name, I was, too. She called me Lowenna."

Rayshell set her empty cup beside her. With potent eyes arrowed straight at Trish, she muttered, "Lowenna and Navaryn, huh?"

"Yeah. I don't know the right words to say this, but I think that these dreams and visions we're having are memories of their lives."

The way Rayshell crumpled into laughter was precisely what Trish expected, and it certainly gave her reason enough to reserve some of the other recounts for another day. Though she knew Rayshell often concealed her discomfort with a titter or similar reaction, she counted on a more serious attitude.

"You done?"

After Rayshell's fit settled, she asked, "So what else do you remember from the dream? The one in the library."

Trish swirled her melting yogurt, then glared at her. "Do you even care?"

"Lighten up. Of course I do."

"Then can you please act like it?"

After a small round of silence following Rayshell's half-assed apology, Trish finally continued, "It had more than six floors, and each section was meticulously organized. It was drop-dead gorgeous in there—dizzyingly tall spiral staircases with ornamental carvings adorned with what looked to be gems. Demelza talked about choices in the study for something she called Shahiri. From what I gather, Shahiri is the name given to a group of people who practice exclusive forms of mystical arts, or something like that."

Trish stepped into the recollection as she continued.

"As a Shahiri, you will have access to rare tomes of knowledge," said Demelza in a richly deep voice as she led the way through an aisle packed with hand-bound works. Above her hand, she controlled a floating opalescent orb which she used to light their path. The nuances in her turquoise evening dress shimmered as fiercely as her ruby lips and the golden highlight atop her dewy, ebon skin. "But as you know, one skill set will be your primary focus. Have you had enough time to make your decision?"

"I have."

"What shall it be?"

"Lakena."

Demelza slowly turned and asked, "The art of healing? Are you certain? This category is perhaps the most–"

"Challenging?" answered Lowenna. "I'm aware."

"Is this simply to test your fortitude?"

"No. There's a deeper meaning to my decision, yet I'm uncertain how to explain it."

"Are you aware of the risk associated with Lakena?"

"Risk?"

Demelza nodded, then continued to lead the way. "As you know, not every Celestine can attain their wings. This, I know, is something you can one day reach. And soon. But studying Lakena inhibits that grand transformation. Having barely stepped into adulthood, you run the risk of never being able to call them forth."

It didn't take more than a few seconds for Lowenna to respond, "I guess that's a risk I'm willing to take."

"As your former caretaker, I must ask that you reconsider. At least until you've allowed yourself to break through."

"Demelza. I respect your concern," said Lowenna earnestly. "Really, I do. But the fact of the matter is, this is my decision to make. And there is something that's pushing me. An urgency that I can't explain. And I won't ignore my intuition."

"Very well, my child. Just as you won't ignore your intuition, neither will I. I'm responsible for ensuring you're aware of the repercussions behind your choice." Demelza patted her hands over her buoyant silver-streaked updo, secured with a glittery silk sash. "But then again, I knew it had little chance to sway your decision. You have proven yourself incredibly selfless. A strength that people often mistake for weakness."

"I hope that's something that will one day change. Kindness is not weakness. Nor is sacrifice."

Demelza continued until she reached a section of the library darker than the rest. "Do you know that both Aalrija and I also elected to study Lakena?"

"Of course."

"I must admit, Aalrija is more versed than I am because she studied longer. It was difficult for her to balance the depth of knowledge she took on, along with the heavy regimented training necessary to keep her transformation active."

"So that's why she can't call forth her wings anymore," acknowledged Lowenna with her fingers to her chin. "I remember the first day Navaryn and I trained with Labraid. He had Kumiko demonstrate the transformation. That's when Benson said Aalrija lost the ability. I always figured that meant she stopped training altogether."

Demelza halted at the last bookcase in the row, then commanded the opalescent orb toward the ceiling, where it hung above them. It took her a moment to thumb through the stack of manuscripts until she came across the one she sought. "You'll soon figure out why she had to choose between one or the other," she claimed, then handed her a thick green journal.

"What's this?"

"The first fundamental I'd like you to begin studying. The Principles of Lakena, written by one of the earliest practitioners of this craft, Maja Mayori."

Lowenna ran her fingertips over the intricately stitched cover. "Maja was mentioned in one of my earliest studies after joining the Shahiri. I had no idea her original work was accessible."

"Every tome that Maja created lives right here in this library, as do the impactful works from other scholars, experts, and practitioners. Now I'm sure you appreciate the level of responsibility that comes with this being under your care."

"You're allowing me to take this with me? Outside of the facility?"

Demelza nodded. "It's one of your many privileges."

Lowenna's eyes widened as she scanned the stacks of ancient works around her. She tucked the journal under her bare arm and began skimming through some of the other titles.

"You can take as many of them as you can carry, so long as you start with this one first."

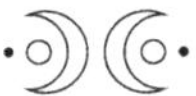

Rayshell didn't realize the instances where she had held her breath during her friend's reveal. Hearing the name 'Aalrija' again affirmed their experiences were linked, though she still didn't understand how.

Trish's eyes hardened as she spoke, "A lot of these visions I get have to do with that library. The works, the symbolry, it's all in my head. But aside from that, there is one other person who fills my head just as much, if not more. A man named Claymar."

The name ignited a spark within Rayshell's chest. "Claymar?" she whispered.

With blushing cheeks that were hot to the touch, Trish continued, "The depth of his blue eyes, I just, I don't know. I feel like I fall into them every time they come to mind. He is someone very special to Lowenna."

"Like, her husband or something?"

"I guess you can say that. I know they love each other. Deeply."

A gust of cold wind hit the pair, sending their hair flailing over their faces. Clumsily, the girls did their best to clear the strands from the sticky cracks of their lips.

Rayshell waited until Trish's face returned to normal before she asked, "What do you remember about him?"

"Lots," she answered, looking at a new crowd heading inside the frozen yogurt shop.

"Well, tell me something."

Trish held her cup, the heat of her hands neutralizing the coldness. As she slowly immersed herself in one of the strongest memories of Claymar, she did her best to recount everything that ran behind her eyes.

·◝◟◞◜·

Shirtless and lying on his side in a bed tucked with black linen, Claymar hummed an upbeat tune with his head propped up in his hand. Lowenna's giggles eased into his ear and broke his concentration.

"Had all you can bear, my lovely?" Claymar pulled Lowenna close and buried his face into her neck, seizing her with laughter.

"Clay!" she yipped as he nibbled her neck.

Their playful tussle ended with a kiss, then Lowenna rested in his arms.

As soon as silence filled the room again, she asked, "What do you want out of life?"

"Such a question at this hour? Are you intentionally avoiding sleep?"

Smiling, Lowenna answered, "Maybe a little." She ran her fingers over his satiny flesh, cloaked in amber candlelight. "So tell me."

"Well," began Claymar with wide eyes. "That's hard for me to answer."

"Oh, really? Why?"

As Claymar combed his thick fingers through her wavy, blonde locks, he said, "Because it sounds like a trick question."

"It's not a trick."

"Well, how could I long for something more than the perfection I already have?"

Lowenna guffawed until she ran out of breath.

"What did I say?"

"I haven't heard you dispense such flattery since the day we met," she replied after her fit settled. "Come on, Clay. I'm being serious."

"Well, what is it that *you* want in life?"

"Me?"

"Well, you seem to think this is such an easy question."

"It's only easy if you've already prepared yourself for it."

"Ha! So you did set me up, you sneaky, sneaky little Dragonfly." Claymar hugged her tightly and then jostled her. "Well then, out with it. Tell me, oh, *prepared one*. What do you want out of life?"

Lowenna's smile slowly evened out as she looked deeply into his eyes. "Change."

Claymar cocked his head to the side. "Ch-Change? In what way?"

"In many ways. Ways that are far larger than us."

"I'm sorry, my lovely. But I'm afraid I still don't understand."

After a hearty breath that calmed her mind, Lowenna continued, "Ever since I was a child, I never had the chance to choose what kind of life I wanted. Though I had choices, they were limited to the paths someone else had laid in front of me. As you know, I've found ways to sneak past so much. But in doing so, I'm living separate lives. Quite honestly, it's exhausting."

"I know, my lovely."

"I shudder to think what Benson or the Tiers would do if they found out I've fallen in love with a Daeva," she confessed, then bit down on the inside of her lip for a moment. "But I'm not the only one being controlled. Limitations are imposed upon everyone. Ultimately, no matter who we are, we all become the product of Benson's wishes. Every single one of us."

"He's a dictator, sweetheart, and Celestine has been governed in that fashion for countless generations. But it's not exactly different here. I mean, it's not like a full-on dictatorship controls the people of Daeva. But we are governed. Someone leads while the rest follow."

"Yeah, but it's the right people who should be the ones to govern. To give choice back to their people and let them live how they want to, whether they be a Celestine, Daeva, or anyone else."

"A noble vision indeed. Yet no one in power will bat an eye at such an idea. An empire is vulnerable if its people simply do as they wish."

Lowenna rolled her eyes. "I'm an example of how that proclamation is false. And so are you."

"Yeah, but we are both products of the very thing you are looking to dismantle. Sometimes it takes such a horrible circumstance to create greatness." Claymar paused as Lowenna slowly closed her eyes in defeat. "I can see the gears turning in that clever mind of yours. What are you getting at?"

"What if ... you and I push for change together?"

"Change? You don't mean ...."

Lowenna nodded. "We'd likely get a better start pitching the idea here. Nikkias," she named, as Claymar rose from the bed. "Killian, Morgan—"

"Nope, nope, *nope!*"

"Clay, listen to me."

"Look, I know you want change. I do too. But our worlds want nothing to do with one another unless it's to settle some outdated score once and for all. One winner, you see what I mean? You and I—we can be happy together just the way we are. If we want change, we can address our own sectors accordingly. I'm afraid that's about as good a shot as we have."

Lowenna's face fell flat as Claymar took her by the hands. "Clay."

"Oh, damn it. Here it comes," he grumbled, then walked to the dresser.

"If you really want true change, we have to aim to unite Daeva and Celestine," Lowenna affirmed over his groans.

"Naming off Daeva's most outspoken progressives doesn't convince me that your plan will work."

"We can at least try."

"I suppose this means you would like me to arrange an audience with Nikkias, then, am I right?"

Lowenna nodded. "He has been the biggest proponent of unification."

"Yeah, but for Daeva alone. Which we already have, more or less. Celestine was never part of the equation," he griped as he slid on a pair of underpants. "So what will you do once Benson figures out your plan?"

"*If* he does."

"*If*, or *when*."

"*If* he does, then we'll just have to wait and see."

"Sounds like the probability of war is ever promising in this endeavor. Swell."

"Don't worry. Things will be fine. We'll have Navaryn and Von on our side, should we need it."

"And I suppose this is a reason to celebrate?"

Lowenna shrugged her shoulders before leaning into her bare thighs.

"You're prepared to put your faith into two of the shortest fuses I know. That couldn't sound any more foolish to me. But beyond that, my main concern is with your dear friend, Navaryn. Sure, she'll make an incredibly powerful ally. But we don't know if she'd end up truly helping our cause." Claymar poured himself a glass of water from a pitcher by the large window, then slugged it down in just a few hearty gulps. After a sigh that lent no relief, he looked to Lowenna. "If you are truly serious about approaching Nikkias, which could lead to talks with the progressive component of Daeva's rule, then we will go about it alone. And we will continue as such for as long as possible. We keep this from Von and from Navaryn. From everyone."

Such earnestness was rare to experience from Claymar. Lowenna looked into his raking stare as she nodded her head.

"Good. Well then, I hope we won't live to regret this endeavor."

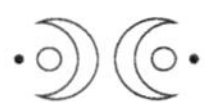

Rayshell disconnected from Trish's recount once her wandering gaze locked onto a man leering at her with intense, emerald-green eyes. He sat at one of the steel tables in front of the frozen yogurt shop, scooping spoonful after spoonful of the irresistible dessert into his mouth from an extra-large cup. Toppings dropped onto his lap and atop the ground, and soon he began to laugh.

Trish turned to Rayshell's contorted face once she finished her delineation. "Damn it, Ray!" she barked as a large group of kids entered the pavilion. "Were you even listening to me?"

"I was, but," she began, unable to find the words to continue.

"But, *what?*"

After the cavalcade of patrons cleared the area, the oddly familiar man was nowhere to be seen. Confused, Rayshell pointed at the cluster of steel tables in front of the yogurt shop. Trish ignored her gesture and walked to a receptacle, tossed in her yogurt cup, then reached into her backpack for her buzzing phone.

"Someone was staring at me, and then he just vanished. This creepy guy. He was *just there.*"

Trish paid no mind to her plea. "Hold on," she uttered as he put her phone to her ear. "Hi, Dad. N-no, not yet. I'm with Rayshell ...."

Curiously and cautiously, Rayshell scanned the pavilion as she walked toward Trish, but could not find any trace of the emerald-eyed man. "Who the hell *was that?*" she whispered to herself with furrowed brows, then tossed her cup into the receptacle.

"Okay, I'm heading home now. I love you, too."

As Trish tucked her phone into the front pouch of her backpack, Rayshell teased, "Uh oh, is someone in *trouble?*"

"No," she bluntly replied.

Rayshell folded her arms while she waited for her friend to say more, but all she did was look at her shoes. "I'm sorry, okay. I was listening to you, but I got distracted by that creep. I'm surprised you didn't hear his annoying laugh."

"It's whatever, okay. Look, I've gotta get across the street to catch my bus. My dad wants me home."

"Promise you're not mad at me?" asked Rayshell as Trish gave her a farewell hug.

"I'm fine. I'll see you tomorrow."

"Okay, but you didn't promise."

Trish shook her head and said lightly, "Bye, Ray."

Rayshell watched Trish bound through the pavilion as a drizzle settled in. She knew that her friend was irritated, or at least to some degree, disappointed. Whether beckoned home or not, Trish usually waited with her for the bus since her stop was across the street. Once heavy raindrops barreled through the mist, Rayshell reclaimed her backpack and was soon off.

·)C·

After a stop-and-go bus ride sandwiched among damp and weary passengers, Rayshell darted through the parking lot to her complex, then up the stairs. The sun had set, making it easy to see the various glowing colors spilling from the row of windows. Jakobe was chopping onions and garlic in the kitchen as she walked in.

"You're back later than usual," he called as Rayshell locked the deadbolt behind her. "I was starting to think maybe you were called in to cover a shift at work again."

"I'm sure you'd enjoy the house to yourself for another few hours."

Jakobe laughed as he scraped the fragrant alliums into a hot pan. "Honestly, I was just looking forward to eating your dinner."

Rayshell chuckled as she sauntered to his side, then peeked over his shoulder. "Whatcha makin'?" she asked while he stirred the contents of the pan with a wooden spoon.

"Spaghetti and garlic bread with, um, mushrooms and spinach. I'm keeping the sausage to the side like usual."

"Thank you. Can I help with anything?"

"I'm done with prep and got the oven preheating. The bread is cut and ready to go in. Water is salted and coming to a boil, and the vegetables are in a bowl over by the sink."

"Dang, you weren't lying. Those cooking shows are sure paying off. Well, I'll be back. I'm gonna go change out of these wet clothes."

Jakobe clicked on a third burner for the vegetables. "Oh, by the way. I saw Mom before she left for work. She said she found some beads on the floor in your room. More in your bed."

"Beads?"

"Yeah, she said a necklace of yours broke or something."

"I don't wear necklaces to bed."

Jakobe poured the tomato sauce into the pan with the roasted alliums, then teased, "Well, who else has been sleeping in your bed?"

"No one," griped Rayshell.

"*Sure*," he called out playfully while she walked to her room.

"Not funny!" she yelled back.

"They're by your jewelry box on your dresser. Maybe you could tell your sneaky boyfriend to come pick 'em up."

Rayshell flipped on her bedroom light and dropped her backpack against the wall by a mesh basket overflowing with dirty laundry. Pursing her lips, she shuffled over to her dresser, and sure enough, a small pile of irregularly shaped stones was lying on top. She scooped them into her hand, then selected one of the larger pieces to examine under the ceiling light. The tones of red were deep, and the sharp edges gleamed as she twisted her wrist.

"But there's no hole," Rayshell whispered.

Suddenly her heart skipped. Tied by feverish wonderment, she recalled the last of her early morning dream, where the sharp edges of sparkling shards refracted into her eyes from her hands.

Rayshell slid to her knees, cradling the glittering red fragments. They were, without a doubt, tangible evidence of what had transpired earlier. Von, the man who journeyed into her dreams and proclaimed he would bring her back to where she belonged, was disproved as a vagary. He was as real as Rayshell's potent trepidation. Despite the surge of curious emotions rattling her heart and mind, she feared letting go of denial's stranglehold.

The space around Rayshell grew warm, and, for a moment, it felt like she had fallen back into a dream. Slowly, she thumbed over the shards' sharp textures while she thought back to the intensity within Von's eager red eyes. For him to call for her by that peculiar name made her suspect she was someone different in her dreams. Unless given the opportunity to ask, she'd never know for sure. Though she was hopeful they would meet again when called to slumber, she wasn't sure she was prepared to learn further details of his plight.

Outside Rayshell's window, atop a long tree branch that stretched above the falling light, perched a solitary crow. Crystal raindrops sat like beads over its silken feathers. It would have been invisible among the dancing shadows had it not been for its glowing emerald eyes. The crow jittered and hopped toward the tree's thick, knotted trunk, where its frame distorted and altogether failed. Amidst a dizzying display of distended, swaying positions, the silhouette of a man took form. He quickly corrected his balance atop the slippery branch and pressed his thick body against the tree trunk. A smile promptly lit his face as he stared down at Rayshell beyond the window through his wiry, tangled black hair. The breakthrough he had so patiently sought had finally surfaced.

3

THE ORDER

The frigid clutches of winter settled into the realm of Daeva's lowlands, a treacherous and unsavory region where only those who wished never to be found would venture. Tucked away in the mountainside and cloaked from prying eyes was Merisek's fortress, a long-since abandoned experimentation site where the souls of many departed Daeva still haunted. Due to his severe transgressions against Daeva's ruling parties, it was only within this domain that he could remain safely hidden from the rest of the realm's inhabitants.

Merisek confined himself to his study and pressed on into his fifth straight day without sleep. A meager handful of tapers lit his work area, keeping him shrouded in darkness. The room had no doors or windows and was accessible only through a hidden portal that he and his apprentice knew how to operate. He employed a plethora of charms to cloak their energy, ensuring their location and actions remained untraceable.

Lying atop the large stone table were two of the three tomes to the Order of Existence, Ananael and Zin, that Merisek had stolen from Celestine. Though they came into his possession easily, thanks to careful planning, the selfless actions of the Celestine warrior, Navaryn, foiled his plan to obtain the third, Iaalprt. In an attempt to coerce her to surrender the book she guarded, he cast a banishment spell on her friend and fellow guardian, Lowenna. The one who would follow in tow for banishment was her mentor, Benson. However, as he executed the spell, Navaryn stepped in its path and was cast away in his place. The key to discovering Iaalprt's location was then lost to him.

Inside his study, Merisek rummaged through the two mysterious tomes. Even though Iaalprt eluded his search, he analyzed the contents of its companions. Much to his dismay, however, he learned that the text found within Zin was jumbled, nonsensical, and shifted around the pages every few moments. Furthermore, he found Ananael's pages completely empty. Confused and frustrated, he obsessively tracked the movements of the text within Zin with hopes that a clue would reveal itself within its contents.

From within the dark, secluded room, Merisek heard the portal opening behind him. In walked his apprentice, clutching his cloak tightly with quivering breath.

"Joro," Merisek uttered. "Greetings."

"It's freezing in here. It's the dead of winter, and you haven't thought to start a fire?"

"No need," he said nonchalantly.

Joro ambled further into the room and stopped at the opposite side of the table to face Merisek. He asked through his chattering teeth, "And how can you see in here with just those two candles?"

"I see just fine."

"I'm starting the fireplace. This is ridiculous," griped Joro as he rolled his eyes.

"Suit yourself."

Weakened from his time spent in the realm of Human, Joro stacked a few logs onto the grate in the fireplace and sparked them aflame, though the fire struggled to grow in the deep cold of the study. The visible vapor of his breath clouded his line of sight until the room started to warm. As the flames grew brighter, the firelight unveiled the darkened shroud that Merisek hid within. Before long, Joro could see him standing at the large stone table in the center of the room with Zin open in front of him.

"Now, isn't that better?" Joro jutted as he rubbed his hands together.

Merisek halted as he reached for the next page. The light from the fireplace illuminated the jagged texture of the pale skin on his hand. He glared in utter disgust at the toll his repeated experimentations took on his body throughout the years.

"I'd ask you how you're feeling, but I'm sure you're pretty tired of that question," said Joro as he smirked. Looking to prod a reaction from his mentor, he leaned in closer. "Though I must say you're looking a bit more ghastly than usual."

A fierce look came over Merisek's face as he slammed his fists onto the stone table. The flames on the pair of candles flanking the books grew wildly, shining a bright golden glow upon his malformed face. Joro's smug countenance faded into a blank stare.

"*What do you want?!*" he roared as he glared at him with his sickly-looking golden eyes.

The eerie visage of Merisek gleamed in the fuming candlelight and lit up the blackened scar cut across his neck. His gnarled veins throbbed violently beneath his leathery skin as he scowled at Joro.

Visibly unsettled, Joro replied, "I've, um, come to tell you there have been some new developments."

The candle flames slowly simmered as Merisek retracted his fists from the cracked table. "Get on with it."

"I've located Navaryn. She is only in the next town over from Lowenna's position."

"And how did you manage that?"

"I briefly detected her presence. Her vessel seems to be friends with Lowenna's as well. We were lucky with that."

"Hardly luck at all," Merisek replied. "Navaryn and Lowenna have had a tether between their essences since they were children. It makes sense that they would remain in proximity to one another."

Merisek turned his attention back to the open book in front of him. Yet again, the text shifted around the pages, creating more nonsensical writing. Curious, Joro stepped closer to the table and watched the words continue to scramble. Once the text ceased to move around the page, Merisek let out a frustrated sigh.

"Anything else?" he uttered as he stared at the open book.

"Yes," Joro continued. "It seems that Navaryn has begun to awaken within her vessel, much like Lowenna already has. This banishment spell of yours doesn't seem to have a permanent effect on either of them."

"I see. And how much time do you anticipate we have until Lowenna awakens completely?"

"Likely not long. She's made substantial progress over the last month."

"We'll need to be ready for her," Merisek replied as he looked back up at Joro. "Stay close and be on alert for any further signs of emergence. There's no doubt she'll be coming for the books when she returns."

Joro nodded. "And what of Navaryn?"

Merisek slowly exhaled as he recalled when she intercepted the banishment spell intended for Benson. The selfless loyalty she exhibited for the sake of all existence spoke to her commitment and fortitude. Though it pained him to admit it, the likelihood of Navaryn surrendering the third tome of the Order was virtually nonexistent.

"I'm beginning to think dealing with her may be a lost cause. If she awakens, she likely won't give up Iaalprt."

"We may have one other option," claimed Joro. "Lowenna and her vessel seem to share memories and flashbacks in a stir of confusion as she continues to awaken. The same is surely happening with Navaryn and her vessel as well."

"Your point being?"

"If I make contact with Navaryn's vessel and coax out her essence, I might be able to extract a clue to Iaalprt's location."

With few options, Joro's plan made logical sense. However, Merisek was all too familiar with his unpredictability and destructive tendencies from years past. The trust he had in him to carry out tasks involving Navaryn wore thin, and doing so proved too risky.

"We underestimated Navaryn once already. And for you to bring her essence forth would be unwise. Utilize her vessel for information instead. But have Nathaniel and Eitha do it," Merisek commanded.

"What?! My parents? You must be joking."

"Far from it. They owe me at least that much."

"But they won't last five minutes in the realm of Human!"

"You needn't worry about that. They'll survive just fine if I simply cast them into vessels."

"What?! Like you did with the Celestines?"

"No, you fool. They will simply assume control of them. Not be imprisoned as such. Though I'm leaving it up to you to find suitable vessels."

"But, how? And why go through the trouble?"

"I've taken care of the 'how' already, so do not concern yourself with it. We cannot afford to make our presence known in the realm of Human. Besides, their feeble minds make them dangerous to us. And since Lowenna could awaken at any time, I need you to keep your eye on her."

A brief pause followed after Merisek's order. "Fine," he said with a glare. As he took a few steps to leave the study, he turned back toward Merisek and motioned to one of the books on the table. "Is that Zin you have there?"

Merisek nodded.

"What have you found?"

"Nothing," Merisek replied, then peered back at the book. "The text keeps shifting into nonsense. I've looked for patterns in each change, hoping to decode any lines. There is nothing at all. At the very least, it finally stopped spouting those strange orbs."

Joro looked upon the nonsensical writings morphing across the pages. After only a few moments of observing the text's strange behavior, his mind grew fatigued. He imagined how draining it had been for Merisek to sustain his attention over the past several days.

"What about Ananael?"

"It's completely blank," he said while shaking his head.

"Blank?" said Joro puzzledly. "Do you think it could be a decoy?"

"It's not. It is authentic. Our inability to see the text poses a problem, but should not be completely unexpected." He looked back up at Joro, who stood with his arms crossed and a perplexed look.

"Ananael is the book of secret knowledge," Merisek continued. "Without all three books united, its contents are invisible. However, I did not expect to see this with Zin."

"You must know of something that can help. You've known of the Order for most of your life."

"We need Iaalprt. It's as simple as that," Merisek replied. "It seems that the books are utterly useless when they are separated. This isn't mere arcane diablerie we are dealing with here. It's the power over all that is, all that has been, and all that could ever be. The one thing that perhaps these books are telling me is that no shortcut can be taken."

A defeated look came over Joro. Although the lack of success in finding clues within the books came as little surprise to Merisek, his frustration continued to mount.

"I trust you understand now why Navaryn did what she did," Merisek uttered.

Joro could only jostle his head in response to his point.

"Go now. We're wasting time. Report back to me once you have found the vessels for Nathaniel and Eitha. I will make preparations to transmit them in the meantime."

"As you wish," said Joro with a nod as he walked away.

Silence returned to the study as Joro departed through the exit portal. Though before long, Merisek's semblance of peace was disturbed as the writings on Zin's pages began moving again. He closed his eyes and clutched his talisman, the Augo Mundus, as he tried to calm himself. Gifted to him by his father, the Augo Mundus was the most powerful and secretive item in his possession, crucial in the ascension of his power. It served as a window into an invaluable trove of knowledge that spanned countless realms. Had it not been for its use, Merisek would not have been able to track Navaryn and Lowenna to the realm of Human. Yet despite its unbridled power, the silver medallion, adorned with blackened jewels and a single smoky mauve gem affixed in its center, failed to bring him comfort. No matter how tirelessly he searched, he could not find a single clue that could unlock Zin's or Ananael's power. His only relief came from the memory of a long-since departed woman named Athelisa.

Though Merisek never let it be known to anyone, Athelisa was at the heart of his quest for the Order of Existence. Visions of the beautiful and warm-hearted woman he adored passed through his closed eyes. He recalled how her curly golden hair framed her gentle yet weary face, as well as the light brown freckles strewn across her cheeks that only he cared to notice. The essence in her vibrant green eyes had always managed to shatter any feeling of concern or despair, except for her own. Merisek often wondered, foolishly, what his life would be like if she were still alive. A persistent feeling of regret tore at his fiber as he pondered what more he could have done to prevent her tragic and painful end. Before her untimely death, he had never seized the opportunity to profess his love and admiration for her. Though his feelings toward her were unrequited, for she was wholeheartedly committed to another, he was confident the Order could afford him the chance to bring their paths together as he saw fit. Should he succeed in unlocking the secrets of the Order, a reunion with Athelisa would prove to be as effortless as a mere thought. Through the achingly slow degeneration of his body and mind, the cherished memory of Athelisa's smile became increasingly more challenging for Merisek to hold onto as each day passed. Time was not on his side, and he was more than aware of it.

Zin's words continued to shift as it lay open before Merisek, relentlessly mocking him as he came out of his thoughts. His eyes began to glow angrily as he watched the letters float and waltz around the pages. As nonsensical as the lines of text appeared to be, Merisek saw the sting of his undying regret, coupled with his erratic pursuit of redemption, spelled out across page after page as Zin continued to torment him. Suddenly, he extinguished the fireplace with a swift swing of his arm. The echoing slam of Zin being furiously closed trailed off into the cold darkness as Merisek sat in silence. Only the longing in his cold, withering heart, seeded in vengeance and brimming with hate, kept him company.

4

THE KEY

Warm flames nestled within the fireplace of Navaryn's underground safe room burned gently into the late evening as Von ambled with a glass of wine in hand. In his other, a soft lavender trail of energy flowed into one of several intricate symbols set at various points across the expanse. The time had come to recharge the concealment charms that hid his presence from Celestine's lurking eyes and ears. It was a process he found tedious, yet essential to keep his energy hidden. The charms took on a red-orange glow when fully charged and would last at least a week before needing another boost. Although restoring adequate power to the charms was taxing on Von's energy, his wine did well to replenish his vitality.

In further effort to keep his presence cloaked, Von periodically threw a handful of shed skin from Navaryn's dragon, Onyx, onto the fire, which helped mask the smoke escaping outside from the chimney. It was an accidental yet clever discovery Von made one day while assisting Onyx during a molt.

Given the circumstances, Von had become accustomed to hiding out in Celestine. Although he was far from his home realm of Daeva, the solitude of the safe room offered him uninterrupted focus amidst the familiarity of Navaryn's estate. Her safe room was equipped with tools for conjuration, from essential manuscripts of mystical knowledge and lore to talismans and other complementary items that she had collected over time. Additionally, a pantry full of preserved foods was kept for extended stays. There was even a modest bar neatly situated in the corner. Von regularly kept a stash of his self-made wine, which happened to pair wonderfully with the meat he dried from the carcasses Onyx provided from his occasional hunts.

Various pieces of dark-colored furniture, which muted the firelight, kept the room in line with the motif of concealment. A half-empty bottle of wine sat atop a large, polished obsidian table in the center of the room. Von snatched it up, promptly filled his glass, then sat at the table to ruminate and recharge before addressing the remaining charms.

Upon Navaryn's disappearance, Von sought the help of Aalrija, Navaryn's former guardian and one of Celestine's Tiers, to find her. She was the only Celestine in the upper echelons of the Halryn who trusted him and kept the nature of his whereabouts and relationship with Navaryn discreet. Military presence increased throughout the realm following Navaryn and Lowenna's banishment, especially within the western Halryn borders where Benson, his Tiers, and other esteemed council members resided. This made establishing contact with Aalrija challenging, but Von's patience paid off. After careful attempts over almost a month, they finally met and formed their alliance.

It was then that Aalrija instructed Von in the practice of Laylanailee, an old, arcane technique used to help locate one's essence through their dreams. Given the seemingly endless number of realms in existence and no other way to effectively search and hone in on Navaryn and Lowenna's imprisoned essences, Benson cited the use of Laylanailee as the only possible solution to locate them. The caveat, however, was the difficulty of using such an antiquated and challenging technique, and there was only a short, unpredictable window of time when a subject would even fall into a dream. No one, not even Aalrija herself, had achieved success. Nevertheless, she had unwavering faith that the bond Von had with Navaryn would help him forge a successful connection.

The safe room below Navaryn's castle had become Von's home,

and over the span of four months, he worked relentlessly to develop his skill in Laylanailee. His convenient location also enabled Aalrija to keep in frequent contact through Elemental Paralleling, a covert form of projecting oneself through one of the classic elements. For that reason, Von kept the fireplace in a constant burn.

While sipping his wine, Von reminisced over his efforts and failures. Throughout his concentrated practice, he had only recently found the success he had so earnestly strived for. And after his latest connection, he was sure that he made a breakthrough. Von impatiently tapped away at the side of his chair while staring into the dancing flames, eagerly awaiting Aalrija's projection for more hours than he cared to count. After he slugged the rest of the wine back, wispy embers fluttered out from under the mantel.

"Von?" called Aalrija. Her tall spectral figure was shrouded in a gentle, fiery haze as it flowed out of the fireplace. "Von, I'm here."

"*There* you are!" he boomed as he turned in his chair, "Where have you been?"

"I'm sorry. As you can imagine, it's been a bit chaotic, and I haven't been able to step away from the council for very long," Aalrija replied. Her fiery projection approached Von, casting an orange glow onto his face and revealing his tired red eyes. "Are you alright? You look exhausted."

"I've barely slept," he replied while refilling his wine. "Old nightmares have been acting up now and again. Don't worry about it."

Although Elemental Paralleling was one of many antiquated techniques all but forgotten throughout Celestine, the dazzling display made Aalrija's periodic visits all the more enjoyable to Von. Because of the mystical substance behind the technique, coupled with the purifying nature of fire, the gentle, disciplined flames did not harm anything they touched.

Von was aware that Aalrija made it her duty to catalog, protect, and rehearse such techniques to keep them from being lost to the ages and to have them up her sleeve, ready to utilize should the necessity arise. Elemental Paralleling also offered the security Aalrija needed to communicate with Von without alerting the council, namely Benson.

Aalrija wearily traipsed to the opposite side of the gleaming obsidian table and sat across from Von as he swirled his wine.

"You seem anxious. What's going on?" Aalrija asked.

Von leaned forward. "I have news."

"News? Well, that can only mean you've made some progress in Laylanailee, then?"

Von put his glass down and looked into her fiery eyes. "I found her, Aalrija. I finally found Navaryn."

Overtaken with shock and delight, Aalrija cupped her hands over her face and fell silent for a moment before replying, "Y-you're certain?"

Von nodded.

"Where is she?"

"Far away, in the realm of Human. She, her essence rather, is trapped. Imprisoned within a young girl," explained Von. "She's confused. Her thoughts and memories are detached, and she doesn't know where she is."

"Trapped within another being? That simply can't be possible."

"It is her. I am sure of it," said Von.

Step by step, he recounted the events of the dreamwalk. Although it appeared he had become well-versed in the technique and that a genuine astral exchange had occurred, Aalrija was not yet convinced.

"It doesn't make sense, Von. It could have simply been your own dream. How can you believe with utmost certainty that Navaryn is imprisoned in this human girl?"

"I'll show you then. Wait here," said Von as he rose from his seat, then walked to the end of the room. After a few moments, he returned to the table with a hefty book. With conviction, he placed it atop the obsidian table next to the bottle of wine.

"Iaalprt?" Aalrija said softly. "You had it?"

"Now that you know, don't tell anyone," he cautioned. "It's safer that way."

"But, Von, I-"

"No one. At all. Do you understand?" he uttered sternly. "The more people who know where Iaalprt is, the less safe it will be."

It was then that Aalrija understood Navaryn had entrusted Von with Iaalprt, should she be compelled to lay down her life to protect it. However reluctant she was to swear her secrecy, she understood Von's intention. Just as Navaryn acted to protect the book, Von sought to do the same for the sake of all existence.

Von opened the tome. "It started doing this as soon as I woke from that dream after I made the connection," he confessed as he motioned to the small orbs of encapsulated fire fluttering out from the binding. "I think it's calling to her."

Aalrija's eyes widened as she watched them dance and swirl. There was only one other time she had seen the display: at the ceremony when Navaryn and Lowenna were inducted into the Halryn Tiers, and both Iaalprt and Zin were bound to them for protection. Upon being bestowed to their guardians, Iaalprt and Zin emitted their respective elemental responses of fire and water to officiate their duties. Von was indeed correct in deducing the reason for Iaalprt's behavior, and she could hardly believe it.

"She's there, Aalrija," Von pressed. "The dream I found her in is one that no other could possibly ever have."

"This is astonishing, Von. Iaalprt is certainly aware of your discovery," she declared through excited, quivering breath. As she pulled Iaalprt toward her, any lingering doubt she had in Von's words was extinguished. "What a dastardly banishment this is. We can only assume that Lowenna would be in the same predicament."

Von nodded. "And if I know Merisek, he's working to keep a few steps ahead of us."

"Then we haven't any time to waste," said Aalrija as she quickly rose from her chair.

Von watched as she muttered to herself and paced frantically in front of the fireplace. He then took Iaalprt back to a hidden compartment within the far wall. Not only was it for the added measure of protection, but the fiery orbs were an annoying distraction.

With Iaalprt secured, he then retrieved his glass of wine from the table. "Thoughts?"

Aalrija ceased her mutterings and turned toward Von. "We need to get to the realm of Human right away."

"Obviously," Von replied. "But how? I can't Parallel there. Can you?"

"No, I cannot. And going to my channels to figure out how would no doubt raise suspicion and alert Benson," said Aalrija. "However, I might know of a way to get you there. You need to pay a visit to Fallon."

"Fallon?" he said. "The last time I checked, he wanted me dead."

"You needn't be concerned, Von. He can be trusted," she assured. "I've kept him apprised of all our actions. He offered to help should we need it, and he has something that can assist in getting you where you need to go."

"Does he, now? What is it?"

"I will make sure Fallon explains everything to you," she replied. "You must go to him tonight. Paralleling is out of the question, as you might have guessed, so you'll have to take Onyx to get there."

"A ride on the winged reptile. Great," he muttered.

Aalrija gave Von a puzzled look, "Is something the matter? He still doesn't dislike you, does he?"

"No, we've been fine," said Von. "It's just that Paralleling would save us a lot of time."

"There cannot be one inkling of detectable transmission. As I said, Benson and the council are surely monitoring—"

"I know, I know," Von interjected. "The risk is too great. I get it."

"Take a look at the bright side. It gives you more time to bond with Onyx," she said with a smile.

Von chuckled at Aalrija's lightheartedness because she didn't have all the details behind his colorful relationship with the young dragon.

"It'll be alright. You have Navaryn's cowl to shield your energy, and Onyx knows the way to Fallon. He can quickly and quietly fly you there under the cover of night. Furthermore, this item requires personal instruction on how to use it. You must be present."

"You sure have thought all of this through."

"I've had to, Von."

Von finished his last sip of wine. "Alright, fine. I'll pay Fallon a visit."

"Wonderful!" Aalrija said ecstatically. "And please trust that there will be no hostility directed at you. I won't allow it."

"Oh, I'm not worried."

"Then, I will let Fallon know to expect you."

After a stretch, Von chimed, "Time to wake up the lizard."

Aalrija smiled and positioned herself in front of the fireplace. "Words cannot express how grateful I am. We are a step closer to bringing our guardians back home. And it's because of you."

Von looked back at Aalrija with a grin and waved goodbye as her fiery projection slowly dissipated. As the dancing flames sputtered away, the warm feeling of her acknowledgement washed through his chest. Progress had finally moved forward in his quest, and there was no time to lose momentum. He placed his wine glass atop the mantel, opened a small trunk on the floor beside the couch, and grabbed a black satchel and Navaryn's concealment cowl.

With items in hand, Von closed the trunk and started toward the secluded rear exit of the safe room. After making his way out of the rear entrance of the safe room and following a long dark corridor, he slipped through a small exit hole leading to an underground grotto. A smile found him as he recalled the occasions when Onyx was confined to the safe room as a hatchling. Eventually, he came to use the small exit as he pleased, sometimes bringing back the mangled carcass of an unfortunate cave rodent as a gift for Navaryn. Such excitement, however, was short-lived. Onyx grew quickly, and it didn't take long before his girth prevented him from fitting through the exit.

The damp cavern was dark, and even though Von's sensitive eyes could see the outlines of the jagged rocky walls, the irregular formations made him stumble. He conjured a small flame above his fingertips to light the way. The cavern filled with a golden hue, and tiny glints of various minerals embedded within the walls ignited. Suddenly, a low rumbling from the far end of the cavern caught his ear, and a large black mass stirred and rolled over. Fast asleep on a pile of plush pampas grass was Navaryn's dragon, Onyx.

Apprehensively, Von approached the sleeping beast. Through time and persistent effort on Navaryn's part early on, Onyx eventually grew tolerant of him. However, mounting him like a steed was a different story. Onyx's stubbornness proved to be a test of patience as he typically bucked Von off his back whenever he tried to ride him. Such instances didn't go without their share of laughs to be had. Yet, for Navaryn's sake, he knew better than to endanger Von's life during his shenanigans. Over time, as Navaryn made her feelings toward Von more evident, Onyx's tolerance for him grew more toward true acceptance.

Von draped Navaryn's cowl over his shoulder as he began to coax Onyx out of his slumber. Softly, he called, "Come on, sleepy head, we gotta go," as he patted Onyx's plump belly.

Onyx let out a grunt as he remained still. His breaths were long and calm, as if he was having a peaceful dream.

"I know it's late, but I need your help now," Von pressed.

Onyx nudged Von away with his tail and proceeded to groan.

"Oh, c'mon. How can you possibly be sleeping at a time like this?!"

The startling sound of his voice made one of Onyx's sky-blue eyes spring open. His piercing oval pupil glared at Von, then slowly looked away. Lying just outside the nest of pampas grass was a skeleton of a large animal picked clean of all meat and sinew, and formations of rock excavated of all minerals.

"Right. I almost forgot you're still a growing boy," said Von as he glanced over the remains of his meal. "Had yourself a late-night snack, eh? Think you're overdoing it at this point."

Onyx typically became enthusiastic whenever it came time to eat and responsibly enjoyed the occasional late-night outing to fetch a morsel from the open grounds of Celestine when he tired from foraging for gems and other precious deposits within the cave. Devouring the animal he had caught from the forest earlier in the evening exacerbated his lethargy. The tired look on Onyx's face was apparent, though it couldn't veil the sadness in his eyes.

"I miss her too, Onyx," said Von as he patted the scaly armor plating on his shoulder. "Which is why we need to get going. Fallon is expecting us."

Onyx perked at the mention of Fallon's name. He was always thrilled to visit him, since he always had unique treats to share, as well as various obstacles and contraptions to keep him entertained. Having not visited Fallon's estate for several months, the prospect of going there made him turn his complete attention to Von.

"It'll have to be a quick visit. We don't have a lot of time to spend there."

The elation left Onyx almost immediately as he stared blankly at Von.

"I know you're disappointed. Believe me, I wish time were on our side," he continued. "But Fallon has something that can help us find Navaryn."

For a moment, Onyx seemed to be in disbelief. Yet, his eyes began to brighten with hope.

"I promise there will be time for everything once things return to normal. And you can help with that by helping me now."

Von watched Onyx's pale blue eyes pan left and right as he sat in thought. Through his encouraging words, it appeared that the despair hidden deep within his eyes began to dwindle.

"What do you say, huh?" asked Von with a smile.

With a flame spurt from his nostrils, as he snorted, Onyx rose out of his plush nest of grass onto his four sturdy legs.

"That's my guy," Von uttered with satisfaction as if speaking to an obedient child.

Von and Onyx strolled side by side down the winding corridor toward the cave exit. The adolescent dragon unfolded and stretched his massive wings, though they dragged against the walls as he barely reached half-span.

"Looks like you're gonna need a bigger cave pretty soon," said Von with a chuckle.

As they approached the cave entrance, a clearing in the corridor provided enough room for Onyx to stretch his wings properly. There was just enough of a runway before the cliff dropped off to a ravine below, which he always used to warm his legs up with a few laps. Von thought back to the handful of times he would watch Navaryn delight in taking off on Onyx when she was coaching him on how to fly.

The shadow of night normally cloaked the remote sector in darkness; however, the pair of full yellow moons at their late-night apex cast plenty of light on the cliffside. Von took the opportunity to gaze at them while quickly recharging the pair of concealment charms affixed to both sides of the cave entrance. Onyx noticed Von smiling as he recalled how Navaryn would always make him stop and stare at the moons with her. He sighed and turned to Onyx, who waited for him at the edge of the cliff. Just then, Von slipped his arms into Navaryn's cowl, a faint scent of her musk still lingering in the cloth. Although the fit was fairly snug, the material felt soft and secure. Ironically, it seemed to correct Von's slipping posture as well.

Onyx seemed amused by Von wearing Navaryn's cowl, though seeing it gave him comfort. Knowing she had given it to him made it all the easier to bear trust in him.

Von pulled the oversized hood over his head and asked, "Think this will go smoothly?" as he ruminated on his last encounter with Fallon.

Onyx's inquisitive eyes shifted in thought, then squinted before he stretched his legs in preparation for his take-off jaunt.

"Yeah, tell me about it. I'm sure he's still pissed at me," he said as he opened the thick, black hide satchel, then reached inside. Out came a pair of exquisitely crafted gauntlets, obsidian in color and adorned with precious red orbs. After affixing them to his hands, he asked, "You remember the way, right?"

Onyx slowly reared his unamused face toward Von.

"Just thought I'd ask. No need for dirty looks."

Von ascended Onyx's outstretched wing like a staircase and vaulted onto his back, his armor-plated scales providing the perfect footholds. Once past the cave's boundary, the cowl was the only thing keeping his energy secure.

"You ready?" asked Von, to which Onyx replied with a jovial nod and a shifty eye. "I know that look. Don't even think of bucking me off this time. It's annoying." He then nudged Onyx's shoulder with his foot. "Let's go."

The mischievous dragon blustered what Von interpreted as a snicker as he galumphed in a circle away from the edge of the cliff and soon returned to it at full speed. He quickly tightened his grip around a stubby pair of spiked horns protruding from Onyx's scaly neck and held tight as they spiraled downward towards the gorge.

Onyx extended his wings to slow his momentum and ascend in the air, narrowly avoiding clipping the scattered trees and careening into the jagged rocks.

"South, Onyx. Remember?" Von yelled as he tugged the spikes in his neck to the side, "Made yourself dizzy back there, didn't you? You know, if you had taken one second longer, I'd have had to act. Would've Paralleled us both to Daeva in that case."

Onyx nonchalantly banked to the right and corrected his southward path toward Fallon's shop. Although he tried to play off his miscalculated direction, Von knew all too well he was simply trying to show off.

"Guess I'm gonna have to steer, huh?"

Von's grip on Onyx's spikes loosened as his flight smoothed out. The quiet night air brought a peaceful calm to his mind after several long and taxing months. However, it didn't take long before his mind started to churn with thoughts about his impending encounter with Fallon. He had met him only once before, briefly and unexpectedly. Considering the disastrous outcome, Von wondered what Aalrija could have said to convince him to offer his aid.

As Von's contemplation trailed off, he looked to a small town below him. "Oh, shit. We're too low!" he snapped and stiffly patted the side of Onyx's neck.

Realizing the error as well, Onyx swiftly shifted out of sight above the rolling clouds. However, a pair of weary eyes caught a slight glimpse of Onyx's tail.

"Hey, Teagan. Look!"

Teagan, the tavern's keeper, who was taking a breather from a heavy crowd, replied, "What did ya say there, Kumiko?"

Sitting atop the dew-filled lawn, Kumiko peered back up to the sky. "I thought I saw ... wait. No. It couldn't have been."

"Couldn't have been what?" Teagan pressed as he strode down the steps toward Kumiko.

"Never mind," he whispered.

Teagan squinted at the night sky. "Boy, you make me wonder sometimes." His laugh was hearty as he rummaged through his thick, wiry beard.

Kumiko's violet eyes were exhausted and distant as he replied, "I make myself wonder, too."

"I know that lovesick look of yours. Trust me, we'll get Navaryn back," Teagan encouraged. "Lowenna, too."

"Sure hope you're right," he replied as he sipped his ale.

"Why not come back inside? Your mates are playing a game and wondering where you are."

"I'll be along soon."

"Well, you've been sitting out there for about an hour now, and I'm sure your britches are soaked."

"Britches?" Kumiko griped. "I don't wear britches."

"Jus' foolin' there. You can do as you like, you know that." Teagan repeated his hearty laugh, though it failed to make Kumiko grin.

Kumiko looked back to the sky as his mind churned with memories of Navaryn, his long-time training partner and friend. Although they had tried and failed at a romantic partnership, he was determined to remain an integral part of her life. Not long after their split, Kumiko discovered her secret relationship with Von, one of Daeva and Celestine's most wanted. Feeling betrayed by her recklessness and deviant wanderlust, he strove to expose Von as the demented soul he was rumored to be, even if it meant that Navaryn would despise him forever. Though afforded the opportunity on several occasions, his words failed to make the impact he intended.

Kumiko stood up and turned to make his way back into the tavern. After dusting off the damp sprigs of grass from his pants, he slugged back the remaining ale from his glass. Teagan looked his way as he approached and gave him a nod. With a labored smirk, Kumiko casually ascended the steps to the tavern to make his reentrance, but not before taking one last skyward glance.

From atop Onyx, Von watched the clustered domains below

become fewer and further apart as they flew through the night. The billowing clouds thinned as they entered the familiar forest region on the outskirts of the Halryn border, which meant they were nearing Fallon's shop. The cover of darkness was enough to keep them hidden as they descended toward the dense canopy of trees.

"Almost there, Onyx. I'll guide you the rest of the way," said Von to his scaly steed.

Though Onyx enjoyed the dark, namely because he loved viewing the moons just as much as Navaryn, his night vision was underdeveloped since he was still plenty young. Von hardly had difficulty seeing in the darkness, so he surveyed the vast canopy to locate their destination. The large span of the forest area leading up to Fallon's Shop was uninhabited, offering him the distance and solitude he desired. The shimmery moonlight cast a gentle luminance across the trees, keeping everything beneath the canopy unseen. The only impending indicator of the shop's location was a discreet lookout tower protruding just above the canopy. Naturally, Von located it at a distance with ease.

Fallon had a mandatory rule that all his guests had to follow. Paralleling and other visual travel to his domain were restricted to a distant perimeter of the forest line, ensuring that any would-be onlookers couldn't learn of the precise location of his shop. Just as Navaryn did when they came to Fallon's shop together, Von guided Onyx to a suitable place to land to venture the rest of the way on foot. Shards of moonlight managed to pierce through the thicket, yet it was still much too dark for Onyx to see clearly. To avoid an aimless trounce through the forest, Von had a different idea.

"Alright, here's the plan," he said gently. "Just keep your eyes closed and run straight ahead."

Onyx grunted and reared his head backward toward Von in a puzzled manner.

"I know, I know. But Fallon insists we land this far away, and we need to hurry."

Von felt the brushing of Onyx's rear legs on the soil, which was the giveaway that he was preparing to buck him off his back.

"You throw me off, then you can forget about sticking around at

Fallon's," he warned.

The gleam of Onyx's widened blue eyes seemed to pierce through Von as he looked at him giddily.

"Yeah, you heard me. You've been great, and you got us here a lot sooner than I anticipated. We can spare some time at Fallon's, but we need to hurry."

Onyx swung his head forward again.

"Trust me on this. I can see for the both of us," he pleaded. "I'll steer you through the trees, and we'll be at Fallon's in no time."

Although Onyx was unsure of Von's idea, he reluctantly agreed with an affirmative snort. Von grabbed hold of Onyx's stubby horns, then firmly planted his boots in his armored plates. Braced for a romp through the trees, Von gave his reptilian ride the signal to dart full speed ahead. With his eyes tightly closed, Onyx sprinted into the forest as quickly as his legs could manage.

As Von carefully steered Onyx through the trees, he was reminded of when Navaryn first brought him to the forest. Aside from the familiar winding limbs and the fluttering of insect wings, he distinctly remembered the scent of the native tree bark as they traversed the forest together. The same smell hung over him, and he relished the rejuvenating sylvan aroma filling his lungs.

Out in the dark distance ahead, a trail of purple floating orbs came into view. Von slowed Onyx's pace and had him reopen his eyes. Though Von was initially cautious of them, Onyx immediately knew what they were for. He quickly followed the loose trail leading deeper into the forest. Just beyond the last series of orbs was a discreetly lit clearing in the woods. Standing at its center was Fallon, holding one of the signal orbs in his hand. Onyx sprinted straight toward him with an elated look in his eyes. As he closed in, Fallon tossed it into the air. With a quick reaction, Onyx disintegrated this target with a spittle of flame from his nostrils.

"Well done, Onyx," said Fallon with a grin as he tossed the butchered leg of a forest animal to the frisky dragon.

As Onyx excitedly devoured the morsel of meat, Von hopped off his back and walked toward Fallon. He wore a fitted shirt, thick pants, and a long, dark blacksmith's coat that covered panels of hard leather armor. Von surmised he had recently finished working in his forge, judging from the soot spots on his weathered hands and face.

"Hello, Von," Fallon greeted with his hands clasped behind his back. "It's been a while."

Surprised by such a warm and welcoming demeanor, he apprehensively replied, "Indeed it has."

Fallon took notice of Von's guarded stance and instantly recognized the fearsome gauntlets affixed to his hands. "I take it you've discovered the secret in using those, perhaps?"

"Maybe. You care to find out?"

His warning made Fallon furrow his eyebrows. "Don't be alarmed, Von. You are not my enemy today."

"If not today, then how about tomorrow?" he quipped snidely. "Does that work better for you?"

"There is no need for hostility. I am here before you as an ally. Should your continued efforts further demonstrate your honorable intentions, I shall stay that way."

Von chuckled. "I must've played this meeting out in my head about twenty times on the way over here, and not once did I expect you to be so welcoming."

"Am I wrong in being gracious to you in this time of need? I care no longer that you stole from me. Our present situation bears far more importance."

"You are missing the big difference. I did not *steal* these from you. They are rightfully mine, and I took them back," Von affirmed, clenching his fist.

"Which you no doubt had discovered only after the fact," Fallon replied with his index finger pronounced.

"Look. I didn't come to split hairs with you about this. I'm here only because Aalrija sent me."

"Indeed. She told me you managed to make contact with Navaryn through Laylanailee. I'd be a fool not to call that impressive. But I can't say that I'm surprised."

"Is that so? Why?"

"Simply put, it illustrates the bond that you and Navaryn share. You are the only one I've encountered who has successfully used that technique in this endeavor. It gives me confidence that you could be our hope in bringing our guardians back to us."

"And you have something that will help me get that done. I will trust you that far."

"And I am willing to put my trust in you as well. Navaryn and Aalrija surely have. Not to mention Onyx, here. That is enough reason for me right now," said Fallon, motioning to the gluttonous dragon still gnawing on the animal flank.

"Glad we have come to an understanding of sorts," said Von with careful gratitude. "Care to lead the way?"

"Of course," he replied with a motion of his hand. He took another glance at Von, recognizing the fabric shrouding his head. "Is that Navaryn's concealment cowl you have on?" he asked.

"*Heh.* Yeah, it is," said Von, rolling his eyes.

"You look uncomfortable. And ridiculous," said Fallon with a chuckle. "I have something that will suit you better."

Von and Onyx followed behind Fallon as he led them to his shop, where he lived and worked. Just beyond the clearing stood the familiar grand stone edifice of the main showroom. Onyx flew off to trounce about the open estate grounds as they reached the entrance, though he was cautioned not to make too much noise.

"Do pardon the mess," said Fallon as he opened the door. "I've been a bit busier than normal."

The shop's main showroom was much as Von remembered, though now there were even more valuable pieces of armor and weaponry on display. Each one was crafted entirely by Fallon with exquisite quality and attention to detail, making it impossible for Von to hide his appreciation.

Although he was primarily a craftsman of weaponry, Fallon was also adept at using them, having a hand in training Navaryn.

As Von dawdled around the aisles of armor, Fallon reemerged from behind his work desk with a shiny piece of metal in his hand.

"Here. Catch," said Fallon as he tossed a medallion to Von. "Wear this instead of that cowl. It'll offer you the same protection."

Von held the small amulet on a silver chain in his hand and delved into a tense yet oddly fond memory. As he looked over the intricate patterns in the forged metal, he began to chuckle.

"What's so funny?"

"Nav was wearing this when we first met."

"Is that right?" Fallon replied as he pondered. "And just how did you two meet each other?"

Von looked at Fallon's inquisitive face. "I'll, uh. I'll tell you later. Can we get on with what you have for me?"

"Certainly. I'll just be a moment," he said as he started toward a curtained archway behind him.

After Fallon disappeared behind the deep blue fabric draping the doorway, Von pulled the amulet over his head. Not typically one for wearing talismans or jewelry of any kind, he slipped the amulet inside his shirt and removed Navaryn's cowl. He found instant relief after shedding the restrictive cloth, jostling his head back and forth to crack his neck. Fallon then promptly reemerged with an object large enough to be carried with two hands. Nestled gently in his palms in its raw form was an elestial cluster of crystal, translucent yellow with specks of pale blue suspended within. The unsuspecting crystal didn't appear any more useful than a paperweight, but Fallon handled it with extreme care as if it were delicate glass.

Puzzled, Von blurted, "This is it? A rock?"

"Do not be fooled by its appearance," said Fallon with a smirk. "It's incredibly powerful."

"What is it?"

"Delavine Crystal"

"Alright, so, what does it do?"

"It can take you across planes of existence. To other realms."

"Like inter-realm Paralleling?"

"Not exactly. Even Paralleling has its boundaries. With this crystal, there is only one skill to learn. Master that, and you may go wherever you choose."

Fallon carefully passed the crystal into Von's cupped hands. It felt cool to the touch as he looked it over. Specks of blue reflected the chandelier's light above, giving the yellow clusters a glowing hue. Although initially unimpressed with its unrefined state, he felt an unmistakable force pulsing through his arms as he held it.

"You're not lying. There is a lot of power coursing within these formations."

Fallon nodded. "Traveling by way of this crystal is undetectable, I might add. Unlike Paralleling."

"Where did you get this?"

"This Delavine Crystal sat in the council's archives until Benson ordered all of them to be destroyed several years ago. Aalrija secretly took it from there and entrusted it to me."

"Why would he want to destroy them?"

Anticipating Von's query, Fallon turned and sat on his work stool. "As you are aware, not everyone can Parallel. However, anyone can learn to use a Delavine Crystal," he explained. "Since the advent of the Parallel, using the Delavine Crystal as a method of transmission was deemed obsolete and therefore was no longer used. Benson sought to further his control over Celestine by doing away with these crystals completely, thus preventing those not sanctioned by the Halryn council from leaving the realm."

"Aren't you doing the same thing by keeping this stashed in your shop?"

"There can be an honorable purpose in safeguarding a secret, Von," Fallon replied. "One day, Benson's rule will come to an end. Then, and only then, can the populace have this knowledge safely returned to them. The risk of trusting more than myself and Aalrija to keep this secret is great. So now I'm trusting you to preserve it just the same."

Fallon's outlook resonated perfectly with Von, for his scenario with Iaalprt was the same. To see eye-to-eye with Fallon, a member of the Halryn council himself, was as unexpected as it felt natural. As pragmatic as Fallon presented himself, his words framed him as a potentially sound and fair leader. There was, however, no ambition for him to pursue such a role. Although he knew the value of freedom and the means to preserve it, his work and his isolative nature were enough for him. Nevertheless, in his anticipation of Kumiko's rule, he kept the dream of seeing a more just and free Celestine in his lifetime alive.

"So, is it possible that more of these crystals are out there?" asked Von.

"It is, though this is the only one I know of," Fallon replied. "Frankly, there's no way of knowing if anyone has one in their possession. If someone does, I'm sure they are doing well on their part to keep it hidden."

"An untold secret," said Von.

"Precisely. Not even Navaryn knows of it. Not by her teachings nor spoken of by either myself or Aalrija."

Von embraced the energy emanating from the crystal as it created a gentle tether to his core, responding to his will and determination. The sensation felt natural in essence and caused him no alarm or tension. Fallon was pleased with how quickly the crystal responded to Von's energy, as it would make the instruction of its use easier.

"Aalrija mentioned you located Navaryn in Human," said Fallon.

"That's right. Are you familiar with the realm at all?"

"Not personally, but I have records of it. It is a realm of weak mystical energy. A fact that may pose a challenge for the crystal."

"Okay. I guess that calls for the next order of business. How do I use this thing?"

"I'm glad you asked," said Fallon with a grin.

Fallon noted that the practice required a quiet mind and extraordinary focus to enter a proper meditative trance, a test of patience far beyond what Aalrija had instilled in him. Following a few quick lessons, Von made several successful incremental projections ranging from just outside Fallon's shop to the doorstep of Navaryn's castle. However, Fallon did caution that traversing into another plane would be a far more challenging feat. Although his practical training was short, his bond with Navaryn gave him an advantage.

Von knew well that Onyx was enjoying himself while he received training from Fallon, but it had come time to leave. With the Delavine Crystal secured in his satchel, Von called Onyx over with the help of another treat.

"Be prepared, Von," said Fallon. "With the limited time I've had to instruct you, a successful projection into the realm of Human will take more than a few tries to get it right. You must be persistent."

"I'll give it my best," he replied. "It's for Navaryn."

A warm smile found Fallon upon hearing the humble determination in Von's voice. "You love her."

Von gave a subtle smirk before nodding affirmatively.

"You know, it wasn't long ago that I would have been proud to have your head. I've severely misjudged you, and for that, I am sorry."

"Oh, come on, don't do that," said Von. Not wanting to linger for further embarrassment, he turned toward Onyx, waiting patiently with his wing outstretched, then vaulted onto his back.

"Before you go," called Fallon, "would you humor me and tell me how you and Navaryn met?"

"It's sort of a long story," he replied.

"Spare the details, then."

Von grinned as he came up with the most succinct yet humorous explanation he could give him. "We tried to kill each other."

Fallon gave Von a perplexed look as his jaw fell agape, yet he couldn't muster a response. Von simply replied with a shrug. Before the silence became any more awkward, he gripped Onyx's horns and directed him back through the forest.

Given Fallon's position within the Halryn council, Von was surprised he did not know about his first encounter with Navaryn. It only further illustrated Benson's grasp of who was privy to specific events. Regardless, Von preferred to keep as many details about his life as discreet as possible, so he paid little mind to the situation. His focus remained steadfast on the task at hand. After their jaunt through the thicket, he and Onyx darted into the clouds hanging low in the night sky. Mid-flight, he whispered to the dragon a promise of more delicious morsels in store for him the sooner they made it back to Navaryn's castle. Onyx streamlined his body and cut through the air like a knife as he picked up speed, making Von grab a tighter hold of his spikes.

Fallon inhaled the sweet night air, then proceeded to straighten up his lanes of training targets. As he waltzed patiently through the grassy clearing, he felt a sense of gratification he never thought he would experience in lending assistance to a Daeva, especially one as notorious and feared as Von. Following their rendezvous, Fallon could no longer accept the notion of Von being an enemy. Their mutual goal of bringing Navaryn and Lowenna back to Celestine sparked the possibility of unity between their two kinds, however distant that remained. Standing his last training target upright, he turned his attention to a looming presence within the trees.

"I know you're there, Kumiko," Fallon called into the forest. "You can come out now."

A few seconds later, Kumiko revealed himself from skulking in the shadowy canopy above and leapt to the ground. "You knew I was here?" he asked as he furiously strode up to Fallon.

"Ever since you arrived. The ale on your breath explains your inhibited energy suppression," Fallon said as lightheartedly as he could manage. "Surprised I was the only one to notice."

There was evident anger in Kumiko's stance and expression. Unable to shake his suspicion from seeing Onyx mounted and flying overhead back at Teagan's tavern, he decided to follow his heading. Just as he had expected, he found Onyx traversing the grounds when he arrived at Fallon's shop, but stayed out of sight to survey the area for his obscure companion.

"Well, since you've been up there for a while, I'm sure you have questions," said Fallon.

"That's an understatement," Kumiko snapped. "Just what are you doing with that Daeva scum?"

"Kumiko, listen. Von has located Navaryn."

"What are you talking about?" he griped. "Just how long have you two been conspiring together?"

"Did you not hear me?" As Kumiko's irritated groan cut the air, Fallon continued, "As it stands, Von is our strongest lead in getting her back. And with any luck, Lowenna as well."

"I don't understand. What's going on here?"

Fallon took a deep breath to settle his nerves. "There are clandestine plans in motion to see that our guardians return to us. Von is playing a crucial role in this, and I am assisting him."

Flabbergasted, Kumiko berated, "This is ridiculous, Fallon! Since when do you trust the word of a Daeva?!"

"Since Aalrija has."

"Aalrija?!" Kumiko yelped. "She's involved in this, too?"

"She is. And now that you know, you must swear to keep this from Benson."

"Why shouldn't I tell him of this? He's my father, after all, and he has made finding Navaryn and Lowenna his main objective."

"And how close has he come? How close have you, for that matter?"

"How dare you?" Kumiko growled. "We have tried everything we could. For months! I fail to believe how a Daeva could succeed where we have failed."

"I can't help but see what is before me, Kumiko. Von worked tirelessly to find Navaryn and has succeeded, while you've apparently resorted to indulging in ale and feeling sorry for yourself. I implore you to see things as they are." With crossed arms, he continued, "Your father has become inept. Delusional, even. You know that just as well as I do."

Such bluntness came as a blow to Kumiko. After a tense and dismissive pause, he spoke, "How could this be? How can that putrid Daeva possibly be the key to all of this?"

"Say what you will about Von, and all of Daeva, for that matter. That is your right. But you must think beyond yourself and your standing in Celestine and consider what is at stake here," reasoned Fallon with intense yet pleading eyes.

Fuming with frustration, Kumiko began to pace as he battled the thoughts he tried earnestly to deny.

"Should Benson be made aware of our plan, he will bring ruin to Aalrija and me," Fallon continued. "Besides the obvious consequences we would face, do you honestly think he would accept the possibility that a Daeva would be successful in saving two of our own? He is far too arrogant and would sooner disrupt our plan than admit to being powerless in finding them."

Kumiko had no further retort, for Fallon had been familiar with Benson's character for far longer than he had. It was a brutal truth at times, but he reluctantly agreed with Fallon's assertion about his father. His leadership had grown increasingly weak over the years, yet his inner circles continued to place their confidence in him out of unquestioning loyalty. Beyond the apparent degradation of his father's rule, Kumiko had fought against his increasing disdain for him.

"So," Fallon continued, "what will you do? Foil our chance at bringing Navaryn and Lowenna home, or keep your father in the dark and let us do our work?"

Kumiko slowly exhaled with a stern look before replying, "What is this plan of yours?"

"I have said all that I will to you about that. Am I to guess you wish to assist in this endeavor?"

"Yes. I want in."

"Well, should you conclude that you will not breathe a word of this to your father, then go speak with Aalrija."

Fallon waited with anticipation for Kumiko's compliance. There was no question in his mind that Kumiko's desire for Navaryn's return was compelling enough that he would keep it a secret from his father.

"Benson won't know a word of this. I swear it," Kumiko pledged. "I will consult with Aalrija."

"Go quickly then," Fallon urged. "Parallel if you must. Every moment saved is another moment closer to the return of our guardians."

Kumiko dashed into the trees without hesitation and vanished under a bright flash of white, arcing light. At last, the sound of silence returned to Fallon's remote corner of the forest. He turned back toward the stone edifice of his shop and ran his fingers through his thick, dark hair. Only the sound of his slow, steady breaths and the crunch of the grass beneath his feet found his ears as he paced forward. Having so deftly coaxed Kumiko into lending his assistance was an unexpected yet crucial addition to the plan. It only further assured Fallon that they would find success. For the time being, until beckoned again, he returned to his shop and back into the solitude he had become so accustomed to.

5

THE OPPORTUNIST

Inside a large, gleaming, tiled room, a young man in a towel stood before an L-shaped counter and lit a series of tapers. He carefully placed them into branching candelabras as steam continued to fill the room.

After he lit the last one, he turned around and asked, "Hey, Nav. Got any more candles?"

Navaryn, who sat atop a thick basin rim in a plush black robe, looked away from the surging hot water and pointed to a low cabinet. "There might be some spares in there."

"If there aren't enough, Abyl, let me know," called Lowenna from across the room. "I can go grab some new ones from the closet down the hall."

Abyl pushed aside small bins of odds and ends long forgotten, then came upon a thin paper box. "Ah, these will do just fine."

Navaryn watched him fish out a handful of tea lights. "So that's where those have been."

With a smile, Lowenna turned back to the glass cabinet against the wall and knelt beside her friend, Catriona. "Did you find the phlox?"

"Did I? There are fifteen different varieties. Is this just from Navaryn's garden?"

"Both of ours, actually. And we might still have some things in there from Aalrija's garden, too. She grows more flowers and herbs than anything else."

While Catriona nabbed a few more jars, Lowenna walked to the large tub with the salts. She refastened the sash of her satin robe, then sat down beside Navaryn. "You okay? You haven't said much since we started setting up in here."

"I'm fine."

Lowenna's grin remained unfazed as she affirmed, "This is a big step, I know. But if they don't show up, we'll still have a relaxing evening as planned."

Catriona lined up a plethoric selection of dried botanicals as Navaryn turned off the water. "Okay, before any of you say anything, I'll have you know that, yes, we need to use all of these tonight."

As Catriona dropped a few dried orchids into the steamy water, Navaryn looked at Lowenna and said, "And I thought you were bad."

The women had their laugh while Abyl walked over a few bottles of wine and set them into the basin's outer nook. A few moments later, Kumiko entered the room carrying two glass pitchers.

"Look who I found," he announced while shuffling to the counter. "Spotted these two in the back garden through the window while I was filling the water." Once he set the pitchers down, he quickly grabbed his towel before it came loose from his waist.

"Aww, damn. Looks like I lost my bet," a deep, playful voice clamored behind him.

"Yeah, and now you owe me a round at Teagan's," Kumiko added, pointing back at him.

Navaryn jumped to her feet as the couple she had been anticipating entered the room, wearing matching dark blue satin robes and white sandals. "Mila. Mathias. I'm so happy you made it."

"Sorry we're late," said Mathias as he scratched nervously at his thick hairline. "Well, we've actually been here for a while now. But, you know Mila and her flowers."

Mila closed the door behind her, then said, "I recognized a familiar scent right after our Parafall. Night Phlox. But not just any variety. You have Crystal Black Night Phlox. My mother grew that variety when I was little. Their aroma is a treat to the senses, like a decadent dessert." Mila readjusted the straps of her cloth bag and then continued, "I've been trying to find some for my garden for years."

Mathias chimed in, "We've been to every nursery and seed bank within the Halryn border," then cupped his hand and whispered, "and as many as we could journey to beyond it."

"And no luck. Were these native to your property?"

"Technically," Navaryn replied. "I stumbled on a cluster of them in the woods a couple of years back when I was walking back from some evening training. I dug some out of the ground, then transplanted them into a new section in the garden where they managed to survive."

"I hope you don't mind, but I helped myself to some seed," confessed Mila as she pulled out a velvet sack from the inside pocket of her robe.

"She never leaves home without that thing."

"A good section of your row wasn't deadheaded, so I think there should be some viable seed in here," she said, then tucked away her sack.

"No problem. And if they don't germinate, let me know. I have some seed saved from last season."

The room quickly grew quiet. Mila's eyes danced around the room, then settled back upon Navaryn's strained smile. "Um," she began as she slung a cloth bag off her shoulder, "Mathias and I brought a couple of bottles of wine and some dried fruit and nuts for snacking. I wasn't sure if food was necessary, but—"

"It's perfect," Navaryn interjected. "Thank you."

Kumiko took the provisions and filled them into a decorative wooden bowl while Navaryn set the wine beside the rest of the collection. Catriona and Lowenna teamed up to put away the jars of botanicals as the others gathered in front of the large tub.

"Aromatics are in, and water is to temp. Let the soak begin," Navaryn announced.

Mathias chimed, "Let's not be bashful now," as he dropped his robe. When he stepped onto the bench seat inside the basin, his face instantly contorted. "To temp, you say?! You mean, on *fire*?!"

His bulky, tan body flinched as the water crept up his legs. Instinctively, he cupped himself before the splashing water hit his low-hanging, sensitive flesh. The collective guffawed and watched as he lowered his butt into the water while wincing.

Once Lowenna finished helping Catriona bundle her thick brunette locks into a bun, they followed in after Abyl and Kumiko. Navaryn and Mila stood on opposite sides of the tub. Following each other in similar movements, they slid their robes to the floor and took their partners' hands as they stepped inside the basin. Though it was customary to share a soak, especially after training, Navaryn couldn't help but study Mila's physique. Every tight muscle was meticulously defined beneath her lustrous dark skin, proclaiming her careful dedication to her craft.

Abyl poured generous amounts of wine into stemless glasses and passed them down until everyone had one. "So, what do we toast to tonight?" he asked as the last of the bottle dripped into his glass.

Mathias answered, "*To taking a break every now and then,*" while raising his glass.

Abyl shook his head, "Not again. We toast to that every time we're at Teagan's. Anyone got something better?"

Mathias slowly lowered his glass, narrowing his eyes as the others burst into laughter.

Catriona raised her glass and asked, "How about, *to growing our group?*"

Together, Navaryn and Mila shouted, "No!" in the same serious voice, then looked at each other and giggled.

"Okay, *fine,*" replied Catriona as Lowenna put her arm around her.

"What about, *to health?*" asked Abyl.

"Lame. What are we? The Elders?" griped Catriona.

Kumiko chimed in with his thought, "*To patience and acceptance?*"

Both Mila and Navaryn rolled their eyes and groaned.

"I'll be finished with my wine by the time we find something to toast to," muttered Abyl after he snuck a little sip.

"I got it!" announced Lowenna. "How about, *to strength, and always striving for ascendance.*"

The others whispered and nodded amongst themselves. One by one, they raised their glasses.

"*To strength!*" they cheered amidst their clinking glasses.

When Mathias finished his wine, he set his glass down and reached for a decanter of warmed oil. "If I may," he said, then moved to the opposite side of the basin and squeezed between Abyl and Lowenna. Mila smiled as he reached for her foot.

"This is an amazing room, Nav. I think we should get into the habit of coming here more often," said Abyl as he sank until the waterline reached his throat.

"You can say that again," said Mila with closed eyes. "This is bliss."

Though it still felt unusual to hear Mila sling a compliment her way, Navaryn smiled contentedly.

Glasses clinked over more small talk and laughter as they sipped wine and nibbled treats until the tapers burned down to nubs. The steam in the room had cleared by the time Navaryn's guests took their leave, until only Kumiko remained. With hazy eyes, she watched as he split the remnants of the last bottle of wine between their glasses.

"That certainly went well, didn't it? It's hard to think Mila and I used to be at each other's throats."

Kumiko nodded and professed, "You see? Things can change for the better when you put forth the effort."

"I still think back to the first day we met."

"Maybe in time, you can put that behind you. There's no sense in hanging onto bad memories."

Navaryn nodded. As she put the glass to her lips, Kumiko raised his hand to stop her.

"I've thought of something we could both toast to. A result of all the positive changes I have witnessed around us for the past few seasons." Kumiko cleared his throat and held his glass her way with a smile. "To *new beginnings*. Each and every one of them."

"*To new beginnings*," concurred Navaryn.

After their glasses clinked, Navaryn slugged back the modest offering, then reached for some water in the nook behind her, inadvertently missing Kumiko's intense gaze. "Whelp. I'm beat n' ready to call it a night." Carefully, she stepped out of the tub, then wrapped herself in one of the plush gray towels from the stack atop the far counter.

"What? So soon? We don't train tomorrow."

"But we did today, remember?"

"I know."

"Plus, I think it's the wine. I'm more accustomed to ale after training, to be honest. It doesn't make me as sleepy."

Kumiko searched the room for something to delay their departure. Poking out from behind the corner of the tub was the glass decanter holding the infused body oil. To his delight, it was still half full, and the candle beneath it was aflame. "Before you call it in for the evening, I can smooth some hot oil on your shoulders. It'd be a great way to top off the night."

Navaryn patted her hair dry and replied, "Well, my skin has been feeling a little tight lately."

She tossed Kumiko a towel, then stood before him as he sat on the basin's thick outer rim. With a subtle smile, he motioned for her to turn around, then clipped up her long and unruly dark brown locks.

As soon as the hot oil met Navaryn's skin, she realized how cold the room was. Goosebumps flocked her arms and legs, but the aromatic scent of the oil and Kumiko's stiff strokes quickly relaxed her nerves. Breath by breath, her arms became slack, and she slowly drifted atop a calm ripple deep within her mind. Almost as silent as Kumiko's breath, her towel fell to the floor.

His delighted hands passed over her shoulders and back in a manner more sound and confident than his anxious mind. After he replenished his palms with oil, he journeyed the firm scape of her behind and thick leg muscles. Navaryn became thoroughly entranced by the warm and tingling sensations of the oil that accompanied his firm pressing and careful pulling between her thighs.

Following Kumiko's gentle nudging, Navaryn turned to face him with closed eyes. Leisurely, he rehydrated every delectable curve before him. While his hands skillfully slid over her hips and ribcage to the sides of her breasts, he slowly stood to his feet and pulled her into him. Navaryn broke from her meditative state with wide eyes the moment his lofty appendage inadvertently jabbed her. Instinctively, Navaryn pulled away and shielded her breasts from his lustful eyes before she could summon words to berate him with. Holding her breath, she hurriedly knelt to the floor for her towel. In a classic fashion, she misjudged her distance and smacked face-first into Kumiko's perfectly poised cock.

"Oh, for fuck's sake!" she clamored, then covered her forehead.

Embarrassed, though halfway expecting her adverse reaction, Kumiko bent down for his towel. His disappointment kept him from anticipating her jolting movements, and they knocked heads together. The pair shuffled backwards and resumed their awkward efforts to shield their private flesh from one another. Cupping his steadily deflating package, Kumiko yanked at his towel from under Navaryn's feet until it slipped free. His forceful tug made her lose her balance, and she fell backward into the tub of lukewarm water. She worked furiously to recover her position amidst her flailing and splashing, but lost even more control when Kumiko reached for her.

Navaryn reclaimed her footing and averted her eyes from his naked body. "I'm fine! I'm fine!" she shouted with outstretched waving hands. "Just stay over there."

Kumiko sighed, then chimed calmly, "Navaryn, I don't understand why you're still so nervous over the smallest shred of sexuality between us."

Dramatically, Navaryn dropped into the bath until the waterline covered her ears. Kumiko's muffled words reverberated in her chest and didn't stop before she needed to come up for air. "We're *not* having sex, Kumiko!" she yelled after sputtering off the lukewarm bathwater from her lips. "I don't know how many times I have to tell you. I'm just not ready for that."

Kumiko fastened his towel to his waist with a grimace. "You could have fooled me."

"What do you mean? Are you referring to the massage?" With deeply furrowed eyebrows, Navaryn rolled her eyes at Kumiko's wordless reply. "If I was supposed to act like it didn't feel good, then fine. Fine!

I'm sorry I led you on. So you're not mistaken again, no more oil, and no more massages."

"Is that *really* what you want?" After waiting a few moments for her to respond, Kumiko shook his head and went about the room to gather his belongings. "Fine. I can take a hint," he said before slamming the door behind himself.

In a bleary daze, Rayshell shot up in her bed as the echoing slam from her dream reverberated in her head. Her breaths were quick and shallow, and her mouth was parched. Groaning, she reached atop her nightstand for some water. After clearing the remnants of all three dusty glasses, she exhaled and rummaged through her sweaty locks. Her body was shaky and tingly in a very off-putting way. Just as the effects of the dream began to subside, she turned to sneak a peek at the time. Before her eyes could make out the numbers, the alarm sounded, sending her heart straight into her throat.

After fumbling with the device for a moment, she turned it off and then flopped back onto her bed. Though she desired to close her eyes, she couldn't. Sleep no longer felt like the blissful escape it used to. In an unprecedented fashion, Rayshell slipped out of bed and opened her curtains. She stared into dawn's deep blue firmament with troubled eyes, wondering how much worse things would become over the coming days.

·)(·

"I think the warning bell went off, Ray," said Jakobe as he sipped his cup of hot chocolate.

"Well, we would have been on time for once if it wasn't for the shitty coffee. I mean, how was anyone else even willing to drink it?" ranted Rayshell.

"It wasn't that bad."

"It tasted like it was brewed with toilet water. I wasn't gonna pay for that. And I know they took their sweet time to bring us our new order—just because we're 'kids,' I'm sure."

With her cup of tea cradled between her knitted hands, Rayshell continued to voice her piece of mind as she watched the kids scamper to the double doors and funnel inside. She reluctantly stepped off the curb to cross the street once she saw a break in traffic.

"Watch out, Ray!"

Before she could answer, Jakobe grabbed the top loop of her backpack and yanked her toward the curb before a white IROC-Z sped by. Rayshell's tea slipped from her hands as she looked at the descending passenger-side window. Inside, Stephanie held out her middle finger in front of her sneering face. The block was then set afire by her echoing profanity. From the students who whispered nearby to Rayshell's bewildered expression, everything felt like it moved in slow motion.

"Um, Ray. Are you, uh, okay?" Jakobe asked and finally released her backpack.

Shawn pulled his car into the student parking lot, and just as Jakobe expected, his sister's eyes locked on target. Once Rayshell stepped in their direction, he called, "Hold up," and latched back onto her backpack. "We gotta get to class."

"Let go," she softly and coldly demanded.

"You know if you start anything, the cops will be over here in a heartbeat."

"I don't care. Now let go of me before I make you."

"Goddamn it, Ray! Stop being so fucking stubborn, will ya? If you do anything stupid, then it's *both* our asses."

"What do you mean? This is *my* problem."

"It's mine, too," Jakobe snapped back. "And it always will be. So unless you want to go at this together, let's get to class."

Though it took some time for Rayshell's gaze to disconnect from the two shit-starters, Jakobe managed to lure her across the street to campus.

"Coward!" belted Stephanie.

Her laughter racketed through the air and made Rayshell's face hot and prickly. She looked to her brother with a stern countenance and confirmed, "I wouldn't have done this for anyone else. Remember that."

Jakobe wasn't sure whether she was just stating a fact or implying an underlying threat, but smiled softly in return. He let go of her backpack, believing she would keep walking toward campus. "Look," he said and stared at the impending glass doors. "They're so close."

"*Wee* ...."

"Aww, come on, Ray. You should be proud of yourself. Not only are we on time, but you made a very mature decision just now."

"Please don't remind me."

"Okay, okay. But one thing out of this won't change."

"Oh yeah? And what might that be?"

"That I'm proud of you."

Rayshell rolled her eyes, then pantomimed her famous rendition of retching, rousing her brother to laughter.

"Whatever, dork," he jutted, then gave her a tight hug before they took off in their respective directions for class.

·)C·

"You will *never* guess what happened today!" Rayshell blurted as she swung open the doors to the music room.

Trish paused her playing and looked at her with lowered brows. "You quit smoking?"

"No, no, no."

"Well, you got me," Trish said and poked around at the keys with a stale gaze. The jarring entry broke her concentration, and the new segment of music vanished from her mind.

After delineating the incident with Shawn and Stephanie, Rayshell pulled out a shiny green apple from her front pouch and asked, "So, where were you this morning? I had to smoke my cigarette alone."

"Ah, so is that all I'm good for?"

"Come on. You know that's not what I meant."

Trish took her fingers off the keys, then replied. "I wasn't able to wake up this morning."

"That's weird. You sound like me."

"I know, right?" She tucked her cold hands into her pants pockets, then continued, "It's hard to explain. It was like I was stuck in my dream or something."

"What happened?"

Trish exhaled an uneasy breath as a few frames of her dream passed before her eyes. "It was awful. Everything around me was either on fire or exploding. People were dying ...."

Rayshell held the masticated apple pulp between her tongue and cheek as she watched Trish's eyes well.

"There was so much blood," she whispered.

Rayshell put her hand on her friend's shoulder, at a loss for what to say.

"I'm fine."

"Does this have anything to do with the stuff from yesterday?"

Trish nodded. "I don't know if you even want to hear any of this."

"Of course I do," Rayshell assured. "Look, I'm sorry about yesterday. There was just someone there who spooked me. That's all."

Trish chewed on the inside of her bottom lip for a moment, then said, "Fine. You got another apple in there for me?"

"Yes, ma'am. Fuji or green?"

"Fuji, please."

As Rayshell walked to her bag, Trish pushed away from the piano. The trauma that bled from her dream felt real, as though she had experienced it firsthand.

"I was, I mean, Lowenna was in the middle of some kind of attack. As I understood it, outsiders had invaded local territory and wreaked havoc upon the town's civilians. Men, women, children—it didn't matter. Everyone was a target. And whoever they were, they seemed to know that the townspeople would be no match for them, like they knew they had no power."

Trish looked at the dusty floor and recounted the most virulent sector of her dream.

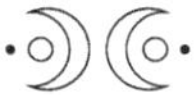

A small shimmering projectile flew past Lowenna and exploded against a crumbling stone edifice. Below the compromised structure was an older woman with one of her legs twisted backward at her knee, clutching two children tightly in her arms. Soot and blood smudged their terrified faces, and the two children wailed. Her eyes bore a hole straight through Lowenna before she lowered her head to the children, sobbing. After a brief interruption by two steadfast assailants, which ended with their swift and expert obliteration, Lowenna heard the woman scream. The ghostly white haze over her striking blue eyes flickered as she turned to witness the structure come loose from its support channels.

"*No!*" Lowenna belted as the deadly debris descended.

Once the white haze disappeared, she immediately called forth one of her specialized techniques. A dazzling amethyst barrier quickly formed around the civilians just before the first slab of stone and concrete crashed down. Lowenna witnessed hope ignite within the woman's teary eyes following her conjuration. Though the ground rumbled and cracked around her, and the massive slabs continued to stack, the barrier held strong.

Lowenna focused her energy as a neighboring building beside them collapsed. Her posture strained as she attempted to open the barrier without compromising its integrity. Slowly, a small pinhole continued to expand just above the buckling pavement.

"When the barrier opens wide enough, I need you to crawl out!" Lowenna shouted.

The woman nodded, then slowly scooted across the ground with the children tucked tightly in her arms. Once the opening reached a hand's diameter, an assailant blindsided Lowenna with a battle mace to her ribcage. With the wind knocked out of her, Lowenna tumbled down a pile of rubble and motionless bodies. Her thick, advanced armor kept the spikes from impaling her, but the blow had disarmed her of her staff. The diadem above her brow began to pulse rapidly, causing gut-churning panic.

Stunned, she collected herself as best she could and quickly assessed the barrier. It remained, but had contracted considerably. The tiny shred of relief didn't last long, for the lumbering steps of the same antagonist came crashing her way. Lowenna dodged his swinging mace in a smooth maneuver, and they proceeded to exchange offensive blows until she took him down with a cracking sweep. She kept one hand tense, fingers pronged, keeping the link between her mind and the barrier intact. Quickly, she mounted the brute, then head-butted him with her gemmed diadem. As she wound up for one more strike, another assailant tackled her to the ground.

Lowenna heard the woman shriek as they tumbled toward the barrier. "Hold on!" she screamed as the barrier's integrity waned.

"You'll make this easy work if you keep letting your eyes wander," barked the second assailant.

He torqued her forearm above her head with a grip so intense her tendons felt like they were on the verge of ripping apart. The assailant motioned to take her other hand under his control, but noticed her tense, pronged fingers. He then turned to the odd diablerie in the distance.

"You clever bunny. How are you doing that?"

Lowenna leered at him with an expression that was almost successful at hiding her fear. Just as her eyes began to flicker with the same ghostly white as earlier, igniting the rage deep within her heart, she was hit in the breastplate by a red, cracking energy blast. She again lost her wind, along with more of the barrier's size in the process. Dazed, she counted the slow, scuffling footsteps that came her way.

"I can't believe the nerve of this wench," griped the brute that Lowenna head-butted a few moments earlier. Blood fell from the gash on his forehead and bespattered her brow as he leaned over her. "Let's end her and be off."

"Not so fast. Look at that technique," he said, then pointed to the shimmery, amethyst barrier. "I think she's one of the Celestines that Joro said to keep a watch for. Let's take her back to base once we've worn her down. I could really use that reward coin."

"Nothing would be more rewarding than spilling this bitch's guts!" he declared wildly, then unsheathed his sword. "Now, hold her tight so she doesn't squirm."

While pinned, Lowenna watched the man signal his compliance with a shrug. Her heart leapt into her throat as his bloodied partner raised his sword. Fearful there was no escape, the ghostly white haze in her eyes quickly strobed until her power regained its stronghold once more. The blade, layered in dried blood and grime, descended as intently as the man's objective. Lowenna expertly maneuvered out of the burly assailant's grasp, then lunged out of the blade's path. Radiant crackling green energy engulfed both of her hands. Shot after shot, she pummeled them until they lost their footing. Lowenna retreated and claimed the sword that was left jabbed into the ground. The bloodied assailant aimed to tackle her, but she quickly countered his advance with an upward strike and sent him airborne. While in mid-air, she battered him with a series of high-intensity blasts.

Lowenna was right at his side when he opened his eyes. Before he could utter a word, she jabbed the filthy blade straight through his throat and pulled it down through his axis. She kicked his decapitated head to the side and set out after the other. Once she dispatched him, she reclaimed her staff, then viciously tore through an approaching unit in the same bloodthirsty manner. Standing amidst a mass of motionless bodies, she suddenly recalled the civilians she left within the barrier.

The white haze over her eyes quickly flickered away as she turned to the pile of rubble where the barrier once stood. She fell to her knees once she reached the crumbled stone and frantically began to clear what she could.

"I'm here! Can you hear me?! Please, let me know you're okay!"

Lowenna tightly gripped her staff and imbued it with her diadem's power, then began to shatter the larger slabs of stone with violent swings. Exhausted and doused in sweat as plumes of dust drifted away, she fell into an agonizing sob once a tiny hand nestled in a pool of blood appeared. Her breath quaked with shame on account of the blinding power of her diadem. Disgusted, she angrily ripped it from her forehead and threw it as far as she could. Among the ruins and the war that waged on around her, she wept with a woeful heart and broken spirit.

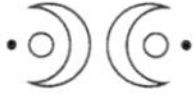

"They died, Rayshell. Under all that wreckage," Trish tearfully concluded with a lump in her throat. She looked to Rayshell, who seemed to have forgotten how to blink, let alone breathe. "How could those monsters be so cold? It was such an awful feeling to wake up from." She ran her fingers through her bangs after setting her elbows atop the keyslip, then groaned. "There's more."

"What do you mean?"

"When I woke up, I felt like I was hit by a bus. My body was sore all over," she said, then pulled up the sleeve of her black and navy checkered shirt. Several grape-sized bruises spotted her forearm.

"Who the hell did this to you?"

"They came from my dream. This was the same place where one of those men grabbed Lowenna. *Exactly* the same."

Rayshell brought Trish's arm toward her for a closer look. "Gah, these look awful. Do they hurt?" she asked, resisting the urge to press down on one of them.

Trish nodded. "But not nearly as much as this."

Leaving all modesty behind, she hopped up from the piano bench and lifted her shirt past her bra line. Across the center of her chest and down her ribcage were deep-purple blotches outlined in a sickly yellow tinge.

While Rayshell continued to inspect the horrifying marks in disbelief, Trish continued, "This is obviously no coincidence. What's happening in my dreams is happening to me. There's no other—"

Suddenly, the glass doors to the music room tremored. The girls slowly turned to the ridiculous faces of three senior boys, one of whom was in Rayshell's second-period class.

"Got any room for us?!" yelled Gilbert as his friends banged on the glass.

Mortified, Trish pulled down her shirt and glued her bulging eyes to the floor.

"Maybe next time," Rayshell shouted back as she waved them away. "*Bye*."

With folded arms, Trish walked to the end of the room and leaned against the wall next to the broken harpsichord. Rayshell and the boys continued to taunt each other until they eventually ran out of quips.

"If I know Gilbert, the whole school will know about you flashing me before the end of the day."

"I didn't flash you! I was just *showing* you the stupid marks."

"Geez, I'm just messin' around," Rayshell yipped after her ill-received joke. "There's nothing to worry about. It's not like your boob was out or anything. Plus, I didn't see any phones."

As laughter erupted between a flock of students passing by the piano room's side windows, the warning bell rang.

"Already?!" Rayshell whined as she looked at the clock. "Didn't lunch *just* start?!"

"Some days just move faster than others, I guess."

After retrieving her backpack, Rayshell gave her a gentle hug and said, "We'll pick this up after school, right?"

Trish nodded. After Rayshell bolted for the door, she yelled, "Be careful this time!"

Rayshell tightly grabbed the straps of her backpack and jogged around the cafeteria. The usual dawdlers crowded the quad, but she avoided eye contact with everyone. Most of what Trish divulged felt incredibly familiar, and the waves of adrenaline it sparked still coursed through her veins. As she ran through the halls, she fought through sections of a haunting, hazy vision from a dashing aerial view. Smoke, dust, and rising plumes of debris veiled crumbling structures and waves of people clashing into one another. Though the bodies were several stories below, the evidence of slaughter was undeniable, from the red-stained ground speckled with lifeless bodies to the moments where shrieks echoed in the back of her head.

·)(·

After a clumsy trek to class, Rayshell hung back next to the door and took a few moments to compose herself before entering. She shuffled alongside a few other students and headed for her computer station.

"Alright!" Mr. Adams yelled over his class as the final bell rang. "Settle down, everyone. Let's get started." He clapped his hands loudly in the air. "You all know your projects are due Friday, so let's get to work.”

Puzzled, Rayshell looked at her teacher and whispered, “Project?”

“Ah, yes. Ms. Stone,” her teacher called as he beckoned her with his hand. “Since you weren’t here yesterday, I’ll need to fill you in on the guidelines.”

Once she reached his desk, a security guard walked in, holding a green entrance form.

“Hey, Dale. Sorry to interrupt.”

“Not a problem. What can I do for you?”

“I got a new kid for ya. I know it’s kinda late in the year. Apparently, he’s been pushing pretty hard for this class. Roxard made it happen since you have a free space.”

“I was full up until just last week,” Mr. Adams added.

“So I heard.”

After taking the entrance slip into his hand, he continued, “Lucky fellow. Alright, let’s get him in here.”

Rayshell kept her wide eyes glued to the red stapler atop her teacher’s desk as the shuffling, popping sound of flip-flop sandals entered the room.

“Welcome, Shawn. You certainly have perfect timing,” Mr. Adams proclaimed. “I was just about to explain this week’s project to one of our students. You can listen in, too.”

While sliding his hand over his frosty, gelled hair, he walked right beside Rayshell and feigned his thanks and appreciation to the teacher.

Shawn’s voice swarmed inside Rayshell’s head like a nest of hornets. She clenched her fists as the teacher gave the rundown of their assignment over the blossoming whispers of her peers who knew their history. No matter how hard she tried, the redolence of his woodsy cologne kept her from believing her misfortune was just a dream.

“Rayshell, are you paying attention?” her teacher asked.

“Yes, Mr. Adams,” she answered as a few kids snickered.

“Well, what are you waiting for? Get to work while I show Shawn to his station.”

In truth, Rayshell was nearly clueless about what her assignment entailed. Dispirited and at a loss for words, she returned to her station and sat down. Every ounce of creative energy evaporated, replaced by a burning desire to escape. She put her hands over her face and stretched the skin of her eyelids as she groaned.

"I've gotta tell Stephanie," Amanda whispered as she promptly pulled her cell from her backpack. "She's gonna flip."

Ryo wasn't much for gossip, but he replied, "Ray's got some pretty bad luck, but I'm not surprised you'd find a way to make it worse," and continued fiddling with the colors on the front page of his assignment.

·)(·

After the longest fifty minutes of Rayshell's life, the dismissal bell finally sounded. She waited at her computer, hoping that Shawn would exit the room, but all he did was linger near the doorway with his friends.

"Great," she hissed and slid on her backpack.

As Rayshell approached, Ryo said his goodbyes, then took his leave with Amanda, who followed in tow with devilish eyes. Shawn stayed behind and leaned against the doorway as students broke off from the hall's cavalcade and filed into Mr. Adams' class.

"My early birds," he announced. "Just what I like to see."

Once the teacher began conversing with his prompt arrivals, Rayshell attempted to exit, but Shawn stuck his hip into her path.

"I'll always be looking forward to this class," he jutted.

"And for the first time, I won't."

"Hey, maybe you can be my study buddy. The teacher did say I'd benefit from a partner. Someone who could give me some quick tips about the program."

"You're insane," she blurted as he creepily panned his eyes over her.

"Say what you want. I know damn well you still want me."

Rayshell's face flushed with embarrassment. Although she thought she could handle another confrontation with Shawn, her confidence waned as she shook her head to disagree. Riddled with aggravation and swollen nerves, her eyes began to burn.

"Come on, Ray. You can't lie to save your life."

"What does any of this matter, anyway? You've made your choice."

Before he could respond, Stephanie walked up and locked arms with him. "Hey, babe. Amanda said you might be around here."

Shawn pulled her in for a sloppy kiss, but kept his eyes open and locked onto Rayshell. Passersby were suspicious of the trio in the doorway and expected a fight to break out. Before long, a small crowd of students who needed to enter the classroom had formed and impatiently stood behind them.

Shawn smiled and put his arm around Stephanie. "You're still here. Enjoying the show?"

Mortified by his comment and the growing titters from the surrounding students, Rayshell spat, "Fuck you both," then pushed through them.

Shawn and Stephanie leaned against one another and cackled while the crowd of anxious students slipped into their classroom. Halfway down the hall, Rayshell looked back at their hysterical faces. The fierce scowl she wore started to buckle under pressure. Tears quickly filled her eyes, casting a bleary glow over their entangled frames. While their laughter echoed, she turned away and headed to her next class with clenched fists.

·)(·

The school day had ended, but Rayshell didn't find Trish waiting for her at the side gates. She managed to distract herself for a few minutes until her patience expired. After peeking inside the A-wing, then looking through the rows of portables, she thought to survey the front of the school. She rounded the corner beside three overturned metal garbage cans, then headed for the bus circle.

"Ray!" a distant voice called out to her.

Rayshell turned around in every direction until the voice sounded again.

"Across the street, silly!"

Trish stood at the corner of the student parking lot with an armful of books next to a tall, dark-haired boy. With a sly look in her eyes and a grin to match, Rayshell trotted off in their direction.

"Sorry, Ray. I totally lost track of time. I was just saying goodbye to my study partner."

After a hug, Rayshell looked the handsome boy up and down.

"Hi. I'm new here. My name is Nico," he said with a smile and held his hand out.

While they completed their handshake, Trish continued, "Nico and I have economics together. We were supposed to pick partners for a project we started yesterday."

"I wasn't there," Nico added.

"Yeah, and since I hate almost everyone in my class, the teacher assigned us together."

"Doesn't look like a bad match."

Even though Trish anticipated Rayshell's suggestive comment, she couldn't help but roll her eyes.

"So, ah, I'll see you tomorrow after school then?" he asked Trish, then unlocked his car.

"Sounds good to me. I've got your cell, so I'll text you later."

Nico started his 350Z and waved to both of them. His deep, emerald-green eyes glimmered as he turned his head away. Smitten by his charm and comely looks, both girls waved their observations away as they watched him zip off down the road.

"Wow. Well, you sure drew the winning hand today."

"Yeah. It was luck after all," Trish claimed while scratching her cheek nervously.

"Well, I hope you have a good time *studying* with him tomorrow."

"I will. Trust me. And I'll think about you being at work," she taunted.

"No, please," Rayshell put her hands over her eyes and pretended to stumble.

"I'll think about how you're unable to leave. Trapped inside with all those *customers*," Trish continued.

"*Oh, the agony!*" Rayshell's playful spirit simmered as she rummaged through the front pouch of her backpack. "But it's still not as bad as what happened after lunch today."

"Yeah, I heard. I have a bunch of Shawn's friends in my sixth-period class."

"This is turning out to be the worst school year ever," she said while lighting a cigarette.

"But it's our last one here. At least that's something, right?"

Rayshell shrugged. "You always try to point out the positive side of things."

"You should try it sometime."

Once Rayshell's chuckle fizzled out, she quipped, "Had any luck in finding out the positive in all these weird dreams we've been having?"

Trish batted at the smoke that wafted her way, then replied, "Well, not exactly like it's a positive affirmation, but the idea I shared with you yesterday—"

"The one about these being Lowenna and Navaryn's memories?"

Trish ran her fingers through her thick chestnut locks, then cleared her throat. "Yes."

Rayshell exhaled a long drag of her cigarette and looked at her friend with a cock-eyed glare. "Well, if that's what this is, then I'm reliving the life of some majorly awkward, emotionally inexperienced chick."

Trish laughed. "Kinda like you?"

After Rayshell's brief rundown of her morning dream, Trish's sides nearly split. Visualizing being hit in the forehead by an erect penis was more than she could bear. With hysterics aside, the fact that she was familiar with each name she mentioned blew her away. It solidified that the journey was one they needed to make together.

"So, now it's your turn."

Trish looked at her quizzically. "My turn? For what, exactly?"

"To tell me one." After waiting a generous amount of time for Trish to respond, Rayshell leaned toward her. "You're gonna leave me hanging, aren't you?"

"Well, as much as you would want to hear a dirty story from me, I don't have one," Trish fibbed. Though she had a plethora to choose from, she opted against humoring Rayshell in order to stay constructive. "But, I do have one you might enjoy."

Rayshell flung her cigarette butt, then folded her arms. "We'll see."

"I was reminded of it when you mentioned Von brought you the moon."

"You remembered that?"

"I do pay attention, unlike some people."

Rayshell moved her eyes to her fingertips as they grazed a hedge of flowering rosemary. "Huh?" she replied after a few silent moments.

"Nice one."

As her friend laughed, Trish settled into the recollection. She pictured two full, milky moons looming high in the dark sky. Accompanying the pair was one much larger, tinged with deep crimson. Trish described the haunting satellite and revealed that the so-called 'third moon' appeared only once every six years.

"The event is celebrated in Celestine far and wide ...."

Lowenna sat on a tufted sofa with her hands folded atop her lap, silent and observant. She wore a lavender off-the-shoulder dress studded with silver and black rhinestones and slip-on flats. Beside her was Demelza, who, just like her, preferred the quiet secondary conversation room over the bustling main hall. The pair turned their heads to the sound of furious clomping heels that echoed their way.

Aalrija, with a glass of wine in one hand and the rest of the bottle in the other, groaned loudly in the air. "That child will be the death of me," she barked, then sat next to Demelza.

Lowenna kept a straight face while she watched Aalrija slug back the entire glass.

Feigning concern, Demelza asked, "What's she up to this time?"

"She's in Benson's garden again, digging in the damn dirt."

Demelza laughed while Aalrija refilled her glass.

"Go ahead, let it all out." She then gestured to Lowenna. "How do I get Navaryn to behave like this? This is the third ceremony these girls have attended, and not once has Navaryn behaved properly."

"Luckily, this is just who Lowenna is. An obedient, well-mannered young lady."

The compliment failed to flatter Lowenna. She looked at her perfectly manicured nails, despising the fact that her outward demeanor didn't reflect the emotions that brewed within.

"Well, I've had it," said Aalrija, unpinning her wavy gray hair. "She can miss Benson's speech for all I care."

Demelza turned to Lowenna. "Why don't you check on Navaryn? Maybe you can convince her to join the festivities. Before Aalrija decides to drink that whole bottle of wine."

"I heard that."

Demelza kept her composure and smiled at Lowenna.

"Okay," she answered lightly.

Silently, Lowenna walked through the festive crowd of gilded guests and the dexterous attendants that maneuvered through them. After a pit stop at the refreshment station for a clutch of grapes and an apple, she continued through the castle's side exit. A handful of guests meandered the terrace near Benson's ghostly white rose bushes, clinking glasses as they patiently awaited the arrival of Hirunae from beyond the distant mountain range. Lowenna gathered her long, puffy flounces, then carefully descended the stairs. Around the first corner of Benson's hedge maze, she spotted Navaryn just before the border of blackberry brambles.

"Thought I'd find you here," called Lowenna as she walked behind her.

"Hey. I didn't think I'd see you out here tonight. Had enough of Demelza and Aalrija's bickering already, or did they send you out to find me?"

"I'll keep you guessing."

Navaryn laughed. "Not hard to know which one it is by that remark," she answered, then went back to poking the dirt with a broken branchlet. She reached for one of the wine bottles at her side and stuffed a couple of glistening objects through the neck.

Lowenna squinted and asked, "What are you doing? Are those *worms?*"

"Yep."

"What? *Why?*"

"I need some more in my garden," she said, holding one of them up to Lowenna's curious face. "Plus, these ones are pretty cool. They're really meaty. Oh, and they have these cool silvery rainbows that show when you look at 'em under the moonlight." After stuffing the worm down the bottle, Navaryn resumed digging in the wet spot of dirt in front of her feet.

"You're so weird."

"I know. So are you."

While watching Navaryn forage, Lowenna quickly munched her apple down to the core and tossed it under a gap at the edge of the brambles. "Want any help?" she asked.

"That's okay. I wouldn't want you to break a nail or anything."

Lowenna silenced her friend's giggles by pelting her with a couple of grapes from the sprig she held in her hand.

"I'm joking, I'm joking!" she wailed with her hands in the air. "I promise. The bottle's almost full."

Navaryn rinsed her hands off in one of the small fountains, then followed Lowenna to a lone stone bench that sat midway down the hedge border. After a few silent moments, she looked at Navaryn earnestly.

"Do I come off as obedient and well-mannered?"

With a mouthful of blackberries pilfered during their stroll, Navaryn answered, "What kind of question is that?"

"Just answer me," she grumbled.

Navaryn wiped her dirty face with the back of her hand. "Of course you do. That's why everyone trusts you."

"But you know the real me."

"That has nothing to do with what you asked me."

Lowenna sighed as she pinched the buoyant grapes.

"So, why'd you ask? Is something wrong?" she pried.

"I just, I don't know. I'm starting to get frustrated with everything." She felt her friend's confused stare beaming at her. "Everyone thinks of me as this perfect example. It's all a joke. For some reason, I can't seem to act any other way around the Tiers or the other Halryn. I sit quietly, attentive and focused because I don't dare to get up and do anything different."

Navaryn beheld the state of her soiled dress with a mildly disappointed gaze. "That's not a bad thing, you know. Aside from not being scolded all the time, it comes with certain perks, if you will."

"Perks? Elaborate, *oh, wise one*, because I sure don't follow you."

"People will never suspect you of misdeeds, for one. And if you get caught, they'll just assume someone talked you into it. Kinda like what happened last week."

Lowenna shrugged.

"Trust me. Image is everything. I know I might not be the best example because, frankly, I don't care about what people think. But you do. That's part of who you are. And let me be the first to tell you that it will come in handy one day as long as you maintain it."

Lowenna was impressed by the profound statement from her typically immature, very impulsive friend. "Thank you," she whispered with a smile, then moved Navaryn's wild, gritty locks away from her cheek.

Before Navaryn could offer anything more, their ears pricked at the clamor from the terrace behind them. They looked at each other with eager eyes.

"*Hirunae*," they chimed in unison.

Without wasting another moment, the pair dashed down the far end of the hedge border and crossed into the field of giant sapphire pampas grass. The waving, glimmering strips flicked them as they maneuvered around the mounds. Joyful titters accompanied their excited gait through Benson's private tea plots, where Navaryn nearly lost her footing over some disconnected irrigation. After clumsily ascending a few flights of steep stone steps, the girls arrived at their private viewing spot, one they had discovered during the last Lunar Amassment celebration when they were nine.

Through a perfect parting in the surrounding trees, where the blood-red haze spilling out from the mountain range ahead was unobscured, Hirunae had crowned. With their mouths agape, Lowenna and Navaryn slowly inhaled the crisp air and looked ahead with delighted eyes. The gargantuan, full-moon beauty continued to rise, casting its haunting, sanguine glow over the valley below. The spectacle delighted them both, but Navaryn was always particularly entranced. Whether it was Hirunae or one of Celestine's two other moons, her eyes always fixated on the first glimpse of a full satellite. Lowenna adored how something so simple and expected could fill her dear friend with such wonder.

"Benson's probably getting ready to deliver his speech," Lowenna warned once Hirunae rose above the forest line ahead.

Navaryn, who had made herself a comfy spot on the ground, simply gazed at the trio in the firmament.

"Did you hear me?"

"Yeah. And if we stay longer, that means we'll miss it. What a shame."

Lowenna smacked Navaryn's arm after her sarcastic utterance.

"Ugh, I'm just messin' around."

Reluctantly, the pair retraced their steps, and it wasn't long until the joyful chatter of the evening's guests became audible once again. Navaryn swiped both of her worm-packed wine bottles, then followed behind Lowenna toward the terrace.

Kumiko, wearing dark-colored formal attire and a presumptuous smirk, came their way in a forthright stride. "I see you've picked up Aalrija's habit," he addressed Navaryn. "It didn't take as long as I expected."

Navaryn glanced down at the two wine bottles she had in her hands, then held one up for him as soon as he was in proximity. His joke was obvious, but Navaryn couldn't refrain from retorting. Sloshing the wine bottle around, she quipped, "Care for a drink?"

"Navaryn, don't," said Lowenna, then reached for her wrist.

"Come on, Kumiko," she continued to tease while fighting off Lowenna's persistent hands. "Just a little taste."

Lowenna ushered Navaryn toward the castle's side entrance. "Trust me, I'm doing you a favor," she claimed as she looked back at a very puzzled Kumiko.

After a few paces, Lowenna succumbed to Navaryn's infectious laughter. They stumbled up the stairs to the terrace as if they both had imbibed, then stashed the worm-filled bottles behind one of the large potted shrubs. Lowenna managed to coerce Navaryn inside with the rumor of her favorite mushroom crostini appetizers. Once inside the main hall, as though everything was perfectly timed, Benson made his appearance.

Lowenna slipped her hand behind Navaryn as she tried to slink back in her steps. "Don't even think about it."

"Damn you." Soon after, she felt a presence close behind her. "Not you, too," she addressed Kumiko.

The pair chuckled and kept Navaryn surrounded to thwart any opportunity for her to sneak away.

"I'll get you both for this, don't worry."

While Benson addressed his guests with his typical ostentatious gaiety, the three friends kept to the edge of the collective. Lowenna smiled, not on account of Benson's words, but of the overwhelming sense of fulfillment and pride that came with being in the company of her best friends, afforded by the Lunar Amassment. The cherished feeling of kinship and unity brought her joy and became the cornerstone of her wish that it remain forever.

Trish turned to her friend at the close of her recollection. "Are you okay?"

Rayshell nodded, then revealed, "Hirunae. That's what Von called it."

Trish smiled at her friend's spellbound expression, which was eerily reminiscent of Navaryn looking upon Hirunae.

"And it's funny to hear you mention Kumiko. In the dream I told you earlier, he was the one with his dick out."

Trish burst into laughter.

"In your story, the girls were what, sixteen?"

"Almost, I think. Kumiko was clearly a bit older."

Rayshell put her fingers to her chin and thought for a second. "They were all definitely older in my dream."

Trish flipped through a few vibrating notifications on her phone as they rounded the corner onto the main street.

"And who is this Benson guy? The leader of some upper-class cult?"

"I guess you can say that," said Trish, intentionally cutting the explanation short.

Rayshell pulled on the straps of her backpack as they crossed the street. Her mind buzzed with the details of Trish's recollection. Even though she tried to prepare herself for what was unfolding, the weight of the alienating experience continued to stack.

"Did you want to get some coffee today? My treat."

Trish flipped through more notifications and answered, "I'm sorry, I can't. I promised my dad I'd help him with something. He's blowin' up my phone, asking me if I'm on my way. I'll see you tomorrow, okay?"

Rayshell gave her a tight hug. "I'll see if Jakobe will let me use his phone tonight. I'll message you or something."

"Good luck. You two argue more than anyone I know. Just call me the old-school way if you need to. Or just buy yourself a damn phone already."

·)(·

Rather than going straight home, Rayshell stopped for some provisions at her favorite grocer, located in the same plaza as her work. She lingered in the produce section, excited to see offerings she had yet to try. After selecting a few new things she wasn't quite sure how to prepare, Rayshell meandered the bakery area, then finally headed for the checkout. The last of the afternoon sun took refuge below the horizon just as she looked ahead to the front windows. She sighed at the sight of another day expended, then slowly retracted her gaze.

"Rayshell?" a familiar voice called out ahead in the line.

It took a moment for her to recognize the smiling red-haired man. "Jack?"

"Betcha didn't notice me through all this hair," he jested, then ran his fingers through his beard. He offered his place in line to the people between them so they could stand together. "How have you been?"

"Good. For the most part. Just busy with school. You know, the usual. How about you? How's Laura and Brian?"

"Laura is well. She's back working at the hospital. And you won't believe how big Brian is now." Jack motioned to his cart. "That little man can eat. I'm sure what's here won't last a week."

"How old is he now?"

"Eleven. Almost twelve. But he has the appetite of three grown men."

As they both shared a chuckle, Rayshell thought back to the last time she saw Jack and his family. He and his wife, Laura, were longtime friends of her mother, and she used to babysit their son, Brian, before school and her part-time job became overwhelming.

"So, did you come here to get some stuff for dinner?"

"Yeah, and lunch."

Jack peeked in her basket. "Not much in there. Just a bunch of green stuff."

"You sound like my mom."

Jack looked in his cart, jam-packed with boxed items plastered with colorful logos, and scratched his head. "Admittedly, I could stand to add more fruits and veggies in the mix. So, what are you? Vegetarian?"

"Yeah. My mom still tries to sneak meat into my meals because she doesn't think what I'm doing is healthy. It's so annoying."

Jack tried to keep his embarrassment from showing as he placed his groceries on the conveyor belt. "I'm sure she means well. How is she doing, anyway?"

"Working like crazy. We hardly see her. Just on her days off."

"She still workin' graveyard, hm? I don't know how she does it."

"To tell you the truth, I don't either."

After Rayshell set her basket atop the checkout conveyor belt, Jack asked, "So, if it's been about three years since I've seen you, that would make you a senior now, am I right?"

"Yep. Last year. And I couldn't be happier."

Jack felt that Rayshell sounded more exhausted than excited. "Do you have any plans lined up for after you graduate?"

Rayshell's mind began to spin. Though they've talked about it, there was no way her mother could afford to send her to college. She was waiting for Trish to confirm her out-of-state college plans and had the idea of tagging along to find a job nearby so she could afford to attend. "It's kinda complicated," she finally answered.

"Say no more. I totally understand. It can be a little scary when you're on the cusp of your next big decision in life. I know whatever you choose, you'll do amazing."

With the best smile she could feign, Rayshell replied, "Thank you."

Rayshell followed Jack into the parking lot after they both finished checking out. The evening chill quickly greeted the pair, reminding them that winter was approaching.

After Rayshell quickly slipped on her gloves, she said, "It was nice to see you, Jack. Tell Laura and Brian I said 'hi.'"

"I will. But how would you like to tell them in person? Perhaps Saturday if you're not busy."

"Well, I do work Saturday. But only until seven."

"Perfect. We can have you over for dinner. We'll whip something up meat-free if that will seal the deal."

"Sounds like a plan."

As Rayshell motioned to hug Jack goodbye, he waved his finger. "Now, what kind of responsible adult would I be if I just let you take the bus home? I know it's only six, but it's dark."

"It's okay. I take the bus all the time. I'll be fine."

Behind them, a man in a gray hoodie walked, smoking a cigarette. He scowled at the pair once he noticed their curious eyes upon him.

Once he was far enough away, Jack whispered, "You know what kind of riffraff comes out after the sun goes down."

Rayshell squinted as she watched the rough-looking individual continue toward the bus stop. Though she welcomed the notion, she confessed, "I don't want to be a bother."

"Nonsense," Jack confirmed as he finished loading the trunk of his tan station wagon. "It'll take but a moment."

The man with the gray hoodie turned around just in time to watch Rayshell settle into the passenger seat. With his emerald eyes gleaming under his shadowy hood, he took a long drag of his cigarette and leaned against one of the plaza's decorative trees. With a smug grin, he patiently waited for the pair to pull out of the parking lot before dissolving into the jittering, colliding shadows surrounding him. The cigarette he held between his fingers dropped atop landscape stones with the smallest of sounds, where it burnt away as inconspicuously as his bizarre departure.

6

THE DEFIANCE

Another uneventful meeting of the Halryn Tiers concluded in the late afternoon. Tensions between Benson and the council steadily mounted with each passing day, and the weight of Celestine's peril began to strain more heavily on his shoulders. He didn't want to admit it, but he knew the strength of his leadership continued to wane. After Navaryn and Lowenna's banishment, Benson recklessly deployed several battalions to the realm of Daeva in search of Ananael and Zin. He ignored his constituents' repeated pleas to halt the assaults. Having failed to formulate a sensible plan to recover the tomes, much less unveil a single clue to Merisek's whereabouts, the Celestine army's loyalty and numbers continued to dwindle.

Celestine, however, wasn't alone in the search for the culprit and the artifacts he stole. The leaders of Daeva's united populace had their own hunt underway for Merisek on account of his transgressions, and for irresponsibly pushing Daeva into full-fledged conflict with Celestine using his radicalized militia. Several months into the chaotic fray, Merisek remained in hiding while Daeva's legions responded to Celestine's unsanctioned invasions with brutal force. Meanwhile, Merisek's militia, branded as apostates, remained scattered across the realm. Abandoned, leaderless, and without direction, they stood at odds with Daeva's forces, with nowhere to turn.

As the meeting adjourned, Benson was the first to take his hasty leave while the last of the Tiers shuffled out one by one. Aalrija followed Labraid, Ailbhis, and Demelza, walking with an exhausted gait, gently massaging her temples with her index and middle fingers. She walked over to a window overlooking the vast lands of western Celestine, where the setting sun cast a warm orange glow across the lush landscape. Aalrija couldn't help but see the irony in looking upon such a beautiful, serene visage, knowing full well the turmoil etched within it. Word of the realm's troubles spread quietly among the people of Celestine, and there was little that could quell their fears. The urgency in her quest with Von felt ever more daunting with each passing hour.

The last Tier to emerge from the council chambers was Kumiko, awaiting the chance to approach Aalrija away from prying eyes and ears. After he closed the double doors, he gingerly approached her while she stood on the lookout.

"Aalrija," he called out. "I need a word with you."

She sighed. "Can it wait, dear? I'm exhausted, and that meeting took everything out of me."

"It's important," pressed Kumiko as he lowered his voice. "I know of your dealings with the Daeva."

Aalrija was stunned. Her mind began to race as she tried to discern how Kumiko discovered her secret agenda.

"You should know I've told no one," he continued. "But if I am to keep it that way, I'm going to need an explanation."

"Not here," Aalrija said softly. "If we are to discuss this, we must meet somewhere more discreet."

"Then meet me at Teagan's. At sundown."

"Really? Teagan's?" she questioned, to which Kumiko nodded earnestly. "Well, if you insist."

·)C·

Teagan's tavern was a popular meeting place among the Halryn soldiers and was an establishment frequented by many of Kumiko's peers. After grueling reconnaissance missions and seemingly endless training sessions, Kumiko would often be found there alongside

Navaryn and Lowenna with brews in hand and small bites to share. Teagan created a safe place where the Halryn could decompress and vent their frustrations about their instructors. In recent months, even though Teagan maintained his tavern's welcoming presence and energy without fail, its patrons struggled to shake away their mounted despondency in losing their comrades.

At the precise moment of sundown, Aalrija arrived and received a warm greeting from Teagan. Considering the tavern's clientele and environment, senior members of the Halryn council were typically hard-pressed to be in attendance. Just as Aalrija expected, nearly all the patrons' eyes widened as she set foot inside. After she scanned the room, she found Kumiko sitting at a booth against the far wall with a mug of ale in hand. She walked over and seated herself across from him just as Teagan promptly brought her a glass of wine.

Sparing not a moment, Kumiko told Aalrija of his unexpected exchange with Fallon the night before. Naturally, he let loose his disdain for Von and their alliance. Yet, no amount of berating could change how Aalrija felt about Von, and she soon cut Kumiko's badgering short. In turn, she praised Von's efforts where Celestine had failed with Laylanailee, explained her use of the Elemental Parallelling to communicate with him, and outlined their plan to reach Navaryn with the Delavine Crystal.

"So she's trapped within a being from Human," said Kumiko as he peered into his mug of ale. "How are we going to get her out?"

"We are learning more as this unfolds, but I feel Von may be onto a clue soon enough," said Aalrija.

Though Kumiko tried, he could hardly conceal his contempt for Von whenever he heard his name. "If what you say about the Daeva is true, then I want to offer my assistance however I can," he said.

After clearing her throat, Aalrija replied, "Forgive me. But considering your feelings toward the situation, I fear your involvement will further complicate the matter."

"What does that mean?"

"I think you know," Aalrija said with a smirk.

"Look, Navaryn and Lowenna are my friends. I want nothing

more than to get them back."

"Then I ask that you trust we will bring them home. I don't wish to involve anyone else in this, namely Benson."

"My father is unhinged, I know. But I know his concern for Celestine is beyond measure. Losing Ananael and Zin was tragic enough. And need I mention we have no clue where Iaalprt is? For all we know, it might have already fallen into Merisek's hands."

Aalrija fidgeted slightly yet remained tight-lipped at the close of Kumiko's sentence. Although she stopped short of assuring him of Iaalprt's safety, he was privy to her tells.

"What is it?" he asked. "What are you hiding?"

Hoping to calm her quickening heartbeat, Aalrija reached for her glass of wine and took a generous sip.

"It's Iaalprt. You know where it is, don't you?" Kumiko pressed.

"Keep your voice down."

"*Where is it?*"

"I cannot tell you."

"But why?" Kumiko prodded. "If not me, then why not tell the council to ease their minds?"

"Kumiko, you must understand. Informing the council of Iaalprt's location would only further endanger it. Keeping it hidden is the only way to ensure its safety."

"You're a Halryn Tier, and you have a duty to the council. The more you keep from us, the less effectively we can protect our realm."

"*Don't you tell me about my duty,*" Aalrija snapped as she pounded her fist on the table. "This goes beyond the council and far beyond Celestine. All of existence rests on keeping that book safe. Navaryn knew exactly what needed to be done to protect Iaalprt, and I refuse to have her sacrifice be in vain."

Kumiko sat silently through Aalrija's lashing as their argument came to a head.

She continued, "We owe it to Navaryn to bring her and Lowenna back safely, and I will do what is necessary, just as Von is trying to do. But the council has become weak, and we cannot trust Benson to see that through. You heard him in the meeting, Kumiko. He is operating solely on his own with complete disregard for what we have to say, and has no reservations about sending more of our soldiers aimlessly into Daeva and to their deaths."

The pair steadily grew quiet, hoping the droning chatter in the tavern would resume muffling their conversation.

"I think I'm going to need another drink," said Kumiko.

"I might join you in that," Aalrija replied, resting her head on her palm.

Just then, Teagan's familiar, warm, and comforting voice wedged into the climbing tension. "I'm way ahead of you two," he called with a chuckle as he approached the booth with refreshed glasses. "On the house, okay?"

They thanked Teagan as he set them down with a genuine smile. A few more silent moments passed as they sipped their drinks, trying to break through their palpable frustration.

Aalrija added, "Now, I refuse to spend any more time pursuing this discussion if it stays wound by futility. Are you going to continue to sound off self-righteously, or would you rather tell me how you intend to help?"

Kumiko and Aalrija leaned back in their seats to pause and take a breath. While Aalrija drank her wine and calmed her trembling hands, Kumiko delved into thought and considered what assistance he could offer. As he ruminated, he began to reflect on how he had approached the situation. Even though Navaryn's opinion of him had become less than favorable, he knew his actions would cause her even greater disappointment. The only recourse he saw fit was to act as selflessly as her.

"Give me a day or two. I think my father might have something in his study that could be of assistance."

"What does he have?" Aalrija questioned with an unsure look.

"A few years ago, I spotted some old books he had made some notes on. They looked to be regarding Kaimaharaa."

"Kaimaharaa?" Aalrija said in a near whisper. "Don't tell me you're thinking about—"

"Yes," he interjected. "I could use it to reach the realm of Human."

"For the sake of discussion, I will humor you. Continue."

Kumiko set his drink aside and placed his palms on the table. "Merisek still needs Iaalprt, so we can safely assume that he is looking for Navaryn. If I can get close to her, possess someone familiar enough to the human girl, I'll be able to protect her, all while shielding myself from the Realm's degrading effects."

"You make a valid point, Kumiko. Putting yourself in a position like that may give us a better idea of Merisek's efforts," Aalrija replied. "However, you'd simply be trading one danger for another. There's no telling how long this might go on for, and I don't have to remind you of what prolonged exposure to Kaimaharaa can do to you."

"That's a risk I'm more than willing to take."

"But what will Benson think of your absence?"

"I'm not worried about that," he said grudgingly. "Truth be told, I'm sure he'd hardly notice I was gone." His confession made Aalrija's face sink, but he quickly continued, "Never mind that. The other advantage we'd have is that my energy would be concealed—my presence would be completely unsuspected. No one would know where I am, not even Benson."

Kumiko's idea was enticing, though Aalrija still could not compel herself to agree with his proposal. For him to pursue such a dangerous craft meant he was likely never to be the same again. Such a thought weighed heavily on her conscience, even though he made the suggestion of his own volition.

"So, what are your thoughts?" he asked after a bout of silence.

"I certainly had not considered Kaimaharaa to be an option. Nor would I ever."

"But it could work, could it not?"

"Yes, I suppose it could," Aalrija reluctantly replied. "It's a dark art, Kumiko. I can't reiterate enough of the great risk it carries."

"If the Daeva cannot succeed with the Delavine Crystal, then what other choice do we have?" argued Kumiko. "Besides, I'm sure you've become familiar with taking risks yourself."

His snide remark had little effect. "See what you can find out then. In the meantime, I'll need to inform Von of your involvement.

He will be able to find you a vessel."

"Very well," Kumiko replied.

Aalrija finished the last of her wine and hastily rose to her feet. "I must be forthright with you. Should you say a word of this to anyone, you will jeopardize all involved."

"I swore to Fallon that my father would not learn of this from me. And that includes the rest of the council. I swear the same to you," he assured.

"Good. Keep a fire burning. I will call for you when the time comes."

Aalrija walked away from the booth and out through the tavern doors with a wave to Teagan, leaving Kumiko sitting with clenched fists and teeming with discontent. Time grew short, and the prospect of evoking Kaimaharaa was far more than a simple undertaking.

Kaimaharaa was a devious yet powerful art, with potentially harmful consequences. Once evoked upon a subject, the user stood to unlock every facet of their being. Having access to their knowledge, thoughts, feelings, and memories made posing as the subject a seamless task. However, with sustained practice, the subject's mind would often overlap with the user's. The effects could range from simple confusion and frequent unwanted flashbacks to a complete amalgamation of the mind, where the user could no longer distinguish the subject's thoughts and memories from their own. In the rarest of instances, though most discussed, gradual madness would ensue until the user lost their memory altogether.

As dangerous as Kumiko knew Kaimaharaa to be, he also knew it was possible to resist its detrimental effects on the mind with enough mental fortitude. Success could be found in his confidence, though the price he would pay remained uncertain. Regardless, he was prepared for whatever outcome was meant for him, so long as his efforts entailed the safe return of Navaryn and Lowenna.

Kumiko left the booth and finished his drink as he walked toward the bar. He moved his gaze to the sullen faces of Halryn soldiers scattered among the tables. Some looked to have a steady discipline in their eyes, though he wondered how much longer they could keep their morale intact. The privilege he held as Benson's son kept him from joining the waves of Halryn soldiers deployed into Daeva, but it was something that he would no longer take for granted. Their aimless situation demanded change that Benson failed to see, much less bring. Aalrija and Fallon's words rang crystal clear as he repeated them to himself. Retrieving the guardians would give hope and reprieve to the Halryn army and, in turn, would affirm Benson's incompetence. For the first time in several months, Kumiko found himself with a genuine chance to help bring Celestine's misery to an end and gain the proper recognition for it.

As Teagan cleaned off the bar's long countertop, he saw Kumiko approach with his empty glass.

"Now that's the look of a man with a job to do," he said with a grin.

With an uneasy look, Kumiko began, "You got a sec? There's something—"

Before he could utter another word, Teagan hushed him, then took his glass before he could set it down. "Now, son, before you say anything else, I will remind you that this is a place of sanctuary, and what is said here will never leave. Your business with Aalrija is your own, so you'd best keep it that way."

Though Kumiko was wise to the rule, he pondered the possibility that Teagan overheard details of his conversation with Aalrija. Nevertheless, he offered him a reassuring look, conveying his discretion.

"Right," uttered Kumiko with a nod as he turned to leave the tavern.

The evening air was cool and crisp, which was just what Kumiko needed. He closed his eyes and relaxed his fists after taking a deep breath to gather his senses. Fallon's earlier words echoed in his head, imploring him to be honest with himself. To join Aalrija's endeavor meant turning against his father and the council to which he had pledged his unquestioning loyalty. Doing so entailed his second act of defiance: obtaining the tomes of Kaimaharaa from his father's study. Kumiko then vanished under white arcing light as he Paralleled back to Benson's castle to await his opportunity.

7

THE MANIFESTATION

After a gentle knock, Trish's father opened the door to her dark bedroom and peered inside. He took a few careful steps, then called, "Trish, honey. You awake in there?"

In a low and groggy voice, she answered from her bed, "Yeah, Dad."

"Are you feeling any better?"

Before answering, she discreetly looked her father up and down. He was wearing his work shirt and had his car keys in his clenched hand. "A little."

"I want you to take it easy and rest again today, okay? I'll call the doctor if you're not feeling better by tonight. I know you'd prefer some company, but I gotta get to work. Boss won't let me have another day off unless it's an emergency."

"I know. It's okay."

Trish's father walked to the side of her bed. After moving her wild locks away from her face, he kissed her atop her forehead. "I love you."

"I love you, too, Dad."

"Remember, there's noodle soup for lunch in the fridge. And if you get your appetite back, I left you some pad thai and spring rolls. Everything is in the plastic bag on the middle shelf. I'll call to check on you later in the morning." After Trish nodded, he continued, "And

I'll call the school on my way to work and let them know you'll be out another day."

"Okay," she rasped. "Have a good day at work."

He slowly closed her bedroom door and gathered what he needed for the day. Lying in bed with wide eyes, Trish listened to every one of her father's clumsy movements echo through the dark house until he locked the front door. Anxiously, she awaited the fading sound of his rumbling truck. Once in silence, she sprang to her feet and shuffled to the large window in the living room that faced the street, then poked her fingers through the blinds. Relieved she was finally alone, Trish ran back into her room and pulled out a stash of notebooks and binders from underneath her bed.

Trish felt guilty for feigning illness, but what she had experienced since Tuesday night warranted some time alone. Her visions had become more frequent and excruciatingly painful at times. And the information she gathered was extensive, to say the least, having filled three new notebooks on Wednesday alone.

Sitting atop her bed, Trish thumbed through the last half of one of the notebooks containing rushed, heavy-handed writing. Since her father was home during most of her episodes, she tried her best to keep the notes stealthy in case he came to check on her. As she turned another page, her phone began to vibrate. Just as she suspected, it was a message from Rayshell using Jakobe's phone. In a brief reply, she assured her worried friend that she was feeling better but wouldn't return to school until Friday.

Trish resumed flipping through the notebook and refreshed herself on the details inscribed. On the last page of the notebook, she found a couple of lines she didn't recall writing. Squinting in disbelief, she brought the page closer to her curious eyes.

Seal your domain.
They're looking for you because of me, and you cannot be found.

A feeling of dread washed over Trish. She slowly set the notebook atop her bed and zoned out while she repeated the cryptic message to herself. In doing so, she mentally retraced her steps earlier in the week, from her journey to and from school to the errands she ran with her dad. In retrospect, there were a few odd-looking people whose strange energy caught her attention momentarily, but she never felt it was anything to be concerned about. Upon pondering the message again, Trish considered that perhaps it was her stalkers' goal to avoid being seen. Everyone was a suspect, whether a simple passerby or someone who blended inconspicuously into the background.

"Seal off my domain? How?" she asked herself.

Her restless mind raced through random faces still imprinted in her memory from earlier in the week, until the message suddenly made sense. Feverishly, Trish flipped back through the notebook to a section charted with various symbols. She rummaged through her backpack for a pack of colored tabs and marked a few areas, then continued through the rest of her handwritten work.

Trish reviewed the tagged sections within the array of binders and notebooks strewn atop her bed. Some of her earlier notes mentioned how Lowenna sealed her domain, as did other high-profile individuals, including Kumiko, Benson, Aalrija, and Demelza. They used particular charms to prevent people from materializing in a room through a supernatural method of travel known as Paralleling. There were also charms for containing energy, ensuring privacy, and for things she didn't yet understand. She reached for a notebook full of symbols accompanied by nearly illegible details scribbled beside them. As she slowly turned each page, the handwritten note 'close-off' caught her eye.

While skimming the bulleted points, she muttered some of them aloud. "... used to contain the dweller's energy inside a given space ... cloaks most forms of energy and Shahiri workings ... will not cloak a dweller's Parallel ...."

Trish marked the symbol, along with a few others, with a tab, then took the notebook into the kitchen. After pulling the stepladder out from beside the spice cabinet, she selected a knife from the wooden block and set up a working space in front of the living room door.

"Alright. Here goes nothing," she said, then put the knife tip to the door casing and carefully inscribed the tagged symbols in the top corner.

Noon came and went in the blink of an eye. Not long after Trish finished carving the symbols as inconspicuously as she could manage, her father called to check on her. His routine questions reminded her she had not yet eaten anything. After their brief call, she heated the soup she fibbed having already eaten. She slurped at the aromatic broth and admired her handiwork from a distance. The symbols were barely visible, and with any luck, her father would never notice them. If he discovered them, she had a plausible explanation ready. With a smile, she forked a wad of rice noodles into her mouth, then started down the hallway back to her room.

Without warning, Trish's head began to throb. The severe, undulating pain brought her crashing to her knees. Groaning, she put her hands over her ears as grating dissonance culminated.

"Okay, Nav, now it's your turn," Lowenna's familiar voice cut through the whirlwind of sharp sounds in her mind.

Clenching her teeth, Trish opened her dizzy eyes. Dark crimson pattered atop the carpet.

"You're not even listening to me, are you?"

At the close of Lowenna's inquisition, the discord trapped within Trish's head had settled. Slowly, the familiar elements surrounding her dissolved into the parched scape of a struggling garden.

Navaryn had a shimmering jumping spider on her arm and wore a subtle smile. She turned towards Lowenna at the sound of her grumbly exhale. "What'd I do?"

Lowenna flicked her damp blonde hair away from her neck and walked to a spot under the melon trellis for some shade. The hot afternoon reminded her she still had her training armor equipped. She unfastened the plethora of buckles and ties while Navaryn chose a safe leaf to place her new friend.

"What's the last thing you remember me saying?"

Navaryn put her finger to her chin. "Um ...."

Lowenna rolled her brilliant blue eyes after a string of seconds passed. "Wanna pay attention this time?"

Navaryn folded her bare arms. "I don't understand why I need to know this in the first place. I mean, the garden is doing fine."

Lowenna gestured to a few failing vines behind her.

"Whatever."

"And there's more than just that. Some of your tomatoes look like you lit them on fire, your cucumbers are falling from the vine before they have a chance to mature, and the—"

"Alright, I get it," Navaryn interrupted, then poked at one of the crunchy leaves that dangled above her head.

"All I'm saying is your garden can use a helping hand from time to time. We train so much, and there are only so many hours in the day to give it the attention it needs. Material Displacement provides that help."

Navaryn squinted her eyes and leaned toward Lowenna. "This isn't a trick, is it?"

"A trick? What are you talking about?"

With pursed lips, she slowly leaned away. "After the whole episode with Benson trying to force me to perform Mass Displacement, I've noticed you and Kumiko have been testing me in your own ways."

"You're just paranoid."

"Am I?"

"What I am trying to show you isn't even the same thing."

"But it's a component of it. Material Displacement is the root of Mass Displacement."

Lowenna smiled, then sarcastically jutted, "So you do pay attention after all."

"Contrary to popular belief, yes. Yes, I do. And if you're trying to get me to hone my Material Displacement skills so that I can achieve Mass Displacement, don't waste your time. That's something that I will never let happen. Not again."

"Nav," Lowenna said defeatedly, "I've been trying to teach you this technique long before that crazy shit you conjured on the island during crossover." She shook her head, then tossed the last piece of her armor harder than intended. "The technique is rudimentary at best, but it's important. And there are no hidden motives here. If you want to be as adamant as you are against learning any Shahiri techniques, fine. I'll stop trying to show you."

A warm breeze sailed between the pair. Lowenna listened to the jostling, crunchy leaves scrape against each other amidst Navaryn's tense exhalations until she finally spoke.

"Maybe Aalrija rubbed off on me more than I realized," Navaryn said with her eyes downcast. "Just like Demelza has rubbed off on you."

Lowenna nodded. "Eerie to realize it, huh?"

After some more thought, Navaryn groaned and reluctantly called, "If I try the stupid technique, will you stop badgering me?"

"Perhaps."

"That better mean you will."

Lowenna led Navaryn to one of her grow boxes, recently packed with rows of pea shoots. She had a hard time concealing her disappointment upon seeing their condition. Aside from not being properly watered, Lowenna suspected that Navaryn had neglected to amend the soil to start. She bent down, touched a few limp and struggling tendrils, and sighed.

"This isn't the best time to start them, I know."

"Well, if you know that, it's best to give them the attention they need, or your work will have been for nothing."

Navaryn agreed with a simple, silent nod.

"This will be a harder example since we're not simply boosting a healthy plant. Ready to take it from the top?"

Feigning the best grin she could manage, Navaryn gave a thumbs-up, then pulled her long, dark brown hair into a bun.

"Unlike simply diverting the healthy energy within a plant to its less active channels, here we'll have to displace the energy thriving under the soil below the roots and direct it upwards. Follow me?"

"Yeah," Navaryn replied, then knelt beside Lowenna in front of the wooden grow box.

"I'll take this corner row, and you take the other. Now, place your hands on each side of the row, like me." She watched Navaryn mimic her hands' position, then added, "The only thing you have to do here is make sure your palms and fingertips touch the ground. That's all. You can place your hands however you want."

A swell of embarrassment quickly flushed Navaryn's cheeks.

"Just get comfortable. That's probably the most important starting point."

Navaryn relaxed her shoulders and spread her fingers apart atop the hot dirt. Once she closed her eyes, Lowenna smiled triumphantly.

"I want you to feel for the energy below your fingers. Open every one of your senses and search deeply."

With as advanced as Lowenna was, she didn't have to try very hard to lock onto the writhing energy beneath her fingertips. After a matter of moments, sparking sensations rose and culminated in her peripheral veins.

"Search for one of Celestine's many pulses," she added, hoping it would help Navaryn find focus so she could discover and harness her inner sight.

Attentive and patient, Lowenna waited for any indicators that Navaryn had locked onto something, but she soon broke from her concentration.

"What is it?"

"I can't do this shit."

"Yes, you can. You just have to be patient and follow your instincts."

Navaryn muttered, "I can follow my instincts just fine."

"I'll explain it again. Then we'll take it from the top, okay?"

Lowenna ceased to be distracted by Navaryn's seemingly uninterested expression. She simply nodded, then took a moment to gather the concentration she needed. It took an entirely different kind of focus to hold onto the energy for as long as she did, but she grew accustomed to it whenever she was training someone. In time, she came to consider it part of her conditioning.

"Like I've said before, you have to know how much to take and how much to bestow so you don't disrupt the balance."

"What happens when you do?"

Lowenna tilted her head and answered, "You know what happens."

"I told you, I don't remember that night. Now stop trying to insinuate that I do."

"Quit being so defensive. I wasn't even talking about that. Don't you remember the last time Demelza used this technique in your garden?"

Navaryn flicked at chunks of dry dirt and smiled. "Oh, yeah. When she and Aalija were at it again. A bunch of things got messed up for the whole growing season."

"Geez," Lowenna griped as she shook her head. "As I said, you have to be careful with your pull. For instance, this delicate row of peas can't handle much. If you try to bestow too much energy, you will harm it. Likewise, pulling from a source that isn't bountiful enough for your objective will harm what's around it. Understand?"

"Yeah."

"Good. Now put your hands on top of mine. I'm going to see if I can channel the energy to you, then have you release it."

Navaryn repositioned herself alongside Lowenna and placed her dusty hands on hers.

"Now, I'm going to pass it through to you slowly. But don't let it go right away. I want you to hold onto the energy first. Ready?" After Navaryn's confirmation, Lowenna continued, "You're going to feel a hot and tingly sensation, and it may be difficult to move your hands."

Lowenna watched Navaryn's face cycle through a multitude of elated and ponderous expressions until it appeared she had settled into a state of concentration. With her pull tethered to a sweet spot deep within the soil, Lowenna refilled her reserves just in case Navaryn had a mishap with her channeling.

"Now that it's yours to command, I want you to slowly and *carefully* release it to the plants in this first row."

Navaryn's eyes skimmed over the sad-looking specimens in the three-meter row and nodded. Slowly, she stretched her tense fingers and curled them under Lowenna's. After a few moments, the first few plants ahead began to jostle as if caught in a tender breeze. The limp, deflated leaves rose one after another, then flooded with deep green.

Lowenna smiled right along with Navaryn and admired the gyrating tendril protractions. "Great work. Now go ahead and send some of the energy down the rest of the row."

Navaryn followed Lowenna's direction with steady aim and careful intention until halfway down the row.

"Nav, take it down a notch. You're giving them too much," warned Lowenna when she noticed the energy given was more than what a gentle revitalization called for.

With an eerily thirsty smile, Navaryn disregarded her friend's warning and cemented her focus. Greedily, she claimed Lowenna's reserve energy for her own. Curling, writhing, and sprouting with purple and white flowers, the pea shoots continued to develop.

"What the fuck, Navaryn? Take it easy."

Lowenna leaned forward to face Navaryn, and her heart sank. The white flicker she had come to fear was dancing inside her eyes. As she held her breath, she felt the strong pull of energy Navaryn had manifested. The nerves along her arms and fingers panged. Although she tried to inhibit the draw, Navaryn's might prevailed.

Clenching her teeth, Lowenna looked back at the raised bed and watched the augmentations carry over into the remaining rows. Dense clusters of flower buds overwrought the flailing shoots and exploded into bulging pods. The spectacle continued until each plant reached the same excessive metamorphosis, then vitality departed just as fast as it came. The overabundance of swollen pods dried and shriveled, and the entire box withered to a crisp.

Lowenna ripped her hands away from Navaryn and shoved her back. "What is your problem?!"

After her backward crash landing, Navaryn disconnected from her trance. Rubbing the back of her head, she barked, "What was that for?"

"What was that for? What was that *for*?! Take a look for yourself, you lunatic," Lowenna roared and pointed to the bed of desiccated remains.

Navaryn stared blankly at them. "I did this?" After Lowenna helped her to her feet, she confessed, "I'm really losing it, aren't I?"

·◦))(◦·

The same grating dissonance that heralded Trish's vision had overpowered Lowenna's response. Color by color, the garden scene faded before her eyes, and her house's familiar elements slowly reappeared. She winced until the noise had finally departed. Blood bespattered her forearm and hands, and the broth from her noodle soup had absorbed into the carpet. She wiped the crusty blood from her nostrils and chin, then cleaned up her mess.

Three passes over the maroon carpet, and she could no longer tell what had happened. Though the event left her fatigued, she knew she wouldn't be content simply lying in bed or thumbing through her social feeds. With a freshly cleaned and moisturized face, she poured herself a frosty glass of water with a squeeze of lemon, then headed outside for some air.

Smoky clouds blotted the afternoon sky. Trish placed her cup on the glass patio table and sat in one of the weathered fabric chairs. Leaning back, she took a moment to close her eyes and embrace the mild breeze. Her face was hot, and the brisk air was welcome, but the silence that followed was a pest that kept her mind from relaxing.

Trish's leg bounced as fragments of the vision she had just experienced erupted over her eyes, her thoughts waging war within her mind. She sprang forward, took a sip of her water, and then chose to abandon her outdoor retreat. Before walking back inside, she stopped at the row of mint that grew by the door and harvested a few tender leaves to use in her water. Then she froze as a hot sensation cascaded down her arms, reminding her of the fantastical concept of Material Displacement. It was among the many mystical techniques clearly delineated in her visions. Trish knelt before the edge of the brick border and set her glass beside her. As she placed her hands atop the dirt, she couldn't help but feel that such a feat was impossible, even though there were several instances when she had disproved such doubt. After a deep breath, she recounted the instructions from her vision and grounded her concentration.

A prickly sensation reached Trish's fingertips while a clamor of blackbirds passed overhead. Holding her breath through a lull of stillness and a swell of determination, she opened her crystal blue eyes. Looking at the columns of fragrant mint, she did her best to remain calm and centered while her hands and arms started to tingle. Spreading her tense fingers, she willed the mild wave of energy forward, causing the anterior columns to twitch and wriggle. One after the other, they extended slightly. Netted veins on the mature leaves swelled and hardened, and the sprigs formed new leaflets. The augmentations continued until Trish released the modest amount of energy she had gathered.

The tingling sensation dissipated, and Trish dropped to her butt in disbelief. She snagged her water and stared in awe at the altered plant before her. Carefully, she plucked one of the newly formed leaflets and scrutinized it with triumphant but fatigued eyes. It appeared utterly ordinary, and no one else would be the wiser. Though she felt the urge to boast about the phenomenon, she resolved to protect the secret knowledge.

8

THE KISS

Several hours passed since the sun dipped below the horizon. Exhausted from her shift at work and unprepared for the homework that awaited, Rayshell unlocked the front door to her apartment, surprised to find the lights off.

"Jakobe?" she called out into the empty room as she pulled off her shoes, then dropped her backpack to the floor.

There came no answer. Since it was their mother's last workday of the week, Rayshell was sure her brother was enjoying a night out with his friends without a supervised curfew. Nevertheless, she was confident in Jakobe's responsibility and expected his impending return. She walked into the kitchen, relieved and nervous about the moments of solitude ahead.

The clock on the wall chimed, prompting Rayshell to make a quick dinner and dive straight into her homework. She fished out a few bags of produce, made herself a colorful salad topped with nuts and the last of some homemade vinaigrette, then grabbed a protein bar from the snack drawer. Even though her feet were tired from walking laps around the department store all evening, she paced the room as she munched. She thought of calling Trish, but the late hour kept her from picking up the phone. Without an outlet, her stream of intensifying visions and dreams grew harder to bear.

After a sigh, Rayshell jabbed her fork into her salad, then pulled a red shard out from her pocket. Pinched between her fingers, she looked at it with intense eyes. The hole deepening within her heart became harder to fight against with each passing day. Though Von never proclaimed his relationship to Navaryn in her dreams, the amorous desire between them transcended the need for an explanation. The persistent traveler's commitment was unwavering and admirable. Rayshell studied the stone and recalled Trish's conclusion. Though the notion seemed absurd, the glittering fragment dispelled any further doubt, accepting they were experiencing fragments of Navaryn and Lowenna's memories. Though the question of 'why' remained unanswered.

Alone in her apartment and stifled by the confusing thoughts that raced through her head, Rayshell succumbed to the sinking feeling she had tried to avoid. Pining for another glimpse of Von's tenacious crimson eyes, tears conquered her view and blurred the sharp corners of the shard she held between her fingertips.

·◗◖·

Worlds away and fueled by the very persistence imprinted in Rayshell's memory, Von lit a row of half-burnt candles inside Navaryn's safe room. While he finished the last of the wine in his glass, he knelt at the outer edge of his work circle and tidied the contents' positions. Earlier in the day, he found Navaryn's amplifiers packed inside one of the inset shelves furthest from the fireplace. Much like any, the set consisted of three small, charmed mirrors affixed to an ornamental brass stand intended to reflect the summoning energy back to the conjurer.

From candle and incense cone to the trio of amplifiers, everything sat around the elestial Delavine Crystal in perfect symmetry. Von set his glass atop the obsidian table, then stepped inside the circle of candlelight. A decorative cushion lay beside the inner border, patterned with golden embroidery and glass beads. Hanging onto every shred of hope possible, he took his position and stared into the crystal's icy blue inclusions shimmering within its translucent yellow body.

Despite Von's failures over the past two days, he was nowhere near defeated. However slow it was, he recognized his progress. Once he understood how to quiet his mind and enter a trance-like state, he could project himself vast distances. However, the only places he could reach were various regions within Celestine, Opiri, and Daeva, where he and Navaryn had accompanied each other in the past.

Von realized why he couldn't project himself further. His longing kept his attempts strangled by retrospection, preventing him from gaining the focus needed to disconnect from familiarity. His red eyes hardened as he stared at his reflection in one of the amplifier's diamond-shaped mirrors. To have any chance of correcting everything Mersiek upheaved, he needed to master the Delavine Crystal's power by tapping into the cynosure of focus—something that stemmed from something more profound than recollection or anxious yearning.

Slowly, Von closed his eyes. With every breath, he envisioned blowing out a candle, extinguishing one of his colliding thoughts. He continued until the point he considered his mind to be clear, just like all of his previous attempts. Acting as a spectator within himself, he detected a pulse hiding deep behind the darkness in his mind. It was inconspicuous to start, but the longer he focused on the sensation, the more unmistakable it became. The mournful tone boasted his sadness, frustration, and every other uncomfortable emotion that had stirred within him since Navaryn's disappearance. Everything was there, clustered into a single channel, including the guilt he harbored.

There was no way Von could have predicted the turn of events that ultimately led to Navaryn's current circumstance, as well as her choice to sacrifice herself to Merisek's diablerie in place of Benson, but he assumed the blame regardless. His desperate search for Claymar, who had disappeared days prior, made him conclude that he had been baited away from her with perfect timing. He clenched his teeth as he helplessly dwelt upon his carelessness.

The extinguished wicks surrounding Von's mind reignited one by one, and soon after, his searing rage broke loose through a tumultuous stream of cacophonous thoughts. With disharmony nearly drowning his intention, the candles erupted into violent flames. No matter how intense the firelight was, it did little to penetrate the vast, encompassing darkness. Without Navaryn, he was just as empty as his inner projection. At that moment, he prepared to embark on the only path to resolve.

Hanging on to the hope of reaching Navaryn, he began to sever the ties that bound his spirit to guilt. He cut away thread by daunting thread until the sea of clashing thoughts calmed. As the blissful silence reclaimed his headspace, the candle flames receded until their amber glow disappeared.

It was liberating for Von to experience weightlessness once the burden had lifted from his conscience. He took a much-needed breath and realigned his concentration as he exhaled. Locating Navaryn's energy in an unfamiliar world seemed impossible, but he wouldn't let it discourage him. With a mind that was truly clear for the first time, he projected his inner sight and set out on his quest.

Von's perception ascended beyond familiarity into a firmament studded with constellations unknown. The vastness ahead seemed infinite, but the pull he felt from within coaxed the patience he needed to withstand the journey. Scintillating in his eyes with undeniable brilliance, the hordes of distant stars continued to recast. With a vigilant heart and a tranquil mind, Von followed the faint pulse of Navaryn's energy through the revolving celestial planes.

After what seemed like several hours, a powerful current flashed through Von's nerves. The arrangement of astral bodies settled, and soon he felt the pull of gravity rush through his limbs. His projection sent him soaring from behind a modestly sized moon toward a small planet curiously encircled by floating metal objects. At first glance, its land masses looked disjointed. Pristine verdant forests covered some sections, whereas the vast majority appeared scarred, parched, pillaged, and divided. The descent continued into a sector of the world draped in the shadow cast by nightfall. The pulse Von followed now surged through his veins. Like a moth drawn to flame, he followed heedlessly above the strange silhouettes of starved, lanky architecture and clusters of sickly orange city lights. In a less-than-charming part of town, his projection slowly descended upon the corner-end residence atop a two-story complex.

Von's stomach tightened as he touched down on the carpet inside a tiny, vacant bedroom. A single buzzing light illuminated the stark white walls of the cramped living space. He cautiously inched away from a pile of garments at his feet and toward a colorful poster that hung on the back of the door. As he leaned in to study the gamut of illustrated characters, the door swung open. Frozen in place, he darted his wide eyes to Rayshell as she entered. His entire body felt like it had caught fire when he looked into her hazel eyes. Not only was she proof that he successfully managed to project himself to the realm of Human, but she was undoubtedly the vessel that housed his beloved Navaryn. However, the joyous feeling was fleeting. Anticipating her startling scream, Von held out his hands only to discover them to be transparent.

With her eyes on the floor, Rayshell passed by, then rustled around in her backpack for a textbook and a small pencil bag. She maintained her pensive countenance as she retraced her steps, this time passing through him. Once she arrived at the open door, she leaned against the jamb and scanned the room with suspicious eyes. Von held his breath and wondered if she experienced the same icy, electric sensation he did. After a few moments, she flicked off the light and closed the door behind her.

"She can't see me," said Von inside the dark room.

Rayshell strolled into the living room, then sat back at the table with her half-eaten salad on one side and her binder and crinkled protein bar wrapper on the other. Her eyes were red and itchy, and the last thing she wanted to do was homework, but she made an effort nonetheless. Von tiptoed down the hall with his transparent hands out in front to quell his nervousness and stood just behind her. Rayshell took a few bites of her salad and leaned into a comfy nook in the chair. With curious eyes, he watched her scribble her name at the top corner of the paper.

"Rayshell?" Von uttered.

A violent chill shot through Rayshell's feet as the soft utterance caressed her ear. In an instant, she jumped to her feet and grabbed her thick textbook with both hands. "Who's there?" she shouted, turning about the empty room. "Jakobe?"

No answer came as her eyes traced the room. With the textbook gripped firmly in her hands, she ran down the hall and opened each one of the doors while calling out her brother's name.

Von stood still, fighting to maintain his focus. There were moments when his nervousness seemed to induce a strange pulling sensation, as if it would unravel his projection. At a loss for what to do or say next, he turned toward Rayshell's advancing frame. She intended to check the deadbolt and knob lock, which she hoped would give her peace of mind, but all thoughts of safety dissolved. Two glimmering red specks hovering in mid-air caught her eye. Left to rely on her instincts alone, she cocked the book back and swung. Von chose to stay in place, but it didn't take long for him to regret that decision. The book swiftly made contact with his jaw and sent him to his knees.

Amazed that she actually hit something, Rayshell stood with the textbook held high, ready to strike again. The strange translucent mass at her feet took the form of a top-naked man with long black hair that dangled messily over his face. The book that turned her knuckles white slipped from her hands as he parted his curtaining locks. Holding her breath, Rayshell fell to her knees. Her wide eyes overflowed with disbelief as she studied his familiar frame.

"V-Von?" she whispered.

Elated that she remembered his name, he answered, "Nice arm," as he rubbed his face.

"I-I … I'm so *sorry*," said Rayshell with trembling, outstretched hands.

"Don't be. If anything, I'm impressed." He rotated his pale hands in front of his face. "I'm shocked that this even happened, to be honest. This was just supposed to be a projection, after all."

"Just a, *what*? A projection? What does that even mean?" Before Von could reply, Rayshell continued, "Okay, so, why are you—I mean, how are you even here?"

"It's a lot to explain. Just try to relax."

Rayshell stared into his crimson eyes with a twitchy smile and burst, "*Relax*? Is that the best you can say? Something happened to me the morning you came to my dreams, and I really thought I was losing my shit. So many things are flooding my mind. People with these strange names I've never heard of before, but faces I know I've seen. What's happening to me?"

"Navaryn," whispered Von.

"And who the fuck is *Navaryn*?! My name is Rayshell."

Von exhaled and attempted to collect his thoughts.

"This whole week, I wondered if you were real. If *any* of this was real."

"I am real. And this is not some dream," he confirmed, taking her by the hand.

Von's icy touch made Rayshell flinch. As she sat, looking into his patient, sincere red eyes, a turbulent stream of warmth expanded deep in her gut, then flooded her limbs. Part of her wanted to bolt out of the house and keep running until she had no breath left in her lungs, while the other wanted to lunge forward and embrace him. When her anxiety came within seconds of overtaking her, Von's sweet and undeniably familiar redolence claimed her focus and slowly calmed her nerves.

"What do you feel?" asked Von.

"Confused," she responded as tears dropped from her eyes.

"What else?"

"Sad. Something inside of me hurts. It wants to burst through my chest," said Rayshell, gripping her black overshirt. "I feel trapped. I feel alone. And when I feel this way, all I can do is think about you."

Von's face brightened as he looked into her flickering eyes. "Navaryn?"

"Am I Navaryn?" she asked nervously.

Her inquisition wasn't something he could easily answer, and quite honestly, he dreaded trying. Much like he knew he couldn't instantly explain his appearance, the truth would take time and, most importantly, a patient, receptive mind.

Unsatisfied with his silence, Rayshell inched his way with a fierce brow and added, "You asked me what I felt, and I answered. Now, I need you to do the same. *Am I Navaryn?*"

"She's inside of you," Von confessed as he leaned in close. "And right now, I'm looking right at her."

The flickering celestial lights that danced within Rayshell's eyes continued to expand into a blanketing ghostly glow. At that moment, her vision surrendered to the sleeper within.

"Von ... it's really you," she whispered.

Her utterance sent chills down Von's spine. The rich voice that departed Rayshell's mouth was unquestionably Navaryn's.

"I knew I found you."

Tears streamed down Rayshell's face even though she continued to smile, but it wasn't long before her seizing breaths took over.

Instinctively, Von pulled her close to ease her sobbing. Though Rayshell's frame fit differently in his arms, the familiar buzzing warmth was undeniable. He embraced her until the shaking within her core softened.

"I thought I'd never see you again."

Rayshell slowly leaned forward until their lips met. Admittedly, Von felt incredibly uneasy kissing the face of the human girl who hosted Navaryn, but he couldn't reject her timid embrace. Locked within a delicate balance of hesitation and completeness, Von closed his eyes and hugged her tightly.

As Rayshell's lips slowly parted for a deeper kiss, the weight of his arms abruptly vanished.

"Um, Ray? What the fuck are you doing?"

Rayshell's eyes sprang open at the sound of her brother's voice. Now that the ghostly white glow had receded, her vision was her own again.

"I guess I should be happy now that Terrence couldn't come over for dinner tonight," said Jakobe as he locked the door behind himself. "What are you doing anyway? Practicing for drama club or something?"

"I u-um," she stammered.

Jakobe saw the half-eaten salad atop the table and growled, "Damn it. You made salad again? What about the stir-fry we talked about?"

At a loss for words, Rayshell stood and apologized with her eyes on the floor. Before Jakobe could say anything more, she turned around and headed straight for her room. Her brother curiously raised an eyebrow as her door slammed closed. It wasn't the first time he had witnessed his sister's strange behavior, but he knew when to let her be. With a disappointed sigh, he headed to the fridge and gathered everything he needed to make a quick dinner. After what had happened, he was sure Rayshell would confine herself to her room for the remainder of the night, even if it meant leaving her homework incomplete.

9

THE FIRE

Friday afternoon was warmer than expected for the season. Usually, Trish and Rayshell would be singing their fortune for such a fantastic occurrence, but they were too distracted and tired to care. The recent events had even managed to stunt their typical end-of-week giddiness. While they waited at the bus stop, Rayshell leaned against a telephone pole, looking entirely checked out. Even though she was exhausted, it was hard to miss how nervous and hyper-aware Trish appeared.

"I'm glad your dad said it's cool for me to stay the night," said Rayshell.

Trish forged a smile since she, in fact, didn't ask for his permission. Her father messaged earlier that he was pulling a double shift again. Though she preferred to have the evening to herself, she felt it was time to bring Rayshell up to speed on some new developments.

"Weren't you going to study with Nico today?" Rayshell asked as she peeled off another one of her brittle nail tips.

"I told him I had other plans. We'll catch up tomorrow, so it's no big deal."

"Sounds better than being at work. Wanna trade?"

With a half-assed smirk, Trish gestured toward their approaching bus by lifting her chin.

The lingering commuters converged as the doors opened. Rayshell shuffled for her pass with a smile, looking forward to the change of scenery. The girls settled into the corner seats at the back of the bus. Wearing nearly the same faint smile, they rested their heads against the back paneling and closed their eyes in relief. Between the two, Rayshell's mind was the most fatigued. Von's appearance the previous night stunned her to the point of insomnia. Even her homework, which she snuck out to retrieve after her brother went to bed, lacked the power to compel her mind to slumber. On the other hand, Trish managed to get plenty of sleep due to the draining effects of the mystical technique she practiced.

As the bus droned on, making frequent stops for passengers along the way, Trish thought of how to schedule the evening around the topics she needed to share. Aside from the immature reactions expected from Rayshell, she knew to be cautious to keep from rousing the volatile side of her counterpart from slumber.

Unaware of the events Trish planned to orchestrate later in the evening, Rayshell opened her stinging eyes. Disappointed that she had yet to grasp a single comfortable thought to keep her mind at ease, she quietly exhaled, then turned to Trish sitting in the corner seat. Her long chestnut locks covered half of her face, and she appeared to be in the middle of a peaceful dream. She thought it best to let her friend continue to rest while she kept an eye on their journey home.

At the next stop, a large, muscular man dressed in dark clothes boarded the bus. After tossing in what sounded like more coin than was necessary to board, he combed his wiry dark hair back with his fingers and sauntered down the aisle. The man claimed his spot on the bench seat facing the side windows, two rows away. Rayshell didn't realize how firm her fixation was until the man's alluring emerald-green eyes panned her way. Unfortunately, his attractive face didn't boast the charming aura she anticipated. It was dark, unsettling, and somehow unmistakably familiar.

The man licked his teeth as he forged an unpleasant smile. Rayshell's expression instantly fell blank. She tried to nudge Trish awake in a fit of panic but found that she couldn't move, as though trapped in the clutches of a nightmare. Unable to turn away, Rayshell had no choice but to stare down the tan-faced man while a host of repulsive emotions took her over. Her eyes reflected every bit of discomfort and confusion she felt as they slowly went dark.

Trapped alone inside her head again, a torrent of Navaryn's memory fragments pummeled her. Most glimpses were too brief to make much sense of, but she felt the tethering emotions of disgust, rage, and helplessness. Over the passing moments, flickering images had grouped into their proper timelines, offering a momentary glimpse of waves of bloodshed and destruction. Shrieks and muffled wailing filled her ears, along with electric crackling and the crash of stone and debris. Rayshell isolated the panicked voices of children screaming and the gut-wrenching sounds of the life force departing from the lips of unfortunates as the amplifying racket blended into one intolerable tone. As fast as the culmination formed, it vanished, and everything went dark again.

Shortly after, a disturbing series of memory fragments claimed the forefront of her vision. A muscular, top-naked man with bronzed olive skin leaned above amidst a blurry haze. His messy dark hair dangled in front of his face while his body thrusted with passion unreciprocated. Out of the eerie silence came the sickening melody of his solitary lustful groans. As he corrected his posture and readjusted his grip, Rayshell anticipated the prospect of escape from the wretched sensation burning within her. The memory, however, remained in frame and kept blurring, as if she were looking through someone else's eyes as they cried. The man ran his thick fingers through his wiry hair, revealing his sweaty countenance and glowing emerald eyes.

Rayshell's heart fell to her feet as his face hardened among the distortion. Everything down to the same feverish, maniacal expression was identical to the peculiar man who boarded the bus. In a fit of terror, she ripped from her trance. The disturbing memory segment slipped back behind the surge of the others, all of which now clearly illustrated the same emerald-eyed man as the instigator of destruction.

"*Joro,*" she whispered in disbelief.

Pleased with her utterance, Joro smiled with satisfaction, imagining the likely scenes playing out behind her eyes.

Although Merisek tasked Joro with finding suitable vessels to host his contact with Rayshell, his deviant impulses led him to ignore protocol. Earlier in the day, Joro made a quick shift, scouted for some info, and devised his own means of contact. Confirmation of her progress was all he wanted, but he welcomed the possibility that Navaryn might awaken from the distress she was in.

Trish jolted awake at the sound of Rayshell's groaning. Upon beholding the frightening, familiar face just a few meters away, her heart nearly left her chest. Joro could tell by her terrified blue eyes that she knew who he was.

"Don't worry. I'm not after you. Unless you want me to be."

"Just leave us alone, Joro. *Please*. She doesn't know anything."

"I don't know how much of Lowenna has spilled into you, but you should know damn well you're not in the position to demand anything from me."

Trish did her best to keep herself from buckling under the mounting pressure. She looked at Rayshell's dazed expression and asked, "What have you done to her?"

"Nothing but perhaps trigger a simple memory, or two."

"Rayshell, snap out of it," she urged, shaking her gently.

"I don't think that will do much good," he taunted, pointing at the white lights flickering within her deadpan eyes.

"Fuck," Trish muttered. "Not *here*."

"Why not? It's about time she comes home."

With earnest eyes, Trish replied, "Navaryn won't fully awaken in this state. She won't come home. Not yet."

Rayshell's groaning intensified. She slowly leaned into her backpack on her lap and buried her face.

Trish asked, "Ray, can you hear me?"

"I-I won't," muttered Rayshell.

Out of the corner of her eye, Trish spotted two protrusions rising beneath her shirt from between her shoulder blades. "Ray. Come on. You have to snap out of it," she pleaded.

A few passengers turned toward the rising commotion.

"I won't," she repeated.

"What, Ray? You won't, *what?!*"

While Rayshell sobbed, she affirmed, "I won't rest until he is *dead!*"

Joro leaned forward in suspense. "Then go ahead and try."

Upon hearing the sickening pitch of Joro's voice, Rayshell's nerves caught fire. The protrusions in her back continued to writhe as she slowly lifted her head.

"It's about time we settle a score long overdue," Rayshell spoke in a mature, jaded tone.

A familiar haunting glow erupted from Rayshell's eyes in full force. The essence in her gaze mirrored the immense disgust and hatred Navaryn felt for Joro. Trish grew cold from fear, knowing she had to act fast to prevent the devastating repercussions that would follow if Navaryn's volatile form emerged. With her fist balled and charged with energy, she grabbed Rayshell by the shoulder as she stood. Once Rayshell turned her way, Trish sent her palm flat across her face, stunning her with a green current. After the glowing white vanished from Rayshell's eyes, she hunched forward in a daze.

Trish braced her friend's body and pulled the stop cord. "I'm warning you. Leave us alone," she hissed with fierce eyes.

Joro's expression attested to his unappreciation for yet another demand.

Confused, Rayshell shook her head. "What the—"

"It's okay, Ray. We're leaving."

"What happened? Everything went dark again." Rayshell froze as she turned to Joro. "*Trish,*" she whimpered and latched onto her arm.

"He won't do anything."

Unable to conceal how ridiculous he felt the human girl's declaration to be, Joro leaned back in his seat with a smirk.

The bus stopped at a shopping plaza halfway to their intended destination. A few owl-eyed, curious passengers watched the pair as they headed for the exit doors. After an initial misstep, Rayshell led the way off the bus.

Trish took Rayshell by the arm. "Are you okay?"

"I think so," she answered with her hand on the side of her head.

As the bus hummed away, the girls turned toward the sound of maniacal laughter, then raced across the grassy, landscaped divide. Rayshell continued to sneak glances at Joro's intimidating figure as they entered the bustling plaza.

"Come on, girls. I just want to talk."

"We don't know anything! Just leave us alone!" Trish shouted, hoping to garner the attention of some passersby. Just as Joro quickened his gait, she yanked Rayshell by the wrist and beckoned, "Let's go!"

Hand-in-hand, the pair dashed through the crowd of confused people, dodging their strollers and carts. Their feet tapped hard on the glittering pavement, alerting those nearby of their approach. And if that didn't grab the patrons' attention, the plethora of panicked shouts did the trick. For those who didn't jump out of the path, Joro indiscriminately shoved them aside like ragdolls.

Trish and Rayshell rounded a corner, then sprinted through a strip of tiny shops. Judging by the shrieks and crashes that trailed behind them, they could tell Joro wasn't far behind. Breathing heavily, they followed a narrow corridor to the plaza's outer edge. With a firm grip, Trish steered her friend left and into the open doors of a local grocery store.

Halfway into the produce section, the girls watched Joro round the corner through the tinted panels of bordering glass. In unison, they crouched below a display stand of avocados and grapes as he slowed to a stop just ahead of the door. Undeniable frustration seethed through his eyes while he looked around for any sign of the girls.

Trish squeezed Rayshell's hand to get her attention. "Follow me," she whispered. "And focus on containing your fear."

The girls stayed low and slipped behind the next closest aisle, stocked with dried fruits, nuts, and an impressive offering of local honey and preserves. Once out of the entrance door's line of sight, they rose to their feet and tiptoed toward the back of the store.

"Where are we going?"

"Somewhere where we can hide," whispered Trish. "Remember. Stay focused and calm."

Curious eyes panned their way as they carefully snuck down the dairy section and through the gray plastic doors that read 'employees only.' The girls reset their posture as they tiptoed through the cold, dim room. Two employees conversed in the back corner as they restacked bales of rice onto a pallet. To avoid interrupting them, they paused beside a cart of cereals, prepped for restock. Before either of them could take a much-needed reprieve, Joro burst through the plastic doors.

"Feeling clever? That's cute," he teased, following their shriek.

As he came their way, Trish stepped in front of Rayshell to shield her. "Please, Joro. I know what you want. But we don't know where it is."

"Oh, I know well enough *you* don't know shit," Joro directed to Trish, then pointed at Rayshell. "But *she* does."

"No, she doesn't. Not yet, and I promise you that."

"What would you have me do, hmm? Leave and come back when she's done baking?"

The pair of employees who were working in the back suddenly ran up to the trio. The larger of the two clapped his hands high as if to break up the altercation. Joro sneered at the two men as they approached him, their demeanor intimidating.

"Yo! In case you haven't realized, this area is for employees only," wailed the large man.

"What are you doing messing around with these girls, huh?" his coworker chimed while pointing at Rayshell and Trish. "Get outta here before we call the cops."

"Are you guys okay?" the large man asked the frightened pair.

"That's it, man. You ain't leavin', then I'm callin'," warned the other employee.

As he pulled his phone out of his back pocket, Joro raised his open hand. Out of his palm, he launched a concussive blow of black energy dead center into both men's chests without a second thought.

"Now step aside unless you're bent on taking one, too," Joro threatened, then pulled Trish away by her arm.

Through her bleary eyes, Rayshell watched Trish stumble into an empty gray cart and lose her footing. With a yip, she fell to the floor.

Joro advanced, but all Rayshell did was back herself against a large cement support beam. She felt ashamed to be rendered idle by fear when Trish showed so much courage.

Leaning over her, Joro sloshed his thick tongue over his teeth and presented the same unnerving smile as earlier. Though his breath wasn't especially foul, the eerily familiar scent nearly made her gag.

Relishing in her distress, Joro softly taunted, "Got any more of my lover's energy left in you, kid?" Clear that Rayshell's quivering lips prevented a response, he angrily took her by the collar of her shirt. "Come on out, Nav. I know you're ready for another round. You keep me waiting any longer, then this girl will have to do."

He reeled her teary face toward his for what she feared could be a kiss or something worse. Packing all of her panic and trepidation into an amplified sensation, she lifted her tingling hands. Trish's eyes widened at the dazzling display of green current around her fingers. With a roar that sounded every bit like the young woman she was, Rayshell shoved him back.

Joro flew through the air like a toy, slamming into a wall of unpacked boxes. Without a second thought, Rayshell shook the static sensation away from her hands and quickly ran to help Trish to her feet. Moments later, an employee, accompanied by three security guards, rushed in.

"He ran through here!" she clamored, then pointed at Rayshell and Trish. "He was chasing them."

"Call an ambulance," one guard called. "We've got two employees here, unconscious."

"Where did he go?" the second guard asked the girls.

Rayshell pointed at the pile of toppled boxes, discovering Joro had vanished.

While his comrade went to inspect the area, the third guard approached the girls. "Are either of you hurt?" he asked in a warm but concerned tone.

"No," Trish answered.

"That guy caused quite the ruckus, I heard. Is there any reason why he would be chasing after you like that?"

Trish shook her head and explained, "He just started following us once we got off the bus. We got scared, so we ran here to get away."

"That was good thinking," he praised, then ushered them toward the plastic double doors.

Trish's heart skipped a beat when she spotted a security camera lens pointed in their direction. If the stockroom was under active surveillance, there was a good possibility that the cameras captured the energy attacks.

Once outside the store, the guard retrieved a leather-bound notebook from his back pocket and said, "I'll need to get a few words from you both about the incident."

Fearing he may detain Rayshell for questioning, Trish pointed at the vehicle stalled at the streetlight ahead. "Actually, I see our bus coming," she uttered. "We really need to get home."

Trish took Rayshell by the hand and dashed off toward the main street.

The guard called after them and motioned to give chase, but the fear in their eyes persuaded him to let them leave. His only hope was that they would make it home safely.

Rayshell and Trish arrived at the humming bus as the last passenger boarded. As late in the day as it was, there were no seats left. They each grabbed a cold metal handrail and tried to catch their breath.

·)(·

The girls stayed silent and watchful for the rest of their journey homThe girls stayed silent and watchful for the rest of their journey home. Nothing suspicious grabbed their attention along the way, though they still felt like someone was following them. At moments, the warm afternoon air carried sweet nuances reminiscent of spring. But the browning leaves that fell from the lofty tree limbs above reminded them that winter was only a few weeks away.

Trish pulled out her keys as they approached the front door to her house, happy to find nothing out of the ordinary. After they stepped inside, she turned on the light and promptly secured each lock. Relieved, she closed her eyes and exhaled as she slid against the door to her fanny.

"Trish," said Rayshell with her back to her. "How could he just disappear like that?"

Trish picked at her nails, nervous to answer back. "If you truly knew who that was, you wouldn't be asking that."

Rayshell turned around with a perplexed expression. "How much more do you know about what's going on?"

Grumbling, Trish ran her fingers through her hair. "A lot. Okay? I know too much. Like I've told you, since the beginning of summer, I've had these strange visions—dreams, whatever you want to call them." She let their frustrated eyes battle for a moment, then continued, "Well, in case you haven't figured it out on your own yet, they're more than just that."

"No shit. So where did he go?"

"Joro didn't just disappear. Not without the obvious sign of a Parallel." Trish skipped past qualifying Rayshell's knowledge and broke it down as a term used for a type of travel, one where you simply materialize from place to place. "So, my guess is he never left," she confessed.

"But he was gone. How is that possible?"

"Because. Joro is a Shifter."

One of Rayshell's eyebrows arced so high that Trish thought it would fly away. "A Shifter? You mean, a *Shapeshifter?*"

Trish nodded, then watched her friend buckle into laughter. "For fuck's sake, Ray! Even after what just happened, you still can't take things seriously," she barked as she picked herself off the floor. "I need a drink."

"You sound like my mom," she teased during her outburst.

"Looks like I've discovered why she needs it."

Rayshell chose not to address Trish's sarcasm. She met up with her friend in the kitchen as she opened a bottle of wine, and chimed, "Oh shit. You were serious."

Trish quickly poured two glasses and handed one to Rayshell. "Yes. Care to try it yourself?"

Rayshell looked at the dark crimson in her glass and exhaled. In a calm and somewhat dispirited tone, she replied, "Fine."

"Great. Then let's cheers to cooperation, and I'll tell you about everything I've dealt with since summer."

After they clinked glasses, Trish suggested they continue their discussion while they prepped dinner. Rayshell pulled out every vegetable she could find from the crisper and a few potatoes and onions from the hanging basket. She then went to work scrubbing everything down while rehearsing the list of questions racing through her head.

"You'll have to excuse me," said Trish as she took out a packaged slab of bright red meat from the refrigerator. "Usually, when my dad pulls a double shift, I'll try to cook him something for when he gets home. That way, he doesn't eat out."

Rayshell cinched her lip and muttered, "Gross. Why don't you get him to eat some tofu?"

"If tofu even tasted good," Trish teased as she flopped it into a bowl. "He will eat some vegan things, especially if they're disguised well enough. He's at least gotten better."

"That's more than I can say about my mom. She wouldn't touch any meat substitutes even if they were served to her by James Hetfield himself."

Trish lost herself in a fit of laughter as Rayshell pantomimed serving a dish with a routine of his famous 'yeah yeahs.'

Not long after silence claimed the room, Rayshell dried off her hands and said, "So, about earlier. You told Joro you knew what he was looking for and that I didn't know anything. What is he looking for?"

"Well," Trish began as she rummaged through the spice cabinet. "He's looking for a book."

"A book?" Rayshell leaned against the counter while Trish simply nodded. "Why the hell would he do this for a stupid book?"

"Because it's not just a stupid book. It's one from a set of three. When they're together, whoever has them can do some pretty serious shit."

Rayshell rolled her wrist, gesturing for Trish to elaborate.

"You would essentially become the author of existence. You can do as you please: destroy planets, wipe people from existence—literally anything. Imagine what could happen if some psychopath got ahold of them.”

“But you could use them to do good stuff, too, right?”

“Yeah, of course. But if you’re insinuating that Joro has good intentions, you’re wrong.”

“So why does he think I know where this book is?”

With an armful of spices, she claimed, “Because Navaryn was guarding it.”

The kitchen light above them hummed as they resumed their prep under an uncomfortable cloak of silence. While Rayshell skewered the hunks of dripping veggies, she let her eyes wander over the elements in the house that had changed since the last time she visited. There were a few new frames on the wall and a vining houseplant that looked suspiciously large. It sat on a black iron stand beside the front window and crawled along supports the same color as the dark walls.

“What’s to stop Joro from just tearing in here, huh?”

Trish washed the fork she used to poke holes into the meat and answered, “Like everyone else I’ve come to learn about, Joro is some sort of, I don’t know, mystical being, for lack of better words. There are ways to protect yourself against them.”

“How the hell can someone like us protect ourselves from someone with *mystical powers?*”

Trish rolled her eyes at Rayshell’s mocking hand gestures, then pointed to the corner of the room by the front door. “That’s how.”

Perplexed and slightly annoyed that she had to search for the answer, Rayshell scanned the living room until something peculiar in the top corner of the door case caught her eye. She quickly rinsed off her hands and walked over for a closer look.

Trish watched her friend keenly as she tossed thickly sliced potatoes in a bowl with salt and olive oil.

“What are these?” asked Rayshell as she ran her fingers over the three vertical sigils carved into the door case.

“Charms. For protection. Each one does something different. The top one prevents unwanted entry, including a direct Parallel inside this house. The one in the middle masks energy. Think of it like, once you get inside, you disappear."

"But don't you more or less disappear when you walk in, anyway?"

"Your body does, sure. But your essence can still be detected by these mystical beings."

Studying the charms, Rayshell muttered, "Essence?"

"This one might be tough to explain because I've only recently grasped the concept." Trish roughed up her hair as she walked to Rayshell, then continued, "Imagine that you and I have a light inside us. People like Joro can track you by your light, no matter how many doors or walls you're behind. Setting up a charm like that one there will hide your light."

"So, more or less, that charm makes you disappear from someone's radar?"

"Precisely."

"A whole lot of good that does," Rayshell whispered. "I'm sure that Joro knows where we both live by now."

"Yeah, but," Trish looked to the floor, anticipating persistent difficulty explaining things, "if we really are connected to Lowenna and Navaryn, this will keep their light hidden if it breaks out. So long as we're here, that is. And, the third charm is an extra measure to maintain privacy. It keeps whatever we say in this house out of the ears of anyone who could be listening in, by *any* means. I've also taken the liberty of doing the same thing in the backyard. That way, we can barbecue safely."

Rayshell returned to the kitchen to finish skewering the vegetables she left behind.

Trish folded her arms and asked, "You're not going to freak out on me, are you?" as she followed behind.

"No," she answered, though quite honestly, she wasn't sure. "I'm just processing everything you've said and wondering how the hell you know all this."

"Fair question. Give me a sec," said Trish with a finger raised, then walked to her bedroom.

Rayshell listened to the strange shuffling sounds echoing down the hall. A few moments later, Trish reappeared with an armful of binders and notebooks. She set them atop the dark wooden dining table, one after another, then flipped them to different sections marked with tabs.

"About a week into experiencing these strange dreams and visions, I decided to write everything down. *Everything.* I had a tough time in the beginning because things were fuzzy and hard to remember. But as time went on, it became a hell of a lot easier," Trish confided as Rayshell tiptoed over with wide eyes. "These are all the instances that I wrote about sigils of any kind."

Rayshell scanned the variety of sketches and handwritten words. Among the extensive list were the three sigils Trish had carved into the door case. But Rayshell spotted another version that supposedly prevented unwanted entry. Tapping beside it, she looked to Trish and asked, "This does the same thing as the one you used, right?"

"Yeah. But the one I used is supposedly better, I guess," she answered, recalling the memory of when Lowenna feverishly replaced the sigil inside her dwelling with the same variation she used. She had yet to learn what prompted the revision, but figured it was important.

"So what made you go through and flag all these things?" Rayshell asked after flicking up one of the green tabs. "Did you see Joro before?"

Trish shook her head. "I've never seen him anywhere other than in my head."

"Then why?"

Trish grabbed one of the notebooks and flipped to the very last page. "Because of this," she replied, then set it in front of Rayshell. "Read it."

In a monotonous voice, Rayshell read the words, "Seal your domain. They're looking for you because of me, and you cannot be found."

"I came across this warning yesterday morning. I don't know exactly when it was written, but it can't be more than a couple of weeks old because that's when I started using this notebook."

Rayshell slowly walked back into the kitchen for her glass of wine. "So this was a warning written for you. By who?"

"My best guess is, Lowenna."

Rayshell promptly downed the rest of her wine.

"Take it easy," said Trish while Rayshell started to guzzle her refill. "You need to eat if you're going to drink all that. Come on. Let's get the stuff on the grill."

Trish turned on the back porch light and cleaned off the table as Rayshell brought out the food and wine.

"Did you grab the crackers, too?" she asked as she removed the grill cover.

Sarcastically, Rayshell replied, "Yes, Mom," with her mouth brimming with them.

"Good. I don't want you feeling like trash in the morning. Don't you have to work?"

"Yeah, but not until eleven. Shit. Or was it ten? Maybe I should check. I have a copy of my schedule in my backpack."

While Rayshell scampered back into the house, Trish grabbed the briquettes from the shed, wagering the bag was over two years old, and proceeded to fill the barbeque. Back before her father's work schedule became a nightmare, they grilled nearly every weekend, rain or shine. She smiled as the familiar odor called forth a team of fond memories, including her father's dramatic reaction the night she asked her dad to add broccoli to some of the skewers.

Rayshell walked back outside to ask Trish if she wanted a jacket, but stopped when she saw her standing at the grill with her hands spread above the unlit grate. An eerily warm zephyr sailed by while Trish lowered her head. Rayshell held her breath as the hair on her head, arms, and neck pulled in her friend's direction. Tiny glowing flickers materialized just below the palms of Trish's hands and descended atop the briquettes until enough energy culminated to ignite them.

Quietly, Rayshell tiptoed behind her friend, then sharply asked, "How did you do that?"

Close to jumping out of her skin, Trish barked, "Shit! I didn't know you were back already." She clenched her fists a few times to alleviate the uncomfortable tingling sensation and continued, "Well, basically, I studied what I wrote down in my notebooks."

Rayshell slowly nodded. She would have been more shocked to witness the ability if she hadn't manifested the strange electric energy that launched Joro backward.

"I haven't been able to do anything close to what you did to Joro, though. That was pretty amazing."

Smiling, Rayshell replied, "I don't know how it happened, honestly."

"For you to be able to do something like that within your first week of experiencing all this tells me you may be up for a tougher time than me."

Rayshell asked, "What do you mean?" as Trish sipped nervously at her wine.

"Well, I might just be overthinking it, but if you're able to tap into Navaryn's energy as early along as you are, I assume that means you will end up experiencing some *side effects*."

"Side effects, eh?"

Trish brushed the floating ashes from her pink and white plaid shirt. "The reason I wasn't at school Wednesday and Thursday wasn't because I had the stomach flu."

"Ha! You lair. I knew it."

"Hold on a sec. I still wasn't feeling good," Trish defended as Rayshell sarcastically pursed her lips. "Lately, these visions have been getting out of control. The pain. It's just awful, like my head's splitting open. And now I can't seem to function until they pass. Yesterday I got a bloody nose from one of them. Today I blacked out in class. Thankfully, it was in the middle of a lecture. I don't know what's gonna happen next. And truthfully, I'm scared to death."

Rayshell held her glass to her lips as she followed Trish to the barbeque. "So, you think I will experience something even worse than you?"

"I'm not saying it's certain," Trish answered, then placed the slab of meat on one side of the pit. "But it's something you should know, just in case." She continued to neatly arrange the vegetable skewers to cook before throwing on the potatoes.

They stood around the grill's mellow orange glow, watching the vegetables sizzle. The tempting aroma made Rayshell realize how hungry she was. She quickly reached for the box of woven wheat crackers on the table behind her, then proceeded to cram her mouth. While Rayshell snacked away, Trish regaled her with more intrusive memories that reminded her of an instance she had yet to divulge.

"Have you ever taken anything back with you from your dreams?"

Rayshell nodded as she worked on chewing down the wad of salty crackers. "The time when Von came to me in my dream. Remember, I told you that he transformed into a creature? He was upset because we didn't get to finish our conversation, so he tore open his forearms. I woke up and found spots of his blood all over me." Rayshell touched herself in the places she remembered as she fell into the memory. "I thought I was losing my mind, honestly. Did I tell you his blood drops turned to stone?"

Trish shook her head.

"I have some of them," said Rayshell. She reached into her pocket, pulled out a small jagged red shard, and handed it to Trish.

"This is amazing," she whispered as she inspected it under the firelight.

"I had a bunch of these in my hand just before I woke up. Somehow I took them with me."

Trish handed the shard back to Rayshell. "This makes what I have to show you so much easier."

Rayshell tucked it away as Trish took the skewers off the grill and replaced them with potatoes.

"This is what I took back with me," she said, then pulled up the back of her shirt.

Poking above the right side of her pants line was a meaty, discolored scar. Rayshell couldn't control her recoil. Not even the firelight had the power to soften its appearance.

"It goes all the way down the back of my leg. I guess I'm lucky I don't like wearing shorts or skirts."

"Wait. So this is something that just appeared?"

Trish nodded. "Just like the marks I showed you in the music room earlier this week. After a horrible nightmare." She pulled down her plaid shirt, then took the skewers to the table. "This was what prompted me to start writing everything down."

Sporadic and violent flashes of Trish's nightmare passed behind her eyes. Silvery wisps of smoke surrounded Lowenna as she frantically surveyed the bleak, cavernous hall that she found herself in. Out of the darkness, a pair of glowing yellow eyes appeared as she readied her weapon. The mysterious figure dashed toward her with lightning speed and clashed against her staff with a set of violet energy blades. She held the rapid succession of attacks at bay until the assailant found an opening in her defenses and quickly disarmed her. The burn of the caustic energy blade ran through the back of her leg and forced her into submission. Blood pooled at her grounded knee while she belted a blood-curdling scream. Lowenna turned to find the golden eyes glaring down at her. Before the assailant dealt a deadly strike, the nightmare came to an abrupt end.

"I felt what it was like to have my flesh torn open, and I woke up screaming. But the pain didn't go away. When I moved the blanket away from my legs, there was blood everywhere."

With wide eyes and bulging cheeks, Rayshell chewed down the savory vegetable skewers in suspense.

"My dad heard me scream and came barging into my bedroom. I gripped my sheets, darted into the bathroom, and jumped in the shower as fast as I could. He banged on the door and yelled for me to tell him what happened. As I stood in the shower, still clinging onto the bloody sheets, the best thing I could come up with was that I started my period."

Rayshell wanted to laugh, but the gravity of her friend's experience kept her from it.

"He eventually left me alone. But then, the strangest thing happened. While I was in the shower, the wound healed into this gross-looking scar almost instantly. And it's been there ever since."

Trish walked to the grill and pulled off the meat, hoping she didn't overcook it. After rotating the potatoes, she closed the lid, then snatched up her glass of wine.

"It was an emotionally draining day, to say the least, and I still get chills when I think about it."

Rayshell squished a puffy cherry tomato between her fingers

until the skin separated from the meat. "Last night, Von told me that Navaryn is inside of me. I didn't want to believe what he said, just like I didn't want to believe you."

"Why don't you want to believe it?"

"Because. I'm scared. If they're inside of us, what happens when they leave? Will we die?"

Trish looked to her feet as she skimmed her mind for something comforting to tell her friend, but sadly, she had nothing. And she would be lying if she said she didn't think the same on occasion. Soon her eyes widened with an impossible idea.

"What if we go to where the answers are?"

Rayshell almost choked on a hunk of mushroom. After fighting to clear the food to one side of her mouth, she asked, "What the hell are you talking about? The only one who could possibly know anything is Von."

Trish replied with a nod.

"That's impossible."

"Hear me out," requested Trish with her finger in the air. "Von is actively trying to reach you. There's no denying that. But I think someone is facilitating your contact. And his list of allies is small. If I'm right, then I know where he might be."

As Trish dashed into the house, Rayshell yelled, "You're even crazier than I thought!"

Trish returned with an armful of her notebooks and the container of lighter fluid. While she worked on tagging new sections, Rayshell took over the grill.

"Now, if we're talking about a Celestine here, the only one who would assist Von is ... Aalrija," said Trish after skimming a list of names grouped in circles and color-coded with lines that linked one to another.

"Aalrija? Navaryn's caretaker, right?"

"Well, previous caretaker. Her role dissolved once Navaryn became an adult." Trish moved her eyes back to the pages of scribbled details under the dim light. "Aalrija, like any Halryn, wouldn't dare travel to Daeva. That means Von is likely posted in Celestine."

Another warm breeze dashed by. Holding onto the tongs with

folded arms, Rayshell looked at Trish with an overwhelmed gaze. She had yet to fully understand the terms 'Halryn,' 'Celestine,' and 'Daeva,' but did her best to follow along.

"There's only one place in Celestine where Von could be. Navaryn's safe room."

Trish flipped through more pages while Rayshell removed the potatoes from the grill with a tester sticking out of her mouth. "What if you're wrong?" she asked after she set the plate down at the corner of the table.

"Then I'm wrong, and we go back to the drawing board."

"But what if something bad happens?"

"Look, I get that you're scared. But if we can be proactive and figure things out on our own, we should try. It sure beats waiting around for something else bad to happen."

Rayshell couldn't disagree with Trish's proclamation. "How do we get to him, then?"

With a mischievous smile affixed to her face, Trish grabbed the bottle of lighter fluid and confirmed, "With this."

After the girls pulled their chairs in front of an old fire pit, Trish doused a stack of firewood in a hefty amount of lighter fluid. Though Rayshell had no idea what was in store, she maintained patience and slowly sipped her wine. Under the table, in a magnetic box, Trish pulled out a box of matches.

"Aren't you going to do what you did earlier?" asked Rayshell while she mimicked a magical hand gesture.

Trish tossed a lit match into the pit while she shook her head. "Nope. I don't want to waste my energy. I'm going to need every bit I have." She tucked the matches back where they belonged, then selected a few notebooks from the stack.

Rayshell leaned over to skim the page Trish had turned to. Most of the words were illegible, but she managed to discern the heading titled 'Parallel' followed by the names of the four elements prepended by bullets. "Wait a minute. Don't tell me—"

Trish nodded, tapping her finger against the word 'fire.' "I am going to try to Parallel to Von."

The buzzing excitement within Rayshell's stomach fell flat at the sound of her proclamation. "You've got to be kidding me."

"I know that there are many methods of Paralleling, and the only one I think could garner success is one rooted in the elements. I'm going to project myself through the fire, traveling from our realm to Celestine."

"You're insane! How could something like that possibly work?"

"I don't know. Quite honestly, it might not. But, I'm gonna try. I think I can figure out how from what's written here."

"As if anybody can read this," teased Rayshell, studying her friend's shoddy penmanship.

"In a nutshell, I'll try to project myself through these flames. But it will only work if a fire is burning inside the destination. Thankfully, I'm sure that won't be a problem."

When Trish finished reviewing the newly tagged sections of her notebooks, she handed them to Rayshell to set back on the table.

"I'll be honest. I don't know how long this could take. But I will keep trying until I know for certain I can't do it. I need you to watch the fire to make sure it doesn't go out. Douse it with more fluid if it gets too low. And, one more thing. I need you to stay quiet. No questions, no anything."

"Keep the fire going and shut my trap. I understand," affirmed Rayshell. "What if the sun comes up?"

"Then let it," she answered back.

Rayshell grabbed a glistening potato from the plate and dangled it in front of Trish. "One last bite for the road?"

Immediately after Trish devoured the offering, she shook out her arms, took a few deep breaths, and then closed her eyes. While clearing the salty bits from her teeth, she calmed her mind and rehearsed the limited instructions indexed in her memory.

Rayshell shifted around in her chair until she found a comfy divot. Pleased, she watched her friend with attentive eyes, smiling at her rotating, tense expressions. As they sat together in silence, the cooling air grew still, and the creatures that thrived under the shadow of night slowly began to emerge. Along the fence crawled a family of opossums.

Rayshell nearly squealed in delight as the fuzzy cavalcade took refuge behind the ivy overgrowth.

Though the chipper melody of nightingales and crackling fire were soothing to hear, they also created the perfect platform for Rayshell's racing mind to run free. Once she finished her plate of potatoes, she grabbed one of Trish's notebooks, hoping the contents could prevent her anxiety from rearing its impatient head.

The passages were challenging to discern under the waving firelight, but she soon fell onto a section of tight, neatly curled handwriting that was noticeably different from her friend's.

Claymar. Why haven't you come for me?
Through my soul, I've called for you. Every night. But you don't answer.
Something is wrong. Dreadfully wrong. And yet I can do nothing.
I sit as a prisoner in this body, but I will find a way to break free.

Rayshell held her breath as her eyes trailed off into the fire. While she experienced the resonating sadness locked within the delicate string of words, she didn't blink. Quietly, Rayshell thumbed through the tagged sections and tried to make sense of the confusing emotional recounts and internalized assumptions, while her friend struggled to concentrate.

After what felt like hours, Rayshell reached the final pages of the last notebook in the stack. She had come to decode most of her friend's rushed and untidy penmanship with ease. In the light of the refreshed flames, she read a playful recounting of Lowenna and her friend Catriona until a strange sensation seized her attention.

Rayshell watched as each one of her arm hairs pronged skyward. Apprehensively, she reached for her tingling cheeks only to find her long, shimmery locks suspended in the air. She turned to Trish with curious eyes, maintaining her silence, and watched her thick hair unfurl and fan open in the same delicate fashion. Flecks of iridescent light flittered from the fire and into the surrounding darkness. Suddenly, the same strange pull that Rayshell had felt earlier, when Trish lit the grill, returned. The feeling intensified as the moments passed, nearly prompting Rayshell to interrupt the process. A single moment away from succumbing to her anxiety, the feeling simply vanished.

A warm and hazy halo expanded around Trish's silhouette as the apparition of a woman's face leaned forward. Her beautiful visage was calm, and her eyes were filled with determination. Rayshell's jaw fell as she watched the golden figure stand to her feet. In the very moment their eyes met, time slowed to a crawl. A thick pulse reverberated through Rayshell's veins as she sat silent, asphyxiated by light, wonder, and weightlessness.

Lowenna, Rayshell thought to herself as the shimmery apparition closed her eyes.

After a slow and heavy exhale, the phantasm disintegrated into a flock of shimmering particles that drew toward the rippling fire. Time slid back into place once the last fleck departed, and Rayshell gasped for a breath. Clutching the arm of her chair with wide eyes, she looked to Trish, then into the fire for any sign of Lowenna.

·)(·

Topless and sprawled over one of the tufted chairs, Von munched on a large speckled apple while he fought away the dreadful call for slumber. Each bite became more sloppy than the next, and there was only so much wetness he could wipe away with his sticky wrist. He had just finished another series of unsuccessful attempts to project himself using the Delavine Crystal, and his mind was exhausted.

His repeated failure stemmed from the discovery of Joro within the realm of Human. Though he was able to catch a glimpse of Joro's ambush and the girl's successful evasion, he had no idea if they were still safe. And it was nearly impossible to feign a focused and controlled mind while the vile, despicable fiend roamed free to stalk his prey. But he felt as if something else were keeping his projection from manifesting, though he lacked the proper insight.

One thing was certain: Joro was after details on Iaalprt's location, and it was impossible to decipher Navaryn's current standing within the human girl. Although Rayshell hadn't become aware of any information that would be useful to Joro, he feared the lengths that he would go to pry whatever he wanted out of her. While picturing his delighted and smug visage, Von squeezed the half-eaten apple until it popped under the pressure of his electric hands. Bits of juicy, sticky-sweet fruit exploded over his chest, pants, and as far as the obsidian table by his feet. Every bit of displeasure and fear reflected out from his sunken, red eyes. Though it was foolish, he welcomed the seemingly inevitable confrontation with Joro. But it would only occur if it fell within his promise to Navaryn, deeming it the only resort to keep Iaalprt safe.

The low rolling fire behind him churned with the same crackling sounds he became accustomed to hearing upon Aalrija's entry. He began picking the apple chunks from his body so he could stand.

"Your visits are becoming later and later, Aalrija," griped Von while he fed himself the bits of collected fruit.

"Von?" a soft voice called.

Von nearly choked on his mouthful of masticated apple as he looked at the blazing projection of a nude woman. Unable to maintain any semblance of refinement, he fell to his knees and coughed the fruit onto the floor. His astonished eyes barely left her.

"*Lowenna!?*" he managed between his fits. "Is it really you?"

Lowenna looked upon her fiery arms, amazed that Trish executed the technique. The breadcrumbs she left for her human host were misleading, as Trish was never meant to be the one to cross over into Celestine. Nevertheless, she was pleased to see a familiar face.

"Are you okay?" he asked as Lowenna winced.

"I'll be fine," she said, then shook the dizziness from her head. "Where's Claymar? Is he with you?"

Unprepared for her question, Von shook his head. "He's been missing since before you and Navaryn were banished."

Lowenna paced frantically in front of the fireplace as she strived to contain her rising concern. Before Von could unleash his swirling barrage of questions, she quickly turned and faced him. "I'm not sure how long I have, so I'll get to it," she began. "Joro is in Human, and he has found us."

"I know," Von confirmed. "I've seen him myself."

"You have? How?"

Von pointed to the rough elestial crystal situated between the amplifiers on the floor beside the chair's shadow.

"What is that?"

"A Delavine Crystal. I got it from Fallon. It was a peaceful meet, I swear," he assured once her eyes darted to him, then gave her a brief rundown of its power.

"So this is how you were able to appear before Rayshell."

Lowenna inspected the crystal's icy-blue inclusions shimmering prominently through its golden, translucent body. After Von concluded his explanation of its ability, her curiosity suddenly sparked. She then urged him to use its power to locate Claymar.

"Out of the question," Von affirmed.

"But we need his help! Joro's on our tail!"

"There's no time!" he snapped. "Getting you and Nav back is our only objective right now. We'll have to manage without him."

Lowenna curled her hands into fists. "Von, listen to me. He could be in trouble."

"Don't you think I know that? I'm the one who went looking for him in the first place. And what a grand diversion that was, too. While I was preoccupied figuring out what the fuck happened to him, I lost you and Nav to Merisek's cunning. I'm not going to let that happen again."

"I swear. If I make it out of this and he's gone—"

Before Lowenna could finish her threat, the flames within the fireplace sputtered and rolled. A thick silhouette of a naked woman emerged from an unstable wall of bright yellow fire.

Flabbergasted, Von uttered, "N-*Navaryn?*"

"Von!" she cried ecstatically.

As Navaryn bounded toward him, rippling flames caught the corner of her eye. Confused, she stopped and studied her fiery apparition in a panic.

"It's okay, Nav," he assured. "You're in an Elemental Parallel."

The delight in Navaryn's demeanor shifted to disappointment upon realizing her presence in her safe room was not in the flesh. She reached to feel Von's touch but could only watch as her hand phased through his. Not letting the moment get the best of her, her quivering lips managed to crack a smile as she fixed her amorous gaze into Von's red eyes. Lowenna walked to her with a grand smile and congratulated her on her first success at an Elemental Parallel.

As Navaryn prepared to speak, the spectral fire of her projection hissed, crackled, and distorted into a jarring display. Disoriented, she fell to her knees as her fiery apparition slowly ruptured.

Von dodged the torrid bluster of shooting flames and barked, "What's going on?!"

Lowenna trotted to her friend's side and dropped beside her. "I-I don't know."

Though Navaryn's comrades continued to prod her for information, she couldn't reply. She began to squirm and groan as her projection faltered. Yearning to remain with Von, she pulled from the dark energy deep within herself to keep her connection intact. The room began to quake as a blinding white haze eclipsed her eyes.

Navaryn suddenly hunched over in pain. Instinctively, both Lowenna and Von looked to gauge the efficacy of the glowing set of charms affixed to the corners of the room. The sigils' vibrant luminance intensified as the strength of their hold increased. At that moment, two sizable protrusions suddenly jutted out of Navaryn's upper back.

"I think something's happening to Rayshell. I've got to disconnect her before these charms give out," said Lowenna.

As Navaryn wailed, Von conceded with a nervous nod.

"I'll find a way to reach out again," she continued. "Until then, I'll try to keep her safe."

As Lowenna's projection began to disintegrate, Von chimed, "And I'll see what I can do about Clay."

Lowenna's earnest eyes met Von just before her fiery apparition vanished.

Von turned to Navaryn and quickly knelt before her as the room continued to quake. Helpless to quell her agony, his heart ached to see her in despair. Unsure of what to say, he uttered, "Navaryn, can you hear me?"

Curling over the ground, Navaryn groaned in pain with her hands clenched into fists. Flutes of flame hissed and sputtered from the protrusions pulsing between her shoulder blades. Surrendering his sense of self-preservation, Von put his hands atop the jittery projection of Navaryn's scorching wrists. He was all too familiar with her white-eyed counterpart. The strange manifestation that greeted him with such fervor many years ago remained a constant challenge. Although they had worked together to manage the affliction, it was not entirely under her control.

"Von," she whimpered from under her curtaining, fiery locks, "this is all my fault. I'm sorry."

"No. Don't apologize."

Navaryn gritted her teeth as the painful protrusions continued to writhe, then, suddenly, her projection vanished in a crude, ghastly display of fire and light. Left alone in the safe room again, Von sighed defeatedly, then angrily pounded his charred, blistered fist into the floor.

·)(·

As Trish shook Rayshell to break her from her trance, a torrent of glowing flecks shot out from the fire pit. The golden embers of light absorbed into her body with such force that she flew backward in her chair. Trish dropped to her knees to help steady her writhing friend, careful to avoid touching the pair of glistening patches on her back where the protrusions wormed.

"Ray, are you alright? Say something!"

Bordering the yard's perimeter, the series of safeguard charms swiftly activated in brilliant purple. Once Rayshell opened her eyes, the ghostly glow that emanated confirmed the volatile essence trapped within her had assumed control.

A surging gust cracked the air and knocked Trish off her feet. As she gathered herself, she looked to her friend with mounting trepidation. Writhing in pain, Rayshell tore her fingers through her hair and wailed until she emptied her lungs. Opalescent energy swelled around her as the surrounding charms fractured in a frightful display.

The wall of ivy and behind the shrubs thrashed, and silvery wings split from Rayshell's back. Panicked and bespattered in glimmering blood, Trish dashed to the patio table.

The volatile visitor inspected her host's small, youthful hands and understood that her transformation was incomplete. Disappointed, she rose to her feet against the disorienting balance of her outstretched wings. Just as she began to scan the yard, listening to her blood patter atop the grass, a sharp white light took everything away from her eyes.

A neon electric current unraveled from the empty wine bottle Trish held cocked to the side, then dissolved into the air. Rayshell crashed to the ground, and the wings slowly receded into her back. After Trish quickly reaffixed the charms that bordered the backyard, she carried her unconscious friend inside the house and set her atop her bed, thankful to discover her wounds were actively healing.

Hours slipped past while she cleaned the property free of blood and disarray. Trish sat at Rayshell's side, clutching a glass of water. Before she realized how late it was, she heard a set of keys jingling at the front door. Quickly, Trish tucked the soiled linen into her laundry hamper, then grabbed a blanket to toss over Rayshell and herself. She listened to her father's footsteps loop around the house until she finally fell into much-needed slumber.

10

THE SHIT BUCKET

Inside the cold confinement of his study, Merisek sat at the stone table with dim candlelight as his only company. Through countless hours spent painstakingly working to extract a clue to unlock a mere inkling of the Order's power, his drive for success was fraught with frustration. The prospect of obtaining Iaalprt and the hope of correcting the course of his history felt increasingly distant with each passing day. He repeatedly deprived himself of proper rest, languishing his body and mind. Dreams accompanied his brief, intermittent dozes, though he felt them to be nothing more than mere hallucinations. The most common variation was the haunting cacophony of jumbled, indiscernible voices, as though he were listening to the static sound of violent rainfall. Since he was always teetering on the cusp of consciousness while he experienced them, he strove to pick the jumbled, nonsensical voices apart, similar to his efforts with Zin. And much the same, he was unsuccessful and saw it as another way for his failures to haunt him.

A soft blue glow emanating from across the room continued to pry Merisek's eyes from the pages of Ananael and Zin. Once the distraction became more than he could bear, he folded the tomes closed and ambled to his alchemy station against the wall. The glow came from a vial of blue liquid that he had recently synthesized.

Impatiently, he snatched it from the rack, then rummaged through the collection of other mysterious liquids until he found a silvery one more viscous than the rest. He held it up to the dim candlelight and watched the suspended opalescent flecks collide. It was a hauntingly beautiful substance to behold, and he couldn't help but recall his daunting undertakings with it in the past. With a smirk, Merisek retrieved his cloak and prepared to leave his study.

After emerging from the stale confines, Merisek took a breath of fresh air, hoping for an uninterrupted opportunity to quiet his mind. However, Joro's hasty footfalls approached him from behind.

"I need to talk to you."

Merisek quickly slid the two vials into his cloak to hide them. With his eyes closed, he slowly exhaled before replying, "Yes, Joro, what is it?"

"I'm not liking this idea of yours to get my parents involved. They are not confident in the plan, just as I am not."

"That's interesting. I spoke to both of them about it, and they were very much on board to assist."

"You think they would object to *you* of all people?"

"Answer me this, then. What other option do we have?"

"We find others to go instead. And we leave my parents out of this."

"And just who would you suggest? The whole realm of Daeva is against us. We haven't an ally left, and it's all thanks to you!"

Merisek strode through the halls of his fortress with Joro in tow as he made his way to what used to be the mess hall of the facility. He gathered a few pieces of stale bread and filled a bowl with grits and various nuts. Their food supply was meager and growing more scarce by the day, which concerned Joro more than it did Merisek, though it would last through the remainder of the season with careful planning. As he turned away from the pantry, he looked upon Joro standing in the light of a torch to warm his hands.

"Your clothes. Why are they torn?" asked Merisek.

Joro realized he had foolishly and unintentionally given away a hint of his actions within the realm of Human. He searched his mind for a lie he could hand to him, but Merisek had already sensed he had gone against his orders.

"You idiot! What did you do?!" he roared with glowing eyes.

"It's those brats," Joro replied. "Somehow, they've managed to channel the Celestines' power."

"I warned you not to engage them!"

"Nothing came of it."

"They know you're actively pursuing them now, you fool!" Merisek yelled. "This is precisely what I was afraid of. If you cause an incident in the realm of Human, there's no telling what would become of our plan."

"Relax, old man. I already told you—"

Merisek's fist swiftly slammed into Joro's cheek, sending him stumbling into a daze. "Insolent shit. I will not have you derail our actions *again* and put us in an even worse position than we *already are!*"

The jostle in Joro's head blurred his vision as he tried to recover his stance.

Once again, the fierce glow of Merisek's eyes intensified, igniting Joro's contorted face. "Surveil them, and *nothing* more. Nathaniel and Eitha will handle Navaryn while you report to me on Lowenna. Do I make myself clear?"

"*Perfectly,*" he answered, reciprocating Merisek's glare.

The angered afterglow in Merisek's eyes gradually dissipated as he swiped his bowl of food from the counter. "Now, I assume you've found suitable hosts for your parents?"

"Yes," Joro replied flatly.

"Good. Summon them to the study and wait for me there. I'll be back in an hour," said Merisek as he sauntered off.

"Where are you going?"

"To check on our guest."

Joro stood by the torchlight, wincing with his palm against his cheek as he watched Merisek round the corner of the doorway out of sight. The taste of blood met his palate as he tongued tiny, bony shards of tooth, then spat them onto the ground. After hastily tending to the wound in his mouth, he left to retrieve Nathaniel and Eitha.

·)(·

Three floors beneath the study stood a massive wing packed with cells Merisek believed to have once held a variety of testing subjects, from small animals to fellow Daeva. He and Joro had rummaged through the dilapidated rooms and discovered expired supplies, discarded media, and various textiles. Only a few remaining designations were locked and tidy, yet draped in sheets of dust and time. He continued down the eerily quiet halls and imagined the types of chatter and woeful cries that had once racketed among the stone walls.

Merisek arrived at a dimly lit cell located in one of the central blocks where he held one of Daeva's fiercest warriors prisoner. "Good evening," he said as he unlocked the heavy metal door and walked inside.

Sitting propped against the far corner of the cell in a disheveled mess, Claymar raised his head and looked at him through his dirty, matted locks. "Ah, Merisek," he replied in a scratchy and weakened voice, "how I've missed your face."

Merisek smirked as he closed the door.

Although severely weakened, Claymar steadily rose from the floor and took a few shaky steps forward. His aqua-green eyes glared through his long brown hair as it swayed with his staggered gait. "There's something different about you. Fancy new cloak, huh?" he said, tilting his head. "I guess you've decided to look the part to rule over your little kingdom of two."

"I see your time spent here still hasn't affected your knack for smart remarks," Merisek said, unfazed. "I'll admit I'm somewhat thankful for that, oddly enough."

For nearly six months, Claymar remained locked away in the bowels of the fortress. It took the dual efforts of Joro and Merisek to lure and capture him. By dividing the quartet, they hoped to better their odds of obtaining the last remaining tome of the Order. Just as Merisek had anticipated, Von sought to investigate Claymar's disappearance, setting his plans into motion. But the well-intended, swift teamwork turned into a shitshow fast. Instead of entering Celestine alone, Joro led an unsanctioned invasion with his renegade recruits. Both sides suffered devastating losses, but the Halryn army under Navaryn and Lowenna's command ensured that the steep price yielded no payoff. Unable to obtain Iaalprt and at the brunt of Daeva's fury over their reckless abandon, Merisek and Joro were forced to retreat into hidden isolation. Given the circumstances, they kept Claymar locked away with them to ensure their whereabouts remained unknown.

Embedded in Claymar's neck was a sophisticated yet crude-looking collar affixed with small tubes and clamps inserted deep into his flesh. Leading off the collar was a thick chain that trailed up to the ceiling, effectively making it a leash. On both sides of the apparatus were switch valves with coupling mechanisms to attach various instruments, tools, and machinery. The device's intended function was to carefully administer the various formulas Merisek had been synthesizing from C-Poison; the naturally produced toxin sourced from within the wings of Celestines.

Ultimately, the dastardly, torturous device prevented Claymar from using any of his mystical abilities. The inner probes of the device stopped short of completely severing the connections vital for channeling energy between his head and body. At the same time, the bulk of the collar kept them superficially attached. His once-toned, muscular frame had withered on account of malnourishment and his crippled ability to regenerate.

Merisek revealed the bowl of bread and nuts from within his cloak and placed it on the table.

"Joining me for dinner? How sweet," said Claymar with playful inflection. "You know, I'd have an easier time eating if you'd take this fucking thing off my neck."

"Out of the question," Merisek replied. "Either eat with it on, or not at all."

The cell fell quiet as the two started into their helpings of food. Claymar leaned against the cold stone wall and crunched on rancid nuts while Merisek took slow bites of stale bread.

"So, have you given any thought to returning to the fold?" asked Merisek. "Doing so can make things *easier*."

"After everything you've done to my friends, and to Lowenna? I'd rather have a troll shit down my throat for the rest of my days."

The visual made Merisek qualm, and he held the bite of bread between his teeth. "Claymar, you must understand—"

"*Speaking* of which," Claymar interrupted. "I need my shit bucket changed."

"Your what?"

"Over there," he said as he slowly turned his head to a bucket sitting by the adjacent corner of the cell. "It's been a while since you've changed it, so I had to put a sheet over it."

"*Ahem.* Yes, well ...."

Claymar playfully continued, "I mean, I suppose I don't smell much better, but ...."

Merisek was unable to break his gaze away from the vessel of festering excrement, not purely out of disgust, but because he hadn't noticed it in previous visits to the cell.

"Wait," said Claymar as he halted his chewing. "You can't smell it, can you?"

It was an odd occurrence that Merisek kept to himself, but his sense of smell had indeed faded away. Although the revelation was peculiar, Claymar couldn't keep himself from painfully chuckling.

"It's a shame you're unable to appreciate this wonderful fragrance," he continued. "Your nostrils must be as scarred as your putrid fucking face."

Merisek's countenance quickly fell flat as he clenched his fist.

"You're nearly a walking corpse, Merisek. Why not just take a step outside and let the—"

Before Claymar could finish his lashing, Merisek viciously clutched his lower jaw and raised him off the floor. "Come now, Claymar. Don't you think that mouth of yours has gotten you into enough trouble?" he seethed as he slowly drew him close. "I'd say you're done eating."

As blood pattered onto the ground from Claymar's mouth, Merisek reached into his inner coat pocket. "Oh, great. *This* again," he griped through his clenched teeth.

Out of Merisek's cloak came the pair of glass vials Claymar became accustomed to seeing each time he came to his cell. He inserted the top ends into the collar and locked them into place. One contained the C-Poison, the thick, shimmery liquid instantly recognizable by its signature silver color. Within the other vial was a glowing blue liquid, which Claymar assumed was another new potion Merisek wanted to test.

"A new flavor this time?" Claymar joked, then spat his bloody saliva to the side. "What is it? Bogfish? Joro's ass, maybe?"

"Shut up and hold still," Merisek griped as he triggered the first injection.

The mechanisms on the collar began to shift as the potion emptied from the vial. Claymar braced his body after the strange blue liquid prompted a soft yet uncomfortably cold sensation in his veins.

"The last time we did this, you nearly killed me. Going to finish the job this time?"

"Let's hope not, hm?"

Merisek released his grip on Claymar's face as he triggered the injection of the second vial filled with C-Poison. As Claymar fell to his knees, he could feel his heart race. Like in every previous instance, his body descended into painful shock and horrid degeneration. The effects of the viscous silver liquid were instant. Webs of blackened veins drew out from the injection site over his cheek, face, and chest, followed by the sickly discoloration of his flesh. Between the knotted, veiny mess, his flesh writhed, split, and erupted into slimy boils.

But then, almost as quickly as they came, the effects of the C-Poison subsided. The degeneration and discoloration reversed, the lesions on his body had closed, and the convulsions of his muscles released. Not only was the reversal of the C-Poison's effects a relief, but the healing factor that the formula carried was remarkable.

Merisek marveled at the latest results of his work. Despite the C-Poison's effects being halted and reversed, there was still the troubling instance of a debilitating reaction taking place to begin with. Even though the antidote was still far from perfect, he remained confident in his progress.

"How do you feel?" inquired Merisek as Claymar returned to his senses.

"I feel," Claymar muttered in a shaky voice. "I feel like I want my shit bucket changed."

Vexed, Merisek sighed. "Damn it. I need you to be serious, Clay."

"Did that not sound serious to you?" he hissed. "You know it's been a while since I've seen your little lapdog. Why don't you send him down to take care of it for me, hm?"

"As much as I'm sure Joro would love to entertain you, I'm afraid that's an impossibility," Merisek replied as his eyes drifted toward the cell door.

Merisek began to slowly pace in frustration while pinching the bridge of his nose as Claymar denied him the information he wanted.

"How's this for serious?" Claymar resumed. "Let me out of here. Right now."

"So you can inform Sidwell of my whereabouts? You know I can't do that. Not before my work here is complete."

"Face it. Every plan you have in that head of yours will be foiled. Just like every other one you had before, and you know it. Get it over with now. Turn yourself in, and let Daeva have their justice."

Merisek came within an arm's reach of Claymar. With a swift motion, Merisek took hold of the collar and disengaged the clamps from his neck. The pain was excruciating as the collar came off, but he was taken over with relief as the bloodied hunk of metal fell to the ground. He winced as he wrapped his hands around his clammy, gnarled flesh.

"If you want to leave so badly," instigated Merisek as he casually opened the cell door, "go right ahead and see yourself out. There's a way out at the end of the next hall. I won't stop you."

Thoroughly puzzled by Merisek's unexpected action, Claymar was at a loss for words. Hesitantly, he walked toward the door, keeping a wary eye on Merisek, then peered into the empty hallways. He gave Merisek one last glance, then started off. After making it barely ten paces from his cell door, Claymar was stopped in his tracks by an unusual sensation deep in his chest and stinging pinpricks on his skin. He turned to Merisek's eerily placid face as he painfully gasped for air through his bleeding and collapsing airways.

Unable to speak, Claymar buckled to his knees. Sweat beaded his brow, and his aching heart viciously raced. Merisek sauntered over with a disdainful, sharp glare.

"Gullible idiot," barked Merisek with folded arms as he watched the body of his former pupil writhe and convulse. "The day I surrender myself to any authority will be everyone's last. I doubt you'd want to see that."

Three whole minutes passed before Merisek jutted Claymar back into the cell with his boots, then slammed the door closed. Concealed ceiling vents opened to pull contaminated air out of the space. "Now, breathe," commanded Merisek. "You must clear your lungs if you don't want to die."

Just as Merisek had urged, Claymar steadied his breathing and calmed his pounding heart. "What just happened?" uttered Claymar through gurgled groans.

"It looks as though you are still sensitive to taking the poison in through your breath," he deduced. "We're nearly there, Claymar. Soon I'll be able to formulate this antidote to give you invulnerability to every medium of C-Poison."

"You mean," said Claymar through fits of coughing, "the halls? You filled the halls with C-Poison vapor?"

Merisek nodded. "That's right. I suspect that if I hadn't given you my latest synthesis, the vapor would have surely killed you."

"So, you've managed to become immune yourself?"

"Correct again," said Merisek. "A *permanent* immunity. Something far more dangerous to attain than a temporary one."

"Well, good for you. It only cost you your sanity. And clearly, your dashing good looks," Claymar said as he broke into a chuckle.

Merisek knelt and yanked Claymar's head by a handful of his hair, "You just won't stop, will you?"

Just as Claymar feared, Merisek aggressively latched the collar back onto his neck. He cringed as the icy metal spike re-punctured the wound on the back of his neck and settled against his spine. The jagged locks then pulled into the rest of his mangled flesh. Once his panging nerves settled, he ceased his belligerent wailing.

Merisek looked on indifferently as he watched Claymar writhe on his knees. "You should be honored," he claimed. "Don't you realize that your role is vital to the betterment of Daeva? Once I have perfected the antidote, I can bring immunity to the entire realm. This. This is my gift to you."

With all the strength he could muster, Claymar pounded his shaky fist and cracked the stone floor. "You can fucking keep it!" he fired back, then slowly teetered to his feet.

"How can you say that while this odious fluid makes you wriggle on the ground?"

"It's simple, Merisek. The only one you aim to help here is yourself. If you think all will be forgiven simply because of this mere countermeasure you've made, then you don't know the people of Daeva. And you surely don't grasp the magnitude of your treasonous acts," lashed Claymar. "It's clear to me that the C-Poison has affected you more than you're capable of realizing. Daeva will never see you as anything more than a madman, and they will never forgive you for what you've done!"

Claymar's voice echoed through the outside halls and trailed off as Merisek stood stoically with his hands clasped behind his back. Such a reaching insult forced him into a recollection of his bloodthirst and rage, which he had long wished to forget. A slight hint of nervousness found Claymar as they both stood before one another.

"Well, my friend. I'm afraid our time is up for today," Merisek coldly and dismissively affirmed. "We'll have more work to do shortly. I suggest you get some rest." After he stepped out of the cell, he turned and gave his prisoner one last gleaming stare. "Have patience. In time, you will see it's not forgiveness that I'm after."

The ominous tone in Merisek's foreboding was impossible to dismiss. Having said all he cared to, for the time being, he secured the heavy lock to the cell door and left Claymar in a state of nervous confusion.

"Hey!" Claymar yelled after him. "What about my shit bucket?!"

Just as Merisek avoided every instance Claymar mentioned his defecation vessel, he continued to ignore him.

Claymar's scratchy, clamoring voice faded from Merisek's ears as he angrily ascended the stairwell and exited the cell block. Even though progress advanced in the right direction, it was nonetheless incremental and far from satisfactory. Yet he remained steadfast in his pursuit of success. With only a few gaps in his formula remaining to be solved, perfection felt within reach.

11

THE FEAST

Exhausted and thankful that her shift at work was over, Rayshell walked toward the stockroom at the back of the department store to clock herself out. Despite the excitement of having the rest of the night for herself, she was almost too tired to care. With her mind freed from the distractions of unruly customers and scattered merchandise, she thought about what had transpired the night before. She didn't remember much of what happened after Lowenna's apparition dissolved into the fire, and Trish only vaguely answered her racing questions.

Rayshell broke away from her thoughts as she entered the break room, where a few coworkers congregated. She then walked over to a computer terminal and clocked out.

"Man, I'm beat," Tanya, Rayshell's friend and fellow schoolmate, declared and clocked herself out next.

"Yeah, same. Nothing like dealing with crazy customers on top of having to deal with school, huh?" Rayshell replied, then yawned.

"At least it earns you a few extra bucks," a deep voice commented. Manny, their mutual friend, seemed to appear out of nowhere like always. He stepped in line to clock himself out as well.

"So, are we all still on for tomorrow?" Tanya asked and started for the exit door.

"I definitely am. I just gotta call Justine and double-check with her," Manny replied. "Hey, Ray, is Trish coming?"

Rayshell quickly removed her bouncing name tag, then slid it into the pocket of her hoodie. "Nah, you know she's not into pool."

"You should talk her into giving it a try. She might actually have fun. Shit, I remember how long it took you to finally come around," confessed Manny, causing Tanya to laugh.

Rayshell groaned and rolled her head back. "Give it a rest, will ya?"

Manny's chuckle trailed off as he reached into his backpack for his cell phone.

"Oh, I've been meaning to ask you," said Tanya. She slowed down to create a little distance between Manny. "I heard a rumor that you and Shawn were fighting earlier this week. Was that true?"

"How did you end up hearing about it?"

"I overheard Stephanie during fifth period. She was talking about it for more than half the class."

"I swear I'm gonna sew her fat ass mouth shut," Rayshell hissed as they exited the store. "Shawn picked a fight with my little brother, and all I did was break it up."

The ominous sky was dark, and the cold wind howled through the parking lot. Although Rayshell would be more than content to head home, she looked forward to spending time with Jack and his family after so long without seeing them.

"Alright, I see my mom's car, so I gotta go," said Tanya. "Don't forget about tomorrow, okay?"

"I'll be ready."

As Tanya bounded toward the rumbling red minivan, Manny unchained his bike, gave Rayshell a farewell hug, then quickly took off down the street.

Rayshell's teeth began to chatter as the cold inched through her jacket. While she patiently waited over twenty minutes for any sign of Jack or Laura, a mixture of frustration and worry swam through her mind, assuming they had forgotten about the evening's dinner plans. With no way to contact them, Rayshell set off for the nearby bus stop. She reached into her backpack and pulled out a cigarette, thinking it would help distract her from the persistent winds and unpleasant thoughts. Just as she lit the tip and took a deep drag, tire rubber screeched, and the honk of a failing car horn blared from behind. A familiar weathered tan station wagon pulled up alongside her.

"Hi, Rayshell!" called Jack from the driver's seat. "I'm sorry I am late getting here."

Quickly, Rayshell yanked the cigarette out of her mouth and snuffed it with her boot. After she discreetly blew the remaining smoke out of her lungs, she walked toward the passenger side of Jack's car.

"Hey, Jack," she said as she opened the door and climbed in. "Kinda thought you forgot about me."

"Oh, I couldn't do that now, could I?" said Jack as he chewed the last bits of a cream-filled cake in his mouth, then licked the remnants from his rusty-red beard.

Rayshell looked down at an open box of snack cakes sitting on the console and a handful of empty wrappers stuffed inside one of the cup holders. "Having your dessert before dinner, I see."

"Would you like to try one?" he asked as he reached for another. "They're amazing!"

"N-no, thanks. I'm not much of a fan of sweets. I had no idea you were, though."

"Oh, you know, I like to try new things."

Rayshell nodded puzzledly.

Jack crammed another cream-filled cake into his mouth and shifted the car into gear. As they passed through the parking lot, Rayshell heard a subtle grinding coming from the wheel well. She reached over with her left hand and released the still-engaged parking brake.

"Ah, I forgot that again."

Rayshell chuckled. "You've been driving for, what, thirty years, and you still forget to release the E-brake?"

Jack replied only with a playful shrug.

Through a few confused turns, they exited the parking lot and started home for dinner. It was only about a ten-minute drive, though the trip felt much longer.

"So," said Jack as he tensely gripped the steering wheel, "how are you doing? How was your work today?"

"Eh, it was work," Rayshell replied unenthusiastically. "Just happy I have the next couple of days off."

"That's good to hear. Then you have more training after?"

"*Training?* I have school if that's what you mean."

"Yes, yes. That's what I meant. School," Jack responded with an awkward smile.

Rayshell giggled. "How is Brian's training going?"

It took a puzzled glance at Rayshell's smiling face for Jack to understand the lighthearted joke. "He's keeping up nicely," he said. "He talks about you a lot, especially after finding out you're spending the evening with us. Maybe you two could get married one day."

"Um, what?" she said with a sideways glance.

"What is it? You don't currently have a suitor, do you?"

"Well, no. But, it's just—"

"Just a joke," Jack nervously replied after a forced titter. "No need to be embarrassed, Rayshell."

Jack's odd behavior was mildly concerning. Though she didn't think him to be a drinker, she couldn't help but suspect he was intoxicated in some form.

"Are you okay?"

"Yes, I'm fine. Why do you ask?" Jack replied as he jostled the steering wheel.

"You're just acting a little unlike yourself, I guess."

"I see. I don't mean to be. I've just been busy lately, so my mind is a bit out of sorts."

"We can do dinner another time if you'd rather go home and relax. I'm fine taking the bus home."

"Nonsense. I couldn't disappoint Laura and Brian. They will be so thrilled to see you."

After the bout of reckless driving and awkward exchanges over the short trip, Rayshell released her tight grip from the panic bar and exited the car. Laura stood outside the front door of the second-story apartment, smiling and wearing a soiled apron. They gingerly walked to greet each other, but Rayshell stopped short of hugging her to keep from smearing various food remnants onto her clothes.

Laura gently cupped Rayshell's face and looked into her eyes. "I'm so happy to see you. And my, have you grown," she said with a grin.

"It's good to see you, too. You haven't changed at all."

"You're too kind, dear," she replied with a light chuckle. "Come on inside. Dinner's almost ready."

"Awesome. I'm starving after the day I've had."

Rayshell followed Laura as they walked up the staircase to the second level, leaving Jack to gather his snacks out of the car. Upon entering their apartment, an overwhelming mix of conflicting aromas instantly met her nostrils; among the most noticeable were sizzling meat and the heavy scent of dirty frying oil. Layered beneath were savory, briny, sweet, and tangy smells that battled for dominance over the other. Naturally, there was the unmistakable smell of fried bacon wafting through the air that she could single out since her brother ate it nearly every day when they were younger.

From down the hallway came Brian with a cheerful look on his freckled face. Rayshell spotted his gleaming blue eyes as he gingerly trounced toward her.

"Hi, Rayshell!" he called out. "You remember me, right?"

"Oh my gosh, Brian! How could I possibly forget? You've grown so much since I last saw you."

"About three years' worth," he replied with a grin.

"Your dad wasn't kidding. You turned into a giant!" She followed Brian into the dining area, where the menagerie of scents intensified, and found a spread large enough to feed upwards of twenty people. "I didn't know you had planned a party. How many people are coming?" asked Rayshell with widened eyes.

"A party?" said Laura with a snicker from the kitchen. "No, no, dear. It's just the four of us."

"I know Jack said that Brian's a big eater, but I didn't think this big."

Rayshell panned her eyes back to the large rectangular table covered with various foods. Pizza, corn dogs, cookies, french fries, barbeque chicken, brownies, candied fruit, and countless other items layered over one another on plates too small to contain the offerings.

"Did you make all of this yourself?" Rayshell called out to Laura.

"Oh no, dear. Not all of it. Jack had some things delivered," she replied from inside the kitchen. "Does everything look okay?"

Before Rayshell could retort, the front door loudly shut, and Jack entered with an arm full of his leftover snack cakes, which he pulled from the car. "Smells great, Laura. I'm starving," he said as he licked his sticky fingertips clean.

"Why, thank you," she called out as she fumbled with the oven door.

"There's still more?" Rayshell muttered to herself.

While she prepared the last of the dishes, Rayshell sat at the table next to Brian. Though she tried to relax her expression, the heat emitting from the sizzling plates stifled her.

"Looks good, eh, Rayshell?" said Jack as he walked into the dining room and sat down, "We just found out that we can order food on your phone and have it delivered. Isn't that amazing?"

"Yeah, sure," she said as she exhaled, then wiped droplets of sweat from her forehead.

"Is something the matter?" he asked.

"It's just that, I told you, I don't eat meat. And that's about all I see and smell here."

"Oh, silly me. I must have forgotten," he replied, nervously scratching his head.

"Is it alright if I have a salad?"

"Yeah. Me, too," chimed Brian.

"Yes, of course. I'll be just a few moments," Laura replied as she glanced at Jack.

"Here, Rayshell," said Brian as he passed her a silver bowl. "There's mashed potatoes."

As the evening went on, the duration of the meal was mostly devoid of conversation. Rayshell kept her small talk restricted to Brian, seated beside her, while Jack and Laura devoured multiple servings from the smorgasbord before them like gluttonous barbarians. Brian avoided watching his parents sloppily gorge themselves with overdone sirloin steaks, greasy pizza, and platefuls of seared bacon, among other calorie bombs, while Rayshell nibbled on her salad.

"Sorry, Ray. This is kinda embarrassing," Brian whispered as he motioned to his parents, who delved into a platter of spaghetti and meatballs with cheese piled high.

"No, it's alright. They just seem to be enjoying themselves, I guess."

"I mean, they're just not normally like this."

They continued to converse as they munched on their leafy greens and helped themselves to another helping of mashed potatoes, cooked to perfection.

"After dinner, can I show you my card collection?"

"Sure. What kind of cards do you collect?"

"Let me show you," he replied, reaching into his pocket. "I just got these today from the comic book store. You can play different types of games with them."

Brian held ten trading cards in his hands, each featuring impressively realistic artwork of a mystical-looking character or creature, along with a brief description of their abilities and traits. As Rayshell delightedly looked them over, she cocked her head to the side as though they reminded her of something.

She glanced back up at Brian's freckled face. "These are really neat. How many more do you have?"

"About a hundred and thirty, I think. I'm even making my own money by mowing lawns so I can buy more."

"Pretty smart," complimented Rayshell. "I wish I thought about doing that when I was your age. I would have been able to buy all the manga and stickers I wanted."

"I can buy you some," Brian said with a smile.

Rayshell giggled. "You don't have to do that. I have a job, too. Maybe we can check out that comic book store you mentioned sometime."

"Yeah! We go there every few weeks to see what new cards they have. Right, Dad?"

Jack was too focused on spooning a pile of macaroni and cheese onto his plate to hear Brian address him.

"Dad?" Brian repeated.

Laura looked back and forth between them and nudged Jack in the arm with her elbow until his attention finally broke away from the pile of food on his plate.

"Hey, uh, yeah. That's really good of you," Jack mumbled with a mouthful of meat taken from a turkey leg.

A confused, disgusted look crossed Brian's face, prompting Rayshell to chuckle.

"Anyway, if you want, I can show you how to play one of the games later."

Smiling, she replied, "I'd like that."

Jack and Laura dove straight into dessert while Rayshell and Brian neared the end of their salads.

"Oh, Brian," Jack mumbled with melted ice cream dripping from his mouth. "Have you shown Rayshell the drawing you made?"

Rayshell turned to Brian. "You still draw? I remember you being pretty good."

"Yeah, and I've gotten a little better since then."

"Go on and show her, Sweetie," said Laura with a chocolate brownie clutched in her hand.

After Brian excused himself to his room to fetch his drawing, Rayshell tapped her fidgety fingers as she watched Jack and Laura exchange a look of affirmation. The ongoing subtle actions between them seemed increasingly odd in an already unusual evening in their company, and she suspected they were up to something.

A few moments later, Brian returned with his art piece and handed it to Rayshell. Shaded with colored pencil and ink-lined, the finely detailed picture showed a young woman wielding a large sword as she rode atop a black dragon.

"Wow, this is great, Brian. Did your cards inspire you?"

"Well, a little bit. Most of the ideas came from Dad. He basically told me what to draw, and I—"

At that moment, Jack broke into a coughing fit as hunks of saturated brownie flew out of his mouth. Laura aggressively patted his back to try to quell his choking.

"Are you alright, Dad?"

"Y-yes, I'm fine. Just, uh, need a little bit of juice here," said Jack, reaching for a glass in front of him.

"That's soda," Brian muttered.

While Jack struggled to compose himself, Rayshell remained fixated on Brian's drawing. A sense of familiarity overtook her as she studied the armor-clad warrior and the sword with a trio of conjoined red gems affixed to the hilt. Undoubtedly, the woman in the picture was none other than the Celestine warrior, Navaryn. Suddenly, Rayshell winced as a sharp pain crept into her head.

"Ray, your nose!" yelped Brian.

One after another, drops of crimson fell from her nose and onto the drawing. Jack and Laura halted their noisy smacking and watched as she cupped her nose.

"I'm so sorry," uttered Rayshell. "I, um, I'll be right back."

After she promptly excused herself to the restroom, Laura asked, "Sweetie, could you please bring Rayshell a towel and some water?"

Brian hopped out of his seat and ran to the kitchen. After filling a glass with ice water, he sprinted to the hall closet to look for a towel. Once he was out of earshot, Jack turned to Laura with wide eyes.

"Eitha," he said to his wife, "You don't think she suspects anything, do you?"

"As long as you stop making a fool of yourself, she won't have reason to suspect a thing," she replied.

Dwelling within the bodies of Rayshell's trusted family friends like parasites were the essences of Joro's parents, Nathaniel and Eitha. Though Merisek had successfully transferred their living energy into Jack and Laura, they struggled with mirroring their hosts' behavior.

"I wonder," Nathaniel continued, "do you think showing her the drawing was too much?"

"Nonsense," Eitha replied. "What makes you say that?"

"Remember, she is human. And fragile. Navaryn's essence seems to be causing her harm."

"All the more reason why we need to get a move on with releasing her from her vessel. Joro said Merisek is growing impatient."

"But you saw what just happened, didn't you? If anything happens to this girl, Navaryn will be lost forever, and Iaalprt with her."

"We can't afford to dawdle here. We must do what it takes to awaken her, and quickly."

"I just—I don't want to be responsible should anything happen to her."

"Having sympathy for these beings will get us nowhere, Nathaniel," Eitha snapped. "The sooner you realize that, the better."

Rayshell sat atop the bathroom toilet lid, sobbing and trembling with her nose cupped in a hand towel. Trish's words echoed in her mind as she recalled her warnings of the awakening symptoms. The pain and flow of blood intensified, then, just as she feared, another vision flashed through her mind.

As Brian's drawing so explicitly depicted, Rayshell saw through the eyes of Navaryn atop her dragon, Onyx, soaring through clouds of smoke billowing out from buildings below. The sword she wielded was the same ruby-hilted blade stained with dripping blood. Bodies of Celestine citizens lay strewn about on the roads and fields while buildings burned and crumbled away. Indiscernible cries for help echoed in her ears as Onyx swiftly flew through the air. Enraged with a vengeful stare, he frantically surveyed the grounds, sought out the menacing invaders below, and incinerated scores of Daeva soldiers in his path. Navaryn then directed him toward a grand castle situated prominently among clusters of surrounding stone structures. A steady stream of intruders advanced toward the fortress, and Onyx laid flame to all beyond the main gates. With an assertive motion, he quickly ascended to the highest tower, where Navaryn sensed an imminent threat.

Navaryn leapt off his back onto the stone pathway, cutting and slashing away at the throats of conflagrant Daeva intruders as she sprinted toward the tower ahead. In a matter of moments, smoldering, headless corpses lined the path. She dashed inside and raced to the top of the tower with lightning speed. Navaryn could hear indistinct yelling as she neared an ornate door, recognizing one of the mingled voices as Benson's. In anticipation of a fateful encounter, she unsheathed her dagger strapped to her leg and paired it with her sword. With a running charge, she burst through the door and found Lowenna with her weapon drawn and her mentor, Benson, standing to her left with a tear falling down his cheek. His angered gaze fixated on a cloaked man standing just before the open balcony with his hands clasped behind him. Casually, the man panned his gleaming yellow eyes toward Navaryn and spoke in a deep, gritty voice, "Well, well. You're right on time, *Guardian*."

Rayshell's nosebleed had finally coagulated, and she took a moment to splash herself with cold water from the sink. Her heavy breaths fogged the mirror in front of her while the pinkish water swirled down the drain. Relieved that the graphic scenes had faded, she patiently waited for the lingering adrenaline to work through her veins. However, the haunting yellow eyes of the cloaked man she saw in the room remained etched in her mind. For a moment, she swore she could smell the burning sinew of the scorched bodies within her vision, but she concluded it was the wafting scent of fried chicken sticking to the bathroom walls. Not wanting to leave Brian worrying for too much longer, she gathered her senses and finished the remainder of the ice water he had left by the bathroom door. After bunching her frizzy hair into a bun and cleaning the hand towel as best she could, she exited the bathroom to rejoin the family still situated in the dining room.

"I'm sorry about your drawing," Rayshell said to Brian.

"It's okay. Really. I made it for you anyway. Are you feeling any better?"

"A little bit. I think the week is just catching up with me."

"Why is that, Dear?" asked Laura.

"I fell at school earlier in the week. Jostled my head a bit, so I've been getting headaches."

Jack wiped a string of brownie crumbs from his lips. "Should you have someone inspect that?"

Rayshell turned to Jack, "You mean, like a doctor?"

"A doctor, yes."

Rayshell shook her head. "My mom has enough bills. I'd rather not trouble her over a little bump."

Jack and Laura exchanged a confused look, though Brian conveyed concern. "Do you want to stay the night? Dad can take you home in the morning."

"Not tonight. There's a project for school that I need to work on, so I can't stay too much longer."

"How about next weekend?" said Brian as he tried to hide his disappointment.

"I'll see what my work schedule is like."

"Well, before you go, you wanna see my card collection?"

With feigned excitement, she replied, "Of course!"

Brian and Rayshell washed their dishes, then headed down the hallway to his room. When the bedroom door clicked shut, Eitha turned to Nathaniel and shoved his arm.

"Fool. Was that drawing the only part of your plan tonight?"

"I don't remember you offering any other suggestions. Besides, I'm sure it's working."

"I hope you're right, or Merisek will have our heads."

Nathaniel and Eitha rose from the table and began the gargantuan cleanup process. After clearing the dining table, they piled the cookware, dishes, and silverware along the kitchen counter. Had it not been for the substantial amount of to-go boxes and bags from the food deliveries, the mess of dishes would be far greater. With the sink packed and the garbage can on the verge of overflowing, Nathaniel casually walked out of the kitchen and started down the hallway.

"Where do you think you're going?!" yelled Eitha.

Nathaniel paused in the hallway, "I, um. I have to, uh ...."

"Get back in here and help me with all of this," she barked. "I am *not* cleaning all of this myself, *again*."

Nathaniel threw his head backward as he reluctantly returned to the kitchen to do his part of the cleanup. The box of donuts in the bedroom would have to wait for him a little longer.

"So what do we do next?" asked Eitha as she vigorously scrubbed congealed barbeque sauce off a platter.

"You heard her earlier. She's coming back again to stay over with Brian."

"That's not for another seven days! And it wasn't for certain, either."

Nathaniel gave Eitha a blank look. "Well, that gives us time to make another plan, doesn't it?"

"*If* she doesn't figure us out before then."

"I'll think of something," Nathaniel said with a sigh.

Across from Brian, Rayshell sat on the carpet. He neatly organized his card collection into piles between them as he explained the gameplay mechanics. The room décor was much as she expected. Posters emblazoned with comic book heroes matched his bedspread and pillowcases. Statuettes and figurines of various monsters and creatures sat atop large shelves filled with comics and manga. Stacks of video games lined a TV stand in the corner, catching her attention as she entered the room. For the first time during her visit, Rayshell felt entirely at ease. His room had the only tinge of normalcy in the entire apartment. Even though the evening had played out in a less-than-desirable manner, she was content to spend time with someone who had common interests and shared her trust.

"Hey Brian," Rayshell started. "This might sound weird, but do you ever think that your dreams could sometimes be real?"

"Sure," he replied. "My mom tells me that a lot. That whatever I dream of, I can make happen."

"That's not what I mean," Rayshell said with a snicker. "I mean, like, say you have a dream. And somehow, you know that whatever happened in the dream has actually happened."

"That sounds kinda like a flashback to me."

"Not a flashback. When you wake up, you find things around you that tell you that something happened, or someone was with you."

"Hmm, I don't think that could ever happen," Brian said with scrunched eyebrows. "But that does sound like it would be fun, huh?"

"That's one way to put it," said Rayshell with a grin. She realized that her question sounded like nothing more than a whimsical thought to Brian rather than one he would reciprocate with an inquisitive answer. Though she could tell his mind began to wander as he stared blankly at his piles of cards.

"Hey, is something wrong?"

"It's just what you said about dreams," said Brian as he broke from his stare. "I guess for the past few days, I sort of felt like I've been stuck in one."

"What do you mean?"

"I'm sure you know," he continued, motioning toward the door, "my parents are acting weird."

Rayshell nodded. "I mean, I know they act kinda goofy sometimes, and it's funny. Maybe they're just stressed with work or something."

"I don't think so. It's something else," Brian said as he scratched his nose. "I wasn't going to tell you, but Dad wanted me to ask you about something. Something about a book."

"A book?" said Rayshell suspiciously. "What kind of book?"

"I don't know. I didn't understand what he was talking about. It had a funny name. Does that mean anything to you at all? Did he give you a book a while ago, or something?"

All that ran through Rayshell's mind was the mysterious, sought-after book Trish had mentioned and why someone like Jack would try to garner information about it. "Nope. Not that I can remember. I'm not much of a reader anyway. Unless it's manga."

"I'm sorry, I shouldn't have said anything," said Brian, rubbing the side of his arm. "It just sounded really important to Dad."

"Well, now you know what to tell him if he asks, *right?*" The playful inflection in Rayshell's voice put Brian at ease, and slowly he cracked a smile. "Tell ya what. Let's play a quick round of this game before I have to go."

Brian happily obliged, then dealt their cards.

·)C·

About a half-hour later, they emerged from the bedroom giggling as they recounted their victories. Jack and Laura were still immersed in their post-dinner cleanup, though the pile of dishes had significantly dwindled.

"Hey there," said Jack. "Did you two have fun?"

"We did, yeah," Rayshell replied. "I actually should be getting home now. There's a bus stop just a few blocks away, so you don't have to drive me."

Jack gave a subtle shrug. "Well, okay. If that's your decision."

"Are you crazy?" said Laura as she nudged his arm, then turned to Rayshell. "It's late, and it's dark. Please, let Jack take you home."

"Don't forget your drawing," said Brian as he handed her the blood-stained picture.

Rayshell carefully rolled up the heavyweight paper and secured it with a spare hair tie from her wrist. She hugged Brian tightly, then opted to wave at Laura, avoiding coming in contact with her soiled apron. Even though she could not eat most of what they offered, she thanked them for dinner. After she said her goodbyes to the family, she walked out of the apartment with Jack. Erring on the side of caution, she followed behind him on their way down to the car lot.

"So, um, do you remember where I live?" Rayshell asked.

"Yes, of course. How could I forget?"

When Rayshell released the parking brake, Jack chuckled and nodded with bounding eyes, then reversed out of the carport.

The ride was awkwardly quiet. Rayshell glared at the passing street lights above as she rested her head against the passenger window. She could feel the cogs in Jack's head turning as he tried to think of something to say. Once she heard him take a breath, she chimed in with the first thing that popped into her mind.

"Your son's a great kid," Rayshell said.

"He is?" said Jack as he glanced toward her.

Rayshell nodded with a snicker. "You and Laura have done well with Brian. He's really smart and talented."

Jack was unexpectedly caught off guard and fell silent for a few moments. Within Jack's body, Nathaniel thought of his own son, Joro, and had to remind himself that she had referred to his host's son. Yet, Rayshell's comment prompted a brief moment of reflection. Although his son was very dear to him, Nathaniel could not deny the character he had ultimately become.

"Well, yes. Brian is a good son," Jack eventually replied. "Certainly has a warm heart. Not one bit of ugliness to be found in him."

"Yup, you got that right," said Rayshell as she subdued her confused look.

Nathaniel sank into thought as he sat in Jack's body. His memory took him back to when he was locked away with Eitha in a towering prison called Belturris. Joro was merely a teenager then, yet he played a crucial role in their escape. Although they were eternally grateful for his aid and the new life he gave them, they no longer saw the devoted son in him as they had once known.

"You're a nice girl, too, Rayshell."

She smirked at his compliment. "You sure about that?"

"Sure I am," he replied as his eyes shifted across the road.

"Well, I appreciate that, but I'm kind of a brat. Mom calls me that all the time."

The car grew silent once again. As Jack refocused on the road, he could not shake the thought of Rayshell suspecting his unbecoming behavior. Consciously occupying the body of a human had proved to be more of a challenge than he expected. Overcome by the pleasures the realm had to offer and the unfamiliar complexities of the human condition, his restraint fell by the wayside.

"Here we are," called Rayshell as they approached the dimly lit apartment complex. Surprisingly, she saw her mother's bicycle chained up by their front door. Knowing she was home put her at ease and gave her an idea. "Looks like my mom's actually home tonight. Did you maybe want to come inside to say 'hi?'" she asked.

"To your mother?"

"Yeah, it's been ages. She would be so happy to see you."

"Um, I would. But, uh, it's late, and I think I should be getting back to Eith- I mean, Laura and Brian."

"I understand. Another time, then?"

"Another time," he said with a nod.

Doing her best not to break character, she quickly hugged Jack, then bid him good evening. After she closed the car door, the window rolled down beside her.

"You know, Brian sure misses you. You should come by more often," Jack suggested. "How about tomorrow?"

A chill crawled up Rayshell's spine as she searched for an excuse not to oblige. However, she remembered she didn't have to come up with a lie. "I can't tomorrow. After work, I have plans with some friends. I'll call and let you know if I can stop by sometime this week."

"I'll wait to hear from you, then."

Rayshell watched as Jack drove away and gave him a wave. As soon as his taillights disappeared, she started toward her apartment. The light patter of her footfalls lent a calming static sound to her ears as she walked along the pavement. After a slow ascent to the second story, she carefully retrieved her keys from her backpack to keep them from jingling.

The sound of a meteorologist giving the weekly weather forecast emanated from the living room TV as Rayshell quietly walked in. She turned and found her mother asleep on the couch. Rayshell was relieved that Jack had refused to come inside for a visit, though it only added to her list of suspicions. She bent down to pull a blanket over her mother, yet she stirred awake once her shadow blocked the TV's glow.

"Hey, you," said Elizabeth lowly.

"Hey, Mom. I didn't expect you home tonight."

Elizabeth sat upright and brushed her hair from her face. "Guess the boss thought I looked exhausted and needed a break. What does she know, huh?"

Rayshell chuckled. "Right."

"Plus, I think I've worked enough overtime to compensate for it, so it's fine, I guess."

After a quick stretch, Elizabeth switched off the TV and went into the kitchen with Rayshell to get a glass of water. After cutting up some lemon and mint, she sat and conversed with her daughter at the small dining table by the kitchen. It was a regrettable rarity, but it always seemed to happen at rather fitting times.

"So, did you have a good time at Jack and Laura's?"

Rayshell struggled to keep a straight face. "It was fine."

"That's all? Just fine?"

"Yeah. Long story," she said with a sigh. "There just wasn't much they made that I could eat. It was kinda nauseating."

"Really?" said Elizabeth as she gave Rayshell a puzzled look.

"It was just meat, meat, meat, and fried everything. Not to mention there was enough food to feed a whole football team."

Elizabeth pursed her lips as Rayshell rested her cheek on her fist. "I'm sure he was just trying to be overbearing with the best intentions."

"Yeah, but I told him earlier this week that I don't eat that stuff."

Figuring her daughter would continue to pick apart her rationalizations, Elizabeth changed the subject. "Did you at least see Brian? How is he?"

"He's a giant. Still a sweet kid, though. It was so good to see him."

"Remember when you used to babysit him?"

"Sure do," Rayshell replied.

In perfect timing, a rumbling sound came from Rayshell's stomach right as the dining room got quiet. Both she and her mom burst into laughter while the sound trailed off.

"Well, there's some leftover pasta and veggies in the fridge if you're not too nauseated to eat."

Rayshell grinned as her mouth began to water. Not wasting another moment, she grabbed the container of leftover pasta from the fridge. She was delighted by the sight of angel hair tossed with olive oil, garlic, parmesan cheese, broccoli florets, and peas. With a fork in hand, she devoured the pasta without spending precious time reheating it. Elizabeth cracked a smile as she watched her daughter sit so contentedly while she ate. After all, the dish had been Rayshell's favorite since she was a toddler.

They sat and talked for a further forty-five minutes. The nourishing meal perked Rayshell up enough for her to forget how exhausted she was, but it eventually caught up with her when she gave a long yawn, which her mother reciprocated. They looked at each other with droopy, half-closed eyes.

"Well, I'm heading to bed," said Elizabeth as they both rose from the table. "Don't stay up too late."

"I'm not far behind you," Rayshell replied as she hugged her. "Goodnight, Mom."

Elizabeth left the kitchen and walked down the hall to her bedroom. Thoroughly satiated, Rayshell washed her dishes, then headed to her room to wind down. After changing into her pajamas, she went into the bathroom to wash up. As she readied her toothbrush with paste, she finally found herself in a moment of quiet as her thoughts on the evening lined up. Brian's mention of the mysterious book and its unexplainable importance to Jack was far too specific to be dismissed as a mere coincidence. The evening's strange events could only mean that the forces at play that Trish warned about were closing in on her, and the time to recognize the need for caution was at hand. Before Rayshell's thoughts could sink into a feeling of dread, a sudden and frantic knock on the door jolted her.

"Ray, are you done yet? I gotta pee!" Jakobe yelped from the other side of the door.

"Shut up, Jakobe. You're gonna wake Mom," Rayshell snapped. "I'll be out in a minute."

Rayshell shook her head and chuckled at the sound of her brother's fussing as he walked back down the hall. She welcomed the short-lived humor that distracted her in the midst of coming to terms with the essence of the Celestine warrior she carried within her. In a way, she felt an inexplicable responsibility that came with her circumstances, though accepting it was easier said than done.

Once her heartbeat returned to a steady pace, she glanced up at the mirror above the sink and pleaded to her reflection, "I know you're in there, Navaryn. I promise I'm not going to ignore you anymore. Just please, help me out a little here."

12

THE ESCAPE

Von's nightmares had become more frequent and vivid under the strain of the Delavine Crystal's use. As time crawled along, he opted for simply abstaining from sleep to avoid plunging into the frightful depths of his mind. Because he naturally attributed the stressors of Navaryn's circumstance to be the cause of his insomnia, it seemed pointless to assume any other meaningful correlation. After all, what truly mattered was using every waking moment to close the gap in Merisek's lead.

As late afternoon came over Celestine, Von hastily dressed by the fireplace with a long coat at his side. The image of Claymar he had seen through the Delavine Crystal moments before had etched itself in his mind. His friend was weak, pale, and in a state of immense suffering. After Von fastened the last clasp to his rugged footwear, he slugged back the rest of the wine in his glass. He muttered a set of directions to memorize as he threw on his coat, then walked over to the trunk by the couch. Just as he opened the lid, a wisp of embers fluttered out of the fireplace behind him.

"Can't talk right now, Aalrija," said Von as a fiery apparition entered the room.

"*Ahem.* Hello, Von," called a deep, unexpected voice.

"Kumiko?" he replied after spinning around. "What are you doing here?"

"Just wanted to let you know that Aalrija will be along shortly. I met with her just now, but Ailbhis pulled her away for a chat."

"I won't be here."

"What do you mean? Where are you going?"

Von turned back to the trunk and retrieved his gauntlets. "I'm going to get Claymar."

"You found him?"

"Merisek has him, and he's not doing well," Von revealed. "If I don't get him out of there, he'll likely be dead in a day or two."

Kumiko quickly deliberated the situation as Von affixed his gauntlets. "Then, I'm going with you," he said.

Von gave a sideways glance. "Don't take this the wrong way, but this is gonna be dangerous. You should stay here."

"You think I can't hold my own?"

"The idea is to do this as quietly as possible. That won't be easy with the two of us."

"You know, we're supposed to be a team. And since this is Merisek we're talking about here, you're going to need my help."

"Fine," said Von as he slammed the trunk lid closed. "You wanna help? Then meet me in Daeva at Mount Korviniah in twenty minutes."

"Where's that?"

"You're smart. You can figure it out," Von replied as he slung a bag over his shoulder. "Bring a weapon and keep your energy suppressed. If you're not on time, I'm going in without you."

A red flash engulfed Von as he vanished from the safe room, free to Parallel trace-free thanks to the amulet Fallon lent. Kumiko, frustrated by Von's dismissive attitude, contemplated letting him go on alone but decided not to let his nerves get the better of him.

"*Bastard,*" he hissed as his fiery form dissolved from the room.

·)🌑(·

Atop the snow-capped peaks of Korviniah, Von stood by as he looked at the steep mountainside ahead. The icy winds were somewhat calm, though slated to strengthen in due time. A few moments later, he felt a Parafall close behind, followed by the sound of quick footfalls through the snow.

"You made it," said Von with a smirk.

Equipped with light armor, which did little to protect against the cold, Kumiko made his approach. "And you didn't think to mention it would be freezing here?" he said through chattering teeth.

"That's on you. You saw me wearing this coat before I left," Von replied nonchalantly. "And if I remember correctly, I did say this was a fuckin' mountain."

"Whatever. Can we just get a move on?"

Von smiled as he reached into his bag for a spare scarf. He had a habit of packing something extra for Navaryn, who was notorious for misjudging the weather. "Here," he said as he offered Kumiko the flapping garment. "It's not much, but it's all I got."

Still getting used to an inkling of kindness and camaraderie between them, Kumiko accepted the scarf, then thanked him awkwardly.

Von pointed to a ridge in the distance, though it seemed he was pointing to nothing. "His fortress is there. Along the mountainside, cloaked between visible planes."

"So, how do we get in?"

"There is a defect in this mountain that leads to a passageway through a rift in the cloak. We can get inside that way."

They traversed along the mountainside until they came upon a split in the jagged rock formations. The opening was tight but not impossible to fit through. Cautiously, they crawled through the lengthy crack in the mountain, which opened into a corridor tall enough to kneel in. Von retrieved a pair of torches from his bag and lit them with a match.

"You might have already guessed, but no Paralleling and no conjuring of any kind now that we're this close. It'll alert Merisek."

"Well, this should be interesting," Kumiko replied as Von handed him a torch.

"Not a fan of doing things the old-fashioned way, I see?"

As they reached the end of the corridor, they stepped into an open cavern with scorched walls and wrecked equipment strewn about.

Construction of numerous planned sublevels had been underway decades past, but had ceased due to a tragic explosion that claimed many lives. They stood amidst the devastation of the blast that, in turn, formed the opening in the mountain.

"Do you hear that?" Von whispered.

The distant scuttling sound of claw against stone found Von's ears, though it was still too far for Kumiko to detect. Even the faint sounds of ragged, rebounding breaths echoed to him through the network of caves.

"There's something down here. Be on your guard," Von warned.

With his heightened eyesight, Von led the way through the cavern. An old assembly of scaffolding stood ahead, leading to the levels above, so a cautious ascent was in store. Jarring, splintered creaks emerged beneath their feet as they stepped aboard the rickety tower. They stood for a moment to quell the teetering joints and surveyed their surroundings. Scattered remains of the perished workers covered the ground below the scaffolding's base, though curiously, the bones appeared to be picked clean. As they climbed a decrepit stairwell lit with soft blue lights along the beaten walls, Kumiko detected a faint yet familiar floral scent.

"Not much further now," said Von. "Clay should be—" He was suddenly halted in his tracks by a burning sensation in his lungs and dropped to the ground.

"What's the matter?"

"I-I can't breathe," he managed to reply as his muscles locked. "I can't, m-move my body."

Kumiko's confusion turned to alarm. He quickly scooped Von under his arms, dragged him back down to the previous sublevel, and then propped him against a wall. Several minutes passed while Von fought against the tightness in his chest.

"You alright?" asked Kumiko.

"I'll be fine," he replied, reaching for a bottle in his bag. "I don't know what happened. My chest feels like it's going to cave in."

"There's C-Poison vapor wafting through the halls."

"C-Poison?"

Kumiko nodded. "I thought I recognized the scent."

Von acknowledged Kumiko's assertion. "But how?"

"Maybe another Celestine found this place. Who knows?"

Von uncorked the bottle, then held it to his lips for a few seconds.

"Healing elixir?" Kumiko asked.

"Yes. My own recipe. Though I was saving this for Claymar."

"Well, by the looks of it, you're going to need my help after all, eh?"

Von recited the remaining directions to Claymar's cell so that Kumiko could carry on with the rescue plan while he stayed behind.

With his sword drawn and torch in hand, Kumiko proceeded through the dank hallways and ascended a spiral stairwell through the sublevels above him. The flowery scent of the C-Poison grew to its most potent when he reached the next cell block. As he stepped lightly through the halls, he came upon a dimly lit cell with a small grated opening on the door. He peeked inside and saw Claymar sitting in a contorted position against the wall.

The cell door had a simple yet secure lock that buckled under enough pressure from his sword. Vents in the ceiling automatically engaged when the door opened, funneling out any C-Poison. However, the stench from the festering bucket of filth in the corner still caught his nose. Kumiko rushed over to Claymar and straightened his body against the wall to snap him out of his daze. As he gently cradled Claymar's bruised head, his eyes widened as he beheld the metal collar embedded in his flesh.

"Unbelievable," Kumiko whispered to himself, prompting a jarring reaction from Claymar as he awoke.

"G-go away, Merisek. I've had enough of your f-face," he mumbled as he flailed.

"Relax, Clay. I'm getting you out of here."

"Wow," he uttered as he forced his eyes open. "W-when did you get so handsome, Boss?"

"What? Claymar, it's Kumiko. Can you hear me?"

"K-Kumiko? Oh, no. I'm fucked now, aren't I?"

"Ugh, snap out of it. Can you stand?"

"Only s-so much," he said before his head drooped to the side.

"*Great*," Kumiko muttered as he readied his sword.

With a well-placed strike, Kumiko split the chain links attached to Claymar's collar. He wrapped him in a tattered sheet and hoisted him onto his shoulders. As they prepared to leave the cell, Kumiko directed Claymar to hold his breath until they reached the stairwell. Kumiko sprinted back through the hall and down the steps to the lower sublevel, where Von stood with his gauntlets engaged.

Von knelt beside Claymar after Kumiko set him against the wall. "Clay, can you hear me?" He turned to Kumiko after he received an indiscernible response. "What's this around his neck?"

"A shackle, I think," Kumiko replied. "Curiously, it is of Celestine origin." He thumbed over a discreet emblem engraved on one side. "It appears authentic, yet with some modifications."

"Can you remove it?"

"I think so. But, may I suggest we get out of here first?"

Von nodded, then reached into his bag for the remaining elixir. Even though Claymar was on the verge of fainting, he reacted in horror once he saw the bottle.

"No! No more formulas. Get it away," Claymar deliriously mumbled.

"Just drink it, you idiot," snapped Von as he uncorked the bottle and held it to Claymar's lips.

Moments after the warm liquid funneled down Claymar's throat, an invigorating sensation channeled into his core. His eyes became focused, and the clouded confusion left his mind.

"Von? W-what just happened? How'd you find me?" he asked, then looked at Kumiko. "And why is this guy here?!"

"That guy just busted you out."

"Wait a minute. You two are working together?"

"We are. We'll bring you up to speed later."

"I must already be dead because, this, this is *insane*," blurted Claymar as he swiped his matted hair backward.

Kumiko and Von exchanged smirks as they tended to Claymar and his remarks, though they were astounded that he was still alive, given his putrid condition. Infected lesions, blackened veins, knotted clumps of displaced muscle, all of which were adverse effects from the latest would-be antidote decaying in his blood that Merisek had yet to see.

"You look like you've been trampled in a pile of shit. Repeatedly. Smell like it too," Von said, thoroughly disgusted.

"How rude of me. I would have washed up had I known you were coming," he replied sarcastically. "It's nice to see you, too."

Von and Claymar's reunion was nothing short of what they both expected from one another, a display of genuine gratitude full of comments directed at one another, partly in jest.

"You're armed," Kumiko said to Von, realizing he had equipped his gauntlets. "What's going on?"

"We're gonna have a tough time getting out of here," he replied as he stared at the cavern floor. "There are strange creatures down below. A couple of them almost made it up here."

"Let me guess," Claymar chimed in. "Six legs, big teeth, meaty hairless bodies?"

Von nodded. "Friends of yours?"

"Hardly. They've had their hungry eyes on me for some time. Though I imagine they stopped coming by because of the smell. Ugh, and I hate the way they shriek."

"We're wasting time. Let's head back through the rift. We can Parallel out of here once we're through," Kumiko suggested. "Clay, can you move?"

"Barely. My body still feels like rubber. Got any more of that elixir, Von?"

"That's all I had left," he replied with a shake of his head. "Kumiko, if you can carry Clay, I'll take the lead and clear us a path."

With a nod, Kumiko took Claymar back over his shoulder while Von drew a pair of crimson blades out of his gauntlets. In a speedy, forward dash down the scaffolding, Von hacked and clawed through the oncoming horde of ravenous creatures. Every swipe and slash that tore through the beasts' flesh fed his dormant fury. Kumiko followed closely behind and clutched Claymar tightly, though he caught the approaching sound of another wave of creatures closing in from behind.

"Watch out!" shouted Von before a pair of the beasts lunged for Claymar.

In a fluid motion, Kumiko tossed Claymar to a clearing between him and Von. Just as he drew his sword for a counterattack, one of the creatures pounced and pinned him to the ground. A slobbering mouth fuming with putrid breath clamped its jaws on his sword, keeping the beast from sinking its crowded, jagged teeth into his neck. Not a moment too soon, Von hurled one of his blades through the creature's skull. Kumiko kicked the hairless corpse off of him and quickly regained his footing.

"You two better not leave me here for dog food!" Claymar shouted as he shielded his head.

"Shut it, Clay! Little busy here!" Von clamored.

Standing back-to-back, Von and Kumiko shielded Claymar as they fended off the beasts in a brutal and bloody fashion. However, after having decimated two waves of the beasts, a third and even larger one was headed directly for them. Their window of escape was closing, and decisive action was needed quickly.

"Burn them, Kumiko!" Von yelled. "Set the corpses ablaze to create a wall of flame!"

"You said no conjuring!"

"After all of this, we're not leaving here without sending Merisek a message," Von replied with fierce eyes. "Light 'em up!"

Without further hesitation, Kumiko spewed flames from his hand and engulfed the piled carcasses in a blazing inferno. Meanwhile, Von fused his blades into a massive two-handed sword and eliminated the remaining creatures that barricaded the exit. After paving their escape path with the mutilated and charred corpses of the beastly hounds, Von unleashed an energy blast that bore a tunnel through the mountain. Together, they retrieved Claymar and then sprinted through the defect.

"Not bad, guys," said Claymar from atop Von's shoulder. "Merisek's gonna be so pissed!"

Once beyond the barrier, Von quickly placed his hand on Kumiko, and together, the party of three vanished under white arcing light.

·◗◖·

Back in the security of the safe room, Claymar had finally found himself in comfortable silence, yet he was still far from complete relief. Von and Kumiko stood beside him as they curiously studied the collar clasped around his mangled neck. No simple mechanism would unlock it, and it was equipped with failsafe measures that would prove fatal for Claymar if triggered.

"Please tell me you know how to get this thing off," said Claymar as he knelt by the warm fireplace. "I mean, Merisek seemed to have no trouble operating it."

"He might have had a charm that disengaged it for all I know. Just relax and don't move," Kumiko replied as he carefully tinkered with the collar. "As much as you might not believe it, I'm actually trying not to kill you here."

"Oh, sure. After enduring nearly six months of this thing, what's another few minutes, right?"

Von swatted the back of Claymar's shoulder and urged, "*Quiet.*"

Kumiko went to work using a few eating utensils at his disposal. It wasn't an ideal set of tools, but he nonetheless grew confident after carefully disengaging two of the six clasps on the collar. The remaining four were each placed closer in succession to the back of Claymar's neck, which required even more caution. While Kumiko continued his work on the collar, Claymar managed a full five minutes of silence before the urge to speak compelled him.

"You know what sounds nice?" said Claymar. "A sponge bath."

"Shut up, Clay," said Von.

"You know I can't do that."

"Then at least say something constructive," Kumiko jutted in. "I'm trying to concentrate."

"How about I fill you in on all the fun little details of my vacation with our favorite sociopath, then?"

As the three sat in the firelight, Claymar explained the use of the collar in Merisek's experiments and outlined his harrowing experience of being subjected to the various concoctions he had developed and their varying effects.

"So, Merisek captured you to turn you into his test subject?" asked Von.

"Not at first. It turned into that," he replied. "He and Joro got me out of the way so they could have their way in Celestine."

"The invasion," chimed Von. "That's what happened after I went looking for you."

"Drawing you away was part of their plan," Claymar confirmed. "But after the total failure that whole thing was, he kept me locked up so I couldn't disclose his whereabouts to my uncle or anyone else. Then, that's when he *really* went crazy."

Another two clasps suddenly and simultaneously disconnected from Claymar's neck. Kumiko moved his hands slightly away, to which Claymar gave a nervous look in his direction. Once Kumiko's nerves settled enough for him to proceed, Von kept Claymar occupied in discussion.

"These formulas he tested on you. What were they for?"

"For imbuing immunity to C-Poison."

Von immediately recalled the effects he felt upon contact with the noxious vapor.

"It filled the halls around your cell," Kumiko chimed, "which means that Merisek has attained immunity, right?"

"Correct," Claymar confirmed. "At most, I might have built up a small resistance to it. But as for how he managed it, I have no idea."

"But what for? If he's immune already, then why create these antidotes?" asked Von.

"I think maybe it's part of a backup plan in case he has to go all in to obtain the last book of the Order."

Kumiko's eyes widened at the mention of the heavily secretive tomes, which no one outside of the realm of Celestine was to be privy to. Claymar sensed Kumiko's pause in tinkering with the collar and looked toward him.

"Yes, Kumiko, I know about the Order, too," said Claymar. "Guess it's not as much of a secret as you thought, eh?"

Claymar managed to coax a slight but nervous chuckle out of

Kumiko.

"My guess is, if Navaryn doesn't give up Iaalprt, he will aim to enable Daeva with C-Poison immunity," Claymar continued. "If that happens, then they'll be poised to tear Celestine apart until he finds it."

"I'll hand it to him. He's always been ambitious," said Von. "Though that quality seems to have made him even more dangerous than we thought."

"That's for sure. He's grasping at any half-brained idea he can muster to stay ahead. He even tried to convince me to rejoin him. Amazing, huh?"

Kumiko kept his thoughts to himself as he carefully disengaged the two remaining clasps, though the collar didn't immediately come loose. The last remaining measure was the metal spike inserted through the back of Claymar's neck, which could open into a fan of blades and sever his head if not handled with caution. Using only the makeshift tools, Kumiko avoided triggering the deadly trap and removed the collar. He quickly tossed the sophisticated piece of machinery to the ground, which jumped into the air as the fan of blades sprang open.

Von pressed cleansing bandages to Claymar's mangled neck with a squinty face. Before long, profound relief neutralized his searing pain. His jubilance would have been impossible to contain if not for his severely weakened state.

"Stay off the couch until you get cleaned up," Von told Claymar.

"Yeah, yeah," he griped while clutching the bandages to his neck. "I'm just gonna walk around a bit."

As Claymar slowly ambled around the safe room, Von approached Kumiko, who was vigorously wiping off the blood from his hands. "What you did back there in Daeva, and with that contraption," he began. "I want you to know that I appreciate it."

Though Von's gratitude was begrudgingly given, it was no less sincere. Given their violent history, the offer came as a surprise to Kumiko.

The exchange was far short of extending an olive branch, but it marked a rare instance of levelheadedness between the two. What they had accomplished together would spell utter disbelief to their rivaling realms. Yet Von and Kumiko held steadfast in their minds that their truce was, for the moment, still temporary. As the moment ceased, Claymar limped over with his hands on his hips.

"Alright," he said, "who's giving me that sponge bath?"

Von and Kumiko looked at each other unamused.

"He's *your* friend," Kumiko asserted. "And on that note, I'll be on my way. There's still work to do."

After wiping his hands as clean as he could manage, Kumiko tossed the bloodied rag on the ground beside the collar and bid farewell to the pair of Daeva with a swift exit through the rear passageway. A comforting silence filled the safe room, though the sight of the collar on the floor continued to instill a sense of dread in Claymar. Disposing of the device would need to happen, but Von elected to save that for another time. Getting Claymar back to health took priority, and the safe room was well-equipped to do so.

Eager to cleanse himself of the filth he had stewed in for several months, Claymar removed his clothes piece by piece as he started toward the washroom.

"Care to oblige, dear friend?" said Claymar as he turned to Von.

"Don't look at me. You're on your own if you want that bath."

"Some friend you are," teased Claymar as he hobbled away.

"Shut up before I put that collar back on you," Von quipped, turning his head to hide his grin.

·◗ℂ·

An hour later, Von entered the sweltering washroom with a bottle of his healing elixir and a few helpings of fruit and nuts. The gentle scent of vetiver and sage drifted through the candlelit room. Von grimaced at Claymar's tattered and filthy clothes crumpled in a pile by the wall, which he noted to throw in the fireplace at his earliest chance. Through the steam that hovered over the glossy pool surface, he saw Claymar calmly floating on his back, half-submerged as he stared at the ceiling. His eyes had a longing seldom seen, yet it was intimately familiar.

Von studied his dear friend's emaciated frame, then asked, "How are you feeling?"

"Like all of my limbs are attached with tiny threads. But the pain is finally gone," he replied as he slowly waded in the calm water. "Very wise of Navaryn to have this bathhouse in the safe room. Gotta say, these Celestines sure know how to live."

Von smiled lightly as he uncorked a bottle of elixir. During his isolation in Celestine, he had tinkered with alchemy and concocted a brew that surpassed the healing power of his own wine. Claymar gently indulged himself in the offerings as Von sat along the edge of the steaming pool.

"So. You and Kumiko, on the same side," said Claymar. "Things must have gone to shit."

"It's a temporary truce at most," said Von as he bit into an apple. "And yes. Things are obviously disastrous right now, which is exactly why I need your help."

"You know I'm with you on this," affirmed Claymar. "But are you sure that Kumiko is?"

"C'mon, Clay. If it weren't for him, you'd still be in that putrid cell."

"Exactly my point," Claymar replied.

"What does that even mean?"

"Think about why he decided to go with you." Claymar kept his vivid aqua eyes on his friend, who stared back vacantly. "The C-Poison," he continued. "He had to have known that I was surrounded by it and that you would have no chance of getting me out of there."

"So, what are you saying? That Kumiko and Merisek are connected somehow, that he knew you were locked away in his hidden fortress, and knew exactly how you were confined. From the start?"

Claymar's eyes swept from side to side before he gave a light shrug.

"Then why would he even bother to help me get you out of there?"

"You're no good to him dead. Well, for the moment, at least. He still needs you to get Navaryn and Lowenna back, and there was no guarantee you'd survive."

"It doesn't add up, Clay. Have you forgotten Merisek is the one who banished Navaryn and Lowenna?"

"Maybe you're right. It's just that I never would have imagined him, of all people, being the one to lend you a hand."

"This goes beyond just Kumiko. Even Fallon has broken rank and offered his help."

"*Fallon?*" Claymar uttered in disbelief. "I take it back. Things really *have* gone to shit."

"*Everything* is at stake, Clay," Von affirmed, "and it's time we tip the scale back."

"Okay, hero. How do we do this?"

After Von did his best to explain Navaryn and Lowenna's situation in the realm of Human, he earnestly stated, "We'll free them from their vessels and bring them home safe. After that, I'd say anything is fair game."

Claymar leaned forward. Lowenna was at the forefront of his mind, just where he had always kept her, and he yearned to reclaim the time taken from them. "Merisek," he grumbled.

Von raised an eyebrow. "I take it you're going to give his location to Sidwell."

"Oh, I don't think I'll trouble my uncle with that," Claymar said with a smirk. "I want Merisek for myself."

"I was hoping you'd say that," he replied with a sharp-tooth grin. "Once Navaryn and Lowenna are back, we'll take him and Joro out together."

"Works for me, Red Eyes. But before we continue the fun, I'll need to go to Daeva for some things."

Von shook his head, "I'll go. You need to rest and recover before you collapse. Plus, you don't have any clothes."

"What are you talking about? I have those over there," said Claymar, pointing to the putrid-smelling wad of clothes on the floor.

"They're going into the fire. There's no saving those disgusting rags."

"Well, just spare the pants, then? Those are my favorite."

Von shook his head and stressed, "Into. The. Fire."

Claymar reluctantly agreed, "Fine," as he stepped out of the pool.

"I'm sure you know what to bring then."

Von nodded as he averted his eyes.

"Splendid. I'd say you'll find me in the steam room when you get back," said Claymar as he slowly walked away.

Von exited the bathhouse and reentered the main room with Claymar's soiled clothes wrapped in the tattered sheet over his shoulder. He tossed the bundle into the fireplace with a hunk of Onyx's shed skin. A pungent odor briefly wafted away from the burning grime before it neutralized. While Von watched the flames reduce the withered clothes to ash, the rancor and disgust he had worked so hard to contain resurfaced as he reflected upon the degraded state of his closest friend. The way Merisek mistreated Claymar was not only detestable in and of itself, but it was yet another display of his disregard for the ones Von held dear. However tempting it was for him to entertain his tendencies, he quickly quelled his rage and calmed his racing heart. A time for retribution was not yet ripe, though he was ever more eager to manifest and deliver his fury to Merisek.

13

THE GAME

"Hurry up, Ray. You're *so* late!" shouted Tanya from the gray vinyl couch in the break room. "You'll probably be late to your own funeral."

After punching out, Rayshell barreled through the crowd of night shifters to grab her belongings from her locker.

"What happened? I've been waiting here for more than twenty minutes."

Rayshell griped through the slam of her locker, "I had a customer who just wouldn't shut up. It's not my fault." She rounded the corner and stood in front of Tanya. "She was a lunatic! First, she wanted to return something that wasn't even from our store. Then she wanted to buy something with popped tags. I had to call a manager over, which took forever. I couldn't exactly tell her to get the hell out of the store so I can leave because I'm late for playing pool, now can I?"

"*Well*," Tanya teased with a giggle, then stood to greet her with a quick hug. "Come on. Everyone's waiting for us outside. The group chat is blowin' up my phone as we speak. Look at all this."

Rayshell glanced at the series of memes, gifs, and strings of capitalized text. "Makes me even happier I don't have a phone," she confessed with a sly eye. "Hey. You didn't work today, did you?"

"Nope."

"Ah, I see."

"See what?"

"Sounds to me like someone was too nervous to wait with *Jesse*."

Tanya blushed. "I don't know what you're talking about."

"Come on, girl. I'm not the only one who's seen the way you look at him. Just ask him out already."

As they walked through the department store, Tanya finally confessed, "I've hung out with Jesse before, and I've tried, okay? But he kept dodging the subject. I don't think he likes me the same way I like him, and I don't want to push it. Not when it might mess up our friendship." As their friend Justine approached, she hurriedly whispered, "Please don't say anything. I know how you get when you feel like you should step in."

Before Rayshell could answer, Justine wrapped her arms around them with an excited smile. "Hey, you two. How's everything? I haven't seen either of you since summer break."

Rayshell and Tanya answered with hand gestures and mumbled their affirmations of moderate satisfaction.

"How's everyone at good ol' 'SC'?"

"Fine, I guess. Though some people need a brick to the face," muttered Rayshell as Tanya put her arm around her.

"Don't listen to her. She's just dealing with a rough spot with '*you know who*.'"

Justine winced. "Yeah, I heard about what happened over summer break. I'm sorry, Ray. I could only imagine having to finish high school with those jerks."

"Yeah, don't remind me."

"How's your new school, Justine?" Tanya chimed in, intentionally switching the subject.

"It's pretty mellow. I can tolerate it. Kind of a bummer to have to finish at another school for my last year, but whatever."

"I'll trade you," Rayshell offered.

Justine scratched through her dark hair nervously. "C'mon, the boys are waiting outside. They sent me to go and grab you two in case you were looking at the bras again."

As the girls made their way through the automatic doors, their collective laughter blended into the loud music that blared through the windows of Jesse's gray van. He clicked off his hazard lights once he saw them walking his way.

"Come on, ladies. Hurry your buns before that security prick comes back around to talk more shit," griped Manny from the passenger side window.

"Did you guys tell him that you were waiting for your grandma again?" blurted Rayshell as they approached the van.

"Hey, you stole my spot. I wanted shotgun," Justine whined.

"Well, you moved. Finders keepers," Manny teased and pointed at her with a stiff finger.

The group decided that Tanya was best suited for the front seat because of her ridiculous shoes. Justine slipped into the back of the van and scooted to the end beside the window while Manny leaned against the door.

"You must be crazy if you think I'm sitting in the middle," he told Rayshell.

Annoyed, Jesse turned around and barked, "Just get inside so we can hit the road already."

When they pulled out of the parking lot, Rayshell chimed, "So everyone remembers the rules, right?"

Justine whined, "Oh, no," as the others silently expressed their unenthusiasm.

"Oh, *yes!*" Rayshell cheered as she pulled a jewel case out of her bag.

"Can't we at least vote?"

Rayshell looked at Manny and said, "No. We've already agreed on this before. Everyone hates the middle seat."

Her friends continued to groan.

"... so to make them feel better, they get to choose the music. Now," said Rayshell and handed the CD to Jesse, "I wanna feel better."

"What is it this time?" he said as he popped in the CD.

Rayshell grinned with closed eyes. "*The Mantle.*"

Annoyed, Manny ranted, "Agalloch? Again? Don't you listen to anything else?"

"Or anything more upbeat?" added Justine, then put her chin against her fist.

Rayshell leaned her head back, anticipating the solemn guitar of the first track. "Just enjoy, will ya?"

Over the years, Rayshell learned to take her friends' criticism in stride. Aside from her brother, there wasn't anyone she knew who appreciated her taste in music. There were occasions where she spent entire trips defending her musical preference over the predictable drivel that everyone else preferred. Eventually, Jesse and Tanya started to converse, but Rayshell didn't care to listen in. She folded her arms and watched the darkness behind her eyes harden into a vast, verdant field of tall, shimmering grass. The swaying movement beckoned her to experience an upcoming vision.

During a long-awaited break from training, Navaryn retreated to the realm of Daeva and rendezvoused with Von. She traipsed beside him through a remote area of open plains and held her fingertips above the feathery growths that crowned the dancing grass. Their texture was a pleasure to her senses, evident by her gleaming smile.

"It's so beautiful," said Navaryn. "I realize just how much I misjudged what the greater part of Daeva could look like."

With his hands in his pockets, Von looked ahead with serious eyes. "There are always two sides to every coin. Beauty and despair, if you will. Leave it to the Halryn to paint all of Daeva like a war-torn, chaotic place." He plucked a tuft from the next plume of grass that came his way. "Let me guess. You probably only know one side to Celestine, too."

Navaryn's eyes widened, for she hadn't considered any other perspective than hers. "Could I be missing a bigger picture?"

Von thumbed the tuft apart and tossed the seed beside him. "Don't be so content with the charming proclamations of Benson nor the other Halryn."

The pair stopped at a grove of peachy, flowering trees for a rest.

Von sat on one of the lumpy trunk growths, then beckoned Navaryn to his lap. Relishing in the warmth of her body, he ardently lost himself in the amber glow of her eyes as she watched the sun descend behind the distant mountains. After a shared embrace, a playful zephyr twirled between them. Von smiled as the distinct lavender fragrance in her hair danced to his nose and helped clear the wild strands from her contorted face.

Having bided his time long enough, Von compelled himself to confess his blissful desire. "Stay here with me," he gently pleaded. "Forget about Benson and The Halryn. We can start a new life here."

"Stay in Daeva? I just—I can't, Von." She looked into his earnest crimson eyes and could tell that wasn't the response he was looking for.

"Why? What's stopping you from leaving Celestine?"

Navaryn clenched her jaw as she pondered how she should answer him. Although the trust they shared was strong, the depth of her responsibility to Celestine kept her from divulging the truth.

Von took Navaryn by the chin to wrangle her distant eyes to his. "What is it?"

"I-I want to tell you, and maybe one day I will. But, right now, I can't," she said as a panging sensation roused between her shoulder blades. "Besides, you know our lives would be no different than back in Celestine."

"You know we can't do this forever," he whispered, moving her wind-strewn locks to the side. "We have to come up with a plan soon."

"Can we please just stop talking about this?" she urged. "Let's give ourselves a few days of peace while we're here. Please. That's all I want."

"I'm sorry, Nav. Though I don't mean to pressure you, I will say this," Von added. "You owe it to yourself and the people of Celestine to learn through your own eyes. And you owe it to yourself to make your own decisions."

Jesse pulled into the billiards parking lot and knocked Rayshell out of her vision.

"Alright!" Manny called out. "Let's get our pool on!"

"I have ten bucks, and it tells me that I'll beat you," Justine called out, leaning over Rayshell.

"Well, let's go then," he reiterated, then opened the van door.

As they entered the pool hall, Rayshell was relieved to find it half-empty.

"One table is fine," Jesse told the worker, handing him his I.D. card.

"We're going to that free spot in the back, number *twenty-seven*. That way, we can protect Justine, the 'Scratch-Queen,' from embarrassment," Manny joked and passed Rayshell the tray of neatly displayed pool balls.

"The 'Scratch-Queen,' am I? Well then, bow before your master, mister 'Jester of Geometry.'" Justine pantomimed dignified movements and continued to quip, "Oh, ye 'Great Fool of Physics.'"

"My *heart*," Manny whined while dramatically clutching the breast of his shirt. "You know I always try to make the most of my shots."

After racking the balls, Justine and Tanya called dibs to play the first round against each other.

"Wanna break?" Tanya asked.

"Sure."

"Betcha can't even hit one ball," Manny taunted.

Justine teased, "If you step a little closer, I'd be guaranteed to hit two."

Manny motioned to protect his package as the rest of their group applauded her quip. With her tongue sticking out to the side, Justine gathered her concentration and hit the cue ball as hard as she could. Manny guffawed at the result, though she remained unfazed by his attempt to distract her. After a few rotations, Rayshell stood up for a stretch to alleviate the tightness in her back.

"I'll be back. I have to go to the bathroom," she muttered, then walked away.

"Hey, Tanya," Jesse called after she mistakenly shot the cue ball into the corner pocket. "Is it just me, or is Ray not acting like herself tonight?"

"Truthfully, she's been a little 'off' all week," she confirmed.

Justine walked over to the table and took her time deciding where to make her move. Though she anticipated more snarky comments, Manny took a break from his typical hysterics to help coach her. Tanya sat beside Jesse and said, "They're adorable."

Jesse's expression contorted a bit. "I can't comfortably use that word with Manny's name in a sentence."

Tanya's laugh roused curiosity from both Justine and Manny, who turned their squinty eyes her way. "Can we help you?" grumbled Manny with folded arms.

"No. You Sweethearts can go about your business," Jesse said as he shooed their eyes away.

"Sweethearts? Now listen here, Cupcake. I'm open to giving you some lessons if you're interested."

Jesse puckered his lips and kissed the air. "Please teach me your ways, Senpai."

Suddenly, Justine grabbed Manny's arm.

"Lookin' to make this a three-way session?" he called out playfully.

"No, Manny," said Justine, but his jokes kept coming. "Would you stop for just a minute?"

Genuinely puzzled, he then responded, "What did I do?"

"Come here," she hissed, then hushed over the rest of his questions as she walked him over to the others.

"What's the problem?" Jesse asked, just as confused as the rest.

"Guys. Nine o'clock."

"What? It's not *that* late," said Jesse as he checked the time.

"For the love of—just look over by the entrance," directed Justine.

Slowly, the party turned their heads to Shawn and Stephanie, who were standing at the register with a group of their friends.

"Oh, boy. One of you girls should go and warn Rayshell, or we'll get banned from ever coming here again," said Manny with unprecedented seriousness.

Taking the lead, Tanya said, "I'll get her," then quickly walked away.

The hall's ambiance snuck into the bathroom as a fellow patron opened the door to leave. Rayshell took a few extra moments at the sink to splash water on her face. Once she reached for a paper towel, Tanya walked inside.

"Hey, Ray. Okay, cool, you're still in here," she said while she worked to calm her breathing.

"What's wrong with you? You look like you just saw a ghost." Rayshell dried her face, then rustled out some eyeliner from her bag.

"Oh, just wondering what was keeping you." Tanya forced a smile and pressed her fingers to the purple streaks in her buoyant hair. "I thought maybe you fell in."

"I'm fine," she replied suspiciously. "Didn't think I was taking *that* long."

Tanya paused, drawing a blank on a suitable reply.

After finishing with the liner, she walked over to Tanya and asked, "Alright, what's wrong?"

"Okay, promise not to get mad."

"Why?" When her friend's response didn't come as fast as she wanted, Rayshell started toward the door. "You guys aren't sticking me with the whole bill, are you? I only got forty dollars until next week."

"No. It's nothing like that."

Rayshell paused as a sickly heat wrapped over her face. "It's not what I think it is, is it?"

"*Well* ...."

"Is Shawn out there?"

Wincing, Tanya whispered, "*And* ...."

"That dumb bitch is with him, too, isn't she?"

"I'm sorry, Ray. But promise me you'll keep your cool."

Gritting her teeth, Rayshell eventually conceded. "Can we just get out of here?"

As they returned to their table, Rayshell kept her eyes on the ground until Stephanie's high-pitched laugh caught her ear. Luckily, neither she nor the rest of her group looked her way, and they continued to their usual spot in the corner by the entrance.

Justine's eyes swelled with apathy, and she hugged Rayshell tightly upon her return. "I'm so sorry."

"Don't be. This was bound to happen sooner or later."

"Let's just carry on with our night," Manny called out as he racked up the balls for a new game.

"Hey, Ray, what's that song you always play here?"

"What? You mean, 'Until it Sleeps'?"

"Yeah. Want me to put it on for you?"

"Sure. It beats the hell out of what everyone else usually plays."

"Alright!"

Rayshell cringed. If Justine's response were a text message, it would have a dozen emojis following the single word.

"See, girls. This is how you break," Manny called.

"Hey, nice shot," said Jesse as he inspected his friend's move. "Thanks for making one for me."

After a couple of quick rotations, Manny asked, "Hey, Ray, want my shot?"

Recognizing his attempt to distract her, she accepted with a smile. Her song began to play as she walked to the table, and she realized that she had overlooked the fact that Shawn knew it was one of her favorites. Biting the inside of her cheek, she nervously peered his way.

"Well, this is just *dandy*," she muttered after locking eyes with Shawn.

Opting to distract herself from the imminent confrontation, Rayshell shifted focus back to their game. She stopped, prepared to land a shot with a high margin of failure, and gave it a go. Unexpectedly, her move deftly landed two balls into the side pockets.

"Dude, nice shot!" cheered Tanya.

Rayshell paced around the table, stalking her next move as her anxious thoughts wriggled free. Once she made her decision, she bent over and locked eyes with Shawn. Luckily, it seemed that Stephanie and the others hadn't noticed her yet. Imbued with an uncharacteristic confidence, Rayshell landed another quick shot.

"Alright, Ace. I think you should give the stick back to Manny now," Jesse called playfully, but it fell on deaf ears. "What's the deal?"

"Shawn knows she's here," uttered Tanya.

"Well, shit. We might as well call it a night now before I have to kick his ass."

"Don't worry," said Rayshell, then purposefully scratched. "Just as long as his little groupie doesn't start anything, I'll be fine."

Rayshell handed the stick back to Manny, then took her seat. Her eyes wandered back to Shawn, who conversed with his friends as though he hadn't noticed her. Moments later, Stephanie grabbed her purse and headed for the bathroom.

"I need to go outside."

"I'll go with you," said Justine as Rayshell grabbed her bag.

"I appreciate it, but I just want to be alone right now," Rayshell answered, then quickly headed for the exit.

"It's okay. Just let her go," said Tanya as she took Justine by the shoulder.

Jesse grumbled as he watched Shawn's eyes follow Rayshell. "If he goes after her, I'm going out there, too."

"Guys, just let her be," Tanya affirmed as she walked to the end of the pool table. "She can handle this herself."

The cool evening air quickly calmed Rayshell's swelling cheeks. With her eyes locked on the gum-spotted walkway, she kept a firm pace as she rounded the corner of the building and promptly lit a cigarette. Sucking back breath after breath of the noxious smoke, she continued through a small, dark, and nearly vacant parking section, heading for the short wall bordering the far end of the plaza. By the time she found a place in the recesses to relax, she had finished half of her cigarette. She was dizzy, anxious, and nowhere close to feeling the relief her vice typically afforded her.

With tense eyes, Rayshell examined her smoking cherry as she leaned against the trunk of a young red bottlebrush tree. It was becoming ever more burdensome to continue as usual when her heart and mind were so deeply connected to all that had transpired. From the visions of Navaryn's memories to the host of other strange instances she shared with Trish, her personal life was pale in comparison. She winced as she repositioned herself against the tree. Her hazy memory fought to recall the large block of missing time from Friday night and the reason for the strange aching between her shoulder blades.

"I was wondering where you ran off to."

Rayshell's nerves caught fire the moment Shawn's voice funneled into her ears, but she managed to avoid flinching. Maintaining composure, she looked ahead at the peaceful residential neighborhood draped in orange light.

"So you're just going to wait out here until your friends finish, or what?"

Rayshell flicked her cigarette into the middle of the street. "Why can't you just leave me alone already?" she asked while fishing out the citrus hand lotion from her bag.

Shawn sat beside her. "Because. I can't stop thinking about you. When I'm with Stephanie, I think of you. When I wake up, in class, and everywhere in between."

Shawn's confession, however insincere it was, made Rayshell freeze. She folded her bag into her lap and slowly turned to face him. The tingling anxiety in her chest sparked to fire despite her efforts to repress it. Though her situation with Shawn seemed paltry and superficial, she felt the need to address the dilemma. Yet the passing moments drew her thoughts away from Shawn's profession and back to the severity of her bizarre circumstances.

What Von felt for Navaryn was more profound than anything Rayshell had dreamed of, let alone experienced. Worlds away, the proclamation he made to stop at nothing until he succeeded in bringing Navaryn back made Rayshell long to be yearned for in the same way.

Annoyed by the contrived words slithering into her ears, Rayshell took Shawn by the collar of his shirt. Moments away from demanding silence, her scowl unexpectedly softened. She connected back to the vision she had on the way to the billiard hall, and soon Navaryn's emotions swarmed within her. As her lips slowly parted, Shawn was ready to capitalize on what he thought was a successful wooing.

Quietly, Tanya walked toward the corner of the building, concerned and a bit nervous about what she might find. Being the most objective member in her group, she was tasked with surveying the situation. She stopped at the edge of the side parking lot and scanned the area for any sign of Rayshell. Right when she was about to turn away and continue her search on the other end of the building, two dark figures in the distance caught her attention.

"*Oh, my, god,*" Tanya whispered to herself and quietly stepped back into the shadow of the building.

She adjusted her glasses and looked at the entwined silhouettes again, confirming that the two figures were Shawn and Rayshell. As Tanya walked back inside, she tried to suppress her shocked countenance, aiming to keep what she saw a secret.

Rayshell abruptly disconnected from the vision and Shawn's opportunistic embrace. After a few silent and nervous moments, she pulled the strap of her bag over her shoulder and stood. Shawn followed in tow and reached into his pocket for his car keys.

"Ready?" he said as he licked his lips.

Rayshell looked at him with a crooked grimace. "Ready for what?"

"To go back to my place."

"Don't get the wrong idea," she stated flatly as she started through the parking lot. "I'm not going home with you."

Shawn put his fists to his hips, stunned by her declination. "Then what the fuck was that back there?"

Any remnants of passion and longing had immediately dissolved from Rayshell following his infuriated inquisition. Clomping towards the billiard hall, she blurted, "Truthfully, I don't know, okay?"

"What kinda shitty explanation is that?!" he yelled as he worked to match her furious pace.

"Look. It was an accident."

"An accident? Are you fucking with me?"

"Did you honestly think that one kiss would fix everything?"

Shawn threw open his arms. "Then what about all that romantic bullshit you said?"

Rayshell's heart skipped an irregular beat. She hadn't considered what might have transpired during the vision. Shawn's familiar redolence wafted to her nose and sobered the rest of her mind. She felt nauseated, confused, and uncomfortable standing where she was.

Shawn pressed his lips together and looked at the pavement. "Well, I guess you got me. The thought of sneaking you into my room tonight sounded nice, but I'm sure there'll be another opportunity."

Rayshell's eyes glazed over with the same disdain she was accustomed to feeling. "Oh, is that right?"

"You seem to like playing this game as much as I do."

Rayshell stared at his bitter face, cast in harsh shadows by the unflattering orange backlight. During the silent string of moments, she realized the time had come to release all the anger, sadness, and frustration that coiled her heart.

"I've never played games with you. I loved you, and you betrayed that," Rayshell declared, then walked back toward the bottle brush tree. "Now, enjoy your pathetic existence."

Shawn called after Rayshell as she continued ahead through the quiet neighborhood, watching her dark figure slowly disappear into the shadows.

·)(·

Nearly two hours later, Rayshell arrived at the main street that crossed paths with her apartment just a few blocks ahead. She was fatigued and had a headache from smoking herself sick along the way. Her dry and tingling mouth was bitter and smelled just like the descriptor Trish used to be fond of using: an ashtray's asshole.

In the distance, a clacking sound broke the air and steadily grew louder and raspier as it approached. She looked down the empty street to catch the silhouette of a skateboarder barreling down the opposite sidewalk. Once across from each other, the boarder dropped his tail and came to a grinding halt.

"Ray?!" he yelled.

Rayshell stopped under the streetlight as the boarder jumped the curb and pushed her way. After an intimidating powerslide, the boarder took off his cap and looked Rayshell dead in the eyes.

"*God damn it*, Ray!" Jakobe boomed, kicking up his board. "What the hell happened to you? Your friends have been blowing me up, worried sick because you just disappeared from the billiards."

Rayshell resumed walking, and Jakobe followed after her in stride.

"Dude, you reek," he said and pinched his nose. "Did you smoke a whole pack of cigarettes or somethin'?"

"Close."

"What the hell happened? Did Shawn do anything to you?"

"No," she answered simply.

"I hope you're telling the truth."

"He didn't do anything, okay? We just talked. Mostly."

Jakobe panned his disturbed eyes at his sister. "*Mostly?* Aw, for fuck's sake. You're not dating that loser again, are you?"

Rayshell guffawed and then shouted, "Hell no!"

"Good. You had me scared for a moment." He dug out his phone from his pocket. "Here, want to call your friends back?"

"Nah. I don't feel like talking right now. I'll fill Tanya in at school tomorrow."

While Rayshell continued ahead, Jakobe stood under an overhead streetlight. Though he wanted to pelt her with a string of curses, he took a moment to text the news of Rayshell's return to her worried friends instead.

14

THE IMPOSTORS

The first school day of the week came to an end, and for once, Rayshell wasn't staring down the clock. Nearly half the students cleared the room before she finished packing her materials into her bag. She sighed and looked through the window at the dark gray sky. Reluctantly, she slipped on her jacket and waved goodbye to her teacher while meandering out of the room.

Trish waited by the end of the hall listening to her music. Her long, loosely curled chestnut hair bounced around the sides of her face while she hummed to an upbeat tune. Before the song ended, she spotted Rayshell mid-yawn from down the hall.

"Damn, you look like shit," said Trish, packing her headphones away.

Rayshell pursed her lips. "Thanks for the honesty. Ugh, I can't wait to get home and take a shower."

"How did fifth go?" Trish asked as they exited through the side doors.

"Awkward as fuck. I kept catching Shawn staring at me throughout the entire period. Thankfully, he didn't say anything. When class was over, I basically ran out of the room." She frowned as a cold gust zipped past. "This weekend was just awful."

"You're telling me. What you said about Jack during lunch is insane."

Rayshell's tired eyes skimmed the freshly painted crosswalk line beside her feet as she recalled that evening. "I'm worried about Brian."

Halfway down the street, a loud revving sound broke the ambiance.

"Isn't that Tobias?" said Trish as she turned toward the bus circle.

"Oh, great. Where?"

"Over there."

Rayshell quickly slapped her pointed finger.

"What the hell was that for?!"

"I can't believe you pointed out there like that!" barked Rayshell. "I don't want him to see me, damn it."

The spitting racket grew louder, and Rayshell took Trish by the hand. "Come on," she urged, tugging her into a light jog.

"What are you doing?!"

"What do you think?!"

Trish pulled away and pleaded, "Calm down, will ya? I doubt he's still mad at you over what happened with Shawn. That was months ago."

"Yeah, but it still feels like it just happened. We haven't talked since then, remember?"

While Trish was mid-sentence, Tobias dashed by on his shiny red motorcycle, spun a quick U-turn, then stopped at the curb just ahead of them.

Rayshell delayed her gait with wide eyes. "What do I say?" she whispered.

"How about start with 'hi,' you nerd," Trish whispered back, then nudged her forward as Tobias killed the engine.

Rayshell glared at her snickering friend while he removed his helmet.

"I haven't seen you around school, Ray. How've you been?"

"Hey, Tobias. Pretty okay, I think," she answered, scratching her neck nervously.

"What is this, a job interview? You know I hate it when my friends call me 'Tobias.'"

"Sorry, Toby," Rayshell corrected. "So, how are you?"

He rustled his flattened brown hair and chuckled. "This year is pretty brutal. For me, at least. Sure makes me regret slackin' off so much. Most of my friends have half-days, or just about. Super jealous."

"You are talking to 'Ms. Eight Periods' here, so I know exactly what you mean," said Rayshell while pointing to herself.

"Hello, Trish," Tobias said as he hung his helmet on one of the handlebars. "How's it going?"

"Hey, Toby. Whatcha doin' hanging around so late? I thought you got out at seventh. Get stuck in detention?"

Tobias laughed. "No detention for me."

The girls both looked at him with eyes that beckoned elaboration.

"It's just that ... I've been looking for you for a while, Ray. You've deleted your social profiles and never answered my texts."

"About that. I kinda broke my phone."

"Well, that's a relief to know. If it weren't for all the gossip, I'd have thought you went to a different school."

Rayshell rolled her eyes, assuming it was both Stephanie and Amanda who ran their mouths.

"I found out from Gilbert that you have eight classes. So, here I am," he confessed with a shrug. "I hope I'm wrong, but I kinda feel like you've been avoiding me."

Trish stepped back and repositioned the strap to her backpack, intending to leave them to their conversation, but Rayshell took her by the arm.

"Well, I'd love to stay and talk, but Trish and I were on our way to the bus stop. If we don't make it on time, the next one doesn't come for like thirty more minutes, so—"

"Hey, I have an idea," Trish interrupted with a toothy smile. "Why don't I go so you two can talk?"

Rayshell turned to Trish with fiery eyes. "But we had plans today, *remember?*"

"Ah, don't worry about it. Besides, it's not like he can give us both a ride home, right?" she replied and hugged Rayshell. "Call me later then, okay?"

"I'm going to kill you," Rayshell seethed.

"I'll see you tomorrow, Ray."

"Bye, Trish," said Tobias, waving as she continued down the street.

Rayshell exhaled nervously and picked at her fingernails while Tobias' fidgeting foot grated against the sidewalk.

"So, have you been avoiding me?"

With her eyes on the ground, Rayshell admitted that Tobias' suspicion was true, then explained why she intended to distance herself from the incessant drama. Though her confession brought some relief, she felt no closer to being absolved of her embarrassing misdeed. As she dispiritedly sat at the curb's edge, the cold cement quickly stole away the warmth from her backside.

Tobias sat next to her. "I'm not mad at you," he said and placed his hand on her knee.

She looked into his green-speckled, deep brown eyes for a moment, then turned away.

"You believe me, don't you?"

"No. Not really."

"Dude. Why not?" After waiting a generous amount of time for her to respond, he continued, "What's wrong? For sitting right next to me, you feel miles away."

Rayshell groaned and rubbed the pads of her thumbs over her eyelids, smearing her smoky eyeshadow. "I guess I can't get over how stupid I was. After it all happened, I wanted to crawl into a hole and stay there forever. I never meant to screw things up between you and Shawn."

"I get it. Shawn is one of my best friends. Or was, I guess. But, it is what it is."

His dismissive attitude about Shawn was unexpected, though it lent a peculiar relief. Just as she released her thumbs from the ridges of her eyes and looked at him, he let out a snicker and scooted closer to her.

"I like you, Ray. I've been wanting to tell you for a while."

"What kind of 'like'? Like, a 'like-like'?"

"A 'like-like,'" he confirmed.

"Why?" she asked with squinty eyes.

"Well, you're pretty awesome … and different from everyone here. A bit of a rebel who has a sweet side."

Rayshell pursed her lips at his comment.

"A sweet side that she hates to admit," he added. "I couldn't tell you this before because, well, you were dating Shawn." He paused for a moment, then gave her a good stare. "But tell me this. Why did you go for him over me? I mean, you guys are nothing alike, *at all*."

Rayshell held her breath through his proclamation. Though she knew he intended to jest lightheartedly, she wasn't sure how to answer.

Sensing her discomfort, he quickly chimed. "Well, it doesn't matter. But you know something? I heard everything you said that day, Ray."

Her eyes widened. "You did?"

Nodding, he continued, "I could tell by the look in your eyes that you were telling the truth."

Even more relieved than before, Rayshell leaned her head to his cold, armored jacket.

"So what do you say?" Tobias asked.

"Say to what?"

"Do you want to be my girlfriend?"

A surge of trepidation swelled inside Rayshell's chest. She knew committing to a relationship would complicate her present circumstances and lead to further bouts of drama.

"So …?" he asked and took her by the hand.

"I'm not sure if I can answer that question for you yet," she replied. "It has nothing to do with you, trust me. I just need some time. Is that okay?"

Her answer had nearly the same effect as an outright rejection, but he tried his best to keep it from being obvious. "Sure. I get it. I mean, I did kinda put you on the spot, after all." After helping Rayshell to her feet, he dusted off his backside and asked, "Want a ride home?"

"On that thing? How?"

"What do you mean 'how'? Haven't you ever ridden on the back of a motorcycle before?"

Rayshell folded her arms and answered, "Once. And I was seven."

"You don't live that far, do you? We can take the backstreets."

"Actually, I have to pick up my work schedule and talk to my manager about an upcoming project before we break for the long weekend. Cool if you take me there instead?"

"Was that your after-school plans with Trish?"

Rayshell nodded. "Super exciting, right?"

Tobias handed Rayshell his armored jacket to wear for the ride. "You ready?" he said, starting the engine.

"As ready as I'll ever be. Can you please just go slow?"

"No problem. But, when we get you fitted with some proper gear ...." Tobias teased with a wink.

The ride went smoother than Rayshell anticipated, and they were more than halfway through the trip before she knew it. The infamous Rose Garden was at the end of the brick and iron fence they rode beside. She smiled as the light ahead of them turned red.

While the motorcycle grumbled as it waited in gear, Rayshell watched clusters of patrons peruse the park with delighted eyes. The Rose Garden was one of her favorite places, especially in the spring. She reminisced about the many visits she made there and the plethora of vibrant close-up photos she took, featuring cameos from various pollinators.

The bike pulled forward once the traffic light turned green. Rayshell held onto Tobias tightly and filled her eyes with one more glance at the garden. Even though it was nearing winter, the variety of colorful blooms remained unscarred, as if their beauty were everlasting.

Rayshell calmly exhaled as Tobias pulled into the plaza's parking lot. The brisk air and the happy distraction along the way settled her nerves. She felt more confident about continuing their conversation, yet she anticipated the awkwardness of saying goodbye for the first time since summer break.

Tobias pulled his bike up next to the curb in front of the over-lit department store and waited for Rayshell to hop off before cutting the engine. "That wasn't so bad, now was it?" he asked after removing his helmet.

"I'll admit, it was pretty awesome," she replied, handing him his jacket back. "Maybe we should do this again."

"I have a feeling we will, soon enough. So, is it cool if I pop in to say 'hi' while you're at work?"

"As long as you're not embarrassed to venture through a forest of ladies' underwear to find me."

"C'mon. You know me better than that."

Rayshell shrugged. "Some of my coworkers' husbands won't even set foot in the lingerie department."

He sputtered a raspberry as he slipped on his armored jacket. "Maybe it's just hard for them to admit they'd rather be wearing ladies' underwear. I'll be the first to tell you, they're actually really comfy. I happen to have on my favorite pair," he said and lifted his shirt just above his waistline, then dug his thumb inside his jeans. "They're pink and lacy—oh, and have little hearts and stars."

Tobias watched Rayshell lose herself in laughter, then put his shirt back in place, bringing his ruse to a close.

"I hope this project of yours goes well. I'll see you tomorrow, then?"

Rayshell nodded, then gave him a tight hug. The naturally sweet fragrance of his skin was a pleasure to take in. "Bye, Toby," she said as she repositioned the straps to her backpack.

The sparkle of the shimmery walkway in front of the store matched the elatedness in Rayshell's heart. Though she wished the moment would last, the delightful feeling bubbling in her chest waned as she watched Tobias zip away under the darkening sky. As expected, her smile fell flat as she walked inside the store.

·)(·

Although Rayshell's obligations at the store concluded sooner than expected, she discovered that nightfall had descended. The overhead lights draped the bustling parking lot in a sickly orange tinge. Stopping to unwind, she leaned against the storefront and lit a cigarette. As the entrance doors intermittently slid open, Rayshell overheard a small boy pleading to his parents to visit a nearby comic book store. She instantly recalled her concern for Brian, stemming from the weekend's bizarre visit, and that Jack and Laura's apartment wasn't far away.

Paying no mind to contact them beforehand, she decided to drop by unannounced.

During the trek, Rayshell kept herself occupied by watching her shadow shift across the sidewalk as she strolled beneath the streetlights. Thanks to a quick, steady pace, she arrived at their apartment in just under an hour. She glanced up as the sound of rapping reached her ear. Standing before Jack and Laura's door was a young man who carried more bags than he could comfortably manage. Eventually, Brian answered the door and called for his father. In response, Jack quickly yanked the bags from the young deliveryman and then promptly slammed the door in his face. Shocked, he looked at the door for a few silent moments, then headed for the stairs.

The young deliveryman walked past Rayshell muttering a slew of curses under his breath. As she ascended the stairs, laughter and clinking silverware racketed through the living room window of Jack's apartment. While she mustered the courage to knock on the door, the home phone suddenly rang.

Following an unusual professional salutation, Jack continued, "Oh, it's you, Son. I hardly recognized your voice. Hold on a moment."

Rayshell froze and backed away from the door. Since Brian was Jack's only son, his greeting was all the more suspicious. Hidden in the shadow that cloaked the outdoor walkway, Rayshell retreated to a safe distance from the living room window and leaned against the wall to eavesdrop.

"Brian, go to your room and do your homework," called Jack.

"But Dad, dinner's here," he whined as he yanked a greasy chicken leg from one of the takeout boxes.

"Just do as I say."

"But I don't have any left. I did it all earlier."

"Then go read one of your books until I say it's time to come out. I need to take this very important call, okay?"

"But Dad, I'm hungry."

Impatiently, Jack scooped up one of the takeout boxes and pushed it into his chest. Brian crammed the chicken leg inside his mouth as he fumbled to steady the leaky box.

"Take this to your room then," he ordered while sticking a series of utensils into the jiggling mass of food.

With a scrunched face, Brian ambled away while a trail of red grease drops fell behind him.

"Sounds like you're enjoying yourself," said the caller sarcastically.

"Some days are easier than others," answered Nathaniel, shoveling a heaping bite of gooey, cheesy fries into his mouth. He chewed a few times before continuing, "You're back early. Didn't you just leave for Daeva this morning?"

"No, that was ... nearly three days ago, and—" The caller lost focus while listening to the persistent lip-smacking and chomping. "Would you stop that?!"

Nathaniel froze just before he crammed another drippy handful into his mouth and quickly swallowed the salty wad of potato and cheese.

"If I have to listen to that nauseating sound anymore during this call, I'll Parallel over there and expel you myself! All you've done is stuff your face since you got here. You'd be ahead of the game if that's what Merisek sent you here for." Joro groaned so loud it sounded like a roar. "Cut this shit out unless you plan on killing your host before your job is done."

Nathaniel had silently licked his fingers clean. Earnestly, he asked, "Joro, Son. I understand the urgency. But you need to calm down. You're more on edge than ever."

Rayshell couldn't believe her ears. She placed both hands against the wall to steady herself from the dizzying experience of hearing the despicable name.

"I'm *on edge* because, aside from managing my own plans and keeping tabs on Lowenna, I've got to babysit the both of you."

"Eitha and I have things under control here. Coaxing information from Navaryn will take time. It's as simple as that."

"I want progress!" he shouted. "Now, what do you have to report?."

Nathaniel paced the kitchen while Eitha looked on with concern. "Not a whole lot," he answered plainly and explained the drawing he had commissioned Brian to make to prompt Rayshell's reaction.

"That's it? And when was that?"

Nathaniel curled his fingers as he slowly counted backward, more than necessary. "It's been two nights."

"Get her in front of you and crack open that little mind of hers. *Got it?*"

"Yes, Son. Just remember, the seams of entry have to stay hidden. We cannot afford to shake that little girl up. That means you have to be patient while I work. It's the only way," Nathaniel urged. "I'll find out where Iaalprt is. You can trust that."

"Oh, I'm sure I can," Joro muttered over the rev of a car engine. "When are you supposed to see her again?"

Nathaniel paused to think as he pilfered toppings from the open boxes of food.

"For your sake, it'd better be soon," he barked, then ended the call before Nathaniel could answer.

Rayshell tiptoed backward as the impostors clamored on about the phone call. As she frantically turned toward the stairs, she kicked their neighbors' succulent pots. Rayshell's heart hit her feet as it clanked back into place over the drainage plate. Fearing Jack would come out to inspect the suspicious noise, she darted behind the corner of the far apartment.

The deadbolt to Jack's door unlatched, and Rayshell hid behind a large area palm sitting at the far end of the dark apartment's front door. As she quietly maneuvered the broad fan leaves back into place, a young woman ascending the stairs spotted her. With wide, pleading eyes, Rayshell put her finger to her lips as Jack's rickety screen door creaked open. The young girl's perplexed expression quickly washed away as Jack approached.

"What was that?" he asked as he looked side-to-side. Since Nathaniel couldn't read energy signals the same way Joro could, he was at a disadvantage.

"I think a cat ran past me as I came upstairs."

With both hands clutching a hefty load of white plastic bags, the young woman stood before him as he continued to inspect the area. The narrow walkway had just enough room for her to pass by, but she opted to obstruct his path. After a few uncomfortable moments, a gray cat crossed into the parking lot. Jack muttered in relief after it hopped atop the bordering fence.

"Um, excuse me. Could you help me find apartment thirty-two? I have a deliv—"

"That's my apartment. And *you're* late. What kind of service is this, anyway?" Jack scolded unabashedly.

Taken aback, the young woman followed behind him while he proceeded to berate her with a piece of his mind. Rayshell listened to his stern voice trail off, then took advantage of the distraction. Carefully, she fished herself out of the bushy palm and climbed over the metal railing. With the help of a spindly magnolia tree branch, Rayshell found her footing atop the downstairs cement patio wall and slowly descended.

She waited within the drapery of darkness while the young deliverywoman descended the stairs, cursing under her breath after completing yet another tipless delivery. As she headed for the red sedan she left running, she spotted Rayshell crouched beside a patch of yellow Fortnight Lilies.

"There you are. Are you okay?" the young woman whispered as she trotted her way, but all Rayshell did was look at her with wide eyes. "Don't worry. He's inside if that's what you're wondering."

Rayshell slowly rose but stayed in the shadows.

"Did you escape that guy's dungeon or something?" she asked, meaning to be playful, but the frightened look that remained in Rayshell's eyes beckoned a forthright approach. "Do you live nearby? I can give you a ride home if you need one."

Dreading the thought of walking home alone, Rayshell accepted her offer with a tense smile.

The young woman smiled back and held out her hand. "I'm Lina. You're safe with me, okay?"

After verifying Jack's apartment door was closed, Rayshell followed behind Lina. Her small red sedan, plastered in rideshare decals and activist slogans, sounded beat and in need of an oil change. Lina opened the passenger door and pulled out an armful of insulated takeout bags to make room for Rayshell. Once she set them as carefully as she could among the stacks of other bags in the back, she hopped in the driver's seat.

"I hope you don't mind, but I'll need to make a few stops along the way," she said as she swiped through an app on her phone.

"It's no rush. I can hang back for a while."

The cab brimmed with a variety of salty, savory scents snaking out from the containers behind her. She was almost embarrassed by how badly her mouth was watering. As they continued through the neighborhood, Rayshell's curious eyes wandered around the cluttered cabin. Sitting crooked in the center console was Lina's university parking permit atop crumpled receipts and wrappers.

"So, are you still in high school?" asked Lina.

"Yeah, it's my last year. And a shitty one at that," she admitted while picking at her fingernails.

Keeping her eyes focused on the dark road ahead, Lina replied, "Oh yeah? Let me guess. You're stuck with more classes than any of your friends in order to graduate, am I right?"

Rayshell was shocked by her intuition. "How'd you know?"

"Well, there are only two reasons I can think of that would make someone's last year of high school a shitty one. Either you're one of those kids who are afraid to leave behind familiarity, or you're going through the same thing I did and have to bust your ass twice as hard as everyone else. Hang in there. It might be awful right now, but treat this as a lesson."

"A lesson? You mean not to do anything half-assed anymore?"

Lina nodded with a satisfied grin. "And though you may think things are impossible now, I've got news for you, Sweetheart. Life is harder to clean up the older you get." She reached behind her seat, rustled out a bottle of water and a bag of organic tortilla chips, and then handed them to Rayshell.

"So, how long have you been doing this?" asked Rayshell after she gulped a hearty mouthful of tepid water.

"What? Delivering takeout and groceries? I think it's been more than a year by now."

"Do you like it?"

Lina laughed and tied up her long blonde hair while at a stoplight. "Not at all. But at least my bills and books are covered. Well, unless I continue to get shafted by tipless assholes."

Rayshell kept Lina company throughout her entire route. During that time, they shared stories of their siblings, high school experiences, aspirations, and nearly everything in between. The conversation eased Rayshell's mind, and she found that her anxiety had waned in the same manner as the catastrophe of scents inside the cabin. Though the relief was welcome, she knew it would only be temporary.

Lina's route ended close to Rayshell's apartment, but she asked to be dropped off at the row of rustic-style townhomes a few blocks away to err on the side of safety. She pulled to the side of the road, under the canopy of tall Jacaranda trees, with her hazard lights on, as Rayshell grabbed her bag.

"Maybe we'll see each other around sometime."

"I'm pretty sure we will," Lina assured.

Rayshell discreetly left behind a folded twenty-dollar bill as she exited. By the time Lina noticed it, she was gone.

Cloaked in the shadow of ivy overgrowth, Rayshell stood behind the fence and watched Lina's content expression until she eventually drove away. Once her taillights disappeared from the main street, she reemerged. Dead leaves and other debris scuttled over the sidewalk around her. Grabbing hold of her backpack straps, she dashed across the street and didn't stop until she was halfway through the parking lot of her complex.

·)(·

On the other side of town, Nico stepped out of his 350Z. He ran his fingers through his freshly cut dark hair while he looked at Trish's house. With a quick sniff and cock-eyed grin, he proceeded to the front door.

After an assertive knock, Trish greeted him ecstatically, "You're right on time."

"Are you sure it's okay for me to be here so late?" he said, peeking around at the elements behind her. "We could have gone to another coffee shop or something."

Dressed in pajamas, Trish took him by the arm and pulled him through the threshold playfully. "It's fine. I told you my dad won't be home until morning."

Immediately upon entering, Nico felt a heavy and almost warm sensation. He removed his shoes, trying to keep his suspicious eyes to himself.

"Can I get you something to drink?"

"A glass of wi—" Nico cleared his throat, then continued, "Water. A glass of water, please."

Trish laughed as she walked into the kitchen. "I coulda swore you were going to ask for wine."

While she was distracted, he darted his emerald eyes back to the door. Just as expected, there was a series of charms carved discreetly into the doorcase. Joro, who had masqueraded as Trish's classmate for nearly a week, was no stranger to the charms both Lowenna and Navaryn used to ward off trespassers. He had managed to find ways around this particular set before; however, he found himself struggling to resist its pull. Joro's signature cock-eyed smile crept upon Nico's face again. He admired Lowenna's perseverance, though he was sure he could thwart her efforts, just as he did before.

"There are some snacks on the table if you're interested," called Trish as she filled two glasses with ice.

Nico's expression tensed as he regained his focus. By his side and plated neatly on an embossed serving platter was an array of cheeses and chopped vegetables, some of which he had never seen before. A bowl off to the side was brimming with salt-dusted crackers. Nico picked a couple of them up and scrutinized them under the skylight.

"How did you manage to make these so identical to one another?" he questioned, nibbling at the corner of one.

Trish scrunched her face playfully and replied, "The crackers? What do you mean?"

Nico played along like he knew what Trish meant as she shook the half-empty box around.

"You're so weird. Are your parents paleo or something?"

Nico shrugged. "We just make the things we want to eat with our hands," he replied as Trish brought over the water.

"I guess it's healthier than things extruded from a factory. You don't have to eat them. The veggies are fresh from the farmer's market, though."

Nico set his nibbled cracker aside and reached for the bright orange and purple carrot sticks.

"Alright, so our project is due before we go on break. That's in two days, and we haven't even decided what product we'll try to pitch," said Trish as she retrieved her tablet from under the table. As soon as she opened up their notes, she sighed. "Maybe we can at least hammer that out tonight."

Nico gestured his concurrence with pronged fingers.

"Good. Okay, the last we left off, we couldn't agree on one of two ideas."

With a full mouth, Nico asked, "Okay. And what were they again?"

"Really? Did you honestly forget everything from yesterday?"

Nico swallowed down his food hard, then answered, "No."

"Then, what? If I read them back, would you finally pick one?" Trish's cheeks caught fire as she looked into his dark, verdant eyes as he nodded.

Nico studied her concentrated face while she skimmed their notes for the starting point. As time passed, however, the heaviness in his body intensified.

"Okay, here it is. My idea was for an app that integrates with other social platforms, called WeCare. WeCare would connect volunteers to a network of nonprofits that post where and when help is needed. When you use the app, you can share photos of your volunteer work to inspire others to get involved in their community. Yours, however ...."

"What *about* mine?" he asked as Trish snickered.

"Yours is ridiculous." Barely able to contain herself, she attempted to summarize Nico's proposal. "Your idea is to be able to change the color of your car with the push of a button. I mean, how is that even possible in the first place?"

"Well, when you want something bad enough, you find a way," Nico claimed as he picked his gray shirt free from crumbs.

"Yeah, but there's more to consider," said Trish as she folded her legs. "Let's go over the pros and cons list, starting with your idea."

Nico rested the side of his head on his fist as he leaned into the arm of the couch. "As you wish."

"Pros," Trish began with a finger in the air. "'It's cool. It would give you a boss-ass ride. Style on fleek' ...."

Joro cringed as Trish recited the pilfered bits of slang he haphazardly integrated into their notes. They didn't sound any better leaving her lips than they did from the adolescents he garnered them from. The absurdity of their conversation lent a slight reprieve from the heaviness that persisted, though he reached over for some cheese and manufactured crackers to further distract himself.

"Cons," Trish announced with a sly smile. "No technology exists. I mean, I thought that point was enough, but you made me write more. So, here is the only other one we need. The DMV and insurance companies require you to list your car's color for liability reasons. Now, mind you, I looked this up. Getting two huge institutions to change their foundation is very unlikely."

Nico gestured his mild agreement as Trish took a swig of water. "Okay. Let's go over yours."

"Alright then. Pros. Community building. Moral boosting. It raises awareness and connects those looking to volunteer with more opportunities. Inspires people to make positive changes. Need me to keep going?"

"No, that's fine. I'm ready for the cons."

"Alrighty. Cons. 'It's lame, and people don't want to do good things for free.'" Trish leered at Nico. "You see what I mean? Clearly, you're not taking this seriously."

"Fair enough. Yours is better. Let's roll with it."

"Seriously?" Trish tucked the tablet into her chest. "I was anticipating more of a battle, to be honest."

Nico laughed, eyeing her slyly. "Do you want one or something?"

"I guess in some strange way, I was kinda looking forward to one.

But we should move on."

"Fine. But I don't like the name."

"What? 'WeCare' is great. I doubt you'd have anything better."

"What about 'Waste Your Time Right,'" joked Nico, "or 'Do I Really Care'?"

"Come on," groaned Trish as she walked to get more water from the tap.

"I thought you wanted a battle. How about—"

"No!" Trish interrupted through a titter. "No more joking. Come on. We've gotta create our pitch."

Joro began to sweat as he conceded with a grin. In his mounting discomfort, he feared his wits would not be enough to fight against the sickening pull of the charms any longer. Yet the odd pleasure he took in prodding Trish and the desire to spark an irresistible reaction from Lowenna hindered his urge to break away from his simple task to surveil her. The deranged hunter within him hungered for more.

After Trish took a swig of water, she sat down and put her legs over Nico's lap. As they powered through the next phase of the assignment, the heaviness within his core began to numb Joro's limbs. While Trish waited for his input on her inquiry, he looked at his clammy hands.

"Are you okay?" Trish asked. "I know this is pretty boring stuff."

"I-I'm fine," Nico uttered after a fit of groaning. "Just, um, not feeling like myself right now."

"Want to take a quick break then?"

Before he could confirm, the prickly numbness moved up his throat. Despite his efforts to fight the sensation, it kept creeping up behind his eyes, nose, and ears. The next moment, his breath seized. In a panic, Nico hopped to his feet but was quickly brought to his knees by a surge of electricity. Out of the corner of Trish's eye came a vibrant glow emitting from the charms carved into the doorframe. Frightened, she immediately dashed for something to defend herself with while Nico writhed and clawed at his scalp.

Nico's body frame jittered and distended until it burst into bright, silvery lights. As he shouted into the air, his voice phased between that of a teenage boy and the deep, wretched wailings of the despicable

Daeva Trish grew to detest. The shift continued to fail, affording her momentary glimpses of Joro's true form until his figure ripped apart and dissolved from the room.

Freed from the trepidation of Joro's intrusion, Trish braced herself against the wall and relished the wondrous event she witnessed. "*It works.*"

Expelling Joro filled her with courage, but worrisome thoughts quickly destroyed the fleeting feeling of her victory. Strangely, her hope remained intact amidst her dismantled sense of security. Somewhere within her library of notes were more answers, more clues, and more ammo. She retrieved her notebooks from her room, determined to find more effective methods to protect herself and Rayshell from the encroachment of those who meant them harm.

15

THE DANCE

Tuesday morning's sky was a frosty gradient of blue and pink pastels. Only a few birds clamored amongst the varied canopies overhead, which further evidenced the impending winter season. With jackets zipped and hoods framing their tense faces, Jakobe and Rayshell trekked briskly to campus through the backstreets.

The cherry on Rayshell's cigarette steadily burned toward her cold fingers while she dwelt upon the unbelievable turn of events that transpired the previous night. She took one final drag before flicking her cigarette butt into the air. The intoxicating euphoria she had expected from her morning smoke felt more like sickly suffocation.

Jakobe watched Rayshell pull out her pack of cigarettes once again. Anticipating the sight of her lighter, he was shocked to watch her chuck them into the middle of the street instead. He thought of congratulating her but resolved to stay quiet, just in case it would rouse her frustration. Once they arrived at the corner of the student parking lot, Rayshell saw Trish standing in front of the large glass double doors, bundled in her puffy white jacket. Immediately after their eyes locked, the girls jogged to meet each other. They cringed in unison at the sight of each other's exhausted faces and frizzy locks.

"What are you doing here so early?" asked Rayshell, slightly winded.

Jakobe could tell by Trish's expression that she wouldn't answer while he was present, so he decided to leave them to their conversation. He called, "See you at home, Ray," as he passed them by.

"Later, bro." She waved goodbye with her astonished eyes on Trish. "Dude, how long have you been here?"

"Since zero." Anticipating Rayshell's next question, she continued, "I needed to change my routine."

"Okay, what the fuck is going on?" asked Rayshell as the warning bell sounded overhead.

Trish took her by the arm. "Come on. I'll walk with you to class."

The halls were hectic, but they took their time amongst the swarm. Trish slipped her bag in front of her and pulled out a small white box with a striped bow.

"Happy Birthday," said Trish, then chuckled at Rayshell's wide eyes. "Just because you try to hide it every year doesn't mean I'll forget it."

"Thanks," she muttered. "But I doubt that's why you're here this early."

Rayshell opened it as discreetly as she could manage. Once she had the contents in her hand, she quickly slid the box into her pocket before prying eyes took notice of the bow. She carefully unfurled the cord wrapped around an oddly shaped black stone pendant and brought it up for a closer look.

"It's obsidian," Trish confirmed. "And here, check it out. I have the other half."

"A friendship necklace?"

Trish nodded.

"Well, if this thing weren't so cool-looking, I'd laugh at you. Where did you get it?" inquired Rayshell as she thumbed over the carved textures.

As Trish maneuvered herself out of her puffy jacket, she answered, "When my dad and I visited my aunt down in Santa Barbara over the summer, I found a shop that sold a bunch of really cool things ... handmade jewelry, candles, soaps. I'm amazed I didn't spend all the money I had in that place. Wanna see what it looks like when you put it together?"

"Yeah, of course."

Trish took her by the hand and stopped beside a row of unoccupied lockers. She pulled her necklace out from the inside of her shirt and guided Rayshell's pendant into the corresponding grooves. "Inside the knot pattern, in the center, there is a sun and moon."

"What's on the back, though?" Rayshell asked while she thumbed over a series of irregular, rough edges. "The artist's signature or something?"

"No, not exactly," she answered as Rayshell flipped the pendant over.

Rayshell held her breath while studying the identical symbols engraved on both pendant halves. Suspiciously, she asked, "Is this what I think it is?" Before Trish could answer, she continued, "Why are there charms carved on them, Trish?"

"Because," she began, unlocking their pendants, "we need more protection."

"And this thing is supposed to do the trick? How? Is it like the others?"

Trish nodded and led Rayshell through the sea of students. "I'll tell you more during passing period, okay?"

"Fine," she answered, happy that she could use Trish's reveal as a segue to explain her incident with Jack. "So where will you be until then?"

"The library, I guess."

The pair stood beside the door to Rayshell's classroom and looked at each other with tense eyes. As the moments passed, the halls cleared until they remained the only ones.

"Well, at least you managed to finally get some use out of that engraver that I got you last Christmas," Rayshell teased.

Trish shook her head at the attempt to lighten the mood, then hugged her. "Just don't take it off. No matter what, okay? Meet me at the library after second. We both need to change our routine."

Rayshell gave her a thumbs-up and slipped inside the classroom just as the final bell rang.

The bright fluorescent lights burned her tired, bloodshot eyes. As the teacher wrote a few lines on the whiteboard and hollered for the class' attention, Rayshell slipped into her desk and rested her face in her cold hands. She was approaching her mental capacity, and sitting in a classroom pretending everything was normal made her feel worse. With firm pressure, she pressed against her aching eyes, hoping the teacher would send her to the principal's office for ignoring him. If it happened, she swore to snag Trish from the library and flee the city, then the state, from every familiar thing until she found a way to feel safe again.

·)(·

By the time her fourth class was nearing an end, Rayshell felt like her head would explode. Behind her aching eyes swam every detail of the fiasco with Joro, which Trish had divulged during passing period, and her worrisome thoughts about the charm. The cloaking effect, as Trish called it, was incredibly powerful and sealed away all traces of their energy from everyone, including those who looked to aid them. Rayshell argued that blinding their only allies was counterintuitive and gave Joro, and the imposter Jack and Laura, a potential advantage. Just as quickly as she confessed the obvious, Trish convinced her it was necessary.

"Alright, class. Great job today. I'd be a happy camper if we had more days like this. Y'all can go ahead and leave for lunch, and don't make me think twice by just sittin' there," Mr. Abrams called over the sound of shuffling papers and zipping backpacks. "Oh! And don't forget about tomorrow's quiz."

Rayshell looked at the clock and scoffed at the mere forty-five seconds remaining until the bell rang. Though unimpressed with her teacher's offer, she seized the opportunity. She scooped everything on her desk into her backpack and was among the first to leave the classroom.

With no students in the halls, Rayshell ran as fast as she could. Smiling deviously at the prospect of beating Trish to the piano, she rounded the corner to the library. With a book to his nose, Tobias ambled in her path and turned his head toward her approaching footfalls.

"Ray! It's about time I—"

"If you want to talk, follow me," she called and continued down the hall.

Puzzled, Tobias closed his book and dashed after her. "Where are you going?!"

"You'll see!" she called as the lunch bell rang.

Rayshell pushed through the side door and dashed toward the cafeteria, second-guessing her decision to bring Tobias to their sanctuary. Scrunching her face in excitable conflict, she pondered Trish's impending reaction. Her stride eased once halfway down the hall. Just as she approached the music room's windowed doors, Trish descended a stepstool off to the side. With an arched brow, she watched Tobias enter the room behind Rayshell. While he looked around, Rayshell peeked at the doorcase, freshly scored with a series of charms.

Tobias dropped his backpack to the floor to remove his thick overshirt. "So, this is it?"

"What were you expecting?" asked Rayshell as she worked to catch her breath.

"I don't know. I thought you were trying to be first in line for lunch, honestly."

Trish stood by the doors with an expression that nearly drove Rayshell to guffaw. It appeared she was expecting Tobias to spontaneously combust or be overtaken by some strange phenomenon.

"Hi, Trish," Tobias called with a smile. "I hope you don't mind if I join you."

Trish snapped out of her intense stare. "Ah, it's cool," she answered, then headed straight for the grand piano.

"So this explains why I haven't seen you during lunch," said Tobias as he followed Rayshell to the last row of blue plastic chairs against the window. "Are you two always in here?"

"Yep. Whoever gets here first, plays first. So far, I've never managed to beat her. And I still don't know her secret," finished Rayshell in an extra loud voice to ensure Trish heard her.

"So you guys just come here to play?"

"Yeah, but it's Trish who's the musician," said Rayshell while she dug out a green apple from her backpack. "I'm just a wannabe."

"Well, you're gonna have to show me what you can do so I can judge for myself," he replied with a wink.

Rayshell slowly bit into her apple with a nervous smile and shifted her focus onto the chilly, ethereal melody Trish crafted with her dancing fingertips. It was one of the first melodies she wrote during her freshman year. As her skills matured, the piece took on different versions. Some days she played it faster, creating a rambunctious tune more joyous than intended; other days, slower, and an octave or two lower. Whichever variation she chose, it was always something she warmed up with.

"Wow. Talk about skills," whispered Tobias as he reached into the open bag of veggies and cheese Rayshell offered.

"Seriously. Don't tell her I said this, but I'm lowkey jealous."

Tobias motioned for Trish's attention, but Rayshell stopped him with a nudge of her elbow. She put her index finger to her lips and giggled. Grinning, Tobias conceded to her pleas and put his arm around her shoulder.

"I've been wondering," he began. "Have you given any thought to what we talked about yesterday?"

A few breathless moments passed before Rayshell answered, "I have."

"And?" he prodded.

"I guess I'm not sure."

Tobias' bushy eyebrows furrowed as he tried to dissect her answer.

"I like you a lot, Toby, but there's just so much going on right now. I don't want to involve you in any of my problems."

"If you're worried that shit will pop off between Shawn and me or something—"

Rayshell interrupted him with a playful retching noise. "This has nothing to do with him at all, I swear. I just need some time." With her head tilted to the side, she pleaded, "Please."

Though he felt defeated, Tobias nodded with a smile. "Sure."

Trish, who appeared to be entranced by her keystrokes, had eavesdropped on their entire conversation. To lift the mood, she switched to playing a popular 80s rap song. Immediately, Tobias' ears pricked to the familiar string of plucky notes. He turned to Rayshell with a prominent and eager grin.

"Do you dance?"

Rayshell guffawed as Tobias tweaked his arms and shoulders into different positions, then shook her head to decline.

"Well, I do," claimed Tobias as he shuffled to the middle of the room. "If Trish keeps this up, maybe I can show you a thing or two. How 'bout it?"

Rayshell turned away and groaned under the crystalline rays of sunlight that sliced through the window.

"Come on, Ray," called Tobias after he spun a circle on his heel. "It's not that *tricky*."

"It is!" clamored Rayshell playfully. "I can't dance."

"Trish, hold that beat. We're getting Ray on the floor."

"Roger that!" Trish confirmed.

"Don't encourage this, damn you."

With an unflattering expression and withered posture, Rayshell eventually shuffled to Tobias' side. Step by step, he broke down a series of moves and poses for her to follow. After three disastrous attempts, Trish switched to a poetic and grandiose melody.

"Oh, great. Ballroom dancing, eh, Trish? Well," said Rayshell as she looked at Tobias, "you ready for some crushed toes?"

Rayshell thought her inquiry would end the soirée, but Tobias took her by the hand without a second thought.

"You mean to tell me you don't know how to dance to this either? Haven't you been to prom?" he asked.

"No. Dancing sucks. And I sure as hell don't want to dance to any of the trash music they'd play here."

"But look. You're doing fine," encouraged Tobias as he directed her around the room. "You just need a strong lead."

"Just wait 'til I take off a toe," grumbled Rayshell.

Smiling, Trish dimmed the mood with a soulful, melancholy tale of notes. The melody tempered the pair's pace and eventually drew them close. Having avoided trampling Tobias' white shoes for an impressive bout, Rayshell lowered her head to his shoulder and closed her eyes. Though she would never admit it to either of her friends, the gentle swaying among the skyfall of notes was undoubtedly soothing. Her cheeks pulled high as her mind drifted past the busy discord of thoughts and into one of Navaryn's memories.

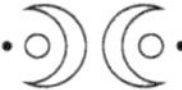

Carrying a golden tray of fruit, nuts, and some haphazardly sliced bread and cheese, Navaryn walked beside Von through a large corridor inside his estate. She lowered her sneaky teeth into a plump cluster of fiery orange and purple grapes as they entered a capacious room. The vaulted ceiling, blanketed in amber candlelight, reverberated with a pleasant, perky melody. Lowenna hammered away at Von's mahogany grand piano near the stretch of curtained windows while Claymar sauntered around playing a spritely tune on his violin.

Von set a variety of wine bottles atop the wall-mounted conversation bar near the musical duo and proceeded to fill everyone's empty glasses. Biting her lip with a grin, Navaryn placed the golden tray between a set of iron candelabras and discreetly masked the evidence of her pilfering by rearranging the stacks of eats.

While pouring the last glass of wine, Von whispered, "You're not fooling anyone, Nav."

"Even I can hear your smacking from here," called Lowenna as she executed her notes.

Claymar stopped bowing and asked, "Is she hoggin' the last of the galaxy grapes?"

Navaryn moved the apple slices away from the half-eaten clutch and yanked off a cluster. "No," she lied.

"Well, let me at least try them. You and Lowenna mowed yesterday's harvest."

Squinting her eyes, Navaryn plucked a few of the shiny orbs from the sprig. "Fine. Catch," she called out playfully.

Claymar dashed for the orbs Navaryn launched into the air and caught each of them in his mouth. With the trio impressed by his nimbleness after three glasses of wine, he took a bow while Navaryn applauded.

"So," Claymar said after he set his violin atop the lace runner sprawled over the piano cover, "I guess Benson doesn't have as tight a leash on you two as I thought."

"What do you mean by a 'leash'?" asked Lowenna.

After retrieving a set of refreshed wine glasses, he continued, "Well, you and Navaryn have been able to slip away from Celestine almost every night this season. I guess I figured it wouldn't be this easy."

"It's not easy, Clay," she claimed as he handed her a glass. "There are countless precautions we have to take. Would you prefer us to have more trouble?"

"Come on, my little Dragonfly. I'm just teasing."

"We're making the most of this while we can," interjected Navaryn with a hunk of fire bread in one hand and Von's forearm in the other. "It's been pretty stressful since we've become Tiers. This is the most downtime we've had."

Claymar stared into Lowenna's serious, blue eyes as she resumed playing. "So you, ah, got any more dirty little secrets about Benson you want to share with us tonight?"

"Clay! Focus. I thought we were supposed to be playing."

With bulging eyes and an overly dramatic head sway, Claymar grabbed his violin and waited for the opportunity to jump into the melody.

"We'll talk about some juicy bits later."

"But I want them *now*," Claymar playfully whined.

With cheeks brimming with bread and the last of the galaxy grapes, Navaryn laughed while Von rolled his eyes.

Lowenna and Claymar ran through their typical cycle of melodies. As the minutes passed, Navaryn tapped away at the oiled, dark wooden bar.

"Please, can you both do anything else but watch? Your eyes are burning holes through me," called Claymar before bowing a sustained note.

Navaryn snapped out of her daze and took a sip of her wine.

"Need me to draw you a picture?"

Von looked to Navaryn and signaled with a sideways smirk. "How about it?"

Navaryn kept her eyes locked onto his while she hastily finished off the rest of her wine. After a deep breath that lent to relief, she answered with a fast shake of her head.

"Don't keep your beloved from his passion," barked Claymar as he continued his revolution around the grand piano.

Navaryn reached for one of the aerated wine bottles, then refilled her glass. "I am not dancing."

"But you're getting better," Von encouraged.

"If stepping on your feet twenty times counts as getting better."

After a few more rounds of badgering from the collective, Navaryn finally acceded. She tightened the purple ribbon crisscrossed up her thigh from behind the holster of her dagger, then followed Von into an open space in the grand room. He couldn't help but smile at her sour expression, for he knew it would only take a moment to assuage her reluctance.

"You should have let me finish the bottle before talking me up here," muttered Navaryn as he took her by the hand.

"Stop acting like Clay," he teased.

"I heard that!" clamored Claymar from behind.

Like a gentle breeze passing through a grove, Von led Navaryn through an arrangement of turns through the harmonic notes in the air. Navaryn managed to stave off her usual clunky, uncoordinated footwork, but it eventually got the better of her. Lowenna and Claymar teamed up to transform their melody into something more playful, improvising a comedic string of notes. Laughter and playful insults ensued until Von and Navaryn finally broke away from the musical duo so that they could practice without distraction.

Navaryn led Von onto the terrace so she could take in the lively nightlife nearby. The air was peculiarly hot, and the pitter-patter from the leaves indicated that a brief storm had recently passed. As Navaryn took off her black training boots, Von unbuttoned his shirt collar in hopes of catching a nearby breeze.

A blanket of soft mossy overgrowth, beginning at the base of the thicket ahead, cloaked the dark stone terrace. Navaryn smiled as she sank her toes in, then sauntered toward a retaining wall beside the outer edge of the estate. Planted in between shimmery plumes of iridescent fairy roses were clusters of tiny white bellflowers. When Navaryn first saw them, she proclaimed them her favorite flower. In the evening, their scalloped, puckered petals unfurl, exposing bioluminescent anthers. If grazed by a passing breeze or the gentle touch of an open palm, the glowing pollen would shake loose and settle at the base of the plant. It was a feast for Navaryn's eyes, and she would make it a point to give one or two clusters a few good taps before she had to leave. But, under the evening's milky, humid sky, she only stared at them in silence.

Von could tell there was something on her mind. "Nav," he whispered. "What is it?"

"It's nothing."

He ran his fingers through her damp, swarthy hair and chimed, "You said we wouldn't do this to each other. Now, tell me what you're thinking."

After composing her thoughts, she finally answered, "Remember when we were out on the plains? When I told you why I couldn't stay with you?"

"Of course."

As the symphony of nocturnal insects amplified in the still air, Navaryn anxiously scratched at the side of her thick, bare arm. She had an idea for how to end the war between the realms without forfeiting her position in Celestine. Though to achieve it, she would have to betray the trust of the Tiers, including Lowenna, who ultimately forbade her intentions.

"What if I told you I know a way to make this all go away ... to repair the standing between Daeva, Celestine, and Opiri, so we can finally be together."

With a raised eyebrow and suspicious eyes, Von folded his arms and looked deeply into her eyes. "What are you saying?"

·☽ ☾·

The warning bell jolted Rayshell's senses, and she quickly opened her eyes. Hovering in front of the sickly bright fluorescent lights were the concerned faces of both Tobias and Trish.

"Fuck, Ray. Are you okay?" asked Tobias as he helped her to her feet. "Two more minutes, and I told Trish we would take you to the nurse's office."

Disoriented and lacking proper balance, Rayshell started to lean to the side. The bold and bright colors of the room demanded that she shut her eyes.

"She's okay, Toby," insisted Trish as she moved in to steady her friend. She had come to expect such occurrences from Rayshell and to know they weren't exactly cause for alarm, at least to the degree she could explain to everyone else.

"I never knew you suffered from fainting spells. That's pretty serious."

Rayshell was moments away from correcting Tobias' claim, but stopped herself when she realized it was likely Trish's doing. "W-what happened?" she whispered.

"Wait a sec," said Tobias as he blotted under her nose with his PE shirt. "You got a bloody nose 'n everything."

"You had one of your episodes while you and Toby were dancing. Luckily, he caught you before you ate tile."

"Thank you, Toby."

"Yeah, sure. No sweat. Do you want to go to the nurse's office? I can walk with you."

"No, I'll be fine."

"Then, can I walk you to class at least? Just to make sure you get there safely."

Rayshell glanced at Trish before answering, "Okay."

"Alright, cool. You coming, Trish?"

"No, this is my next class, so I'm right where I need to be."

While Tobias collected Rayshell's belongings, Trish hugged her and whispered, "Remember what we talked about during passing period. I'll be leaving at seventh today, and you're taking another way home, right?"

"Right."

"Good. How ya feeling?"

"I'm okay." She winced before asking, "Was it bad?"

"A little. You scared the shit out of Toby, though."

"Thanks for the cover," Rayshell whispered just before Tobias returned with their backpacks doubled over his shoulder.

Tobias handed Rayshell her bag of veggies with a look that silently beckoned her to continue eating. She smiled, then noshed on a handful of cut carrots. Once he finished his energetic and promising pep talk about pushing through the remainder of the day, he walked with Rayshell out of the music room. With a satisfied grin, Trish looked up at the charms she had discreetly carved into the frame. She was grateful they provided a semblance of safety in an otherwise bustling setting.

Once Rayshell was safely at her next class, Tobias bid her farewell with a gentle hug. Halfway inside, she turned to his beckoning.

"Sorry, I totally forgot I had this," he said as they met in front of the teacher's workstation.

Rayshell smiled as she reclaimed her backpack. "I was wondering why I felt so light."

"Well, I'll see you tomorrow then."

"Have fun after school," she called back jokingly, referring to the backyard tasks he promised to help his dad with.

As Tobias passed through the threshold, up walked Shawn with a firm grimace. Rayshell held her breath as his icy stare cut through both of them, but thankfully, neither uttered a single word as they passed by. She made a beeline for her station and avoided eye contact with the curious students that lined her aisle. Facing her computer screen, she closed her eyes and tried to quell her anxiety by envisioning herself as the only one in the classroom. Unfortunately, the rambunctious ambiance thwarted her attempts.

"Whatever game you think you're playing, you should stop while you're ahead."

Rayshell's eyes bulged as Shawn's ominous whisper skimmed her ear.

Pursing his lips, he pushed himself away from the back of Rayshell's chair before she turned his way. The familiar stench of his designer cologne lingered in the air, reminding her of their regretful embrace by the billiard hall.

Rayshell jumped at the jarring sound of the warning bell. As the teacher addressed the class, she watched Shawn amble to his station. Confused, annoyed, and moments away from storming out of the classroom, Rayshell turned to her monitor and stared at the plain desktop until her eyes started to burn.

·)C·

Rayshell had difficulty keeping her eyes open on the bus ride home, even though she was standing. The stuffy, hot air inside exacerbated her fatigue, and the last thing she wanted to do was reach through a crowd of irate faces to crack the window. Gripping the railing with her forehead resting against her arms, she observed the passing neighborhood under renovation outside the window. She wagered that the entire route would be nothing but expensive, depthless condos by the time her brother finished high school.

After Rayshell disembarked the crowded, stagnant bus with her eyes on the gray, gloomy sky, she was startled by a familiar voice.

"You look whooped."

"Jakobe? What are you doing here?"

Grinning, he kicked his skateboard up and pushed away from the bus stop pole.

"Did you forget your key or something?" she asked, then dug into her backpack to confirm she had hers.

"Nope."

Rayshell looked at him suspiciously. "You're in an awfully chipper mood for a Tuesday," she said, referring to his toothy smile, "and I can only think of one other instance when you waited for me to get home. That's when you wanted me to buy pizza for dinner. Is it one of those nights?"

Jakobe shook his head and gawked at her with giddy excitement.

"Dude, you're freakin' me out. What's goin' on?"

"This weekend, we're the fuck outta here," he answered with his finger arrowed right at her nose.

Rayshell seized her pace after deciphering his statement. "Wait a second. You mean ...?"

Jakobe nodded his head.

"So, did Mom get that place downtown?"

"Yep!" Jakobe confirmed and closed his beaming brown eyes. "I talked to Mom before she left for work, and she gave me the news. It's official. She signed the papers this morning."

"No shit."

"I know. I thought it would never happen. And the timing couldn't have been more perfect," added Jakobe as he directed her across the street. "Since it's a long weekend, we've got plenty of time to pack. She wants us to start today after we finish up our homework."

Rayshell stopped in the middle of the crosswalk. "Dude, screw homework. This is cause for celebration! Wanna get some pizza?"

Jakobe laughed, for he didn't have to think twice. Arm in arm, the pair dashed back to the other side of the street moments before the traffic lights switched over. Their favorite pizza spot was a few blocks away, next to a small shopping center. As they debated what size to order and the sink-full of toppings that would adorn their creation, Rayshell's mind wandered yet again. The fortuitous turn of events afforded her the possibility to throw a wrench in the cogs of Joro's scheme. Armed with the protective charm Trish had gifted her, she felt empowered to embrace her responsibility and face her foes with conviction.

16

THE VISITOR

At a steady and assertive pace, Rayshell trekked through the bustling halls to her second class. The start of the morning was anything but typical. Instead of staring at the floor, simmering inside her noisy mind, her hazel eyes were confident and arrowed forward. Even though she and her brother were up well past midnight packing, Rayshell felt excited to be on the cusp of a new chapter in her life. She wore a subtle cherry smile, and her eyes were shadowed in shades of black and gray, which her brother lovingly teased were uneven.

Rayshell came upon a buzzing crowd of students lingering in front of her classroom door as she rounded the corner past the library. She rolled her eyes at the thought of shoving through everyone, but the crowd slowly parted as she approached. Rayshell stared back at their varied expressions with arched eyebrows and wondered what she was about to walk into.

With one foot against the doorframe, Tobias conversed with a few of his friends. He wore his armored riding jacket, which meant he had just arrived at school. As soon as he noticed Rayshell, he bid them farewell and walked her way.

"What are you doing here?" Rayshell asked as they hugged.

"What a way to say 'Good Morning.'"

With her head to the side, Rayshell teased, "Good Morning, Toby," in an overly sweet tone.

Tobias brought his arm out from behind his back and presented her with a nosegay of roses. "I wanted to bring you these. You didn't tell me it was your birthday yesterday."

While she fiddled with the satiny crimson petals, Tobias reached behind his backpack and handed her a shiny black motorcycle helmet with a purple ribbon tied through the facepiece. A few curious onlookers clamored with astonishment as she took it into her hands.

"Now we can ride whenever we want to."

"This is really too much. You shouldn't have done this."

"What are you talking about?" he asked through a light-hearted chuckle. "We still need to get you a proper jacket, though. I saw one you might like, but I thought it would be better if you picked it out yourself. We can go after school today if that's alright with you."

Before Rayshell could answer, Tobias kissed her in a fashion that confessed he didn't care if her lipstick would stain him.

"Alright, what's going on out here?" called Ms. Briggs amidst the dramatic whistles and cheers, shooing the crowd away from her door. "Alright, you two, remember you're at school. Tobias, be on your way to class. As a matter of fact, *everybody* get to class."

Ms. Briggs' comment didn't rush Tobias in the least. As the crowd dispersed, he asked, "So, do you like it?"

"Like it? I love it," she said with a smile. "Geez, you've got lipstick all over your face." As she reached to wipe it off, the warning bell sounded.

"Don't worry about it. I'll keep it as a souvenir." After another kiss, Tobias grabbed his backpack. "I'll see you at lunch, okay?"

After they said their goodbyes, Tobias fired a peace sign and then bounded down the hall. Rayshell looked at her reflection in the motorcycle helmet and took a few moments to digest everything that had just transpired.

"So, Ray," said Sheila as she walked up behind her. "Looks like you two are official, huh?"

She looked at her friend with an awkward smile and answered,

"Yeah, I guess we are."

·)(·

After the passing period bell clanged, Sheila gave Rayshell a congratulatory hug before dashing out of the room. Smiling softly, she collected her belongings, then bounded down the halls for Trish, waiting for her at the other end of campus. Her excited steps dashed past various cliques meandering along the rows of lockers until she finally arrived at the far end of the C-wing.

Wearing a new navy blue jacket, a white beanie, and sunglasses, Trish nodded along to an energetic song. It took all of Rayshell's fortitude to keep from laughing at her apparent attempt at a disguise. Once she was certain Trish saw her through the dramatically large lenses, she held up the helmet.

Trish packed away her headphones and took down her shades. The sleek purple ribbon tied through the front caught her attention more than the helmet itself. "Whatcha got there?"

"A birthday present from Toby."

"So, I take it you two are dating now, right?"

Rayshell nodded, then stared at the bouquet of roses cradled in her arms. "I couldn't say 'no' with everyone watching. He met me before second period, like, right in front of my class. I gotta talk to him at lunch because I'm still not ready for this."

Before the pair continued on their way, a loud crash echoed down the hall behind them. They curiously turned to a circle of students forming just beyond the bend. The hostile voice racketing down the hall was unmistakable.

"You've gotta be kidding me," Rayshell muttered. "That's Shawn."

As Rayshell headed toward the commotion, Trish called, "Ray, what are you doing?"

"I gotta see what's goin' on."

Trish groaned, then hastily followed after her friend.

"What makes you think you can pull some shit like this?" Shawn barked as he shoved Tobias into the lockers.

"Look, don't even make this about you and me, alright? It was never about us."

Rayshell peeked around the corner and whispered disappointedly, "Great."

Trish took her by the shoulder once she motioned in their direction. "Absolutely not. I'm not gonna let you walk into the middle of that."

Rayshell conceded but continued to watch from the outer edge of onlookers.

"This was *always* about us," Shawn roared with swaying arms, hungry for a fistfight. "And I ain't about to let you walk away from this, leaving me looking like a fool!"

"You do that well enough without my help," Tobias scoffed. "But I think everyone here deserves the truth, don't you?"

Shawn stepped close enough to see the dark rippling layers of brown within Tobias' eyes. "Fuck you. You ain't got shit to say."

"Oh, I've got *lots* to say, Shawn. Like how it was really you who cheated on Rayshell," Tobias revealed as the surrounding students sucked back their breath. "But not just with Stephanie ...."

Shawn's nervous gaze bounced around to the judging eyes surrounding him as Tobias continued to list his deceitful endeavors.

"You begged so hard for me to stay quiet. Well, I'm done carrying your secrets."

Fuming, Rayshell pushed her way through the crowd. "Wait a sec. You knew about this the *whole* time, yet you said absolutely *dick?!*" she roared.

Tobias spun around in shock. "Ray? Wait, let me explain."

"No! Fuck the *both* of you! I can't believe you'd spill my business to all these people rather than come to me directly." As Tobias shoved through the sticky sea of kids, she added. "Here. Take these presents of yours and shove them up your ass."

The onlookers quickly dodged the rolling helmet while Tobias looked on with pleading eyes.

"N-Ray! Wait a sec, will ya?!" called Tobias as she stormed off. "If you'd just let me ex—"

"Alright, everyone, break it up," called a security guard as he tossed his paper coffee cup into a receptacle behind the commotion. "Break it up!"

With tears streaming down her angry face, Rayshell burst through the double doors. "I can't believe this shit."

"Ray, I think you're overreacting."

"For the first time, I don't think I am. Overreacting would have been me cracking his head open with the helmet instead."

Rayshell's steadfast gait through the side corridor led them to the field behind the school. There was usually a standby guard positioned along the perimeter, but Rayshell wagered the would-be fight had beckoned them away from their post. Once under the bleachers, she reached into her backpack for a cigarette, but then remembered she had ditched them the prior morning.

Trish knew what she was looking for. "You said you were quitting. Don't go back on your word."

Defeated, Rayshell tossed her backpack onto a soft patch of grass.

"I'm sure he wanted to say something. And if you want to stay his friend, just give him a chance to talk."

"I just wanna leave," muttered Rayshell after a bout of uncomfortable silence.

"And go where?"

"I don't know. Maybe we can take a few buses until we wind up on the beach or something."

"Yeah, no. It's freezing."

"Fine then. *You* think of something."

"We're not going anywhere. We're going to stay here like we're supposed to."

"We'll break our routine if we leave," she stated, raising her index finger.

Trish puttered her lips. "Yeah, nice try."

Rayshell sat beside her backpack and leaned back onto the cold, dewy grass. While fiddling with her pendant, she stared at the thick and billowy gray clouds above. Her deep breaths helped settle her nerves and ease the tightness in her chest, but her mind was still ripe with Tobias' confession.

Trish tore off a few blades of grass and said, "So downtown, huh? You're gonna be even further from me than you are now."

"I know. That part sucks. But I'll be happy to have a backyard again, even if it's just for a little while."

Trish pointed her finger at Rayshell and advised, "Remember. Make sure to put up those sigils."

"I will."

"You'd better. I know you've got mixed feelings about them, but protecting yourself is most important."

"We've been over this already," Rayshell griped, "I'll put them up, okay?"

After the warning bell sounded, the pair strolled back toward the cafeteria. Trish could tell from Rayshell's body language that she was nervous about being out in the open.

"I can walk you to class if you want."

"I don't need a babysitter."

After Trish brushed off Rayshell's sarcastic comment, she gave her a hug that went unreciprocated, then set off for class.

·)☾·

The lunch bell sounded, and Rayshell was the first out the classroom door. To avoid Tobias on her way to the music room, she took a path around the rear perimeter of campus. Smiling slyly, she zipped into the side building before a group of students ambled in front of the entryway. Once inside, she abruptly stopped in front of the glass doors to the music room with wide eyes. For the first time all year, Trish was nowhere in sight.

"*I swear*," muttered Rayshell, figuring Trish intentionally skipped out on joining her for lunch.

Promptly after Rayshell slipped inside the empty room, she secured the deadbolt beneath the handwritten sign covered in scotch tape that read '*do not lock door*,' then sat in front of the grand piano. After mowing through her carrots and half of a protein bar in the blink of an eye, she tinkered with the keys. Suddenly, the glass doors jostled in place.

Confused and seemingly distraught, Tobias continued to tug on the handles. Once his eyes darted into the room, Rayshell quickly turned away.

"Ray!" shouted Tobias on the other side of the door with her helmet in hand. "Come on. Can we just talk for a second?"

Rayshell slowly shook her head, then closed her eyes and began to play. As her soft keystrokes grazed Tobias' ear, the unmistakably familiar tune reverberated within his chest. He slowly paced in front of the door, pondering it with a mind that had been piloted by another since he woke for school. Although the visitor couldn't sense Navaryn's essence, the dreadful melody confirmed her presence within the human girl. Tobias watched longingly as she lightly swayed her head to the timing of the notes.

Overwrought with the anxious thoughts of his visitor, Tobias didn't notice that Rayshell had stopped playing until her visage appeared behind the glass.

"What do you want?" asked Rayshell firmly from the other side of the door.

"I just want to talk."

"Go ahead," she urged, then folded her arms.

"Can I please come in?" After Rayshell declined his request, he continued, "I don't get why you're being so damn stubborn."

"Because. I thought we were friends."

"What are you talking about? Of course we are!"

"If you were my friend, you would have told me what that asshole did." Rayshell watched his posture wilt, then barked, "So why didn't you!?"

"*Because.* I didn't want to hurt you."

"Well, what a shit job that ended up doing, huh?"

"Look, I get it. I fucked up. And I know that I can't take back what I did. I just wanted to tell you that I'm sorry."

Tobias' heartfelt apology went unanswered as he stood at the door. Not caring to bask in his embarrassment, he turned and walked down the empty hall. As he neared the exit, a distinct unlocking sound halted his gait. He eagerly retraced his steps, then followed behind Rayshell as she returned to the piano.

Immediately upon stepping through the threshold, a tingling sensation flashed through Tobias' limbs. The charm above the door activated in a purple glow, then quickly expelled his visitor into a disintegrating translucent shimmer. A grating tone racketed in his head, and he took a moment to steady himself before resuming pace.

Rayshell sat atop the piano bench and looked dispiritedly upon the shiny keys, unaware of the phenomenon that took place.

"This is yours," said Tobias as he set the helmet on the piano bench. "That is, if you still want it."

With a sigh, Rayshell poked around at the keys in place of a reply.

"To be honest, I don't know what came over me earlier," he claimed as he sat beside her, facing away from the piano. "I just had this incredible urge to come clean and get the truth out. It was impossible to hold it back anymore."

Rayshell looked at his puzzled expression. "Well, you should have just told me. *Only me.*"

After a further awkward silence, Rayshell reached into her bag for a pair of green apples, then handed one to Tobias. She took an enormous bite while he only thumbed over its glossy skin.

"Where's Trish?" he asked.

"Your guess is as good as mine," she answered with a full mouth and juice dripping down the side of her face.

Tobias nodded with a smirk. "Are you two hanging out after school today?"

"Not today. I've gotta get home and pack. We're moving this weekend."

Concerned, Tobias asked, "Moving? Where?"

Had Rayshell been in a better mood, she would have joked about moving to another state. "Not far. Just downtown."

"Can I give you a ride home?"

After taking a moment to gnaw down more of her apple, she answered, "Fine. On one condition."

"Name it."

"You have to help me pack my room."

·)C(·

After finishing their trip to the cycle shop, where Tobias had Rayshell pick out her jacket, he plugged her address into his navigation display.

"Are you alright?" she asked as he hunched forward

The grating dissonance in his head eventually cleared. "I'm good," he confirmed, then placed his hands on the handle grips. "You ready?"

Their ride home was pleasant despite the mess of impatient vehicles. When they arrived, Tobias pulled into one of the vacant visitor's parking spaces, then killed the engine. Rayshell quickly hopped off the bike and shivered in place.

"Tingly from the vibration?" he asked after they removed their helmets. "Don't worry. You'll get used to it soon."

With her backpack over her shoulder, Elizabeth walked out the front door and unlocked her bike just as the couple cut through the parking lot.

"Hi, Mom!" Rayshell called from below.

"Rayshell? I almost didn't recognize you."

"You're not leaving for work, are you? I thought you took the rest of the week off for the move."

"Well," Elizabeth said as she walked her bike down the hall, "that was the plan. But I was asked to fill in for someone who called out."

"But, *Mom*," whined Rayshell.

"I can spare today," she insisted. "Besides, I need to get in the extra hours while I can." Her green eyes panned over to Tobias. "Would you like to introduce me to your friend?"

"This is Tobias," said Rayshell anxiously.

"Ah, I remember the name. Nice to meet you in person, Tobias."

"Likewise," he said as he shook her hand. "You can call me Toby."

"He's my, ah, boyfriend."

"Boyfriend, no less? *Well*, Toby. You'd better take care of my daughter. Especially on that thing," warned Elizabeth as she pointed to his motorcycle.

After his sincere affirmations to keep her safe, they circled back to the tasks waiting for them upstairs.

"I've given Jakobe a rundown of what I want to have packed tonight. On my way home, I'm gonna grab a U-Haul."

"If it'll help, I can bring my dad's flatbed tomorrow," offered Tobias.

"I wouldn't want you to go through the trouble of doing that."

"It's no trouble," he said with a smile. "It's just an old work truck of his."

"If he doesn't mind, then sure," Elizabeth conceded in order to end the conversation. "Alright, you two. I gotta get to the bus. And Toby, if Rayshell gets lazy, just let Jakobe know."

"Mom! As if Jakobe is *my* babysitter."

She snickered while pedaling out of the parking lot.

Behind a neatly stacked series of boxes, Jakobe popped up with a tape gun in his hand as the scuffling sound of footsteps caught his ear. The pair walked inside, then set down their riding gear. Discreetly, Tobias snuck a glance at the doorjamb. Just as expected, there were no markings of any kind. He pinched his lips as he pondered under the governing thoughts of his cloaked, enigmatic visitor, who rejoined him after they finished at the cycle shop. The visitor was sure that one of Lowenna's charms was to blame for the sudden expulsion from the music room, and feared there would be more landmines lying ahead. Fortunately, Rayshell had yet to seal her domain.

After a typical greeting from his sister, Jakobe walked up to Tobias with a grin and exchanged a couple of slick hand moves.

"So, this means you guys are dating now, right? It's about time," said Jakobe. "So, Ray, did Mom tell you what's up?"

"Yeah. You got a list or something, right?"

Jakobe chuckled and swiped a piece of paper from the table. "You got *hella* shit to do," he said, then held up the list.

"I think your mom also mentioned that you were in charge," Tobias joked. "Wasn't that right, Ray?"

"Ew, not even!" she clamored, yanking the paper from her brother's hand. Jakobe and Tobias laughed amongst themselves as Rayshell read over the tasks listed for the coming days. "You know. We can knock out a pretty good chunk of this today. Ready to get to it?"

Tobias and Rayshell grabbed a few boxes and headed down the hall to her room.

"Sorry, it's kind of a mess in here," she said after flicking on the bedroom light. "Jakobe and I were up last night doin' a little bit of packing with the stuff we had on hand."

Rayshell and Tobias assembled a couple of boxes and began the arduous process of packing the room. They started with the vanity and closet, but after an hour, they struggled to recognize a medicum of progress. After sealing an overflowing box of clothes and stuffed animals, their stomachs began to growl.

"Want me to order a pizza? You guys like the place down the street, right?"

"We ordered from there last night, but I would never decline pizza. Neither would Jakobe, honestly."

As Rayshell retrieved a glass of water from atop her dresser, a piece of paper came unstuck from its bottom and fell to the floor. The curious markings intrigued Tobias, and he knelt to pick it up. On the paper was a series of sigils that Trish had given to Rayshell.

"Did you draw these?" asked Tobias.

After snatching the paper from him more forcefully than intended, she fibbed, "Yeah, I did it the other day in class."

Sensing dishonesty, Tobias watched her fold and tuck it into one of her pockets.

"So, since there's no school tomorrow, I was gonna grab lunch with Trish around noon. Wanna join us?" asked Rayshell while filling another box with folded clothes. "Toby?"

The visitor, lost in thought, had momentarily forgotten the auditory cue. He finally turned around when Rayshell threw a balled-up pair of socks at his backside.

"What?" he responded with a blank expression.

Before Rayshell could repeat herself, the home phone rang. She barreled down the hall and beat her brother to it. "Hello?" she answered, picking up the handset.

"Hello? Rayshell?" a deep voice replied, followed by the sound of a metal platter clanging to the floor. "*Damn it.*"

"Jack? Is that you?"

"Yep. How's my little warrior doing?" he replied into the receiver as he picked up the tray of chocolate chip cookies he dropped out of the oven.

Seemingly out of nowhere, Laura walked up behind him and smacked the back of his shoulder in response to his awkward comment, then took over cleaning up his mess.

With a grimace, Rayshell answered, "Um, I'm fine."

Jack crammed a handful of broken molten treats into his mouth. "So, listen. I heard the schools will be closed for a holiday break. I thought it would be a great time to have you over so you can spend some time with Brian," he said between fits of yelping and blowing. "How about I pick you up tonight? You can stay with us for a few days."

"That's, uh, pretty short notice, don't you think?"

"Is it? Oh, I'm sorry. Will tomorrow be better? I can let you pick out what we eat this time."

She quickly thought of a believable excuse. "It would be nice to see you all again, but I'm working the rest of the week. And I also have a couple of big projects to finish up for school."

"Wow, you certainly have a lot of responsibilities here, don't you?"

"Yes, I do," Rayshell confirmed, conscious of the strange way he composed his statement. "Wanna maybe check in on Saturday?"

Rayshell continued to dance around each of Jack's proposals until their conversation finally ended. Following their awkward goodbyes, Tobias slipped back into the room unnoticed. She returned with a bag of chips as he taped down another full box. Though he knew there was something peculiar about the call, he refrained from prying.

"Did you want to do something during the break? Just the two of us?" he asked.

"Sure. What'd you have in mind?"

"How about bowling? They have blacklight lanes on Friday nights. I haven't been in ages."

"I suck at bowling, though."

"We can put the bumpers up."

"Oh, wonderful. I'll be sure to bring my sippy cup, too." Rayshell teased as she accidentally knocked a small trinket box to the floor.

Tobias knelt to help retrieve the spilled contents. While rummaging through the high-pile carpet, he pricked his finger on something sharp. He fished out what he thought to be a piece of glass from between the twisty fibers, then grew wary upon closer inspection. Sneakily, he concealed the shard between his fingers and proceeded to collect the last of the fallen items.

"Thank you," she said as he set everything but the shard into her hand.

While Rayshell finished packing her trinkets, Tobias excused himself to the restroom. With his back against the locked door, he held the shard up to the light. Through Tobias' tense eyes, the visitor scrutinized its translucent red tone. To anyone else, it would appear to be a fragment of broken glass or an embellishment of some kind. But the visitor knew better, for he had picked more than enough of the same shards out of his knuckles.

With furrowed eyebrows, Tobias flicked the damned red shard into the overflowing garbage bin. His reticent visitor suddenly lost the necessary focus to pilot his host's body. The sharp dissonance Tobias had experienced at lunch had returned, and the resonant memory of the visitor instantly vanished. Wincing, he hunched over the sink and tried to muffle his groans. When the pain finally subsided, he looked at his tired reflection. Large wriggly veins, pointing straight toward his irises, cut the whites of his eyes. From his sudden headaches, momentary lapses in memory, and intermittent inability to control his actions, he couldn't deny the peculiarity of what he was experiencing.

After splashing his face with cold water, a sudden knock at the door jolted him.

"Are you okay in there?" called Rayshell. "We didn't pack away the toilet paper, did we?"

"No. I-I'm okay."

"Alright, well, I went ahead and ordered pizza. It should be here in like an hour."

"Okay, I'll be right out."

As Tobias slowly regained his senses, Rayshell returned to her room. Having taken note of the nearly fifteen minutes he had been gone, he vigorously dried his face off with a towel and exited the bathroom. He cooly sauntered back to Rayshell's room, absent of any telling signs of his departed enigmatic visitor.

17

THE CINQUE

After going days without sleep, Von awoke from a lengthy rest and slowly sat upright on the plush black couch at the far end of the safe room. Isolated without windows, he came to rely on the state of the wood in the fireplace to gauge the passage of time. As he looked upon the blackened, ashy logs and their subtle glow beneath the gentle flames, he gathered it was morning.

Von's skill with the Delavine Crystal was nearing perfection with the assistance of Navaryn's amplifiers, though the prolonged use was taxing on his body. Yet, no matter how impeccable his skill had become, he was tested by a peculiar anomaly caused by Rayshell and Trish's charmed necklaces. Having not witnessed the moment as it happened, he had no explanation for why he could no longer latch onto the energy of either of the human girls. Without the tether, his efforts to stay apprised of their whereabouts were now manual. Since their schedule was somewhat consistent and there were only a handful of places they could be throughout the day, he at least knew where to expect them. Regardless, he struggled to fight through the obstacles, though Claymar cautioned against overexerting himself; a warning that went unheeded.

Pushing through the grogginess from his slumber, Von walked toward the pantry dressed only in heavy, dark brown pants. As he cleared the haziness from his eyes, he noticed a bright orange glow ahead of him. At first, he thought something in the room had caught fire, but then he discerned the familiar blazing figure standing by the obsidian table.

"You're early today, Aalrija," said Von.

"Ah, you're awake," she said as she turned around.

Present in her fiery elemental state, Aalrija had meandered near the fireplace while Von slept, looking at the tall, decorated walls. She was in casual attire, which was somewhat unusual, and appeared more relaxed than she had been in several months.

"Been waiting long?" asked Von.

"No, not very," she replied. "I hadn't the heart to wake you, though I would have had to if the fire had gotten any weaker."

Von added a few more logs to the fireplace, then asked, "What brings you here?"

"I was just enjoying the quiet, is all."

"I don't blame you. I'd also need a getaway from my constituents if I were you."

Aalrija chuckled lightly. "Yes, well, Benson called off this morning's meeting, which is fine. It's not like anything gets accomplished during those anymore."

"Ah, that's why you're not all dressed up."

While Aalrija examined her projection, Von chuckled and filled a bowl with fruit from the pantry. The firelight accentuated the chiseled features of his torso as he started in her direction.

"You look, um, rested," said Aalrija as she cleared her throat. "Would you mind perhaps putting on a shirt?"

"As you wish," Von replied with a smirk. "Feel free to have a seat."

Relieved that her fiery apparition hid her blushing cheeks, Aalrija sat at the obsidian table. Von set the bowl down, walked over to the trunk by the couch, and shuffled through some spare threads.

"Where's Claymar?"

"Last I checked, he was wrestling around with Onyx."

"Wrestling. With a dragon. In his condition?" said Aalrija, baffled.

Von shrugged. "He has his ways of regaining his strength."

"I'm not sure I'll ever truly understand Daeva."

"Me neither," Von jested. "Anyway, they're probably both asleep in the cave."

Peeking out from behind the couch, Claymar chimed, "I'm sure you'd prefer that, wouldn't you?" then extended his arms in a stretch.

"Really, Clay? Of all the places you can sleep, that's where you ended up?" Von answered.

With a sly grin, Claymar rose to his feet in the buff and stood behind the couch with the headrest barely covering his groin. He placed his hands on his hips and turned his smirking face to Von. "I just wanted to be close to you," he replied with pursed lips before he broke into laughter.

Von managed to crack a small smile at Claymar's playful remark as he closed his trunk. Aalrija poorly hid the embarrassment on her face behind her hand, but was more amused than anything else.

"What? I happen to like the floor, okay?" Claymar continued, "Makes me feel … *grounded*."

"Just put some clothes on."

Claymar's presence brought a lightheartedness to the safe room that Von appreciated. The effects of Merisek's concoctions had waned, and he steadily continued to recover. However, his sarcasm and wit never left him through his tribulations, and Von was reluctantly thankful for it. Having a friend's company proved more than beneficial for both of them during such a dark and uncertain time.

As Claymar knelt behind the couch to dress, Von returned his attention to Aalrija. "How is Kumiko faring with the host?" he asked.

"So far, so good, I think," she replied. "Creating a tether to the boy you found had its challenges, but Kumiko managed."

"That's good news," said Von as he slipped on a black overshirt, leaving it unbuttoned.

"I must say I'm surprised at your choice of subject."

"Why?" said Von as he returned to the table. "Because the boy appears to be in love with Rayshell?"

"Well, yes. Given Kumiko's history with Navaryn, if you don't mind me saying, the choice seems rather odd."

Von picked up an apple from the bowl and sat across from Aalrija. "The girl trusts this Tobias boy. That's what's important," he stressed. "Kumiko's feelings toward Navaryn are of no consequence to me, nor should they be to you."

Aalrija folded her hands on the table and concealed her worried expression. Peace between Von and Kumiko felt delicate, yet it held together far better than she ever expected. Keeping their relationship cordial was vital to their endeavor, and she felt responsible for ensuring it remained that way.

"Besides, I needed to find someone quickly. We've been lucky thus far, but time isn't exactly on our side since Merisek could be closing in at any moment. I stand by my choi—" Von paused as his ears caught the inklings of distant footsteps.

"I trust you are right, Von," Aalrija replied, overlooking that he paused mid-word. "Now, we must see if Kumiko can handle the weight of Kaimaharaa."

"*Shh!*" snapped Von with his index finger pressed against his lips. "What is it?"

"Uh, oh," chimed Claymar as he approached the table, fully dressed. "Gettin' spooked, are we?"

"Quiet. Someone's here," Von replied softly. "Out in the cave."

"Oh, relax, it's just Onyx coming back from his morning romp," said Claymar as he swiped his hand across Von's shoulder.

"No. Onyx isn't this quiet," said Von as he walked over to the trunk and kicked the lid open.

"Please, Von. Don't do anything brash," urged Aalrija.

"Wouldn't dream of it," he sarcastically replied.

Von retrieved his gauntlets from the trunk and quickly fastened them. Once activated with his innate power, the gauntlets glowed a soft orange hue. From his palm came a dark crimson spire extending to the length of a short sword.

"Von. I-is that your—" Aalrija started.

"Blood. Yes," he quickly replied as he closed the trunk and started toward the recessed cave entrance to avoid further questions.

Aalrija rose from the table and stood beside Claymar, watching

Von head toward the cave.

"There he goes," Claymar said with a chuckle. "Classic Von."

"Aren't you going to assist him?"

"Ha. He'd probably cut off my hand if I stepped in."

"Pardon?"

"He's itching for a fight."

"How do you know?"

"Think about it. The guy's been cooped up here for months trying to get his girl back. I'd be looking for a fight, too."

"Because of Lowenna?" surmised Aalrija with a solemn stare. "I suppose Onyx helped you with that?"

"A bit," Claymar replied with a wink.

Although the presence of an intruder discovering the safe room was cause for alarm, Claymar's playful demeanor effectively put Aalrija's mind at ease. However, it did little to take her attention off the bloodstone blade protruding out of Von's hand.

"Answer me this," she said to Claymar. "Those peculiar contraptions on Von's hands, that spire of blood ...."

"Oh, you didn't know? Von's a Sangromancer."

"Fascinating. I thought them to be nothing more than a myth."

"Yeah. Kind of a lot to get into. We'll chat about it later," he assured.

The hobbling footsteps drew closer as they echoed down the corridor. Von noted the high ceiling cast in shadow above the entryway and quickly scaled the wall to wait in a dark corner. A figure walked through the opening into the cave. Before the intruder could utter a syllable, Von lunged from above and tackled him to the ground, where they tumbled into the visibility of the main room. As Von mounted the intruder, he let out a soft chuckle as he held his blood spire before the man's familiar face.

"Well, what a coincidence. We were just talking about you."

"Damn it, Von! Get off of me!" yelped Kumiko as he winced in pain.

Claymar doubled over as he erupted into laughter, though a fit of coughing hushed him quickly.

Looking amused yet mildly unsatisfied, Von disengaged the blade from his gauntlet and rose to his feet without offering a helping hand.

"Kumiko?" said Aalrija. "Are you alright?"

"I will be," he answered with tired eyes as he slowly stood up.

"You're lucky Onyx wasn't in the cave. He could have torched you," said Von as he reclaimed his apple from the table. "What are you doing here?"

"I came to give a report."

"In person?" blurted Claymar.

"I thought we agreed you were to travel by way of the fire, same as Aalrija," added Von.

"I couldn't, alright?" Kumiko revealed. "I Paralleled over here in a few short spurts, and that about drained me."

"Why? What's the matter?" asked Aalrija.

"My powers are deadened. Somehow, I was hit with an expulsion charm that broke me away from the human boy. I went back later but couldn't hang on for long."

Flabbergasted, Aalrija chimed, "An expulsion charm? Are you sure?"

Kumiko nodded. "Labraid has done it to me enough times during training. I know the feeling pretty well."

"Who could have done it?"

"It's Lowenna," Von claimed. "She managed to communicate with her host. Thankfully, she's been receptive to Lowenna's instructions on using charms."

"Exactly," said Kumiko with a nod.

"Remarkable," acclaimed Aalrija. "Has Navaryn's host done the same?"

"It seems that Lowenna's host has shared the knowledge with her, but she is not using them," Kumiko added, then explained the illustration he found.

"Well, I suppose that works neither to our benefit nor our detriment," said Aalrija as she slid the fruit bowl toward Kumiko, to which Von raised an eyebrow.

"Wrong," Kumiko contended. "She's leaving herself vulnerable to

Joro and Merisek should they decide to take more invasive actions. We need to come up with a plan."

Kumiko's ominous expression alarmed Aalrija. As they brainstormed proactive ideas, Von walked over to the fireplace to toss in another lump of Onyx's shed skin while Claymar sauntered to the couch. After taking the last bite of his apple, Von unfastened his gauntlets with subtle frustration and placed them back in the trunk.

"Shame you got all worked up for nothing, hm?" said Claymar with a grin.

"Tell me about it," he replied, staring into the dancing flames. "Part of me wished it was Joro in the cave so I could put my blade through his throat."

"How romantic. I wouldn't mind snapping off a leg or two. Well, I guess since all he's got is two, I'll just take 'em both."

Von lightly chuckled as he walked back over to the pantry. After taking a few moments to crudely arrange a platter of bread, dried meat, and cheese, he brought it over to share with Claymar.

"Thoughtful!" beamed Claymar as he twinkled his toes. "I don't suppose I should expect a massage after this snack?"

Von tilted his head and batted the back of his hand across Claymar's vulnerable leg.

"Ow!" he shouted in an outburst between a laugh and a cry. "That knee's still cracked a little, ya know."

Their mutterings caught Aalrija's attention from the table. "Is everything alright?"

"Oh, we're fine. Von just thinks I haven't gone through enough torture."

Aalrija couldn't help but admire their peculiar dynamic. Once Von returned to the table, Kumiko regained enough strength to sit up straight.

"So, what's it like, Kumiko?" asked Von as he finished chewing a hunk of bread.

"What's *what* like?"

"Possessing that human boy."

Kumiko gazed down at the shiny obsidian table top as he thought.

"It's the strangest thing. Not at all what I expected it to be like. Our minds merged in a strange way. I began to think like him, and he began to think like me. I'm able to control him, just not how I imagined. We think as one being, rather than me simply being a visitor in his body, taking hold of the reins, so to speak."

"Do you think the boy is aware of your presence?" asked Aalrija.

"Doubtful."

Von noticed a hint of despondence behind Kumiko's eyes. He attributed it to exhaustion, though he wondered if he was exhibiting a lingering symptom carried over from Kaimaharaa. Not paying much mind, for the time being, Von continued to keep Kumiko's attention. "And what about the girl?" he pressed.

Kumiko griped, "She is so sensitive, so unstable, and annoyingly hot-headed. I'll get Navaryn to surface somehow. I just have to keep my cover."

"When the time is right, say or show something that can trigger one of Navaryn's strongest emotions. That should draw her out."

"That should be no problem for Kumiko," quipped Claymar from the couch. "If anyone knows how to piss Navaryn off the most, it'd be you. Am I right?"

Von turned to Claymar and snapped, "Am I gonna have to gag you?"

Claymar cleared his throat. "Just a joke. I'll shut up now."

Kumiko took the remark in stride, or so he made it appear. He kept his composure, which, oddly enough, he had found was easy to manage in the presence of Aalrija.

"Ahem. Before I do, though, I have an idea," said Claymar as he subtly raised his hand. "Thanks to Merisek, I know how to Parallel to the realm of Human. Why don't the two of us just go there? We can handle it."

"Not without a plan. We can't just hang around aimlessly while the realm slowly kills us," cautioned Von as he fidgeted with the amulet sitting atop his chest. "Not even Joro can stay for too long at a time."

Claymar scoffed at the mention of Joro, then stood up from the couch. "Oh, come on. You know we'd last far longer than that shifty twit. I'll go alone if I need to."

"Don't be stupid, Clay."

"What's stupid about trying to help instead of just sitting here? Lowenna needs me just as much as Navaryn needs you. End of discussion."

Aalrija tried to interject, "As much as—"

"You're not even fully recovered. All you'll do is get yourself killed if Joro or Merisek finds you."

"That's why I need you there to back me up. Now, let's *go*!"

Claymar and Von continued to argue over Aalrija's unsuccessful attempts to finish her statement until her patience expired. "Enough! I swear, the both of you act like children sometimes!" she boomed as her fiery apparition surged. "Now, as I was saying, as much as I would love to have you both try your luck in Human directly, we can't risk causing an incident and having you exposed. Doing so could, frankly, spell disaster."

Annoyed, Claymar barked, "What do you mean?"

Before Aalrija could respond, a shuffling sound from the far end of the safe room beckoned everyone's attention. Having successfully avoided triggering Von's heightened hearing, Fallon walked toward the obsidian table.

"To answer that, you must first understand these *Humans*," he called out in his hearty voice.

"Fallon?" Kumiko chimed in disbelief, "What are you doing here? Benson could know—"

"Not to worry. I didn't Parallel."

Von grinned with genuine pleasure upon seeing Fallon. Instead of puzzling himself with how he made his way through the cave without making a sound, he was content with the tricks Fallon had up his sleeve.

"Hello, Von," greeted Fallon as he extended his hand. "Aalrija has kept me apprised of your efforts. Marvelous work."

Von firmly gripped Fallon's hand. "Good to see you again. What brings you here?"

"Well, I ran into Onyx a short while ago. I was on my way back to my shop with some fresh ore, and he must have sniffed out the gems nestled inside it. Then, something told me I should stop by, and Onyx was kind enough to bring me along for a ride." He then looked to Claymar. "And I see we have a guest."

Hesitant at first, the otherwise unbashful Daeva replied, "The name's Claymar," with his mouth cluttered with bread and cheese.

"Ah, so *you're* Claymar," said Fallon with raised eyebrows. "It's a pleasure to finally meet you."

Fallon's arrival was heartwarming as much as it was unexpected. While he acquainted himself with Claymar, Aalrija sat awestruck at the inconceivable congregation before her; two of Daeva's most powerful stood in the peaceful presence of Celestine's elite, working toward a common goal. Though she could only speak for herself, the prospect of viewing the Daeva as enemies had faded entirely from her mind.

"So, Fallon. Tell us," Von began, "what's the worst that could happen by going to the realm of Human ourselves?"

"First off, as you already know, the realm of Human is rather *unique*. Due to the absence of mystical essence, the realm cannot sustain beings like us. It thirsts, and it suffers. Therefore, it overtakes.

"The reason for this is they are a race that has, how shall I put this … forgotten who they are. And, frankly, that is how they must remain. Revealing our presence to them could, in theory, cause them to recall the ways of the mystics. Were that to happen, they would act much like a plague and conquer as far as their reach will take them."

"This doesn't make any sense," said Von. "For a realm that was supposedly so capable, how do you explain their present, utter weakness?"

"It is because the Humans seldom trust what they see in front of their own eyes. And that includes each other," explained Aalrija. "In many ways, they have poisoned their world—tainted it in strange, inconceivable ways. They tend to argue amongst themselves about a great many things, as far too many of them cannot see beyond their narrow and limited scope. They impose disbelief on one another, manipulate, and rationalize in detrimental ways. They're simply lost, afraid, and far too—"

"Stupid?" Claymar chimed.

Von kicked Claymar's shin after his interruption, but couldn't stop himself from chuckling along with him.

"I was going to say, far too impulsive for their own good," Aalrija concluded.

"But that's not to say they are devoid of any redeeming qualities," Fallon remarked. "There are many who are eager and yearn for the betterment of their society."

Von and Claymar glanced toward each other, subtly rolling their eyes at Fallon's remarks. Though it came as little surprise, they were impressed at the level of knowledge the Celestines had regarding the realm of Human. However, given their illustration of the realm, their stance became understandable. They would have to continue to tread lightly, a notion that did not sit well with either of them.

"Nevertheless," Fallon continued, "the realm of Human is one that we've been cautious to avoid. With the way things stand now, they're slated to bring about their own demise. We will not make ourselves responsible by hastening their stride."

Halting mid-sip, Von and Claymar set down their wine glasses and glared at Fallon.

"That's interesting," said Von. "Seeing as how you Celestines have no reservations when it comes to the decimation of Daeva."

"I cannot speak for the conflict between our realms, Von. That began long before my time," Fallon replied earnestly. "But I can tell you that I myself no longer support Celestine's affront on Daeva."

"Nor do I," affirmed Aalrija. "We've learned far too much from you two to hang onto such unguided hostility."

"Good luck convincing Daeva of that," Claymar uttered solemnly.

"Peace between our realms will come," said Aalrija as she leaned forward. "I will see that through, even if it takes me until my dying day."

Aalrija's vow, to which Fallon echoed the same, lent enough appeasement to lower the temperature of the conversation. The five of them knew well and good that such a notion of peace between Celestine and Daeva felt ever distant, but perhaps for the first time, it seemed possible. Keeping faith in Aalrija and Fallon's promise wasn't difficult, though when Von and Claymar looked to Kumiko and waited for him to chime in, he remained silent.

"Almost forgot you were sitting there," Claymar playfully quipped. "It's okay. You don't have to comment."

Kumiko's only reply was a feigned smile that he hoped would appease.

"How soon do you think you can reconnect to the human boy?" asked Von.

"I should have enough strength in a few hours," he replied. "Although I'm not sure how much longer I can continue sidestepping Labraid's training. He might become suspicious of something."

"I'll tell him you've taken ill today. That should buy you a little time and give you some reprieve," Aalrija assured. "In the meantime, get plenty of rest. You'll need your strength."

However doubtful Kumiko was that Labraid would be willing to accept such an excuse, he was nonetheless relieved and agreed to Aalrija's proposal.

"What'll your next step be then?" asked Claymar.

"I have an idea for what to do," Kumiko replied with a stern look. "The boy is meeting Navaryn's host for a meal later today. I'll try my luck then."

"Perfect," said Aalrija as she rose from the table. "I must be off now to find Labraid. Good luck, gentlemen."

"I'll be going as well," Fallon said with a grin. "I'll need to borrow Onyx to get back before he decides to go down for a nap. Keep up the fight and don't let up, got it?"

Aalrija's fiery apparition dissipated into fluttering embers as she took her leave, while Fallon returned to the cave to look for Onyx. The young collective considered the courses of action laid out before them, and time to act was fast approaching. Kumiko slowly rose from the table and addressed Von, standing idly by.

"I need to wash up and rest for a while before returning to Human," he said.

"By all means. Do what you have to do."

Kumiko nodded at Von with subtle graciousness but didn't bat an eye at Claymar. While he sauntered off to the far end of the safe room,

Claymar pulled Von aside for a huddle.

"So, how do you feel about all of this?" he whispered.

"How do you?"

"I don't know, Von. All this talk about not causing an incident in the realm of Human seems ridiculous to me."

"I don't like it either. But you heard what Fallon said. Besides that, I owe it to Aalrija for getting as far as I have. I'll respect her wishes."

"Alright, I'll give you that. For a Celestine, she's a kind woman who seems genuinely on the same side as us," Claymar acknowledged. "But what about Kumiko? Do you trust him? I mean, you remember what he did to you, don't you?"

"You think I'd actually *forget?*"

"I just can't fathom he's being as forthright as he's making it seem."

"I'm not worried about Kumiko, and you shouldn't be either," Von urged. "After all, we're both working toward the same goal. All three of us, for that matter."

"I'm touched. I know he saved my ass," he admitted, "but don't expect me to be friendly with the little sap."

The following few hours in the safe room were quiet, though the silence was occasionally interrupted by minor instances of Claymar's pained grunts as he exercised his injured knee. While Von slipped in and out of his meditative trances with the Delavine Crystal, Kumiko rested on the plush couch. However, unbeknownst to Von and Claymar, he had feigned sleep for the majority of the time he was there. Peeking through the slightest openings of his eyelids, even in his sheer exhaustion, he fixated on Von as he delved into the crystal. The thought of him watching Navaryn's host was enough to make his skin crawl, yet his mind was sound enough to maintain the goal they shared.

Kumiko's time of rest was nearing a third hour when he was suddenly jolted upright by the sound of a burning log cracking in half. Von and Claymar turned toward him with subtly amused countenances. After another few awkward seconds that seemed to pass ever so slowly, Kumiko rose from the couch and exited through the cave without uttering so much as a word.

18

THE NOSTALGIA

At ten past noon, Tobias and Rayshell pulled into the parking lot of a bustling shopping plaza. The sun beamed through the scattered billowy clouds, and the air was especially brisk. Passing patrons were dressed in coats or bundled in comfy sweaters. Tobias considered the weather perfect for riding, and his reticent guest, Kumiko, couldn't agree more.

A loud sputter cracked the air as they settled into the empty motorcycle parking section near a pet supply store. The sound grabbed Trish's attention, who waited for them on the patio of her favorite restaurant. She set her menu down and smiled as the pair walked up hand in hand, wearing nearly identical outfits.

"Dang, you two look great in all that gear," Trish complimented, then sipped at her water. "Might even be inspiring me to get a motorcycle."

"You should totally get one. I'm gonna sign up for classes in the spring," added Rayshell, then hugged Trish. "We can do them together."

"We'll see," she said through a chuckle, then greeted Tobias the same.

"Sorry we're kinda late."

"Not like punctuality is your strong suit, Ray," Trish teased. "But we should still have plenty of time. My dad dropped me off while he ran a few errands."

Rayshell and Tobias removed their armored riding jackets and took their seats in front of the frosty water glasses waiting for them.

"I'm so hungry," whined Rayshell as she grabbed her menu. "Did they give us any bread yet?"

"Maybe."

Rayshell pulled the menu just under her eyes and squinted at Trish. "Did you eat it all?" she asked as her friend chuckled. "You totally did, didn't you?!"

"Relax, relax. They're coming with more in a sec. At least, I think they are."

Rayshell shot the paper covering on her straw at Trish, but it landed nowhere she intended. She jabbed it into her cup with a pouty expression and muttered, "They'd better."

"So, Toby. Have you been here before?" Trish asked with her fingers interlaced.

"I can't say that I have," he replied after taking his eyes away from a group of people who walked their way. "But Ray's been talkin' about it all morning."

"I wouldn't doubt it. This is her favorite place to eat as much as it is mine."

Rayshell excitedly chimed in, "Yeah, and I haven't been here in forever."

"Forever means more than a month, just for the record, Toby," Trish clarified.

Just then, a waitress walked out with a refreshed tray of their signature lemon rosemary bread and a side of warm olives. Tobias smiled and thanked her as she set it down. Rayshell's eyes were sparkling as if she were looking at a platter of gemstones.

"Did you need more time to order?"

"Yes, please," answered Trish.

"One sec," spurted Rayshell with a mouth full of bread as she quickly scanned the menu. "Can we order appetizers?" After the waitress nodded, she continued, "Can we order the pickled veg, the, uh, kabocha chickpea salad, and, oh! This is new. Can we also do the heirloom tomatoes with roasted pumpkin seeds?"

The waitress took down her selections, then walked over to check on the other table behind them. Tobias looked at her with a smile.

"*What?*" said Rayshell as she went for another piece of bread.

Tobias shook his head gently. "Hey, lemme try some."

As he noshed, the girls looked over the menu and commented on the new seasonal offerings. Content to listen to their chatter, Kumiko piloted Tobias back to his watchful eye on the passersby. He felt incredibly anxious knowing Joro had not only located the girls but was brazen enough to approach them face-to-face if given the opportunity. And considering his abilities, his essence was nearly impossible to trace.

"Are you sure you don't want to bowl with us tomorrow?" Rayshell asked Trish.

"Nah. I don't want to be the third wheel on your date, you dummy. You guys have fun."

Just as the girls went back to studying the menu, the waitress walked out with the appetizers and another round of steaming bread. Rayshell looked as if she were moments away from passing out from excitement. The colorful array of veggies, plated with fresh, edible garnish, was a delight to the senses.

"Have you decided on your order?"

"Um," the girls said in unison, then hastily chose their dishes from the seasonal menu.

Tobias then ordered himself something he and his guest had never heard of before: a barbeque jackfruit sandwich with pineapple. Admittedly, it was the pairing of seasoned garlic fries that lured him.

After handing the menus back to the waitress, Trish took a few clicks of their appetizer spread, one of which had Rayshell's grubby hands going right for the bread again.

"This looks fancy," said Tobias as he poked the tines of his fork at the kabocha salad.

The girls took charge of the conversation while they all indulged in their appetizers. As much as Tobias tried to refrain, his eyes wandered again. His guest studied select individuals whose eyes happened to fall upon him. Some challenged his gaze, while others simply looked away.

Although he expected Joro to be somewhere nearby, there was no way he could be sure. Yet, he remained confident in his diligence in keeping the two human girls safe.

Tobias lost focus when the waitress set his entrée before him. He politely thanked her with a smile as she walked for a water pitcher to refill their glasses.

"Where did you go?"

"Go?" asked Tobias. "I was here the whole time."

"Oh, sure," teased Rayshell. "What did we finish saying before you popped out of that trance of yours, then?"

Tobias took a big bite of his sandwich before he could answer.

"Ha! I knew it!" she burst.

"Yeah, you've been pretty distracted since you got here," Trish acknowledged, throwing him a suspicious look. "Is something the matter?" She patiently waited for him to finish chewing so he could answer. Though she didn't expect foul play, she did recognize a notable shift in his behavior.

"Nothing's the matter. I guess I'm just people-watching. It's funny to see everyone dressed like they're entering a blizzard, but we're sitting outside without jackets," he pointed, thinking on his feet.

"You're right," said Rayshell as she scanned the plaza's patrons who walked by their dining space. "It's still really warm. Well, as long as you're in the sun."

Tobias continued working on his sandwich as Rayshell helped herself to a few of his fragrant garlic fries. As she leaned over, her necklace slipped out of her black buttoned shirt. The smooth surface of the medallion's backside reflected the sun and highlighted the hand-carved symbol.

Tobias did his best to keep his eyes from widening under Kumiko's influence. "That's a pretty strange-looking necklace."

Rayshell crammed another couple of french fries into her mouth with a smile. "I'll take that as a compliment."

"Where did you get it?"

"It was a birthday gift from Trish. She has the other half."

Tobias looked at Trish as she clutched her pendant above her bust. Upon noticing the tense look on her face, he averted his gaze as casually as he could manage. "Friendship necklaces?" he said, then laughed. "How adorable."

"They're not just silly little friendship necklaces. We wear them for protection."

Immediately after her reveal, Trish jabbed the heel of her white boot into Rayshell's shin.

"What the hell was that for?!" Rayshell yipped.

With a nearly emotionless voice, she replied, "Oh, I'm sorry, Ray. My foot slipped."

Rayshell glared at Trish as she resumed eating her biriyani.

"I've never seen a friendship necklace that looked quite as killer as that one. They're usually super lame."

"I was tempted to get her the cheesiest one I could find, just to mess with her."

"What, like the heart halves? Or the pizza slices? I'd rock it no matter what."

"You always talk the talk. But can you walk the walk?"

"Is that a challenge?" Rayshell instigated. "Do it then. Find me the cheesiest one you can think of, and watch me never take it off. I'll be buried dead with it."

"Oh, this is *too* tempting," Trish playfully attested, then pulled out her phone. She immediately opened her favorite shopping app, then punched in the keywords 'friendship necklace' and scrolled through the list of results.

Tobias smiled as he watched the two of them react to the offerings while his pilot lost himself to nostalgia. Kumiko couldn't help but reminisce about the times he so desperately missed; times when he, Navaryn, and Lowenna were an inseparable trio. He found the mannerisms of their human counterparts uncannily similar, which made him wonder whether it was truly their unique nature or the essence of their Celestine prisoners bleeding into their personalities.

While Rayshell squealed in delight over the kawaii offerings of one local polymer artist, Tobias inhaled the aroma of balsamic reduction that floated from her lips. He stared into her hazel eyes, fueled by

Kumiko's contentment. It vexed him to accept that their camaraderie was nothing more than a distant memory. If given the chance, he would sacrifice nearly anything to put things back to the way they used to be; the way he felt they were meant to be.

"Toby?" Rayshell called, then pushed on his shoulder. "*Hello ...?*"

Instead of jolting out of his trance, his earthy brown eyes gently panned to hers while his light smile persisted. Rayshell's childish pout instantly dissolved.

She gulped down the garlicky wad of french fries hampstered in the side of her cheek, then asked, "What's up with you today? You seem, I don't know—"

"Distracted," Trish finished.

Tobias placed his hand on top of Rayshell's. "I'm just enjoying your company. Both of you."

Rayshell mirrored Trish's contorted face. "I'm enjoying yours too," she added, then held the phone in front of his face and asked, "So what do you think of this one?"

Tobias studied the pair of polymer bread slices with cutesy faces, one over jelly and one over peanut butter. "That one's okay. But did you see this one?" he said, pointing to a set made of resin and mica shaped like a full moon.

"I was going for cheesy, remember?"

Tobias thumbed down a few tiles. "Okay, I have it now. This one."

Rayshell and Trish leaned in. He pointed to a quintessential pairing of toilet paper and a neatly coiled turd.

"Which one would you be, Ray?" he asked as Trish nearly fell into tears laughing.

"I know which one," Trish claimed through her fit. "She'd be the shit. Because I'm always the one cleaning up her mess."

Rayshell folded her arms, trying her damnedest to maintain a playful scowl, but ultimately failed under the influence of their merriment. "Well, you got a point. Remember that one time you tried to get Mila and me together at Teagan's when we were still at each other's throats?"

Trish's eyes nearly popped from her skull following her friend's recount. "*What?* What are you talking about?"

"Don't even pretend like you don't remember. Teagan nearly kicked me out after that whole fiasco."

Fearful of what Tobias was thinking, Trish continued to deny every word of her recount.

"And you call *me* forgetful?" she smirked with an arched brow. "It was *your* smooth talkin' that got me off the hook."

While Rayshell continued spouting more of Navaryn's memories, Trish took her by the shoulders until her distant gaze broke from the sky. "Rayshell," she said calmly, "I have absolutely *no* clue *what* you're talking about."

Rayshell's furiously churning thoughts quieted, and in the most believable way she could manage, she chimed, "Come on, it was just a joke."

Tobias stuffed the last of his sandwich into his mouth while his mind churned with Kumiko's thoughts. Hearing Rayshell recount Navaryn's memories like they were her own was jarring yet filled him with eager anticipation. Unfortunately, the awkward silence that followed halted his hope of seeing Navaryn continuing to surface.

A few moments after the waitress brought over their check, a man in a red flannel shirt walked up to the metal gate bordering their table. He repositioned his gray trucker hat so the bill no longer obscured his view.

"There's my lil' girl," he proclaimed with a smile.

"Hi, Dad. How was shopping?"

"Eventful. I had a lovely time trying to track down some of the things from your list. Made one of the clerks do a double-take when I asked them to help me find 'a quinoa'."

Trish and Rayshell's eyes teared up from laughter.

"Yeah, yeah. Laugh it up, too, girls," he said with a genuine smile, then looked at Tobias and extended his hand. "Greg."

"Tobias," he greeted with a firm shake. "Good to meet you."

"Did these two get you to try any of their crazy food? They've got something on the menu that is supposed to be like shredded pork, but it's some weird fruit."

Tobias pointed to his white plate, which held nothing but crumbs, streaks of barbeque sauce, and a few cold garlic fries. "That's what I had. It was actually very good."

Greg cinched his lip. "I dunno. Not sure if I'm ready to cross into that territory yet."

"You'll get there someday, Dad," said Trish with her finger in the air.

"I know, I know. You've been slowly working me over. I don't know if I told you, but I chose a tofu noodle salad over one with beef the other day at work. A few of my coworkers gave me some funny looks." Greg looked at the check in the middle of the table and took out his wallet. "You haven't paid for that yet, have you?"

Trish shook her head.

"Here," he said, handing Trish his card. "Lunch is on me."

The trio thanked Greg for his generosity and insisted that he join them next time and try the jackfruit sandwich. Once the waitress brought him the receipt to sign, they all said their goodbyes.

"Have fun with the move, Ray," said Trish after a tight hug. "Call me if you need any help."

Greg put his arm over his daughter's shoulder as they walked to his truck, then waved goodbye to Tobias and Rayshell. They returned the gesture until he eventually turned around.

"That was nice of him," said Tobias as he slipped on his armored jacket. "I was planning on getting the check."

"Greg is pretty awesome," said Rayshell softly, relieved that his initial remark had nothing to do with her strange outburst. "Probably one of the only parents I don't mind hanging out with."

"Well, hopefully, he'll take us up on that offer soon."

As they both grabbed their helmets, Rayshell added, "We'll see. He works way too much. Probably won't get the chance for at least a few months."

Tobias took Rayshell's hand as they walked to his motorcycle. "Ready to get to some packin' now that we're all fueled up?"

Rayshell nodded. "Thank you again for helping me."

"It's my pleasure. Honestly."

·◗◖·

Their trip home was sunny, brisk, and over way too fast. Tobias pulled into their parking lot and into one of the spaces closest to the stairway, next to the moving truck. Elizabeth was outside sipping on a piping hot cup of black coffee with wild locks and an exhausted look. She had just woken up after a whopping four and a half hours of sleep and dreaded all the work that lay ahead. As Rayshell and Tobias walked down the hall, she glanced their way.

Though it was well into the afternoon, Rayshell greeted, "Good morning, Mom," then hugged her, careful not to spill her coffee.

After a yawn, Elizabeth answered, "I'm glad you're back. Jakobe could use your help with the boxes so we can get the first load over to the new place. I need to hop in the shower. Then I'll help load afterward."

Astute to Elizabeth's state, Tobias chimed, "Why don't you leave the heavy lifting to us and take a rest?"

"And leave those two unsupervised?" she replied, referring to Rayshell and Jakobe. "We'll be here through next week if no one is leading the parade."

"Leave it to me. I'll keep them in gear."

"If you could manage that ...." She briefly looked into his earnest eyes, then gazed back at the passing cars. Halfway expecting him to fail, she still conceded. "Okay. Have at it."

Tobias patted Rayshell's shoulder. "Come on. Let's give your mom a hand and blast through this."

The pair set their gear behind the door and surveyed the front room. Jakobe was kneeling, re-taping one of the boxes Rayshell had packed the other night.

"Do you have any more boxes left in your room to pack, Ray?" Jakobe asked after they greeted each other with their usual procession of hand gestures.

"A few. Why?"

"Don't just tape them along the seam, especially if they're heavy. Do it like this," he said, pointing to the perpendicular layers of tape.

"Why? You just waste more tape that way."

"Is that worse than wasting time repacking the box after it collapses?"

Sensing an impending spat, Tobias interjected in a warm tone, "It's best to tape them like Jakobe said, Ray. I know that firsthand."

"*Finally*. Someone who understands," muttered Jakobe as he stood to his feet.

"Hey, Ray, I'll help your brother load these boxes out here if you want to pack up the rest of your room. Just set them out here when you're done, and we'll take care of them."

Tobias smiled at her juvenile body language as she walked down the hall. It reminded his host of Navaryn's nature all too well.

Under Tobias' lead, they tightly packed the first load of boxes in under two hours. Elizabeth took Jakobe along to help unload the truck while Tobias stayed with Rayshell. The sun had set, and they sat together on the floor at the foot of her bed, enjoying a quick breather from taping and stacking. All of their hard work had lent its payoff, and Tobias relished the pleasant warmth of Rayshell's hand within his.

Kumiko smiled through Tobias. He was incredibly content with the fortuitous opportunity to focus on Navaryn's presence for such an extended period of time, as distant as it was. The priority of keeping her safe was straightforward in her predicament, for Navaryn could not object to his protection. His roused confidence gave him the determination to be the one to bring her home.

19

THE COLD

After being ejected by Trish's protective charms, Joro woke up in a heap of mud in the plains of Eastern Daeva. Slews of Sidwell's ongoing patrols spread across the region, and Joro found himself amidst several of them. While temporarily stripped of his powers and abilities to Parallel or shapeshift due to the effects of the charms, he had to resort to classic stealth to evade the militant soldiers. In an ironically fortunate circumstance, the absence of his powers made him virtually undetectable to those seeking his energy signature. Being no stranger to slipping in and out of shadows and blending into unsuspecting crowds, Joro had little trouble avoiding Sidwell's men. However, returning to the fortress on foot in his vulnerable state, given his notoriety, was more than challenging.

A full four days passed until he had finally reached Merisek's fortress in the punishing region of the lowlands. Numbing cold crept through his shredded boots as he tromped through the freezing snow, while painful aches radiated through his body with every step he took along the unforgiving terrain. In the distance, the familiar rugged peaks of Korviniah came into view through the wispy clouds. With no time or place of reprieve given to regenerate, he struggled with every last step to the cloaked fortress. Yet before he could motion to access the hidden entrance, the portal opened to reveal Merisek standing ominously in front of him. He grabbed Joro by his tattered shirt and pulled him inside, nearly making him stumble to the ground.

As cold as the fortress was, it was cozy compared to the harsh elements Joro had braved for days. There was nothing for him to complain about, although the safety of the fortress was no less comforting, with Merisek angrily looming over him.

"Where have you been?" asked Merisek sternly.

"Can this wait?" Joro replied, then motioned to walk away. "I can barely stand."

"It's been four days!" roared Merisek as he halted Joro's departure. "You will answer me now!"

Joro sighed despondently. "I was Snared out of the realm of Human and had to make my way back on foot."

"You were *Snared?!*" Merisek thundered. "How?! By whom?!"

"That little bitch, Lowenna. Her host has gained her knowledge of charm spells and found a way to attach a Snare to them. I resisted the pull for as long as I could."

"Fool. You should have just left once you felt the pull," Merisek said with a grimace. "Why didn't you?"

Fearing an even greater punishment if he revealed his selfish and opportune intentions, Joro attempted to ease his display of stupidity. "I-I don't know."

Merisek naturally saw through Joro's attempted dodge of the question. "Never mind, I'd rather not hear details of your perverse meddling," he said with a frustrated sigh. "Get back there at once. We need to know what's going on."

"I can't. My power hasn't returned yet."

Merisek persisted, "I'll put you in a vessel then!"

"I'll be useless in a powerless body!"

"Joro, *so help me.* You need to understand. Obtaining the Order is more important than ever right now." Merisek gave a slow exhale. "Claymar is gone."

"Gone? You mean he escaped?! How is that even possible?" Almost immediately after Joro posed his question, he knew who was responsible. He had come to know Merisek's distinctive look whenever the suspect would come up in discussion, and it was present on his face that very moment. "Von," he concluded.

Merisek nodded in response. "He found his way in through a defect in the mountain that led underground."

"Wonderful," said Joro. "How could he have found us?"

"That I do not know. What is clear, however, is that he wasn't acting alone. A Celestine must have accompanied him to get past the C-Poison."

"That's impossible."

"I think you mean *improbable*," Merisek corrected. "Regardless, we must assume that Sidwell will be made aware of our location. Our time is becoming ever more scarce."

Learning of the increased urgency in obtaining Iaalprt was not only an irritation but also made the task at hand feel even more distant. The fact that Von gained the assistance of a Celestine was unforeseen to Merisek. Still, it was more astonishing to Joro, who scoffed at any notion of peaceability between the two realms. For as much as his tendencies revolved around creating chaos, peace between Celestine and Daeva was something he could not allow himself to accept, much less believe. It was enough of a development to cause Joro's anger to surge, though his body could not exert as he needed. He stumbled to his knees, clutching his head in pain.

"Are you alright?" Merisek asked insincerely.

Joro shook the dizziness from his head. "I need to regenerate. How's our food supply?"

"There isn't much. Find what you can."

Joro trekked further into the fortress towards the mess hall with Merisek following behind him. As a kind gesture, Merisek graciously lit the torches lining the corridors along the way to give warmth, though Joro paid no mind. The hollow echo of their footsteps created an irritating ring in his ears as he clumsily tried to soften his steps. Merisek then took hold of Joro's shoulder to guide him the rest of the way.

Aside from a few pieces of hardened, stale bread and some cuts of dried meat, the supplies in the pantries were barren. However, there was no shortage of water because of the abundance of snow during the winter, which Merisek had primarily sustained himself on, along with meager portions of simple grains. Reluctantly, Joro took a hunk of stale bread from the pantry and dropped it onto the large marble counter in the center of the room.

"Perfect," Joro said snidely. "No food. Freezing cold. How much longer can we keep this up?"

"The sooner you quit your whining, the closer we'll be to getting ourselves back on track."

"At least we have one less mouth to feed with Claymar gone," said Joro before gnawing the hunk of bread.

"Well, I'm glad you're able to make light of the situation. Need I remind you that Claymar knows where we are and could show up here with Sidwell and his army at any moment?"

Joro shrugged off Merisek's concern with a wave of his hand. "That would have happened by now," he uttered through his teeth as he bit into a rigid strip of dried meat. "It's not Claymar's style to run to his uncle like that, anyway."

"Perhaps," said Merisek as he took a slow breath. "Though, there's something you should also know. With Claymar gone, our hope of redemption with Daeva is lost as well."

"Redemption?" Joro said, confusedly. "What are you talking about?"

At last, Merisek had revealed his efforts in developing the potions to counter the effects of C-Poison and the torturous experimentation he had conducted on Claymar. While not particularly taken aback by Merisek's discretion nor his treatment of Claymar, Joro was immediately critical of his concocted scheme to return to the good graces of Daeva's leaders.

"Well, I can tell you right now that it's not Sidwell you should be worried about. Claymar will come after you himself, after what you pulled."

Merisek avoided pondering Joro's warning as he poured water into his goblet.

"And as for your deranged plan, there's no question it was doomed to fail."

Merisek pulled the goblet away from his lips. "I beg your pardon?"

"You could have killed Claymar. Honestly, Merisek. Do you not see the insanity in your actions?"

"That's a humorous thing to hear from you."

Joro brushed aside Merisek's antagonistic attempt to detract the conversation's course. "For as long as you tinkered with your little experiment, it doesn't seem like it was working."

"It was working!" yelled Merisek, "Had I been able to finish, I could have made Daeva virtually unstoppable!"

"And if you had killed Claymar in the process? What then?"

"I myself have attained immunity, so therefore Claymar—"

"Claymar is not like you," Joro interrupted. "You forget that *no one* in Daeva is like *you*."

Merisek fell silent.

"Don't be stupid. Even if you succeeded in your little experiment, we both know Lady Kyra will never forgive her father's murderer."

Merisek froze as a bloody scene flashed before his glowing eyes, a sight ingrained in his mind that burned with regret. "That's enough, Joro," he warned.

"What happened to you? The once *illustrious* Merisek, who held the answer to any question, now can't see beyond his own hair-brained ideas."

"Stop it."

"No. Tell me, Merisek," Joro ruthlessly needled. "Where would the Realm's graciousness be if Sidwell were to learn you nearly tortured his nephew to death?"

"I said *shut your mouth!*" Merisek shouted.

A cloud of dust fluttered into the air as Merisek forcefully pummeled his fists through the long marble counter, splitting it into several pieces that fell to the ground. The fierce anger bubbling within him came to a head. His face trembled while his fists throbbed with pulsing blood, though Joro stood before him unfazed.

"Just leave me be and get back to the realm of Human as soon as possible," Merisek commanded as he turned to walk away. "I have more work to do with Ananael."

"Why bother? I thought you said that was a dead end."

"It might not be."

"What did you find?"

Merisek clomped down the corridor without saying another word, leaving Joro alone in the mess hall. Thoroughly agitated by Merisek's increasingly volatile demeanor, he scrounged through the storage room for anything he could find to help restore just enough of his power to Parallel back to the realm of Human. He managed to find a suitably preserved serving of soup. Not even the broth's bland taste, pulpy texture, or sickly cold temperature could deter him from hastily indulging. Within moments, Joro felt a slight reignition of his energy signature.

As Joro rested against the cold stone wall of the storeroom, he recounted his heated discussions with Merisek. Although their latest encounter illustrated their deteriorating trust, he nevertheless kept his motivations on the goal at hand. In his mind, the Order of Existence remained the only avenue through which he could attain his deepest desires and fulfill his most extreme ambitions. To wield such a power, however, would put him on a path only an untold few have dared to walk.

20

THE WARNING

Rayshell and her family kept busy packing as Friday slipped into late afternoon. Tobias had arrived to assist them first thing in the morning. He and Jakobe finished loading the moving truck a second time just as five o'clock had moved into its second half. As promised, Rayshell had packed everything on her daily list, and Elizabeth granted permission to enjoy her evening with Tobias. After reaffirming a curfew, she and Jakobe departed in the moving truck while Rayshell stayed behind to get ready.

"I'm gonna go and change," said Rayshell as she tugged at her black and pink pajama pants. The faded pattern on the fabric was discernible only to her. "I promise I won't take long."

"Alright, Ms. Pajamas. I'll be waiting," Tobias said, then kissed her.

As she walked down the hall, Tobias switched over to a different playlist of music on Jakobe's old device.

"Hey, can you turn it up some more?" Rayshell called.

After fiddling with the dial on the Bluetooth speaker, Tobias paced the room for a moment. "Who is this, again?" he asked from the hallway entry.

"Orgy," Rayshell answered back from inside the room.

"That's right," said Tobias, tapping his fingers against the wall to the drumbeat.

"Trish and I saw them right before summer break started," she added. "Her dad took us."

"Dang. Trish's dad really is awesome."

Rayshell agreed with a chuckle as she reflected on that night. "I don't think they were his cup of tea, but he made it through the whole set. I gotta give him credit because he stayed by our side the whole night even though we were front and center." Rayshell popped her head out from behind the door and added, "And we were singing with them the entire time."

One of Kumiko's memories slipped behind Tobias' eyes as the next song, "Platinum," began to play.

Navaryn sat at an ornate white grand piano, dressed in a shimmering gown with a high slit that gave her access to the dagger she kept strapped to her thigh. A modest group of distinguished-looking guests had encircled her as she hammered away at the lower end of the keyboard. She was nineteen, just a year older than her human host, and still not accustomed to being in the spotlight. Nevertheless, her performance always drew a crowd. Kumiko knew that a dim room did well to calm her nerves, so he called away some of the flames from the overhead master chandelier with a set of swift hand movements. With two glasses of wine in hand, he cut through the crowd until no one blocked the line of sight to his beloved Navaryn.

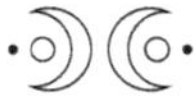

Rayshell, who had been speaking throughout the recollection, flicked off her bedroom light and stood in front of Tobias with her jacket over her arm. Not even her movements had the power to compel him out of the flashback. With squinted eyes, Rayshell pushed on his shoulder with her finger.

"It's a good song, isn't it?" she said. "It's kinda old school, but it still holds up."

For a moment, her eyes looked just the same as Navaryn's. Smiling, Tobias wrapped his arms around her. "You smell amazing," he whispered after filling his lungs with the sweet, earthy fragrance trapped within her hair.

"Toby! That tickles!" she said through a giggle fit as he took another breath close to her ear. "I don't know what you're talking about. I didn't even spray anything."

"You don't need it," he professed. "It's your fragrance that I like."

Rayshell's giggles waned as she slowly stepped away from Tobias. "Okay, no more Orgy for you," she said, then turned off the music. "You're acting like a weirdo."

As the couple grabbed their riding gear, the home phone rang. Rayshell's heart hit the ground as she looked at the dusty and crooked clock face on the wall. There was only one person whom she thought it could be.

"Are you gonna get that?" Tobias asked after the fourth modulation.

Rayshell shook herself out of her blank stare, grabbed the phone, and walked to her room to take the call privately. Tobias turned to watch her with curious eyes and inched down the hall after her.

"Hello?" Rayshell answered in a faint voice.

Through the sound of chewing, smacking, and unsettling heavy breathing, Jack's excited voice beamed through the receiver, "Ah, Rayshell! How's my girl?"

Rayshell's eyebrows folded in defeat. She wanted to throw the phone out the window and forget he ever called, though she resolved to stall him further. After forcing a few fake sniffles into the receiver, she replied, "Hey, Jack. It's been a rough couple of days."

"Oh no. You sound like you're comin' down with something. Have you taken ill?" he asked.

Tobias stood beside Rayshell's bedroom door. With folded arms, he eavesdropped on her peculiar lies.

"Yeah. I think I've exhausted myself ... work and school have been so hard to keep up with."

Though he anticipated the refusal of his offer, Jack said, "Well, if you're feeling up for it, I thought we could get together today. Laura's out shopping with Brian, and they should be back soon. I can come by and pick you up once they get back."

"Aww, that sounds nice, but," Rayshell answered between a few loud coughs, then plugged her nose, "I just don't feel very good. I'd hate to get you all sick. I think Jakobe is starting to come down with something because of me."

"Well, I'm sorry to hear that you're sick. I know Brian was excited to see you. He told me he wanted to try his hand at making dinner tonight."

"He's such a good kid. That's so sweet of him."

"Yep. And he *sure* misses you."

Rayshell rolled her eyes at Jack's clunky persuasions. In a raspy voice, she replied, "How about I cook dinner next week? Monday night, after school. How does that sound? I won't make a very good guest today."

After another bout of loud chewing, Jack added, "You're always great company."

Frustrated that he was not taking 'no' for an answer, Rayshell concluded, "I need to get some rest today, Jack. I don't feel good." She tried to remain composed as she imagined his grimace on the other end of the phone.

"Okay, Ray. I understand. I hope you feel better by then."

After bidding Jack a quick and hollow farewell, she hung up the phone and sighed in desperate relief. Tobias quickly retraced his steps and settled into a chair by the front door.

"Who was that?" he asked as Rayshell exited her room.

"Eh, just a family friend."

Tobias could tell she wasn't interested in answering anything more about the phone call. He ran his fingers through his shiny brown locks, then changed the subject. "Sorry if I creeped you out earlier."

Rayshell looked at him with a puzzled expression. "What are you talking about?"

"Earlier, when I smelled your hair."

Rayshell couldn't keep from blushing. "Don't worry about it."

The traffic was light for a Friday night, but Rayshell figured it was due to the holiday weekend. After a quick trip in the direction of their school, Tobias made a U-turn and pulled into a large plaza across the street from the froyo shop Rayshell and Trish frequented. One end of the strip was full of tiny shops, either in the process of closing for the night or tucked away behind protective bars. Tobias cut through the sparsely lit parking lot toward a large discount grocer, then rounded the corner. Tucked beneath clusters of overgrown trees was the bowling alley.

Once Tobias killed the engine, the pair hopped off the motorcycle and removed their helmets. Instantly, the noxious combination of cigarettes and fruity-smelling vape intensified. Rayshell held her breath as she crossed the parking lot through the rings of smoking patrons, then followed Tobias through the glass doors, greeted by blaring music from a genre neither of them cared for. The black lights were on, and the carpet was a satisfying but equally disorienting neon mess.

"Are we still picking up your dad's truck?" Rayshell asked under the sound of a persistent synthetic snare.

As Tobias handed the scruffy attendant his card to pay for a couple of games, he answered, "Yep. And maybe I can make you something to eat when we get there."

Rayshell laughed as their receipt printed. "Do I sense pizza rolls in my future?"

Tobias scribbled his signature, unaware that it was only half-correct. "Pizza rolls?"

"Did you kick the habit or something?"

Tobias' confusion intensified as Kumiko's thoughts and emotions ran through him at full blast. "I can make other things, you know," he insisted.

"*Sure*," she playfully teased as they walked hand in hand to their lane.

·)C·

Halfway through their first game, Rayshell scampered off to the concession stand and brought back two apples, some water, and a bag of spicy kettle-cooked potato chips for them to share. With a wad of napkins pinched between her fingers, she jammed one of the apples into her mouth as Tobias made his move.

"Damn it," he muttered as her giggles crept to his ears.

"Nice try," she reassured, referring to his admirable attempt to clear a 7-10 split. "You're on a roll. That's the third time."

"I think this ball is cursed or something. I'm getting another."

As he rummaged through the rack behind their lane, Rayshell turned to him and asked nervously, "Hey, Toby. Can you keep a secret?"

"If it's about how to clear those damn splits, then probably not."

"Seriously. Can you?" She opened the stubborn bag of chips, then shoved a handful into her mouth.

With an acceptable replacement ball in hand, he reassured, "Of course I can. Why? What's up?"

After wiping her hands clear of apple juices and flavor crumbs with a crumpled napkin, Rayshell muttered, "Remember this?" and pulled the pendant out of her shirt.

"I remember. And I also remember how Trish kicked you."

She shrugged off his comment, then confessed in a timid tone just loud enough to breach the ambiance, "There are people after me, Toby."

His eyes widened as a hurricane of Kumiko's emotions pelted him. He asked earnestly, "Who's after you? Are they people you know?"

"They're not anyone *I* know."

"Do you know why they're after you?"

"They think I can help them find something. Something I've never heard of until last week."

Kumiko's thoughts fed right into Tobias as his nerves began to surge. Despite knowing she was undoubtedly referring to Iaalprt, he pressed further, "What is it?"

"A special book," Rayshell revealed. "Not something you can find at the library or bookstore, if that makes any sense."

Tobias continued to listen with feigned curiosity.

"But I don't know where it is, and these people seem to think I do. I'm scared because they don't believe me, and they're not going to leave me alone until they get what they want."

Trying his best to tap into relatable advice, Kumiko coaxed Tobias' reply. "Have you told your mom?" Following her adamant declination by head-shake, he continued, "Have you gone to the police?"

Rayshell grabbed her ball from the return, shaking her head. "They can't help me. Nobody can. Especially if I can't explain who I'm being chased by without sounding like a lunatic."

After a fierce gutter ball, Rayshell stayed looking at her frame until she heard her ball come back through the return. On her second try, she toppled two of the far left pins.

"I don't need the police, anyway," she said, then tucked the pendant back under her shirt. "Not when I have this. It keeps them from finding me, somehow."

"Trish has the same pendant as you. Does that mean they're after her, too?" asked Tobias, recalling his earlier observation.

Rayshell nearly choked on her sip of water. She looked him dead in the eyes as he rested his elbows atop the counter.

"They are, aren't they?"

Rayshell indirectly confirmed by blurting, "She's gonna kick my ass if she finds out I told you anything. Do you swear to keep this a secret?"

Tobias nodded. "Of course. I already told you I would."

"We're going through the same shit, and she doesn't know where the book is either. And if I somehow figure out where it is, I'm tempted just to tell them so they'd leave us alone."

"Don't tell them anything," Tobias urged impulsively. "You mustn't."

After Rayshell had as much awkward silence as she could take, she muttered, "You probably think I'm crazy, huh?"

Aiming to give her the confidence she needed, Tobias responded, "Crazy? No. I believe you. But since you won't report this to anyone, I'll stay by your side to protect you."

Something about his proclamation was undeniably nostalgic, yet comforting, since it came from Tobias. "You'd do that?" she uttered softly. "Why?"

"Because I care about you," he professed, then went back to

picking at the crumbly chips on his napkin. "But answer me this. Are you sure you don't know where this book is?"

It took Rayshell a few moments to muster her simple reply. "I'm sure."

"Have you tried to figure out where it is?" he pressed.

Rayshell's eyes widened as his gaze intensified. "It's not me, but what's *inside* of me that knows. That's who they're after."

His prodding softened once Rayshell grew agitated. Rather than continuing to pry, he simply reaffirmed his promise to protect her. The remainder of their evening chugged along as Rayshell's nervousness steadily waned. However, as they neared the final frames, a familiar, pitchy laugh broke the neutral ambiance. Rayshell's heart sank as she turned to the register, where she spotted Stephanie, Amanda, and a few more of their friends. Fortunately, it didn't appear that Shawn was among their party.

"You okay?" asked Tobias on account of Rayshell's tense posture.

"I think so," she answered, then readied herself for what she hoped would be the first strike of the evening. "But it might be wise to wrap this game up."

Just as she wound up to make her move, both Stephanie and Amanda's obnoxious laughter racketed again. After roughly two meters down the lane, her bright pink ball dove right into the gutter. Tobias cringed but quickly reassured her that her next try would be better. Though he ended up being right, it wasn't by much. With a stroke of luck, Tobias managed to avoid yet another split and cleared most of his frame, taking his score into the lead by two points. Reveling in triumph with his hands held high, he turned to Rayshell, already in her outdoor boots.

"No applause? Not even a congratulatory kiss?" called Tobias as Rayshell slipped on her armored jacket.

With a smirk, she muttered, "Nice job stealing my win."

"Uh-oh, don't tell me you're a sore loser," he teased, then worked on swapping out his shoes. "That'll spell no pizza rolls for *you* tonight."

"Oh, no. How could I possibly continue on in life?" she teased in a monotonous tone. "You know, I would have won if they hadn't shown up."

The pair grabbed their gear, dropped their shoes off at the counter, and then took their leave. Before they disappeared behind the corner of the entrance hall, Rayshell peered down to the far end of the alley to ensure Stephanie and the others hadn't spotted them. Her movement wasn't subtle enough to elude Tobias. With a smile, he put his arm over her shoulder and reassured her that everything was fine.

Courtesy of the nearby smokers, the sickly sweet vapor and acrid combustion hovered in the frosty evening air as the couple exited the alley. As they passed between a set of bright orange lights, Tobias mocked a rendition of Stephanie's laughter into Rayshell's ear.

"You're *way* too good at that."

Tobias kissed the side of her head as they cut through the parking lot. While he dug in his pocket for his keys, he spotted an obscured figure sitting atop his bike.

"Yo!" shouted Tobias, then motioned for Rayshell to stop at his side. "You're on the wrong bike, *friend*."

Rayshell clutched her helmet as the dark figure took a more recognizable form.

"You know, I think I'll go for my license, too," Shawn's antagonistic voice called. "That way, I can be as cool as you."

Tobias stood in a defeated posture and responded, "Sure. Do whatever you like. Be whoever you want. Just get off my bike, man."

Shawn eventually heeded his demand, though they knew he wouldn't simply walk away.

"Do you think it will work?" he asked as he approached.

"I don't know. *Sure*, I guess," Tobias replied hurriedly.

"I wasn't talking to you," Shawn said, lifting his chin. "I was talking to your girlfriend over there."

Rayshell clenched her teeth as Shawn's baby blue eyes gave her a quick stab. Rather than dreading their confrontation, she was more concerned by a peculiar sensation that ignited her nerves. Soon, her mind slipped into a persistent numbing darkness.

"This is getting old, bro. Please just back off. We're leaving, alright."

The fact that Tobias wasn't looking for a fight made Shawn all the more eager to antagonize him. "Your snitchin' ass ain't gonna weasel outta this."

"What do you want? An apology?"

Shawn stepped uncomfortably close and replied, "Sure. Let's start there."

"Look. I'm not sorry for anything. You're fucked up for what you did. Not just to Rayshell, but to the other girls, too."

"I don't remember that being any of your fucking business. Or anyone else's."

"Fine," Tobias conceded. "It's your right to blame me for everyone learning who you really are. But it doesn't change the fact that what you did was wrong."

"Fuck you, Tobias!" yelled Shawn. "Mister *Knight in Shining Armor*. You think you're better than me, don't you?"

Tobias' eyes hardened. The influence of his host's temperament kept his nerves from catching fire. "Why don't you just go inside and join your friends while you still got 'em?"

Shawn looked into Tobias' eyes as their hot breath collided in the air. Their bickering garnered the attention of the smoking circles behind them. Shawn scanned the curious eyes that happened his way and balled his eager fists. Before he made his move, Rayshell erupted into hysterical laughter. Puzzled by her outburst, both Tobias and Shawn looked her way. When Rayshell's fit settled, she corrected her wilted posture and looked at Shawn with a set of eyes that were no longer fearful.

Wearing an eerie smile, she sauntered toward him and called out, "Even when the book is closed right in your face, you still don't stop."

"Ray?" Tobias called, hoping to redirect her attention.

"But then again, you've proven incapable of conceding to anything. You, *little boy*, are one of the worst types of people."

As Tobias called for her once more, Rayshell put her hand up to silence him in a fashion his host was more than familiar with. The butterflies in his stomach suddenly dropped to his feet like stones. Before Tobias could compose his racing, anxious mind, Rayshell handed him her helmet and continued Shawn's way.

Fascinated to see such a drastic change in her demeanor, Shawn found himself unable to respond to her eloquent insults.

"... and I'm curious how clever you felt, waiting in the darkness like a rat."

Rayshell stood close enough to feel his body heat reach for her like grabby hands. With her unnerving smile prominent, she looked down at his clenched fists and chuckled. "If you're still looking for a fight," she whispered in a decadent tone, "then fight *me*."

Tobias couldn't hear Rayshell's antagonization, but Kumiko's instincts flooded in once she shifted her weight onto her back leg.

Shawn feigned his intent to back down, then quickly moved in for a sneaky backhand. Guided by Navaryn's keen senses, Rayshell dodged his initial swing and continued to evade his increasingly aggressive attacks. Moments into the scuffle, a few curious bystanders had wandered over to the trio to observe. Every line on Shawn's scowling face had deepened as she deflected his punches one after the other.

"Slow," Rayshell critiqued in a very disappointed tone. "Messy. Too wide. Ugh, are you even *trying?!*"

Frustrated, Shawn lunged with the intent to tackle Rayshell to the pavement. Yet again, she stepped to the side at the perfect moment.

"You're wasting my time. I know children who can fight better than you!"

The surrounding subtle laughter made Shawn's face feel like it was on the verge of exploding. Every advance was expertly out-maneuvered until Rayshell lost her footing over a hunk of crumbled pavement. Shawn seized his opportunity to overtake her and grabbed her by the shoulders. Rayshell smiled in the same maniacal fashion as earlier, then kissed his forehead with hers. As soon as his first uneasy footstep settled behind him, she swept him to the ground.

"You can't even fall right," she added after his head finished bouncing off the pavement.

Rayshell then sat on his stomach and watched him wince and writhe while she cocked her arm back. The stone butterflies at Tobias' feet fell through the center of the earth as she unleashed a series of blunt punches into his face.

"You're not even trying to block me. Have you given up?" she taunted.

"Ray!" shouted Tobias. "That's enough!"

Rayshell ignored his plea and continued to pack Shawn's face in until he seized her by the wrist. Irritated by his interference, she ripped her arm free and socked him once more for good measure. Rayshell smiled as she admired her handiwork and basked in the unprecedented fear in Shawn's eyes. His face was left a bloody, puffy mess on display for all of the spectators to behold.

As Shawn coughed up the blood that ran down the back of his throat, Rayshell bent down to his ear and whispered, "This is your final warning. Keep the book closed and set it on the shelf like a good little boy."

Shawn looked into her piercing eyes just in time to catch a frisky white flicker bounding through her irises. Though it appeared odd, he was too dazed to consider it anything other than the glint of the overhead streetlights.

Tobias firmly shoved her helmet into her awaiting hands, dissolving her devilish grin. They looked at each other for a few tense moments before Rayshell's expression suddenly grew troubled. Through Tobias' eyes, Kumiko could tell she had returned from wherever Navaryn had sent her.

"Let's go," he commanded in a firm voice, then slipped his helmet on.

Rayshell took a moment to once-over the growing crowd and Shawn, who lay bloodied on the ground, then looked to her throbbing, scuffed knuckles. Once Tobias revved the engine, she quickly readied herself for their ride. After cutting through the curious crowd, the pair sped out of the parking lot and dashed down the main street.

Shawn waited for the sound of Tobias' motorcycle to clear from the air before he picked himself up off the ground. His face and body ached, but his shattered ego pained him the deepest. It wasn't until he had finished brushing the rubble from his light blue overshirt that he realized how just many onlookers surrounded him. His face soured at the slew of phones aimed at him, recording every embarrassing moment.

"That chick totally whooped your ass!" one of the spectators called out, rousing the others to laughter.

"Fuck you," Shawn griped, then shoved his way through the wall of bodies.

Ignoring the obnoxious mirth of the crowd was impossible. Shawn doubled his furious pace toward the bowling alley entrance, then stopped before the glass doors. In disbelief of his disheveled reflection, he slowly raised his hand and pressed over the glimmering streaks of red.

Suddenly, Stephanie's astonished face hardened behind his reflection in the glass. She pushed the door open with wide eyes, looking as though she was moments away from crying. "Oh my god, Shawn. What happened!?"

Shawn looked at the drying blood on his fingertips, then shook his head. "Nothing," he answered coldly.

Stephanie folded her arms and waited for him to disclose more details, but all he did was remove his overshirt and use it to wipe the blood from his face.

"I'm out. Tell the others that I needed to leave," said Shawn as he headed for his car.

"Wait a second. I'm coming with you."

"No, you're not. Catch a ride home with Ryo or something."

His reply stopped Stephanie in her tracks. With tears streaming down her face, she called out for him, only to be ignored entirely. Confused and hurt, she watched him peel out of the parking lot and disappear down the street.

21

THE TALK

Saturday was another non-stop day for Rayshell and her family, but their hard work had paid off. By three o'clock in the afternoon, they packed the moving truck with the final load. Elizabeth and Jakobe set out on their way while Tobias and Rayshell stayed behind to wrap up odds and ends. Rayshell would have otherwise been less than thrilled to take on the numerous responsibilities, but with Tobias at her side, she was smiling the entire time. Fortunately, their busy agenda also kept her from thinking about their encounter with Shawn at the bowling alley and the sight of his scared, bloody face.

Tobias took her by the hand just as her eyes fell into the maturing afternoon sky. "Ready?" he asked.

"Fuck yeah!" Rayshell cheered. "I can't tell you how long I've been waiting for this moment."

"This might sound lame, but I'm happy to be a part of it."

After a kiss, they rounded up the overflowing garbage bags.

"Do you need to say goodbye to anyone?" he asked as he led the way downstairs.

Rayshell shook her head. "Nah. There aren't any other kids here, and most of the adults look like creeps."

Tobias rearranged a few donation boxes in the pickup truck while Rayshell sprinted to the office to drop off the keys her mother had packed in a yellow clasp envelope. It was a relief to relinquish them, and she would have recorded the drop for her brother if she had a working phone.

"I can't believe this is it," she confessed. As Tobias reversed the truck out of the parking space, she turned back toward their old apartment door and flipped it off.

"You hated it that much?" he said and slid on his sunglasses.

She nodded while dusting off her black and gray striped shirt as though his comment had sullied it.

While Rayshell listed each of the annoyances that came to mind, Tobias inched out of the parking lot, looking for an opportunity to cut into the intersection.

"... and I've already told you about having to do our laundry across the street. That was the worst. I hated staying while my clothes were washing because people always tried to talk to me, and if I just left, then—"

Rayshell paused mid-sentence as a familiar tan station wagon caught her eye from the left. Once the turn signal started to blink, her face flushed, and a searing urge to flee overtook her.

In a serious tone that grew louder each time she repeated the word, she ordered, "Drive."

"You want me just to blitzkrieg into the middle of traffic? What's gotten into you?!"

"For fuck's sake. Just *go!*" she yelled, then quickly ducked into his lap as Jack slowed to turn into the parking lot.

Tobias was keenly aware that her strange behavior stemmed from the approaching vehicle, but with nowhere to turn safely, he had to stay in place. Jack turned into the parking lot and hit his back tire on the curb on the way in. Hiding his embarrassment, Jack rested his eyes upon Tobias' neutral yet watchful gaze, hidden behind dark lenses. Their eye contact lasted a short moment, but for Tobias and his pilot, time felt like it stopped. Kumiko immediately sensed his unmistakably dreadful Daeva energy. It saturated the air like a vile stench wafting upon decrepit and stifling wind. Neither Kumiko nor his host knew who the individual was, but there was no denying he was someone

Rayshell was trying to avoid.

Mid-day traffic seized again, but Tobias managed to inch his truck through an opening. After they passed through a third traffic signal, he put his hand on Rayshell's shoulder to signal she was safe, though she was hesitant to correct her posture.

"You okay?" asked Tobias as he turned onto the freeway onramp.

"Yeah," she whispered while wiping the tears from her eyes. "Remember what I told you at the bowling alley? That there are people after me."

"Was he one of them?"

Rayshell nodded. "That's Jack. I've known him for as long as I can remember. But something about him just changed all of a sudden."

"Changed? What do you mean?"

"It was like one minute he was the same Jack I always remembered, then just days later, he was different. And the things he said when he didn't know I was listening. I-I'm just afraid to be anywhere near him."

After Rayshell and Tobias dropped off their items at the donation station, they headed to the new house. Silence returned to the cab, and Rayshell looked out the window nervously. Only one more day remained before school resumed, where she would need to act with an even more heightened sense of caution. Sadly, the feeling of sanctuary she anticipated with the conclusion of the move began to elude her.

·)(·

Jack, piloted by the gluttonous Nathaniel, sat in his car for as long as it took him to finish a large bag of spicy onion hot chips, two cans of soda, and a small box of individually wrapped dessert cakes. After stuffing the plastic wrappers back into the colorful box, he shoved it into the pile of trash behind his seat and sucked his messy fingertips clean. The mixture of residual oils and saliva made it difficult for him to grip the chrome-plated door handle, though he eventually managed to exit the car. The brisk air immediately cleared his sinuses of the funky, metamorphic stench brewing inside the cab as he pulled the thick sienna sweater down over his plump belly.

The apartment complex was eerily quiet. Jack looked up to the darkening sky just in time to catch a glimpse of the powdery moon amidst a break in the low, racing clouds. A gust of wind scraped against his backside. Jolted by a chill, he pulled down his sweater again and finally recognized that it no longer fit the shape of his figure the same way it did a week ago.

After a short breather at the midway point, Jack ascended the staircase. His possessor was a bit nervous about interacting with Elizabeth if she were home, but pressed on to investigate, growing increasingly suspicious that something was amiss. To keep his approach casual, he chose to come alone. Once he reached their door, he stood before it until the moment of courage slipped ahead of his anxiety. He rapped, then fidgeted while waiting for an answer that never came. Puzzled, he put his ear to the door but heard only silence. He knocked in waves of growing intensity until he stopped just shy of kicking the door in.

Jack groaned, then took a moment to rest against the banister while he caught his breath. As he pondered where Rayshell and the rest of her family could be, a shadowy figure peeked out of the neighboring apartment.

"Excuse me?" a modest, gritty voice called out. "Are you looking for the Stones?"

"The wh-*yeah*," Jack said, assuming it was Rayshell's surname. "Indeed, I am."

The older woman inched inside the threshold in response to Jack's swift gait. She picked up her large, thick glasses dangling from a thin golden chain over her chest and squinted at him as she put them on. Her grayish-blue eyes hesitantly studied his bulky figure.

"Well, it seems you just missed them."

"What do you mean? Did they go to dinner without me?" Jack belly-rolled and rubbed his hands over his stomach. Once it was apparent there would be no rejoinder, he sighed a heavy breath.

"No, that's not what I meant. I mean, you just missed them."

Jack folded his arms and replied, "I'm not sure I follow."

"They're gone."

Jack pursed his lips. "Gone?"

"They're not here anymore."

"Mildred, you're confusin' the poor man," her husband called out from the front room.

Jack peeked into the dim living room after she threw up her hands in defeat.

"They jus' finished movin'." The older man paused his television and cleared his throat. "Wrapped up the last trip not long before you started poundin'."

Jack struggled to hide his manner of shock. "Do you know where they moved to?" he asked.

"Sure don't. Most we've exchanged were the occasional hi's and byes with 'em."

"I see. Well, ah, I appreciate the help," said Jack as he stepped back onto their welcome mat.

The man put his hand in the air to bid him farewell. Soon after, Mildred appeared out of nowhere and abruptly slammed the front door. Jack closed his eyes as the gust of wind rolled over him. Fighting to control the anxious rage that welled in his gut, he took out his cell phone, which he rarely used for anything else but ordering food, and dialed out.

Sprawled atop their living room couch, Laura wore a completely checked-out look. The blinds were drawn, and the room was dark, aside from the sickly white glow from the television.

"*Now, I know what you're thinking. And yes. This necklace is definitely one-of-a-kind. Quantities are limited, so be sure to call now ....*" the television persuaded as the home phone rang.

Laura groaned as she shuffled into the kitchen on stiff legs. "Hello?" she answered impatiently.

"They're gone!" Nathaniel yelled into the receiver as he walked to the car.

Startled, she nearly lost her grip on the phone. "Gone?"

"Yes. All of them. Gone. I can't believe this is happening. Joro and Merisek are going to be furious!"

"*Slow down!*" demanded Eitha as she turned off the television. "Now, what happened?"

"Well, my *darling wife*," Nathaniel began sarcastically, "I found out from a couple of would-be corpses who live next door that Rayshell and her family moved. They've packed, and they're gone." He swung open his car door and plopped into the driver's seat.

Eitha caught Brian peeking into the room around the corner. "If this isn't a coincidence, then she's a clever girl," she said while ushering him down the hall to his bedroom. "This is all your fault, you know."

"My fault?! How do you figure?"

"Because!" she roared as she slammed Brian's door shut. "This was *your* show to run. Merisek was the one who put *you* in charge. Or did all those sweet treats rot your memory?"

"Oh, so we're going to blame this on the food, now."

"I'm blaming this on you! Not only have you stuck out like such a sore thumb this whole time, but you've also refused to listen to anything I've had to say. If we did things my way—"

"Spare me, Eitha. I'm not going to listen to you badger me." As Nathanial pondered, he scraped away at the gray cakey buildup around the steering wheel. "I have an idea."

"You know what? I don't care to hear it! Just fix this before Joro or Merisek catches wind of your incompetence!" Eitha hissed, then hung up the phone.

Nathaniel's burning rage darkened Jack's blank expression into a ferocious scowl. He tossed his phone into the passenger seat and firmly gripped the steering wheel with sweaty hands. Though it was more palatable to assume that Rayshell's departure was happenstance and that she would soon check in with an update, his instincts sided with the notion that she was wise to their charade. Brimming with frustration, he vented with a short-lived, fiery tantrum and didn't consider his lack of privacy until he finished. Sure enough, he discovered Mildred peering at him from behind her foggy window with judging eyes. He kept his scowl intact as he started his car and then recklessly peeled out of the parking lot.

"Can I, um, help you?" asked a thin woman with stringy hair as she flipped through a stack of receipts behind a plexiglass window.

With a beaming smile and nervous eyes hidden behind dark sunglasses, Jack sauntered to the faux granite counter. "Hello, ma'am," he began in an overly polite manner. "I was, ah, looking for my niece's schedule for this comin' week."

The woman cinched her lip at his inquiry, wondering if he had any idea how suspicious he looked. "Well, sir. " As my other associates have already explained to you, we can only give that information to a parent or guardian," she stated and looked to where she thought his eyes were.

"I'm sorry that I keep asking. It's just that I'm planning a little surprise for her after school. A late birthday present. It would be a shame for me to set everything up on a day she's working." Jack leaned in so that he could read her badge. The words 'department manager' were emblazoned in gold above her name.

"I understand, but—"

"Patricia," he said, then smiled even harder. "My, that's a pretty name."

Taken aback by the disingenuous compliment, she sighed a defeated breath and clipped together the bundle of receipts. "Why don't you just ask her parents for her schedule?"

"Well, I totally could. It's just that I was here to pick up some— socks. So I figured, why not ask while I'm here?"

Patricia dusted the lint off her cerulean blazer, seizing a moment to compose herself. "Are you a parent, sir?"

"Why, yes, I am."

"Then I would hope that as a parent, you would appreciate why I can't simply hand over information to anyone, no matter who they claimed to be."

Apparent that his efforts were futile, Jack decided to give up. His wavering smile held on long enough for a simple yet cordial farewell before departing the manager's station. Muttering a string of curses, he picked up the pace until he was full-blown barreling through the crowded aisles. After carelessly rounding a fully-stocked end cap, he bumped into a postpartum woman and her stroller. Amidst her panicked shriek, she caught her stroller from tipping over. Her newborn began to wail as she shouted after Jack for an explanation, but he didn't so much as bat an eye. Furious yet focused, he continued through the automatic doors in an unheeding gait.

The evening sky was dark, and the frosty air stung Jack's nostrils as he breathed furiously. He plucked the sunglasses from his face just as a young man slipped in front of a slower-moving couple at the edge of the parking lot. Once he hopped onto the curb, Jack spotted the young man's name tag bouncing from the lanyard over his white hoodie. Thinking on his feet, he approached him with a wave.

"Hey Manny, have you seen Rayshell? I thought she was working today."

Manny's curious eyes rose to Jack. "Nah, she has the day off," he answered. "She's scheduled tomorrow, though. Seven to three, I think."

"Got it," he said, doing his best to keep a relaxed demeanor. "Have a good one."

Without losing his pace, Manny took out his phone and started scrolling through a string of notifications. "You too, Frank," he said, throwing up his hand. "I hope you were able to make a dent in that restock for me."

It was then that Jack understood the reason for his good fortune. With a sly smile, he returned to his station wagon and excitedly ripped open a fresh box of snack cakes while he pondered his next move.

·)(·

Illuminated by the dim yellow light of her bedside table lamp, Trish sat against her headboard, half-tucked into her billowy comforter. Plagued by vivid nightmares, relentless intrusions of Lowenna's memories, and a series of odd sensations throughout her body, she didn't dare leave her room the entire day.

She swept the drapery of her unruly curls to the side and stared into her open palm while another bizarre sensation churned beneath her skin. What began as a pleasantly warm swell in her veins quickly transpired into an uncomfortable vibration. Wincing, she watched her swollen hand jitter with tense and wary eyes. Though it felt like her arm would soon split into ribbons, she rejected the urgency to run to her father in the next room.

A long and thin vacillating hand began to trail away from Trish's in what looked like a distorted reflection. The farther the apparition pulled down her arm, the more painful the vibrations became. She closed her teary eyes and prepared herself to embrace the likely departure of the reticent Celestine within her, but suddenly the uncomfortable sensations waned. The phantom hand quickly merged with her own in a final series of tremulous movements. While gasping for air and clutching her throbbing arm, a gentle knock sounded.

"Sweetheart?" Greg called out. "Can I come in?"

Wide-eyed, Trish wiped the sweat from her brow and answered, "Sure, Dad," as she grabbed one of her half-read books from the nightstand.

Before he stepped in, he clicked on her bedroom light.

"Geez, Dad. A warning next time?" she hissed with closed eyes.

After her father apologized, he asked, "Is everything okay? You've been in here all day. I don't even think I've seen you come out to make lunch."

With squinty eyes still trying to adjust to the bright light, Trish answered plainly, "I'm fine."

Once it was apparent there would be nothing more to her statement, Greg leaned against the door casing and asked, "What's got you so occupied in here?"

"Schoolwork. I was just taking a break to finish reading, um ..." Trish quickly read the cover and stopped herself from announcing the embarrassing title. After cramming the would-be romance novel under her pillow, she nervously answered, "... something my friend let me borrow."

With an arched eyebrow, Greg sat at the foot of her bed. "It's getting late, and I bet you're hungry."

Trish rubbed her achy arm with her gaze on the floor, unsure how to tell her father she wanted to be alone.

"Wanna maybe head over to that vegan spot you like so much? It's almost eight and a perfect time for dinner."

Shaking her head, Trish answered, "I'm still in my pajamas, and I don't really want to change."

"That's okay. We can get it to go."

"I'm not really hungry."

Disappointed that she declined her favorite restaurant but hopeful he could still engage her interest, Greg replied, "How about we pull out the ol' 'que? There's a bunch of stuff we can grill up. Like onions, mushrooms, chicken ...."

"Dad," Trish whined as he continued listing ingredients.

"... *broccoli*."

Trish's adamancy vanished once she met her father's sincere eyes.

"I'll even eat it this time," he said as he cracked a smile.

Wooed by his offer, she asked, "Promise?"

Greg reached over and patted her cold, sockless foot sticking out from underneath her comforter. "I promise."

Trish clipped up her rebellious, unbrushed hair, threw on one of her favorite puntastic sweatshirts, then met her father in the kitchen. She grabbed a knife and began cubing some of the vegetables he had just washed.

"We don't have to eat the broccoli, you know," she said as her father held a crown of it under hot water.

With a disgusted expression, he answered back, "No, no. I made a promise. Just try and make it tasty."

"Looks like you're more bothered by the smell than the taste," she teased as she caught a whiff of the sulfuric odor coming from the sink.

Greg sighed defeatedly. "It tastes exactly what it smells like. A nasty old fart. There, I said it."

Trish lost herself in laughter. "You sound like you're four."

"Go on, kid. Laugh it up."

Once Trish got her giggles under control, she wiped the joyful tears from her eyes and resumed chopping the vegetables. They worked in tandem to prepare the skewers, setting the broccoli aside in a foil-lined tray. Trish passed her father the bottle of liquid aminos, but he never took it from her hand.

Puzzled, she looked to her father and asked, "What is it?"

"You, you look so grown up," he said with a peculiar expression.

Blushing, Trish slid the bottle toward him atop the counter, then continued where she had left off. "Come on, Dad. You act like you haven't seen me in forever or something."

"But I mean it. I remember like it was yesterday that you needed your little step stool so you could help out in the kitchen," he said, mimicking the clumsy movements of a toddler. "But now, look at you. In just a few more months, you'll be on your way to college."

Trish smiled uneasily, predicting his following statement.

"Your mother would be so proud of you."

Doing her best to keep a positive expression for his sake, she answered, "I know, Dad."

Opting against lingering in the uncomfortable silence he knew was to come, her father patted her on the shoulder, grabbed the tray of seasoned skewers, and then walked to the back door. "Let's get that fire going. Did you doctor up that broccoli as best as you could?"

"Yes, I did. They won't taste like farts. But they'll still smell a little like it when we cook 'em, though."

It was a windy, chilly evening, but the bordering fence was tall enough to keep the better part of the breeze away. Once everything was on the grill, Trish sat at the table and nibbled on some cheesy crackers. Silence had found them again, and her father knew it was best to dissolve it quickly. He reached over for a few crackers as he assembled what he felt was the best approach to address Trish's recent reclusiveness.

"We haven't done this in a while, have we?"

Trish cracked open a can of sparkling water and nodded her head. "It's been a couple of years."

"It just boggles my mind how fast time flies."

She listened to the vegetables sizzle while her father filled his mouth with another handful of crackers.

"You know, you can always talk to me about anything, right?" he asked, scratching nervously at his thick hairline.

Nodding, she replied, "I know." After her response, Trish could feel the anxiety wicking off of her father. She began to wonder whether he had seen something that would implicate her involvement in the strange, supernatural occurrences she was experiencing.

"Answer me truthfully. Is there something bothering you?"

Trish looked at the table and started to pick at the edges of her cracker.

After a deep sigh, he continued, "I know I work a lot and don't always spend time with you. But that doesn't mean I don't care. I'm not brushing you aside or anything. I'm just busy trying to provide for us."

"Dad, I know. I don't think you're abandoning me or anything."

"Then what's wrong?"

Trish put the crumbled crackers back into the box and then answered, "Nothing. I'm fine. Really. School is a bit of a pain in the ass, but that's it. I'm just trying to focus, you know?"

After her one-sided confession, Trish watched her father slowly nod his head. Luckily, it was enough to satiate his curiosity and ease some of the guilt he harbored. The two then noshed their dinner over the pleasant, long overdue conversation of college plans and fond memories of Trish's late mother.

With a full belly and a brimming heart to match, Trish sat in front of the barbeque and watched the coals die out while her father brought the leftovers into the house. Though she was thankful to be spared from another one of Lowenna's memories during the meal they shared, it wasn't long before the smile on her face straightened. Looming on the horizon was the next unexpected and dreadful experience slated to challenge her fortitude. She was scared and incredibly wary of what would happen to her body and mind when she would eventually separate from Lowenna. Since Rayshell was still so far behind, Trish earnestly hoped her memories would remain intact so she could be ready to provide her with the guidance and support she knew she would need along the way.

Trish smiled as she grabbed the foil-lined tray and the last of the utensils. Her father, despite all his silly faces, kept his promise and ate the broccoli.

22

THE UTSIRRI

Benson called an urgent, late-evening assembly. Keeping the meeting restricted to the Tiers and leaving the Halryn council off his agenda became typical in his efforts to keep certain matters private. The council chambers were uninvitingly dim and stifling. Demelza, Ailbhis, and Aalrija appeared fatigued as they paced the black marble arena floor in their usual ornate garb. The trio slowly climbed the stairs to their designated seats beside Labraid who was already waiting in his typical, proper posture.

On the other side of the arena sat Benson. Though he tried to hide any hint of emotion from his face, he failed to keep his worry from passing through his distant, bloodshot eyes. After Demelza, Ailbhis, and Aalrija took their seats, Benson commanded more candles to flame, then rose to his feet.

"This evening, I have called for the attendance of my Tiers, and it's obvious where my request has fallen short."

Confused, Ailbhis and Demelza whispered to one another while Labraid looked ahead with a stern countenance. Aalrija swiped her soft gray hair from her neck and tried to remain calm, anticipating what Benson intended to discuss.

"This is the fourth day my son has been absent," continued Benson. "What concerns me is that I am unable to sense his energy.

There are a multitude of things this could mean, but at its simplest, he is not here in Celestine. I don't know whether to believe he's in danger or simply embarking on a lead to Navaryn and Lowenna alone. I've called you here to get to the bottom of this. So tell me, who knows where he is?"

The room fell silent until Labraid called out, "I've reported each instance he's failed to show up for training. I, too, have recognized his absence, but regretfully, I have no idea what he could be up to."

Demelza and Ailbhis talked over each other, professing they did not know his whereabouts, while Aalrija picked at her fingernails and patiently waited for her turn to speak.

"At present, I have no idea where the young master could be," chimed Aalrija. "But I'm sure he has good intentions behind his choice to keep his endeavor to himself."

"You sound awfully confident, Aalrija," said Labraid as he leaned forward to lock eyes with her. "So you don't know where he's been, either?"

Aalrija shook her head as she fibbed, "No," and then rearranged her unruly locks again.

"But it was you who reported he wasn't feeling well when I came to summon him for training yesterday morning."

Disappointed that Labraid put her on the spot, she remained calm as she replied, "I happened into his company briefly the other day, yes."

"And I was told you and Kumiko were spotted at Teagan's a few days prior."

Aalrija squinted her yellowish-green eyes and retorted, "And what exactly are you implying by this, Labraid? I happen to enjoy Kumiko's company as well as patron Teagan's establishment."

"I'm not implying anything. I'm simply pointing out that you are the only one who has seen him recently. Surely he's mentioned what he's been up to. If not outright, then perhaps in subtle clues."

"He has not divulged anything that would explain his absence. Whatever his agenda may be, I trust Kumiko has a valid reason for such secrecy."

Over the next few hours, the group delineated a few possibilities that could explain Kumiko's absence. Throughout their deliberations, Benson kept a keen eye on his cabinet, studying their body language and input until one member stood out from the others. Aalrija's lack of viable suggestions and a slew of subtle tells were precisely what he sought. Rather than address her directly in front of the others, risking denial, he chose another direction.

"I'm going to give him two more days to make an appearance," claimed Benson. "If by then he hasn't returned, we must consider the possibility that he too has fallen victim to Merisek, and we will need to escalate the matter accordingly."

"What are you suggesting?" asked Labraid.

"That we use every resource available to figure out what has happened to him. At whatever cost."

Shortly after his ominous statement, Benson adjourned their meeting. The collective silently departed the council chambers, feeling substantially more drained than before.

·)(·

Aalrija promptly returned home, intending to get some rest, but her anxious mind strained under the weight of darkness alone. Dressed in a long-sleeved mauve and gold sleeping gown, she grabbed a fresh bottle of red from the rack down the hall, then ventured to the front conversation room and lit a fire. With a generous pour in hand, she looked at the tender flames while preparing her mind for an unplanned Elemental Parallel to Navaryn's safe room. The critical task at hand was for Von to intervene and contact Kumiko. Not only was there the need for Kumiko to make an appearance to appease Benson, but there was also the concern of his prolonged stint with Kaimaharaa that endangered the well-being of his mind.

After a hearty sip, Aalrija set her glass atop the mantel, exhaled deeply, then closed her eyes. Once she settled her racing mind, the tips of her hair took to the air as if free from gravity, and a glittering halo expanded from her chest. The room brightened with golden light. As her body began tearing away into energetic flitters that sought the fire, a heavy rap came at her front door. In an instant, the phantasm regressed, and Aalrija jolted from her meditative state. She stood in silence until the heavy rap came once more before proceeding toward the door with her wine glass in hand. Although it wasn't uncommon to entertain a late-night visitor, it often meant a pressing matter needed her attention.

Aalrija sucked back her breath and whispered, "*Kumiko.*" She quickly called a few pillars on the wall to flame with a flick of her wrist, then pulled open the large, ornate wooden entry door. Her excited smile slowly uncurled once she beheld the dark figure waiting on the other side. "B-Benson?" Aalrija shook away her apprehensive expression, then fixed her tone. "To what do I owe the pleasure?"

His smile tugged the sides of his lofty cheeks as he asked, "Got a moment, my dear friend?"

Aalrija's heartbeat thumped in her throat. Regardless of the excuse, there would be no suitable way to decline his request. "Certainly," she said, then gestured for his entry. She pounded the contents of her wine glass as Benson removed his cloak and shoes, then closed the door gently behind her. "Forgive me, but I have already down-dressed for the evening."

Benson's light smile remained unwavering. "Not to worry. I'm not offended to find you relaxing at such an hour."

Aalrija lifted the glass to her lips, only to be reminded at the last moment that it was empty.

"If you're keen on refilling your glass, I'd love one myself."

She was highly suspicious of Benson's strange attitude, but continued to play along while she lit a few more scattered wall tapers down the corridor. As they meandered into the conversation room, she picked up a wine glass from the case beside the rack along the way.

Benson sat beside the window as she filled their glasses. "A fire on such a warm night?"

Aalrija's posture tensed as she answered, "I'm sure you, as much as I, appreciate the relaxing qualities of a gentle amber blaze."

"No arguments there," said Benson as she delivered his glass with an awkward smile. He briefly sipped the wine, his steely blue eyes fixed forward. "My dear friend. As a favor between us, I thought it best to spare you the embarrassment of being called out in front of our colleagues this evening."

His ominous comment made Aalrija choke on her wine.

"Knowing you for as long as I have, I've picked up a few of your *tells*, if you will. There's no secret that Kumiko has confided in you about the things he chooses not to do with me. And considering how we've grown apart over the years, I wouldn't be surprised if he were to share a secret agenda with you. That being said, I'm giving you one last chance to be forthright with me. *Where* is my son?"

Aalrija held her breath. Lying was not her strong suit, and she feared the consequences if she kept doing it. After guzzling down the contents of her glass, she reluctantly divulged the details of Kumiko's partnership with Von, as well as his efforts with the Delavine Crystal. However, she did not implicate Fallon in his involvement, disclose Von's location, or admit that Lowenna was aware of their plan. Throughout Aalrija's confession, Benson's expression remained eerily placid.

"So what are you going to do?" she asked timidly.

Swirling the rest of his wine, Benson replied, "Whatever is necessary."

Benson's calm tone rattled Aalrija to her core. His hatred of Von was well known, and the thought of Kumiko conspiring with him was something he could not accept. Given the minimal response Aalrija received from him, she had no clue how he would intervene. After he finished the last of his wine and set the glass atop the table in front of him, he rose from his seat and kindly saw himself out. Alone in unsettling silence, Aalrija fixated on the reflection of the firelight dancing inside the wine glass. With a dreadful expression, she drank heavily from the bottle until she finished it.

·)(·

Once Benson's Parafall cleared, he momentarily looked upon his castle's massive façade. Such a display stood as a testament to his and his predecessors' monumental achievements. In truth, it made him feel just as vacant as the castle had come to be. As the moments passed, the muscles in Benson's face tightened until a full scowl bloomed. His potent, steely blue eyes felt strained, as if he could see nothing beyond his own dismal company. Discouraged, enraged, yet determined to set everything onto its proper tracks, he started for the entrance in search of his personal attendant.

During his trek, he considered the likelihood that Aalrija would inform Von of what had transpired, though it would likely not deter him from his efforts. Having deduced that she would never set foot into Daeva, he suspected Von to be hunkered down somewhere in Celestine under his nose. As much as he relished the thought of tearing Celestine apart to find him, he uncharacteristically conceded to taking a more covert course of action. In the end, Navaryn and Lowenna's safe return took precedence.

After a lengthy clomp through his castle, Benson eventually came upon Ciaran's chambers, where he had just finished bathing.

"How did it go?" he asked while tying his robe in place, though the look upon Benson's face was answer enough.

Benson pulled out a pair of golden amulets from his pocket and simply stared intensely at Ciaran.

"That bad, huh?" he replied, frisking his damp, platinum hair with a plush gray towel. "So, where are we off to this time?"

"Ready some Red Beryl, then meet me in the speaking chambers."

"Utsirri?! At *this* hour?!" clamored Ciaran. "That's taking a bit of a risk, don't you think?"

"There is no time to waste. Not only am I losing members of my cabinet to Von, but I am losing my son in the process."

"To Von?"

"Aalrija told me everything. She and Von, along with Kumiko, have been working together to reclaim Navaryn."

Ciaran sighed, choosing not to test Benson's patience by stating the obvious.

"The last thing I want is for Von to rise from this victoriously. Navaryn will be *ours*. We depart for Utsirri as soon as you ready the Beryl."

"And myself as well, I suppose," he said, then turned to his closet for suitable attire. "Seems I'm having as many sleepless nights as you lately."

"They will come to an end soon," concluded Benson before promptly leaving the room.

·◖)◖·

Benson and Ciaran rematerialized out of flittering ebon fragments suspended inside a contracting diamond formation and into a large receiving dome. Once Utsirri's gravity hit their stomachs, the pair winced and wobbled until they eventually recalibrated to the intensity. Ciaran was the first to straighten his posture. Following a deep breath, he peered through the thick, transparent paneling where distant, towering structures studded with blinking lights spiked skyward amidst an eerie titian haze. Benson, suppressing the urge to retch since his feet met the floor, watched two guards approach their receiving dome. In unison, the guards flipped open a compartment on the wrists of their armored suits. They activated a holographic screen above the unannounced Celestine visitors to both inspect and address them. After a brief security verification, the guards each pressed an identical button on their wrist controls, granting their guests access to the protective gear they needed to reach their destination.

"Dress, then enter the airlock chamber," one of the guards directed. Then, their holographic transmission within the dome promptly ended.

Benson sighed as he unlatched the trunk of neatly arranged protective suits, each equipped with a respirator and a tinted helmet with radio communication. Even though Benson ventured to this sector of Utsirri several times, he was no better accustomed to dressing for the trek than on his first visit. As expected, Ciaran made quick work of suiting up and rested against the edge of the airlock chamber while he waited for Benson to finish.

"You know, I could help—"

"Do I look like a blubbering convalescent to you?" Benson interjected with his intense eyes.

Over time, Ciaran learned to keep his sarcastic utterances to himself. However, on account of a particular subtle smile that pulled at the edges of his lips, Benson recognized whenever he played them out in his mind.

"Something to say, Ciaran?"

A complete smile ripped through his countenance as he replied, "Not at all, sir."

Once Benson finished dressing, the guards activated the airlock chamber and escorted them across a massive bridge suspended over a dreadfully desolate landscape. The enveloping haze obscured the barren, cracked earth below and the series of enormous metal structures towering around them. Sand, pebbles, and other debris pelted their protective gear with such force that the audio transmission within their helmets was nearly inaudible.

The grand, thirteen-story, spired structure that Benson and Ciaran were escorted to was tiny compared to those looming in the distance. Amid the ongoing serenade of clanging debris, they were delivered to a band of guards waiting in front of the armored hyphen, then granted entry.

The party's alternating footsteps echoed down the dim, bleak, sterile corridor. Benson looked ahead as he and Ciaran passed through a series of scanners and blinking lights set up in the very center of the room. After the guardsmen at the other end of the hall processed and approved the incoming data, the sleek, tooth-cut door beside them parted as quietly as a whisper.

The band of armed guards delivered Benson and Ciaran to a young man waiting on the other side of the door in a small, stark room. He gestured his thanks with a bow. Following the guards' exit, the young man sealed off the room with the push of a button. Benson and Ciaran promptly removed their tinted helmets, forgetting for a moment the haunting gray tone of flesh the Utsirri were known for.

"Welcome, gentleman. I don't believe we've had the pleasure of meeting before now. My name is Rajani, Lady Lilija's newest apprentice," he greeted in a very soothing voice while gesturing to the benches behind his guests. "I'm sure you are familiar with the protocol. Please remove your protective suits and the garments you arrived in, then redress in the wardrobe provided."

Benson turned to the oddly stitched beige robe that hung on the wall behind him, then cinched his lip. If given the choice, he would much rather stay in the bulky protective gear.

"I see you'd prefer to learn our names after we've bared our asses."

Rajani's golden eyes hardened. "I'm sorry if my request felt abrupt or otherwise rude, Benson. But as you can see, I do know your name. And I know Ciaran's as well. So if you'd please …."

Without hesitation or the senselessness of shame, Ciaran stripped down to his lean, bare flesh, then promptly redressed in the time it took Benson to remove only his boots. Ciaran suspected Benson was either still acclimating from his transmission or trying to provoke Rajani with his lax pace.

"And, of course, please use the accompanying satchel for anything you wish to bring with you," chimed Rajani as he smoothed down the wild strands of hair that escaped his long braided ponytail.

While Ciaran reached for the coordinating satchel and stuffed it with the offering of Red Beryl meant for Lady Lilija, Benson continued to mutter and moan as he unclothed his bulging waistline. Once dressed in the loose-fitting garment, which felt like part shawl and part robe, he slipped on the tannish-white flat sandals and tied a long teal sash around his waist. Rajani nodded his approval and then ushered them through the next automatic door.

Benson and Ciaran paced down an immaculate corridor of gleaming, smoky marble and flawless oiled wooden paneling. At the end of the corridor emerged a grand indoor pavilion, the most capacious of the five within the compound. It served as a junction between departments and a peaceful commonplace for residents and staff to mingle and relax. Above the trio at the tallest point of the room was the projection of gentle daylight that one could easily mistake as real. Benson and Ciaran slowed their pace and marveled at the lush scenery, much as they did on every visit. Several twisting pillars, draped in ivy and other verdant vegetation, towered among stairways that led to other areas of the facility or to layered terraces where one could relax in a spot of artificial sunlight. The air was crisp, dust-free, and lightly fragranced by the exotic flowers that studded the space. With as much diverse nature surrounding Benson and Ciaran, Utsirri's advanced technology was even more prominent. From the hovering holographic screens, sensors, and blinking lights to the sources that powered the artificial climate, their synthetic oasis was undoubtedly complex. While Benson and Ciaran caught up with Rajani's stride, they scanned the variety of curious eyes in their wake, chiseled with features new to both of them.

This particular faction of Utsirri, known as Iitagai, was led by Lady Lilija and her council of trusted advisors. Compared to other Utsirri empires, Iitagai was a relatively new settlement, formed after a cataclysmic shift in power. Those who fled the older empires were welcomed with open arms, on the pledge of peaceful freedom and protection.

Valgorel, the facility Rajani escorted his guests through, was both a control center for the surrounding vertical cities and an inter-realm hybridization compound. Given the prohibited nature of hybridization between the realms, it was nonetheless an activity Utsirri were notorious for engaging in. The strength of their formidable defenses and skill made it impossible for any opposing force to dismantle their practices as a whole. Valgorel, however, was unique among other Utsirri operations, as its participants were there of their own volition and were not regarded as prisoners.

Garments served as a form of immediate identification within Valgorel. Style, cut, and embellishments indicated one's role and status. From the participants in Iitagai's hybridization to those in high-profile positions, such as Rajani, all donned their appropriate attire. The teal sash that both Benson and Ciaran wore conveyed they weren't average visitors, but rather, esteemed guests of Lady Lilija.

Once through the grand pavilion, Rajani led his guests to a secured elevator at the end of a narrow hall. With a combination of his handprint and the insertion of a clear, chipped acrylic card tethered to a compartment inside his breast pocket, he called the elevator to their floor. The transparent capsule-shaped car he and his guests entered was small and paneled with blinking lights. When the car door closed, a series of holographic controls activated. After Rajani quickly typed a passcode, it swiftly set course for the lounge beneath the primary control wing.

Rajani kept his golden eyes in front of him, and his velvety soft ashen hands clasped behind his back until the capsule emerged through the floor at the center of another grand artificial oasis. Seated atop a transparent, sharp-winged lounge chair flanked by an attendant and an eerily quiet stone fountain was Lady Lilija. As her guests filed into the room, she lifted her intense golden eyes from the glowing projection her attendant had summoned from her crystal tablet. Lady Lilija rose to her feet as her attendant quickly deactivated the projection, straightened her posture, and tucked the transparent tablet under her arm. Her towering, slender frame was draped in fine, crisp linen trimmed in gold and emblazoned with polished gemstones arranged in various symmetrical patterns.

"Welcome, gentlemen," she greeted with open arms and approached her guests with a graceful sway. "It's a pleasure to receive you this afternoon, though I'm afraid I find myself a bit unprepared to entertain you."

As Ciaran beheld Lady Lilija's elegant countenance, adorned with a headdress of sparkling gemstones and dark, curtaining hair, he couldn't help but tense up. Aside from her haunting gray skin and golden eyes unique to Utsirri, she possessed an overwhelming, fiendish essence, akin to the wretched fiends of his childhood.

Lady Lilija was keen on Ciaran's nervous energy. However, knowing his past, she never held it against him. She hoped that her bright smile reassured him that she, nor the people of Iitagai, meant him any harm.

"I am grateful you're willing to host us," replied Benson in a deep tone.

Ciaran stood silently at Benson's side and watched as he took Lady Lilija's long, thin hand. Abiding by Iitagai's formalities, Benson weaved his pudgy fingers through hers, then bowed his head. After Lady Lilija reciprocated the gesture, she directed her guests to sit with her by the fountain.

Teeming with vibrant flowers and lush vegetation, the artificial oasis was even more breathtaking in Lady Lilija's private lounge than within the pavilion below. Ciaran gazed around the room with wide and curious eyes, yet was puzzled by the entirety of the lounge's surroundings. The calm golden light of a midday sun filtering through a dense forest canopy looked completely different from the way it had on their last visit.

After the pair took their seats, Rajani wheeled over a cart brimming with exotic refreshments. Once he brought Lady Lilija a tall glass of mixed juices and hydrated seeds, he walked to her attendant and stood at her side.

As Lady Lilija leisurely sipped her beverage, she shrewdly examined her guests, noting their rigid posture. "Allow me to adjust the environment to something more *comfortable*," she offered, reaching for a small device in the center of the thick prismatic table between them. "I've left it on this scape for several days and could use a change."

Benson raised an eyebrow and fell into immediate awe as the scenery around him rotated. Ranging from mountainous lands in Daeva to the cavernous dwellings of Opiri, the landscape surrounding them morphed at the press of a button. Ciaran was perplexed. Though he had accompanied Benson to Lady Lilija's chambers several times before, not once did he understand that the phenomenal technology surrounding them created such a grand illusion.

Though Lady Lilija had no intention of rousing Ciaran's concern, she liked to keep Benson on his toes. She watched his dashing eyes widen as the landscape surrounding him flicked between the majestic forests of Celestine's western lands, until finally settling onto an open garden studded with prim, white rose bushes. Benson's forehead grew hot as he gazed upon the ghostly blooms swaying ever so gently. For a moment, he swore the scent of their bouquet reached his nose.

Displayed before Benson was his very own rose garden. Though it was clear the projection was dated, judging by the state of growth, it didn't lessen the blow to experience the intimate area within his estate in such a boastful fashion, especially since it was under the protection of his Halryn elite at all times. Even though the Utsirri had cataloged countless realms in search of specimens for their hybridization projects, the fact that he had captured the finite details of his exclusive space demanded explanation. However, Benson's pride kept him from addressing the grand reveal. Even though there was no subtlety in Lady Lilija's affirmation of her powerful reach, Benson coolly carried on as if undisturbed in the slightest.

"Forgive me, but I've noticed some changes here in Valgorel since my last visit. Particularly with the occupants here."

"Oh? How so?" she chimed, then sipped delicately at her crystal straw.

"There are visages with features that are new to me, and others I recognize carry significant bounties," Benson said as he recalled a few shady sets of eyes that followed his venture through the grand pavilion.

Ciaran, who maintained his silence, was astute to Benson's claim. Celestine's Halyrn Tiers were privy to many details concerning the realms they swore to protect, and others who had no idea their spying eyes fell upon them.

"How very observant. Nothing seems to get past you, does it, my esteemed guest." As Lady Lilija pressed her straw against the bloated, slimy seeds in her glass, she continued, "I have recently accepted new members from distant realms into the fold. I suppose some may be perceived as transgressors by whatever intelligence you've collected. But these are folks who were discarded by their homelands."

"Outcasts, then?"

"In other words. But in any case, they seek peace. And, a new beginning."

Benson squinted at her simple explanation. "Peace is only an illusion that the flocks we shepherd strive to attain. For one who treasures their empire, I'd caution integrating such characters into your flock here in Valgorel."

A divine smile cut across Lady Lilija's face. "I'm flattered by your concern, Benson. But a peaceful existence is something we all strive for, no matter what we're branded as. Here, we are *all* Iitagai."

Lady Lilija was content with Benson having shrugged away her half-assed attempt to cloak her true ambition. Iitagai began as a place of refuge for Utsirri back when the shifts in reign and power created rifts within its long-standing factions. Recently, that same invitation had been extended to those from distant realms who sought refuge and amnesty, so long as they pledged their talents to Iitagai's collective force. Such a bold move was part of Lady Lilija's fearless strategy to fortify her empire, making it impervious to the rest of Utsirri's factions and foreign infiltration.

"Well, I doubt you've simply come here to bear your concern for my empire," she chimed as she ran her decorated fingers through her smoky heather hair, anticipating that Benson's unannounced visit was due to his growing impatience. "If you've come here for a status on your endeavor concerning the Chimera, well, I'm afraid I don't have much to report. This venture of yours has required some substantial experimentation, and finding volunteers for Atama Cora has been rather *challenging*, to say the least."

As Benson ruminated on the number of Opiri hands his project passed through before Lady Lilija accepted the challenge, he attempted to fashion himself a beverage. "While the matter of the Chimera will always be at the heart of my concern, I'm here to seek assistance on a different matter."

Benson's face puckered as he sipped at a pungent concoction of bright green and yellow-speckled juices. Promptly after a reluctant gulp, he briefed Lady Lilija on the circumstance that befell both Lowenna and Navaryn. Ciaran watched her gaze grow tepid at the close of Benson's plea, where he highlighted his desire to realign the young women's minds alongside his goal to bring them back to Celestine.

"I'm well aware of *your* talents, Benson. I would figure you'd be able to handle this so-called *realignment* on your own."

Benson forfeited any further attempt to imbibe in the acerbic, neon concoction and set the glass atop the table in front of him. "I'm flattered by your confidence in my abilities," he replied. "Sadly, the method of their expulsion has thwarted me, and I would prefer to solve both problems at once."

"Meaning, you'd prefer to keep your hands clean?"

Benson chuckled with a devious smile. "Is my request within your abilities?"

"Of course. You know as well as I that the Opiri have suffered from similar diablerie, though be it from a different set of circumstances altogether." She slowly cracked a smile as she recalled the briefing with the head of her security personnel. "Well, with as much Red Beryl as Ciaran is toting with him, I assume you're expecting a hasty turnaround, am I correct?"

"If at all possible, I'd like to leave here with a solution."

Lady Lilija finished her beverage, then retrieved the beige canvas satchel from Ciaran. "Of course, you would. And how could I refuse the wishes of my *esteemed* guest?" Before she made her way to the crystal elevator car that her attendant had called a moment before, she grabbed the remote from the table and handed it to Benson. "Please, make yourselves at home," she said, then happened into a titter shortly after realizing the landscape surrounding them.

Benson's forehead tightened as he tried to decide whether or not she intended the joke. "Enlighten me," he called before she stepped into the car. "Why is Red Beryl so important to you Utsirri? After all this time, I still don't know why your kind seeks it."

Lady Lilija's attendant stood beside her and frowned at Benson for such a blunt inquisition.

"A lady never tells a secret," she replied with a wink as the door closed.

Benson managed to prevent a frustrated outburst from escaping his lips if the room was, perchance, under surveillance. After a long bout of silence, Ciaran grabbed the peculiar remote that Benson tossed atop the table shortly after Lady Lilija's departure, then flipped through the wide gamut of Celestine's captured scenery. From the majestic Droplet Trees to the remote islands off the eastern shore, the atmosphere was perfectly harvested. Ciaran closed his eyes, believing for a moment he had caught a whiff of bright, briny sea air. While locked into a peaceful trance, Benson yanked the device from him with a swift and firm hand. Puzzled and a bit perturbed, he glared at Benson's confused expression as he tried his hand at operating the device until he mistakenly deactivated the holographic recreations altogether.

"Satisfied?" asked Ciaran as they sat amidst a stark white room covered in blinking pinholes and strange razor grates from ceiling to floor.

Benson simply frowned, then tossed the device atop the table more forcefully than intended. Rajani, whom Benson and Ciaran had forgotten about, was standing beside the elevator. He watched the remote skid across the sleek, transparent tabletop and clatter to the floor. With a sigh that pricked his guests' ears, Rajani ambled over to retrieve the device. He was genuinely unimpressed by Benson and his combative demeanor throughout the visit. It puzzled him how someone who appeared to be so unstable and reactive was, in fact, Celestine's imperator, the individual who presided over one of the most powerful forces in all the realms.

After nearly two silent hours, Lady Lilija returned with the same straight-faced female attendant in her wake, carrying identical thick, square crystal cases by the handle.

"Was the scenery not a delight to your senses this time, Benson? Or was there a malfunction?"

Rajani arrowed his disappointed golden eyes at Lady Lilija for a moment, hoping that was all it took to reveal his childish behavior.

Ciaran and Benson both rose as Lady Lilija directed her attendant in front of her. She set the crystal cases atop the table as gently as she could manage. Inside, propped atop a clear, supportive arch, rested a gleaming apparatus that housed a bright orb of shimmery dichroic light.

"Is this it?" asked Benson as he gazed upon the seemingly unimpressive devices. "These look a little too simple to accomplish such a grand feat."

Lady Lilija's attendant scowled at his ungrateful remark.

"Must it be gilded on every curve to meet your approval?" she inquired, unbothered by his doubtfulness. "You can either take it and trust me, or leave it behind if you don't. The choice is yours."

Unlike her attendant's raking stare, Lady Lilija's composure made Benson rethink his disrespectful attitude. Once she could see that his pompous and combative energy had retracted, she explained how the apparatus worked and what to expect once the spell was administered.

"I believe our business is done, Benson," she said with her signature smile. "We can discuss matters regarding the Chimera at a later time that suits you."

"I'd be delighted."

After Lady Lilija's attendant draped the cases in fitted silver velvet, Benson rose for a formal farewell, consisting of the same intimate greeting as earlier, followed by a kiss on the cheek. Just as the enchanting scent of her skin departed Benson's nostrils, Rajani walked to his side.

"Shall we?" he chimed and gestured to the elevator car.

Once down in the Pavilion, Benson's neutral expression slowly twisted into discontent. He felt the curious eyes of Valgorel's residents follow his stride. In a matter of moments, disillusion seized him. He feared that everyone therein knew of his business, as though his honor and ability were sullied by carrying the apparatuses necessary to bring his prized guardians home.

The same cold sweat remained with him until he and Ciaran safely returned to the oubliette from whence they came. Celestine's gravity came as no relief to Benson upon entry, and he buckled to his knees, retching upon the gritty stone floor. Ciaran paid little mind to his distress, just as he knew he preferred, and set the velvet-draped cases atop the deep inset counter.

"It's funny," he uttered after wiping away the pasty vomit that clung to his chapped lips. "After all this time, who would have thought you'd be the only one I could trust?"

With a curious expression, Ciaran watched Benson slowly rise.

"My cabinet is tainted, and my own son has formed a forbidden and unforgivable alliance. But, in the end, he'll be the one begging me for mercy."

23

THE ANGELS

"What do you think you're doin', Ray?" clamored Manny as Rayshell punched out for the day. "You still have almost ten minutes left."

Rayshell turned to him with a playfully contorted face. "For your information, I'm actually late clocking out. I started fifteen minutes early to help patch a gap in coverage in the kids department. You would have known that if you got here more than thirty seconds before your shift."

With his phone in sight, Manny followed her to her locker and muttered, "See, that's why I don't come through those doors until there's just enough time for me to walk up and clock in. Ten minutes in that department, and I'd quit."

"Saturdays are worse than Sundays," Rayshell claimed as she pulled out her armored riding jacket.

Manny shivered. "It's shitty no matter what day it is. Most parents are too glued to their damn phone that they miss the ridiculous mess their kids make, let alone their own."

After slipping her jacket on, Rayshell rested her index and middle fingers on the top of Manny's cell and slowly pushed down. Once his curious eyes met hers, she said, "Well, let's hope *you* don't go havin' kids anytime soon."

"Excellent job, roast-master Ray," chimed Tanya as she rounded the corner.

Rayshell giggled with her hand over her mouth as Manny admitted, "That was a good one," then went back to scrolling through his phone. "See you both later."

After he walked away, Tanya smiled at Rayshell and said, "Look at you. That jacket is *awesome*."

Rayshell reached for her helmet atop the span of lockers with a smile. Side-by-side, the pair turned the corner and walked back into the stark white breakroom. A handful of people sat amongst each other, eating their respective lunches, with the television tuned to a repeat of an old 70's game show that no one was watching.

"Are you off, too?" asked Rayshell.

Shaking her head, Tanya replied, "Last break."

After a goodbye hug, Rayshell left the employee lounge and immediately spotted Tobias waiting just outside the hall next to an end cap of fluffy designer towels. Smiling, she gripped her helmet's face guard and scampered to his side.

"Today took forever," Rayshell whined playfully, then kissed Tobias, but his reciprocation was stiff and rushed. "What's wrong?"

He looked at her with worried eyes that she neglected to notice when she first greeted him. "He's here."

His ominous reveal stole Rayshell's breath. "Jack? *Where?*"

"I don't know, but his car is parked outside."

"Fuck," Rayshell muttered. "I can't face him. I'll buckle."

"Is there a back door?"

Rayshell shook her head. "The back is only open if there is receiving. And that's on Mondays and Wednesdays. Any other day, it's locked. I'll set off the alarm."

Tobias adjusted his jacket and peeked around them to ensure Jack wasn't approaching. "Okay. I'm parked close to the front. I'm sure we can sneak by if we're careful enough. Let's stay out of the main aisles just in case, alright?"

They took their time weaving through the racks and table displays along the perimeter wall. Tobias stood beside the glass doors and surveyed the passersby while Rayshell remained tucked discreetly behind a tiered arrangement of sporty mannequins. After a few more moments, Tobias gestured for her hand, and together they shadowed a family of six through the automatic doors.

The late autumn sky was glowing in sultry hues of orange and pink as the sun continued to recede behind the distant rolling hills. Once they stepped off the curb and into the parking lot, Rayshell spotted Jack's tan station wagon two rows over from the motorcycle. Tobias felt her pace seize, so he gently pulled her along, but she dropped her helmet between two vehicles traveling in opposite directions. Once she picked it up, her eyes trailed to the small bakery shop nestled among potted cypress. Jack emerged carrying a bright pink box brimming with donuts in one hand while he fed himself with the other. His jubilation altogether disintegrated when his eyes fell upon Rayshell, who stood nervously in the parking lot.

"Rayshell!"

The car Rayshell stood in front of honked to trigger her gait, but she didn't move.

"Let's go," Tobias ordered, taking her by the arm.

Through Jack's eyes, Nathaniel watched a vibrant violet shimmer quickly cascade over Tobias' earnest eyes. "*Impossible,*" he muttered as the box of donuts slipped from his hands.

Tobias and Rayshell quickly affixed their helmets, then readied themselves atop the motorcycle as Jack breathlessly lumbered after them.

"Rayshell! *Wait!*"

Jack hopped off the curb and ran into the middle of the parking lot, cutting off a white minivan. In an uncoordinated reflex, the driver shrieked and pressed the gas pedal instead of the brakes. The corner of the minivan careened into Jack's hip and toppled him instantly. Fueled by adrenaline, he immediately rose to his feet and called after Rayshell as she and Tobias took off down the other end of the parking lot.

"I am *so* sorry, sir," the nervous woman cooed after exiting her vehicle. "I didn't see you. Are you hurt? Should I call an amb—"

Interrupting the woman with a guttural roar, Jack beat the hood of her minivan.

"Sir, I-I-I'm sorry," she yelped timidly. "Please stop. I have children inside."

Jack banged until his muscles burned and his breath left him.

The terrified woman screamed, "You *maniac!*" before locking herself inside her vehicle.

Jack pounded on the passenger window and bellowed with a disturbingly ferocious countenance. The sounds of the wailing children did nothing to settle his fit. Shaking in panic, the woman fumbled to put the van into drive and then zipped carelessly out of the plaza parking lot.

Like a delirious headcase, Jack squirmed, groaned, and muttered while he walked back to the box of donuts he dropped. Not only did Rayshell's actions confirm she was avoiding him, but seeing the otherworldly violet shimmer in Tobias' eyes proved the interference of a Celestine. Fearing the impending punishment for his negligence, Jack knelt to the ground, stacked the scattered donuts back into his box, and did his best to disregard the wide-eyed, transfixed passersby.

·)€·

Tobias followed the direction of his reticent guest and took Rayshell to his house to ensure the Daeva-ensnared human couldn't find them. When they pulled into the driveway, Tobias didn't see his father's truck and figured he wasn't home from work yet. Rayshell hopped off the motorcycle before he finished parking and nearly ripped her helmet off. She paced frantically with teary eyes, oblivious to the border of marigolds she was trampling.

"What am I gonna do? Huh, Toby?" Rayshell whimpered. "I can't keep avoiding him forever."

Tobias flipped through his keys as he led the way to the front door. "Just stay with me. I'll keep you safe until we figure out what to do."

Rayshell frowned at his reply. "How are you so calm right now?"

"One of us has to be," he answered with a gentle smile, then held the door open for her entry. He drew the curtains as she double-checked each of the locks. "They're fine, Nav. Just relax."

In the middle of slipping off her armored jacket, Rayshell slowly turned to Tobias. "What? *What* did you call me?!"

When his pilot recalled the error, Tobias' eyes widened. "Um, Ray," he uttered nervously.

She threw her jacket to the far end of the couch, then barked, "Who the fuck are you? And don't you lie to me."

Tobias took a breath to calm his nerves as she picked up an abstract table decoration from the coffee table. "No one you would bludgeon over the head, that's for sure."

With narrow eyes, Rayshell answered, "Why don't I believe you?"

His eyes hardened as she cornered him against the dusty mantel. The more his pilot deliberated, he realized the proclamation cusped a fib. After a heavy sigh, he dropped his defensive posture. "Alright, I'll tell you. But please just calm down. I promise I'm not going to hurt you."

Rayshell retraced a few steps but kept a firm grip on the pointy object in case she needed to swing.

"My name's Kumiko."

"K-Kumiko?" Rayshell repeated his name, feeling a bridged connection to the Celestine within her. "What did you do to Toby?"

"I took his body. He's here still, though our minds are intertwined." With a gentle sigh, Kumiko looked into her distant eyes in hopes that Navaryn would recognize him, as if his undying revere had the power to set her free.

"So," Rayshell called as she began to glare, "was it you all along?"

"It was both of us," Kumiko confessed. "Tobias cares deeply for you. And while we are both protective of you, I'm here to find a way to free Navaryn."

The distinctive name of the Celestine that stood before Rayshell filled her with skepticism. Having delved into enough of Navaryn's memories to glean Kumiko's reputation and character, the determination in his intentions felt laced with doubt.

"What about Von? Where is he?"

"The Daeva?" he uttered as he furrowed his brows. "Don't be concerned with him. Just leave this to me."

"Don't be *concerned?* Look, he's one of the only people that this Navaryn person trusts," Rayshell fired back. "And he's the only one who's been upfront with me since this all started. I wanna talk to him."

Kumiko shook his head. "There's no time for that. Right now, I need you to cooperate."

With an eyebrow arched toward the ceiling, Rayshell looked at him with rousing suspicion. "Cooperate?" she barked. "You hijack my boyfriend's body, you follow me around like a stalker, and now you expect me to just go along with whatever you say?!"

"I'm trying to help you!"

Suddenly, Rayshell dropped the abstract sculpture onto the table and then stormed over to the couch.

"What are you doing?"

"I'm out of here. I refuse to be a part of this anymore." Rayshell slipped on her jacket and bounded for the door, but Kumiko stepped in and blocked her path before she could reach for the locks.

"I'm not letting you out of my sight. Not as long as you still carry Navaryn within you."

The subtle shimmer of violet in Kumiko's stern eyes set Rayshell's heart ablaze. Her hands trembled as fury sparked in her core, then swiftly, vibrant green energy encapsulated them.

"Get out of my way!" she shouted, shoving Kumiko into the door. "I don't need your help!"

Kumiko fumbled to regain his stance. "Nav—R-Rayshell," he stammered as she shook away the last of the tingly energy. "You need to calm down! You can trust me!"

"You lost my trust long ago, Kumiko. You should have never come here."

The sound of Rayshell's voice, phasing between tones, immediately drew Kumiko's attention to a white flicker in her eyes. As a trickle of blood ran down her nose, she slowly approached him with fervent anger.

"I'll tell you one last time, you cowering fool," she uttered. "Leave me *alone!*"

Rayshell grabbed a handful of Kumiko's shirt. Before she could hurl him away from the door, her feet gave out, and she collapsed to the floor in a fit of labored breaths and groans. Her body flared with a gamut of fiery emotions alongside a flood of visions of Navaryn's would-be ally. Love, joy, but more intensely, frustration, pain, and fury revolved within her core.

Clutching her face within a cocoon of hair and tears, Rayshell struggled to gather her wits amidst a burning sensation that shot through her limbs. She glared at her clenched fists that jittered with the phantasm of a second set tearing away in both directions at her wrists. As she clamored in pain, Kumiko seized an opportunity to brace her unsteady body.

Clinging onto his arm, Rayshell cried, "What's happening?!"

Before Kumiko could give a predictably palliative proclamation, he spotted a pair of lumps writhing beneath Rayshell's heavy armored jacket. He gingerly helped remove it and found fresh blood seeping through her light blue work shirt.

The protrusions continued to split gruesomely through her delicate skin. "I can't—I can't breathe," she uttered and dug her nails into his forearm.

Consumed by each one of Navaryn's restless passions, Rayshell's body severed from her mind just as a swift procession of silvery feathered wings ripped from her back. Kumiko held her tightly as she screamed, wishing that his touch could not only temper her pain but also liberate Navaryn from within her body. Through distending and blurry shifts, Rayshell's body augmented and matured into Navaryn's thick, sculpted form. Shaking violently, she tore away at the taut, splitting seams of the confining garments until only a few thin textile shreds remained. Kumiko looked at her in disbelief through Tobias' wide eyes. The blazing aura surrounding her was unmistakable.

"Navaryn," he whispered as he looked up to her, "are you ... back?"

Standing in a daze, Navaryn cleared her long, stringy hair from her eyes and surveyed the strange surroundings she found herself amidst. Instead of separating from the host that harbored her for months, she morphed within her. Slowly, she moved her muscular arms in front of her eyes and studied her body, which she had only experienced in her mind until now. She quickly looked toward Kumiko, still posing as Tobias, as he slowly rose to his feet.

"Where's Von?" she sternly inquired.

"Nav, just wait a moment, okay? Let's just get you—" called Kumiko before her furious approach cut him off.

Her long, blood-soaked wings knocked over the free-standing decorations within range as she bounded toward him. "You tell me where he is, right now!"

Riled by the repeated utterance of Von's name, Kumiko belted, "Damn it, Nav. Will you just calm down and focus?! *I'm* here with you, and *I'm* trying to bring you home!"

Following his opportunistic declaration, Kumiko went on to delineate the risks of his seemingly selfless efforts in evoking Kaimaharaa.

Stopping him mid-sentence, Navaryn shouted, "Would you just *shut up?!* I've had enough of this. I need to find Von before it's too late."

"Too late? For *what?*"

"You won't understand, and you'll only get in my way," Navaryn uttered, then locked her eyes on the living room window across the room. Without a second's thought, she defenestrated herself, heedless of any witnesses.

Frantically, Kumiko yelled after her while she bolted down the street until she reached the momentum her wings needed to lift herself into the hazy sunset sky. He belted a slew of profanity and tossed every piece of furniture in his path. Navaryn's frantic jaunt into the open had the potential to send the realm of Human into a superstitious uproar.

Beads of sweat dripped down his forehead, and his heart pounded relentlessly. Moments away from departing his host, Kumiko began breaking the plane barrier between Celestine and Human, a feat in Kaimaharaa that existed as a mere legend in his father's books. Tobias crashed to his knees amidst a strange crushing gravity. Flickers of green opalescent lights danced over his skin, stinging like pinpricks. Clenching his jaw as the weight continued to suffocate him, Tobias watched with teary eyes as a shadowy vapor spewed off his skin. Underneath the haze, Kumiko's physical body pulled away in an excruciating sensation. The haunting flickers of light bloated and shattered as Kumiko planted his feet. Tobias barely caught a glance of his bare, chiseled form before he collapsed to the floor, exhausted from the stress wreaked on both his mind and body.

Kumiko inspected his form with skeptical violet eyes, then quickly found his bearings as the magnitude of the unfolding incident clenched his nerves. "*Fuck*," he hissed, but his modesty stopped him from dashing out the window.

After flipping through a brief chronology of Tobias' memories like they were his own, Kumiko dashed into the kitchen and stumbled through the laundry room door. He mindlessly fished through the dryer for anything that would fit, settling on a pair of silver workout shorts and a purple and yellow sports team jersey. Haphazardly fitted, he leapt through the broken window glass and dashed down the street in the direction he remembered Navaryn ascending.

Kumiko's bare feet tapped hard against the cold black pavement. He kept his eyes on the sky, toward the direction clusters of confused bystanders were pointing, some of them holding their phones in the air. With no way to avoid being immortalized in pictures and videos, he unleashed his immaculate Celestine wings and took to the sky. Opting for the quickest way to bridge their gap, Kumiko focused on Navaryn's position toward the setting sun on the horizon, then Paralleled to her side. The abrupt wispy green flash made her shriek, but her countenance only took seconds to sour back over.

"Navaryn, you've gotta listen to me!" Kumiko shouted through the wind rushing by his face. "You can't be out here like this! Do you even know where you are?!"

"Get out of here, Kumiko! Just go back home. I'll figure this out on my own." She closed her eyes and ascended into a plume of low rolling clouds.

Kumiko then cast aside his cautious efforts and reached for Navaryn's arm. With his hand tightly clutched around her wrist, he initiated a Parallel to get her to safety, but was interrupted by Navaryn's resistance to the rift. The pair sporadically reappeared at various parts of the sky as they grappled and fought against each other's counter-transmissions. Unbeknownst to the combating Celestines, the eyes and cameras of the spectators below captured their bombastic sequence of Parafalls. When they found themselves hovering over bustling lines of traffic along the freeway below, Navaryn expertly maneuvered out of his grasp. While he relentlessly beckoned her for cessation as she outpaced him, she flashed away from the vicinity in a bright green misty haze.

The thick plume obscured Kumiko's vision as his flight path sent him coasting through the remnants of the Parafall. He batted away at the tingly mist and ascended to survey the plane. To his grave disappointment, Navaryn was nowhere to be seen. After several failed attempts to sense her energy, he deduced that she still had the concealment pendant around her neck. In a jarring manner, the sound of crashing metal and blaring horns below pulled him out of his bout of heated frustration. Before he shouted another string of curses, he Paralleled out of view to formulate his plan to track down Navaryn.

·)（·

After a father-daughter afternoon spent shopping, snacking, and holding hands, Trish hunkered down in her bedroom for some alone time with the intent to finish the last of her studies. Their light-hearted activities did a good job of bridging the gap her father's heavy work schedule had created over the last couple of years. She tried to avoid spoiling her relaxed mind by speculating on how long it would be before they shared another afternoon excursion.

Trish had only gotten as far as opening her textbook to the section she needed to review before hopping on her phone to catch up on one of her favorite games. In the typical fashion of becoming thoroughly immersed in gameplay, more than an hour had gone by before she realized the time. After flicking a few notifications up and out of the way of the screen, she committed to quitting the game at the next checkpoint. Less than a few minutes later, her screen flooded with more notifications than she could ignore. In a hurry to swipe them all away, she accidentally quit her game.

"*Trish,*" Greg called from the living room.

Determined not to sound like a testy child, she answered, "What is it?"

"You're gonna want to see this. Come here."

Before trying to log back in to see if her progress was saved or not, Trish tossed her phone to the foot of her bed and opened the door to her dark bedroom. She heard the crack of a beer can and the refrigerator door fall back in place as she meandered down the hall. While she rubbed her eyes to ease the glare of the bright living room lights, Greg guided her toward the sofa.

"You're not gonna believe what's going on. My buddy John called me just a few minutes ago and said to check the news. He's been stuck on the freeway behind some big wreck."

"What happened?"

"Get this," he excitedly said as he turned up the volume on the television. "He says that angels caused the accident."

Trish's heart stopped. "Angels?" she uttered nervously.

"Yeah! See for yourself," he urged while pointing at the television.

A live news broadcast fed them jittery, indistinct recordings of two angelic figures in mid-flight above houses, parks, and the nearby freeway, amid the cooling sunset. The male figure wore an odd pairing of casual threads for the season, while the woman was nearly naked altogether, judging from the pesky, blurry censorship blocks. Trish didn't realize how far her jaw hung until her father patted her shoulder.

"Pretty crazy, huh?"

Trish nodded with the same shocked expression.

"John said he saw them with his own two eyes. He waited too long to get his phone out for better shots, but sent them to me anyway."

Trish strained to focus on the news broadcast while he showed her the photos on his phone.

"He said this shot is when the first one disappeared," said Greg, swiping to a rather strange green blob of mist. "*Poof!* Right into thin air."

The following photo was dark and blurry, but the undeniable features of Kumiko were visible.

"I don't know about you, but this seems like the biggest ruse ever. Probably cooked up by some bored techies with nothing better to do.

What do you think?"

"I-I," Trish stammered when the studio cameras switched to a live feed of a father and son pair standing in front of their house.

Greg turned to the television as the reporter addressed the over-lit pair, pointing to the broken window behind them. After a hearty swig of his beer, he asked, "Wait a second. Isn't that the boy you and Rayshell had lunch with earlier this week?"

Trish's nerves were shot. The internal meltdown she experienced beneath her father's nose had run its course, and the only thing on her mind was getting Lowenna to awaken so that she could help. The necklace Trish spotted in one of the photos was enough to make her believe that somehow Navaryn had eclipsed Rayshell's presence. Suddenly, the same swelling vibration she had felt the day before returned. Following a jitter in her right arm, Lowenna's disembodied phantom hand reappeared.

Trish yipped and concealed her hand inside her sweatshirt to hide it from her father. "I, uh, have to go to the bathroom," she fibbed, then walked toward the hall.

Greg turned to her with curious eyes and asked, "Is everything okay?"

"No. I mean, yeah. Yeah! Everything's fine."

Following her awkward, fishy smile, Trish turned around, bolted down the hall, and then locked herself inside the bathroom. With her back to the door, she closed her eyes and tried to calm her racing heart, but she struggled to catch her breath. The rickety ceiling fan in the center of the room sounded deafening. She put her shaky hands to her ears and closed her eyes.

"You'll be fine. Just let her out," she encouraged herself just before the fiery vibrations moved into her neck, chest, and face.

Trish groaned as she stumbled to the sink and opened her reluctant, teary eyes to the toothpaste-speckled mirror. Her flushed, straining face was paired beside Lowenna's jumpy, distorted apparition, tearing off to the side. Clutching the edge of the sink, she belted a delirious cackle, easily mistaken for a cry. The haunting reflection marked the first instance she had seen Lowenna's beautiful face outside of a vision deep within her mind.

Greg stood at the other side of the bathroom door and listened to the strange commotion. "Trish?" he called, then knocked firmly with the knuckle of his index finger. "What's going on in there? Are you okay?"

On the other side of the door, arcing light popped and hissed, intensifying the farther Lowenna tore away. Trish marveled at the wondrous spectacle while enduring the excruciating pain that accompanied it. In studying the apparition's puckered, wincing countenance, she assumed that Lowenna was experiencing the same awful sensations. A gentle stream of red trickled down both of Trish's nostrils, and her father rapped harder at the door.

"Sweetheart, talk to me."

Trish could not discern his words through her painful utterances and the unbearable grating sound in her ears. Her father stepped back from the door and watched the odd light flicker through the cracks.

"Trish, if you don't answer, I'm coming in."

Cord by cord, the pulling sensation deep within Trish's core snapped, and the tall, lean body of Lowenna materialized into the room. Once her bare feet touched down onto the blue terry mat at the edge of the bathtub, a fury of silvery lights spurted from her chest. With heavy eyes, Trish watched Lowenna's body dissolve within the arcing refulgence. Liberated from agony and her Celestine prisoner, a hot wash of relief coursed through her limbs. She inhaled peacefully with a gentle smile. Just as her father kicked open the bathroom door, her legs gave out from under her.

A fading trail of floating light caught Greg's eye as he quickly surveyed the room, but he quickly dismissed it when he saw Trish lying on the bathroom floor. He immediately dropped to her side. "Trish," he called as he scooped her into his arms. "Can you hear me?"

The gentle tapping against Trish's cheeks coaxed her eyes open.

"What happened?" he asked after a tight hug.

Smiling lightly, Trish whispered indiscernibly, "Exactly what needed to ... a *Parallel*."

·)(·

In a spastic and unrefined burst of white arcing light, Lowenna's Parafall dropped her into a crowded outdoor marketplace in Celestine. She uncharacteristically made the classic mistake of opening her eyes before completing her transmission, just as Navaryn used to do. The vibrant late afternoon sun, coupled with the final potent flitters, left her momentarily purblind, but she still managed to land on her feet. Groaning as she furiously rubbed her sensitive eyes, Lowenna adjusted her barefooted stance and knocked into a neatly stacked tower of metal bowls. She nervously overcorrected her movements, then tripped backward over a trio of wicker baskets into a shallow shelf lined with jars of spices.

Wide-eyed passersby slowed to gawk at Lowenna as she took a moment to find her bearings. The light spots cleared from her vision, and she picked herself up from the mess. A cool breeze sailed between every nook of her naked flesh and sobered her senses. She quickly stood erect and shielded her body from the curious eyes in her wake. Thoroughly mortified, Lowenna snatched the very first tapestry within arm's reach to cover herself with, then dashed down the bustling cobblestone street.

"Hey!" yelled the shop owner. "You thief! You'll have to pay for that!"

Lowenna turned and saw the shop owner giving chase. Rather than spend precious time explaining her situation to the infuriated vendor, she kept running. In her weakened state, Lowenna could not put enough distance between them and began to panic. Mustering as much concentration as possible, she attempted to Parallel back to the realm of Human.

"Damn it!" she barked as the wispy green lights fizzled out, accepting she was far too enervated to execute it successfully.

Lowenna then opted for a second and simpler attempt to Parallel to Navaryn's castle instead, where she remembered Von to be. Unfortunately, her limited energy gave her only a modest forward push. She heard the shop owner's loud footfalls as he closed in behind her.

The lackluster arcing white light cleared, and Lowenna shrieked as her rubbery legs worked to regain momentum. As she turned to survey the distance between her and the shop owner, a young man with a wooden handcart full of restock pulled into her path.

The unavoidable collision sent handcrafted silverware, earthenware, and hand-blown glass crashing to the ground, sounding a disharmonious melody. Lowenna lost her grip on the thick, colorful tapestry and fell away from it as she rolled atop the cobblestone. After quickly picking himself up, the man dashed to her side.

"Are you okay?" he asked as he helped her to her feet, then wrapped her with the mangled tapestry after shaking it free of debris.

"Don't you dare give my wares to that wench!" shouted the furious shop owner, nearly breathless as he arrived. "Just look at this thing! It's ruined! You'd better have the money to pay for this, or I'll hang you with it."

Bewildered, the man turned to the shop owner and belted, "Excuse me?!"

"Step aside, you twit! And stay out of this," he barked, then lunged for Lowenna.

"Absolutely not!" clamored the man as he thwarted the shop owner's attempt to tear away the tapestry.

A growing crowd formed around the scuffle. Lowenna, still dizzy and disoriented, began to step backward, intending to sprint down the next alley.

"You oaf! Have you no idea who this woman is? You should feel honored she decided to settle for your shoddy textiles in the first place."

After the utterance of his statement, Lowenna abandoned the idea of fleeing.

"She's a wretch as far as I'm concerned."

"This is no wretch!" fumed the man impassionedly. "This is one of Celestine's most regarded elite. This is *Lowenna!*"

The shop owner's bluish-brown eyes hardened under the gravity of his proclamation. "*Impossible.*"

"You know what," he said while digging into the sack tied to his belt, "I don't need to convince you of anything. I'll buy this tapestry to get you out of my sight. Take it."

The shop owner looked around at the crowd's disapproving and judgmental eyes as he accepted the stack of coins. Without uttering another word, he hightailed back to his shop.

"You know, it took every ounce of my fortitude not to throw that coin down the street and make him fetch it like the dribbling mongrel he is."

Lowenna chuckled as he looked her way.

"I'm Jayce, by the way," he said, extending his hand with a warm smile.

"Lowenna," she replied, forgetting he already knew who she was. "Where am I?"

"Eastern Celestine. In the small oceanside town of Zhayara."

Lowenna recalled the quaint town as she looked at the setting sun. A small island sat just off the coast where she, Navaryn, and Kumiko used to crossover train with the rest of their clique when they were younger. Her teeth chattered as another chilly gust blew by.

"I'd love to offer you something more fitting to wear, but I have nothing," said Jayce as he gestured to his covered stall. "Though I do have some tea and crackers if you're interested. It's not much, but I'm sure it will help replenish your strength."

She exhaled and looked into his yellow-green eyes, then clutched his shoulder. "I think your kindness was all I needed. Thank you. I'll return soon to repay you for the mess I caused. I guess running through here like a maniac wasn't the best idea, was it?" They both shared a chuckle, then Lowenna worked to center herself. She visualized Navaryn's castle and calibrated her position. "Goodbye, Jayce," she said with a subtle wink.

As he bade farewell, thick, vibrant arcing light leapt from her skin and collided in the air. The flittering channels either dissolved into shimmering flecks or absorbed back into her limbs. Jayce watched in awe at the intimate demonstration before him. Paralleling was a feat only the most skilled Celestine could accomplish, and never before had he seen it performed in such proximity.

Following a few dissonant jitters, the blinding white light stole

Lowenna away. Jayce winced at the single electric crack that immediately followed her departure. He took a moment to replay his interactions with the Celestine elite before kneeling to clean up the mess of broken wares. For a moment, the marketplace was quieter than it was at dawn on a frosty winter's day, when only the most dedicated vendors came to set up shop before the sun had a chance to thaw the city. Once the familiar bustling resumed, the curious bystanders either continued about their business or walked over to offer Jayce their assistance.

·)(·

Lowenna reappeared at the rear of Navaryn's castle, then darted toward the entrance to the charmed cave. Once inside, she dashed atop the new and years-old footprints made by her and her comrades and maneuvered through sharp stones and scattered bones that lined the path.

"Onyx!" she called as a large set of sparkly blue eyes greeted her. "I'm so happy to see you!"

Navaryn's dragon galumphed gleefully in her direction, snorting cinders and short bursts of flames. Though it had only been half a year since she had seen him, she swore that he had since tripled in size.

"Soon, we're gonna need to find you a bigger cave, huh, handsome?" she said as she patted his scaly head. "I'll be back to catch up soon."

Lowenna kissed her scaly friend goodbye, then dashed further into the cave toward Navaryn's safe room. Halfway down the corridor, the ground transitioned from moist, jagged rocks to finished stone. She quickened her pace, keeping a firm grip on the tattered tapestry.

"Von?!" she shouted in a stumble.

As Lowenna entered the dark and quiet safe room, her heart hit the floor. The fireplace she had expected to find ablaze was extinguished, and no one was present. She backtracked her steps, lit one of the wall torches down the hall, and then used it to inspect the room. Aside from a nearly empty wine rack, most everything appeared to be in place. Off in the far corner of the room, beneath the failing glow of the concealment charms, a dark spot on the floor caught her eye. Upon closer inspection, she discovered it was a bloodstained rag. Curiously, she brought it to her nose for a whiff and detected a faint yet familiar musky odor. Puzzled that this was the only thing out of place, Lowenna continued her search in the unlikely event Von was meandering the property. She sighed, unprepared to ascend the several flights of stairs that led to the castle's back kitchen.

Following a break for some water, Lowenna wiped her sweaty brow and glanced over the familiar items inside the dim and quiet room. A sense of nostalgia and the profound pull of homesickness found her. The only foreseeable remedy was for everyone to return to their rightful places.

After an uneventful search of Navaryn's estate, Lowenna cut into the orchards for some fruit and crossed the barrier to initiate her next Parallel. It took a few frustrating attempts, but she managed to transmit herself to her property with the last of her strength. Her shaky legs buckled under her body weight, and she collapsed atop the dewy grass. As she picked herself up, she was met by a gentle breeze carrying the scent of a familiar bouquet of her garden blooms and the nearby forest. Though she could hardly believe it, she was finally home.

Lowenna peeked around the bend to her vegetable garden, expecting to see whatever was in view to be either bolted, dead, or in desperate need of pruning. There was just enough sunlight left in the sky for her to make out a sector of raised beds, all of which looked freshly turned. Curious, she walked over for a closer look. From pot to bed and in-ground plot, everything was immaculate and in its place for the season.

With teary eyes, Lowenna ran her fingers over the span of sugar peas growing in the space before the turned beds. Overwhelmed by the kindness she assumed came from her former caretaker, Demelza, she wept with gratitude. Careful not to let herself get distracted for long, she quickly picked a variety of tender offerings and then made her way inside for a quick shower and a proper fit.

After what Lowenna considered to be the best lather of her life, she quickly rinsed, wrapped herself in her white terry robe, then grabbed a matching towel hanging just outside the glass door. A good shower never failed to rejuvenate her. Smiling, she vigorously dried her sopping, wavy locks and stepped out of the spacious, steamy shower. Intending to dress quickly, she wrapped her hair in the towel and left the bathroom. Upon rounding the corner to her closet, she interrupted the timid gait of both Demelza and Aalrija. The trio stood frozen in each other's tracks with mouths agape.

"Lowenna?!" cried Demelza. "It really is you! *See?* I told you I wasn't imagining things."

Aalrija narrowed her yellow-green eyes and replied, "I never said you were wrong. I just said you *might* not be right."

"I'd recognize Lowenna's energy signal far beyond my last breath!"

Lowenna watched the two older women bicker with a grin, even though she wasn't ready for their company. She deduced that her energy suppression lacked the proper intensity on account of her weakened state. Nevertheless, tears welled behind her eyes, and she walked to them for a firm embrace.

"Seeing both of you makes this even more real," Lowenna whispered.

The women ceased their petty squabble and returned her gesture. "Have you had a look around?" asked Demelza.

"I have. You've taken such great care of everything while I've been gone. My garden. It's like I never left."

While Lowenna and Demelza shared another warm embrace, Aalrija chimed, "My dear, I hate to spoil things by asking, but did Navaryn return with you?"

Lowenna knew to keep her answer simple. She gave her damp blonde locks another pass with the towel and answered, "I'm afraid not."

Aalrija then asked, "Have you told anyone else you're back?"

The women followed Lowenna into her closet, where she rummaged through her wardrobe for suitable attire. She shook her head and answered, "No. But if the two of you were able to sense me in my condition, it won't be a secret for long," she replied, thinking on her feet.

"We can't know that for certain," claimed Demelza. "We should inform Benson. Now. He's going to want to know this."

Aalrija rested against the corner of the wall and sighed at Demelza's predictable reaction. To ensure a few private moments with Lowenna, she fibbed, "I'll need a moment if you want me to go. Paralleling is taking a lot out of me these days."

Demelza rolled her crystal blue eyes and laughed. "I never thought I'd see the day when you'd admit you're getting old."

"That is not what I—ugh. Fine. Take it as you will."

"And so I shall," concluded Demelza with a smirk, then turned to Lowenna as she walked out of her closet. "I'm so happy you're back safe and sound, my child. For now, try not to worry too hard about Navaryn, okay?"

"Thank you, Demelza. I've missed you."

"I've missed you more."

Demelza placed her silky, deep-toned hands upon Lowenna's shoulders, then gave both of her cheeks a kiss before promptly leaving the room. Aalrija looked to Lowenna with a telling expression, confirming her earlier fib. To ensure Demelza was no longer in earshot of their conversation, they waited in silence until they heard her Parallel snap out past the garden.

"Look at us. Resorting to lying."

"I know. As if I'm not exhausted enough as it is." Lowenna tossed the outfit she held onto the bed. "How much does she know?" she asked, then dug out a matching underwear set from the bottom drawer of her nightstand.

While Lowenna dressed, Aalrija walked to the foot of her bed and replied, "Nothing. I'm sure you're not surprised."

"I'm not. I'm sure if she saw what Kumiko was doing right now, she and the rest of the Tiers would be losing their minds."

"You saw him?!"

Lowenna nodded. "Right before I broke free. Leave it to him to ruin everything by intruding."

Aalrija fiddled with the golden trim at the edge of her long sleeves as she nervously revealed, "Actually, he and Von have kind of *teamed up*."

Unable to fathom the alliance, Lowenna froze with her lightly armored undershirt in her hands.

"But there's something else even more unprecedented. Benson. Aside from knowing both you and Fallon are in on the plan, he's up to speed on everything. But the most concerning part is that he's done *nothing*. He didn't react to Von's involvement, and as far as I can tell, he hasn't said a word to the other Tiers."

"I don't believe for a second he's sitting idly by. He's plotting something." Lowenna sat beside her with her diadem in hand, then continued, "I need to get to Von. Where is he?"

"He left once I told him about Benson. He didn't say where he was going, but I assume he's somewhere in Daeva with Claymar."

Lowenna dropped her diadem to the ground and stared at Aalrija, eyes bulging. "Claymar?!"

"Yes. Von found him. He rescued him. Well, with Kumiko's help."

Lowenna's eyes brimmed with joyous tears. "Oh, thank Hirunae," she cried, then hugged Aalrija tightly.

The unexpected gesture startled Aalrija, who was more accustomed to Lowenna's reserved nature. She continued to embrace her until her quaking breaths finally calmed.

"I've got to find them," she said, then wiped away her tears and scooped her diadem off the floor. "I'll be back soon, hopefully with Navaryn this time."

"Wait a moment. You can't be serious. Not only are you in no condition to assist them, but Benson will want to see you."

"Screw Benson! I'm done with the formalities, and I don't care if he finds out I'm involved in this. Plus, I'd just be wasting my time sticking around here."

"Just settle down and let the others handle this."

Frustrated that Aalrija presumed her obedience, Lowenna paused to deduce the situation. Judging from her lack of urgency, she gathered that Aalrija wasn't privy to the present ongoings in the realm of Human, nor that she carried zero influence on Kumiko's actions. Furthermore, his reckless behavior suggested ulterior motives beyond his truce with Von, despite their shared goal.

While Lowenna stood conflicted in thought, Aalrija took her by her shoulders and pleaded for her cooperation. "Please understand, I aim to spare you from the repercussions that will follow your involvement. Celestine needs you. And we can't lose you again."

24

THE COVETOUS

Navaryn peered into the starry night sky as she sat perched atop the south tower of the Golden Gate Bridge, where traffic on both sides had come to a halt. Nearly two hours had passed since her arrival, and a horde of curious spectators from all reaches of the city had corralled behind metal guard rails put in place by the local authorities. Sirens blared amidst the stirring commotion that wailed below, though Navaryn was too captivated by the tiny moon peeking out from behind the misty clouds to pay it any mind.

Exhaustion had set in after repeated failed attempts to Parallel back to the realm of Celestine. While fiddling with the obsidian pendant around her neck, she cursed the tether to her human host, which she believed prevented her from returning home. Lost in a flurry of emotions, her wistful gaze fixed on the glowing satellite, hoping it would bring her the comfort she needed.

Numb to the unrelenting frigid winds sailing atop the tower, Navaryn broke away from the moon long enough to contemplate her next course of action. Under the assumption that Kumiko wasn't far behind, she resolved to continue eluding him. While running her fingers along her pendant, she held it close to inspect its fine details. The gleaming, hand-carved face had remarkable detail, but the fingered edge indicated it wasn't complete without another piece.

Navaryn chuckled at how coincidental it was that the object shared her circumstances. Curious to find the maker's signature, she turned the pendant over.

"This has to be some kind of joke."

Navaryn's insides burned as she studied the engraved sigil. Though she should have been thankful for the protection it afforded her, she viewed it as the reason why Von had yet to come to her aid. Without hesitation, she tore it from her neck and tossed it into the water below.

Shortly after her would-be liberation, a strange whapping sound cut through the air in the distance. Navaryn stood and spread her wings in preparation to flee, but a nauseous sensation overpowered her will. While she recalibrated, her wings caught an agitated gust sent by two approaching news helicopters. Bombarded by every one of Rayshell's anxious emotions, Navaryn failed to center herself and stumbled backward off the tower's edge.

Illuminated by a set of spotlights, the hysterical crowd watched Navaryn corkscrew toward the bridge. In her final moments of descent, she regained enough control to break her fall. Nervous, bleary-eyed, and feeling like she was moments away from vomiting, Navaryn slowly rose to her feet. Camera crews from all local news networks tried to push through the police blockade for a better angle of the mysterious angelic figure. Their microphones and video cameras bumped into the surrounding crowd as glittering white flashes suffused the mass of squashed bodies, who paid little mind to the officers' demands for order.

Navaryn stood amidst a slowly encroaching team of inquisitive yet alert officers who jumped each time she so much as twitched.

"What's your name?" a red-haired officer called in a firm yet nervous tone. "Are you hurt?"

"We're here to help you," another officer insisted as she continued to approach cautiously. "Just tell us your name."

Navaryn stumbled back and put her hands out, hoping it would signal them to ease their pressing.

"Hey, Allen?" whispered another officer to his comrade. "Think this is a real angel?"

"I don't know what to believe," he replied with his hand hovering above his taser.

Navaryn's ears pricked to the familiar sound of Officer Allen's voice as he exchanged light words with his colleague beside the red-haired officer in charge of the battalion. There was an odd comfort in knowing he was present, which she believed came from Rayshell, but the hysterical crowd behind the blockade just ahead reminded her to stay alert.

A crazed man pushed through the blockade while shouting religious tropes with outstretched hands. Two officers tackled him to the ground before he could finish his delirious proclamation and proceeded to cuff him. A handful of spectators fought over the newly formed space in the first row as an older woman climbed atop the folks ahead of her.

"Our day of reckoning has come!" she belted and frantically waved her arms in the air. "Save me, angel! Save us *all!*"

Navaryn's blurry eyes could barely make out the details of the sticky sea of frantic humans holding up their signs with nonsensical phrases scribbled on them. Still, she stared in their direction with a perplexed and genuinely disturbed expression at their odd behavior. Knowing her situation was likely to worsen, Navaryn worked to find the concentration and strength needed to Parallel. Wispy green energy sputtered from her chest, then suddenly, her muscles cramped, and her breath seized. She collapsed to her knees on the filthy pavement and gasped for air. Her wings fanned open, drawing awestruck reactions from the surrounding crowd, then started curling inwards.

The officers stood spellbound as Navaryn's silvery wings bent, snapped, and slowly retracted into her back in a gruesome display. Allen, who initially convinced himself the spectacle was nothing more than a prank, instinctively dashed to her side. His action encouraged a few of his colleagues to break through their hesitation and follow his lead.

Swiping her red hair to the side, Officer Hannigan stood amidst her battalion and radioed for the paramedics on standby to step in and lend their aid. Navaryn clutched onto Officer Allen's uniform and wept.

"Please don't leave me," she uttered through the sickening, syrupy sounds of her bloodied wings as they slipped inside the gaping lacerations on her back.

Allen's eyes grew resolute. For a moment, he thought her voice sounded strangely familiar. "I'll stay with you," he professed through her painful cries. "I'm not going anywhere."

His colleagues made room for the advancing paramedics. Immediately after the vehicle had parked, the team dashed over with blankets and totes brimming with medical supplies. Navaryn pronged the last of the long, silvery feathers sticking out of her back as a warning to those who approached. The sudden jolt sent droplets of blood into the air and bespattered all in proximity, bringing them to a standstill in shock.

"It's okay. They're here to help you. You can trust me," he whispered.

Rayshell eventually influenced Navaryn to drop her guard. As soon as she relaxed her muscles, the last portion of her wings immediately retracted. Navaryn's eyes shot wide open, feeling as though her torso had split in two. As she went limp in Allen's arms, he reassured the nervous paramedics that they could approach. They worked together to gently wrap her naked body with a warm blanket as another paramedic from the team arrived with a gurney. Before they could load her onto the contraption, a ghostly, verdant flash erupted. Kumiko materialized with outstretched wings amidst a wispy electric snap, blindsiding those closest to him with a gust of wind. The crowd erupted into further hysterics at the arrival of a second angelic creature before them. Scattered screams amidst the blinding flashes of cameras made Kumiko's anger steadily rise. He shoved through the unarmed paramedics to get to Allen, prompting the rest of the battalion to take formation.

"Nav!" Kumiko yelled over the hysterical crowd barricaded behind the authorities. "What did you do to her?!"

"W-we didn't do anything. She fell from the tower," Hannigan explained. Her weapon rattled in her hands as she fixated on the deep amethyst gleam in Kumiko's eyes. "We're trying to help her."

Kumiko was cautious about trusting her declaration.

"Who are you? Are you human?" she foolishly asked.

"Do I *look* human to you?" Kumiko replied snidely and looked down the barrel of her gun. "It makes no difference who I am. I've come for my friend."

"Yeah, well, we're gonna need a little more cooperation than that."

Sensing that the tension between Kumiko and Hannigan would only continue to rise, Allen called, "She's okay. At least, I hope she is."

Kumiko walked away from Hannigan, though he barely batted an eye in her direction as she followed his gait with her pistol. When he approached Allen, he folded his wings and knelt beside him, looking upon Navaryn's sleeping face. He knew it wouldn't be long before she reverted to her human counterpart, which would spell disaster should the reckless crowd witness it happen. Assertively, Kumiko took Navaryn into his arms.

"She's lost a lot of blood. She needs a hospital," he said as he looked at Kumiko.

"All she needs is to sleep, then she will be fine," he claimed. "Trust me."

"Hey, excuse me!" shouted Hannigan with her gun still trained on Kumiko. "Where do you think you're taking her?"

Bloodstained and still in shock from the ordeal, Allen hopped to his feet and stood between Kumiko and her gun. "Lower your weapon," he ordered, looking her dead in the eyes. "Let them be."

As the two officers bickered amongst their apprehensive colleagues, Kumiko stood silent and observant. Though he was familiar with the general nature of humankind, he still found himself baffled by their collective ineptitude, hysteria, and bitter disillusion. He knew all too well from his studies that humans were deemed a lost and dangerous species; they were too proud and self-centered to maintain a symbiotic relationship with their flora, fauna, and their planet. Just as well, any hope of them rediscovering their true potential felt infinitely distant. His mind churned with choice lines of advice to bestow upon them in hopes of correcting their detached and misguided ways, but ultimately chose not to waste his breath. Before either of the officers glanced in his direction again, he disappeared under a wispy green current.

Kumiko Paralleled as far as he could carry Navaryn and reappeared with her several cities away in a small clearing deep within a stretch of rolling hills. His substantial expenditure of energy left him weakened to resist the realm's thirstful pull, though the secluded area was suitable enough for a reprieve before plotting another move. Settled amidst a profusion of tall, waving grass, Kumiko knelt with Navaryn in his arms. The air was chilly at the higher elevation, and he was grateful that the humans had enough decency to wrap her in a blanket. He stared contentedly at her sleeping face, relieved that her Celestine form hadn't fully regressed. Her radiant visage had become elusive to him for so long, especially with a look so placid. Giving in to his quiet longing to feel Navaryn's embrace, he tightly wrapped his arms around her and closed his eyes. Even though it seemed there would never be another opportunity to continue from where they had left off, he never surrendered hope.

Having been pleasantly distracted by memories and grand delusions of a future that would never be, a nearby Parafall eluded Kumiko's senses. The skulking presence approached the couple as a swift shadow dancing among the rustling bushes and trees, then as a cluster of scattered leaves that descended inconspicuously behind them. In a sinister, stealthy fashion, the false figures quickly merged and augmented. Kumiko came to his senses and frantically surveyed his surroundings upon hearing the sound of crunching grass. He suddenly turned his head into an outstretched hand with no time to react. A jolt of black and purple crystalline energy blindsided Kumiko and sent him ricocheting off the ground, where his body quickly dissolved from the plane in white arcing light.

The hearty chuckling of the clever and adept shapeshifter broke apart the quiet air. Joro, with potent glowing emerald eyes, opened Navaryn's blanket with his thick index finger. Hundreds of scars visible only to a keen enough eye adorned her skin. Such scars, obtained through numerous battles, were characteristic of both Celestines and Daeva alike. He placed his warm hand beside her breast and ran his sensitive fingertips along her body's curvature to study her imperceptible flaws through her ripped garments. Though Joro had beheld her naked body only once before, he could distinguish every new blemish and defect she had obtained since.

Joro fought through his desire to take Navaryn straight to Daeva. Because her essence was still bound to the human girl, there was no guarantee she could survive the physical strain of an inter-realm Parallel. Until Navaryn could detach from her human host, he had no choice but to seek a place to harbor the melded pair. While pondering what to do next, Navaryn lay unconscious among the dewy strands of grass, unaware of his malicious plans and the unnerving, sharp-toothed smile that twisted his face.

·)(·

Benson called for an urgent meeting with the Tiers as news of Lowenna's return came to his attention. Instead of sitting in their designated places upon arrival, the frantic collective paced atop the council chamber's black marble floor and shouted over one another. Lowenna recalled only a handful of other occasions when Benson held such unorganized meetings. She remained frustratingly silent after her peers concluded their bombardment of inquiries regarding her imprisonment in Human, and any knowledge that could facilitate Navaryn's awakening. Working against any detriment, Lowenna confessed only vague details and, more importantly, omitted knowledge of Navaryn's transformation.

Lowenna remained calm among her panicky peers as she leaned against the marble baluster. Aalrija convinced her not to wear her combat gear to the council chamber to avoid suspicion. Still, she refused to part with her diadem, for her energy had not yet fully replenished. She folded her arms and watched the others bicker about the flaws of everyone's ideas but their own. Interestingly, she noticed that Benson was oddly quiet given the situation and feared whatever plan he had hatched behind closed doors.

The furious, repeated tapping of heels on the marble floor started to make Lowenna's eye twitch. Along with Demelza, she had always been an example of poise and sensibility among her peers, but she was moments away from forfeiting that standing. Her anxious mind feverishly churned as she observed the lack of proper control, focus, and effective collaboration. Just as she opened her parched lips to admonish the congregation, there was a rap at the council chamber's doors. The collective was immediately silenced as Ciaran quickly stepped in.

"Benson, sir. We have a bit of a, uh, *situation*."

The Tiers followed behind Ciaran's stride. When they arrived through one of the rear corridors, Teagan rose to his feet and locked eyes with Benson.

Benson's thunderous footfalls prompted his gathering staff to make way for his approach. Teagan gestured toward the guards and attendants who surrounded a limp and unresponsive body at the center of the hall. With fearful eyes, Benson darted ahead of the group to witness Kumiko's battered state. Half his face was scorched, and a white towel that one of the attendants promptly delivered upon his arrival wrapped his dirty, naked body.

"He's alive," Teagan assured Benson just as Demelza and Aalrija fell to their knees at Kumiko's side. "I'm not sure what happened to him, though."

Benson folded his arms and asked, "Where did you find him?" with an expression that failed to hide his disappointment.

"In the vineyards by the tavern," Teagan replied. "I was making my usual late-night check after closing the tavern. Down one of the rows, I saw what I thought was just another irresponsible lush who got turned around looking for a place to take a piss, then decided to sleep it off until the morning. I wanted to leave him there and let the night frost sober his nerves, but I couldn't do it. I thought my mind was playing tricks on me when I beheld his face. I don't know how Kumiko wound up where he did."

"Did you see anyone else?" asked Labraid from Benson's side.

"No. Nothing at all. And I don't think he was there for very long because I smelled his burnt hair right away."

"We should get him to the infirmary," chimed Ailbhis as he looked at his peers. "Kumiko's a tough young man, but it's best not to take any chances, wouldn't you agree?"

"Fine," Benson reluctantly agreed. "We can at least get him cleaned up and out of this embarrassing state."

A handful of attendants hoisted Kumiko off the floor, then carted him off following Ailbhis' lead. Aalrija and Lowenna's hesitant steps brought up the rear. Before rounding the dark corridor bend, the women glanced at one another with troubled eyes. They suspected someone had ambushed Kumiko while trying to protect Navaryn.

"Aalrija, *please*," whispered Lowenna as discreetly as she could manage. "I need to get back to Human. Something awful is happening. I know it."

"But you mustn't. You need to regain your power."

"This is ridiculous," she hissed. "This can't wait."

"Even if you were to make your way there now, what good would you be?" Anticipating her reply, Aalrija continued, "And if you think that diadem of yours will do the trick, think again. You're going to kill yourself if you use that thing unwisely."

Lowenna folded her arms and furrowed her brows. "Aalrija, you don't unders—"

"Don't forget who we still have on our team. If we want our plan to work, you have to suck it up and play along. Now, we'll talk more about this later. We'll see what information Kumiko has when he awakes."

Before Lowenna or Aalrija knew Benson had his eyes trained on them, he averted his watchful gaze. Their subtle actions made it clear they knew what befell his son. No less fed up with the dishonesty that infected his cabinet, he allowed them to continue thinking he was none the wiser rather than address them outright. Ultimately, their hidden agendas would have no bearing on the future he envisioned. Once Navaryn was safely back in Celestine, by the hand of his disobedient collective or otherwise, she would be the first one cleansed of her deviances.

25

THE CHOICE

A clamor of crows stirred Rayshell out of her deep slumber. Her bleary eyes could see little else but the procession of veining light seeping through the cracks in the wall as she rose. It was painful to move and very uncomfortable to breathe. Panic set in as her eyes adjusted to the dark space around her. Utterly confused, she had no idea where she was or how she ended up in such a frigid and unpleasant place. She clutched the blanket covering her naked body and rose to her feet from a decrepit, compressed pile of hay that smelled stiflingly sour.

With a racing heartbeat, she surveyed the deteriorated condition of the large wooden stable and gathered that she was on an abandoned farm. Dust and cobwebs covered the rows of overhead light fixtures, and the confines of dingy metal and rickety wood bordered the box stall caging her. She hobbled to the door and discovered a wad of chain braided through the fasteners on the other side. Though unlocked, it was secure enough to stay in place when she thrashed the door. Desperately, she reached over the shoulder-high wooden panels and through the metal bars of the door, but her fingers merely grazed the cold, braided metal links. Ignoring the radiating pain in her body, she pounded against the door with her fists and feet, then continued her fit across the stall's perimeter until her muscles gave out. Not a single panel budged from its place. A string of profanity left her lips as she griped at her failed efforts.

Rayshell curled into a ball and sobbed atop the hard, lumpy ground. As she drowned herself in ominous predictions of the horrors that awaited her, vivid memory fragments of her fiasco with Kumiko dashed before her eyes. Painful stabbing sensations accompanied each procession, making her flinch and squirm. Blood began to fall from her nostrils as dizzying glimpses of feathers, flight, and the frightened faces of strangers flickered past. All of the frenetic imagery in her mind convinced her it was nothing more than a dream. However, that notion washed away once she realized the blanket she was frantically clutching was the same one the paramedics covered her in.

When Rayshell finally collected herself, she felt as though hours had passed. With swollen and blurry eyes, she wiped the grime and grit from her face, then nestled into a somewhat comfortable spot in one of the far corners to rest her throbbing head. Covered in her itchy hay-threaded blanket, she studied the stall door for defects to potentially exploit. Her eyes followed the support beam toward the ceiling, where she discovered a fresh carving glowing with mellow purple light just below a curtain of thick webs. Equally intrigued as she was worried, Rayshell rose to better observe the marking. The design was reminiscent of the sigils Trish had cataloged in her notebook, but she couldn't recall them in explicit enough detail to determine if they were the same. Nervously, Rayshell turned about the stall and discovered identical carvings at approximately the same height in each corner.

The markings were out of hand's reach, but Rayshell had an idea driven purely by instinct. She dropped to her knees and dug out a long and thin twig discovered after fluffing the hay pile. With careful patience, she used it to scrape away at one of the glowing sigils. After a few minutes of progress, a metallic jangle came from outside the main door.

Seized by terror, Rayshell froze and dropped the twig to the ground. A large chain clattered through the door's outer metal handles, and then a thick, masculine figure walked in. Instantly, she recognized her visitor and started to whimper. She closed her eyes and pressed herself against the stall corner as if doing so would render her invisible.

After fastening the interior handles with the chain he brought in with him, Joro glanced inside her stall with a smirk. "I was hoping you'd be awake by the time I returned," he called while rustling through a sack with some quick harvest from the nearby orchards. "I was growing bored."

Joro's thick boots clomped over the uneven, dusty floor as he approached Rayshell's stall. He looked her over with his glowing emerald eyes, then offered her a peach through the metal bars. "Hungry?"

Rayshell cringed at his gesture and continued to weep silently. Joro's patience expired before his second breath, and he let the fruit slip from his fingers onto the floor of her stall. He then sloppily stuffed his face with the piece he picked out for himself.

"That was quite the ruckus you caused last night. I'm sure when Benson gets wind of this, he won't be the least bit amused," he said through a sickening symphony of slurping with his eyes arrowed at Rayshell. "You do know who I'm talking about, right? That coward whom that Celestine wench within you serves."

Rayshell took in only a few glances of Joro's intimidating countenance.

"You know what I find hilarious? It's Navaryn's job to preserve this so-called 'balance' among the realms. But all she seems to do is fuck up. *Significantly.* And you'll end up doing the same if you aren't quick to stop your cowering and answer me when I speak."

Joro finished the drippy, overripe stone fruit, then tossed the pit at Rayshell. With all the courage she could muster, she calmed her quaking breath and opened her eyes. However, his sharp-toothed smirk from beyond the rusty metal bars kept her petrified.

"I'll play nice as long as you do," he said, unfastening the chain to her stall.

Rayshell nodded ever so slightly.

"Good. Now that we're on the same page," he said as he opened her stall, "I do have a question that I'd like answered."

Anticipating his inquiry, Rayshell proclaimed with a quivering lip, "I-I don't know where Iaalprt is, Joro."

"And look at that. You know the name. Impressive." He wiped his messy hands down the front of his black shirt, then continued, "Now, how about you pull its location out of Navaryn's head and give it to me? The sooner you do, the sooner you can go back to your meaningless little life."

As Joro sauntered her way, Rayshell casually repositioned her feet to conceal the twig she used to grind down the sigils.

With folded arms, he continued, "I'm not a patient person, Rayshell. Don't make this harder than it has to be."

Hearing her name uttered from Joro's tense lips filled her with dread. As much as she tried to conceal her tells, she couldn't keep her eyes from bouncing to the marred sigil on the beam behind him. With his seasoned experience, it didn't take Joro long to discover what she was hiding. He stepped uncomfortably close and moved one of her shaky legs to the side with his foot.

"You clever little girl," he muttered as he looked upon the chaffed twig. "I guess I can't count on you playing nice, now, can I?"

Hot tears streamed down Rayshell's sensitive cheeks. Before she could make her plea, Joro shoved her to the ground and aggressively restrained her weakened limbs.

"You know, you *do* share some similarities with Navaryn." He snickered as she thrashed below him. "Her cleverness ... even some of her carelessness."

Rayshell's blanket pulled open as she tried to wriggle free from his grasp.

"But you definitely don't share her strength. So stop fighting me before I break your arms," he threatened, then effortlessly secured both of her wrists in one hand.

"I'm sorry!" she desperately wailed. "Please. I-I just want to go home."

Joro looked upon Rayshell's sniveling face in disgust but couldn't help but lose himself to his repugnant fantasies. The sound of her quickened, stifled breaths recalled scenes of blissful torment in his mind. At that moment, he wanted nothing more than to break the defenseless girl down until the stress forced Navaryn to resurface. The thought of looking into the Celestine's panicky hazel eyes and hearing her fervent screams was too enticing to pass up. He had nearly forgotten that the sigils meant to hold her in place were compromised and would likely fail if put to the test.

Rayshell blenched as Joro skimmed her flesh with his hot and thick fingers. His sour musk filled her nostrils as she watched beads of sweat gather atop his brow. When his putrid touch reached below her navel, she quickly locked her knees together.

"Please, Joro. Please don't do this to me."

Joro was equally unmoved by Rayshell's pleading as he was by her tears. Though he hungered for his Celestine rival to appear, the feel of his victim's unripe curves deadened his wanton desire. He pulled his hand away from her trembling flesh and placed his fingertips to his tongue to confirm his speculation.

"Disgusting. You taste nothing like her," he coldly remarked.

Sneering, Joro released Rayshell's wrists and slowly rose. He stood at her feet and watched her shaky hands scout for the edges of the blanket, then proceeded to repair the sigils. Once finished, he exited the stall, rethreaded the chain through the door fixture, and then dug his hand through the bag of harvest.

"I'd recommend you eat that peach before the afternoon is up, or I'll force-feed you myself," he affirmed with a terrifying gaze.

Rayshell continued to sob as she listened to the sound of Joro's boots slowly trail off. She looked to the newly reformed sigils upon the rafters in shame. Although the thought of making another attempt to remove them crossed her mind, the paralyzing fear of an even worse violation by Joro kept her from trying. Her tears fell quickly as the pain in her weakened body pulsed stronger, while the light of her dwindling hope continued to die.

·)(·

Impatiently, Benson watched Kumiko stir beneath two layers of fine ivory linen with a glass of frosty water in hand. He sipped at the herbaceous concoction, filtering the floating particles with his clenched teeth, and rested against the window's deep stool. Across from him, beside the room's entrance, Ciaran took turns rotating his gaze around the room, periodically landing in Benson's intense eyes. At dawn, the pair had received word from the attendants that the wound on Kumiko's chest was nearly healed and that he could awaken at any moment.

Early afternoon had come, and the vibrant rays of light cutting in through the curtains had begun to deepen with a golden hue. Though his stomach felt swollen, Benson slugged back the rest of his water, then furiously paced to the cart beside Kumiko's bed to refill his glass. The rushing trickle panged both his full bladder and his sour nerves until he decided which of the two would be the first to rupture. With a white-knuckled grip on his glass, Benson feverishly slung the contents onto Kumiko's face.

Gasping with eyes peeled open, Kumiko shot up in bed. Before he could process where he was, a jolting procession of his latest memories pummeled him. He hunched inwards and put his fingers to his chest, where he expected to feel a raw, syrupy wound, but he touched only solid, bare flesh. His next recollection, however, stemmed from his human host, Tobias. An outline of Navaryn's bloodied, winged form standing in his living room flashed before his eyes, and suddenly, a suffocating sense of terror overcame him. He then turned to Benson with frightful eyes that beheld him as a stranger.

"W-who are you?! What do you want from me?!" he shrieked, prompting a befuddled look from Benson.

Satisfied that his son was awake, though not the least bit entertained by his crazed flailing, Benson slammed his glass atop the cart and gestured for Ciaran to secure the door. He clutched a patch of Kumiko's hair, then yelled, "Kumiko, it's me! Get a hold of yourself this instant!"

Following a swift swat across the face from his father, Kumiko moved his wet hair away from his eyes. Several moments had passed before he recognized his surroundings as his bedchamber. Just as he feared, he realized that the detrimental effects of Kaimaharaa had manifested. Though the severity of his affliction was unclear, he knew his wits needed to remain strong to combat any further progression. He swallowed a hot patch of saliva and held his breath, nervously watching Benson's furious pacing.

"You've got a lot of explaining to do, Son," he called with folded arms.

Kumiko turned away from his father's intense stare and opted to stay quiet.

"Admittedly, we've grown apart over the years, but for you to defy our values and principles by conspiring with the likes of Von is unthinkable."

Kumiko kicked himself out of the linen, then replied, "It seems you're quite aware of what's going on, Father. What's left to explain?"

A hot rush of rage ran up Benson's spine. He dashed to Kumiko and brought him to his feet by his shoulders. "I have given you *everything*! Ever since the day you were born, I have done nothing but bestow greatness upon you. And *this* is how you repay me?! By defying Celestine's decree?!"

Kumiko's posture deflated as his father tightened his grip.

"By such incomprehensible defiance, you, *Son*, are not only shaming me, but altogether divesting yourself from your future role as Celestine's imperator."

Kumiko wrestled out of his father's grasp and stumbled backward until he found his balance. "Be honest for once. In your eyes, I'll never be good enough to assume the throne of Celestine!" he belted. "This greatness you speak of was nothing more than abusive training and a bunch of elixirs you shoved down my throat. And all it ever did was remind me of how I was never good enough."

Benson straightened his posture and met his son's angry eyes as he berated him.

"I'm just your little project, Father. What you've truly bestowed upon me is the affirmation that I will never attain greatness on my own, and that my power will be insufficient to guarantee the security of our empire."

Benson rolled his eyes and scoffed, "You sound just like your mother."

His proclamation tore Kumiko's heart wide open. "You disgust me," he uttered with tearing eyes.

"Be that as it may, I couldn't care less. You can stand here and wallow in your despair, or you can follow my lead."

"Why would I ever choose to follow you?"

"Because I have a way to realign things in our favor." Benson turned away from his son and paced before the window.

Kumiko's scowl remained in place as he pondered his father's claim. "What do you mean?"

Benson chuckled and smoothed down the ornate fabric scrunched up his arms. "I mean, I am willing to forgive your foolish deeds so that we may start anew. A clean slate, so to speak."

Disregarding the uncomfortable silence of Kumiko's apprehension, Benson sauntered toward Ciaran as he removed the entrance medallion from under his vest. He took it by the long golden chain and held it toward Kumiko. "Care to take a walk with me?"

The polished emeralds and intricate details reflected the golden sunlight into Kumiko's eyes. It had been ages since he had ventured to the oubliette with his father, and he knew he used the dwelling to safeguard secrets from the Halryn council and the other Tiers. Curious to discover what his father was scheming, Kumiko quickly dressed in the garments folded at his bedside, then followed his father out of the room. Ciaran, devoid of much expression, followed behind them in a light-footed gait.

It wasn't until they reached Benson's private study, cloaked under the protection of privacy charms, that Kumiko spoke, "What are you planning, Father?"

"Simply, the preservation of Celestine."

"How?"

Benson gestured to the medallion Kumiko held around his neck. "Come with me, and I'll show you."

Kumiko looked to Ciaran for a moment, who in turn gave him a single nod, then walked to his father until they were close enough for their golden medallions to connect. In a sudden eruption of sparking green energy, the pair was transported into the oubliette, leaving Ciaran alone in the candlelit study.

Ciaran sighed and pulled the ornate wooden chair away from Benson's study table to rest his tired legs. While he skimmed the deranged inked rantings scribbled on the scattered parchment, he reflected on all the ways his dynamic with Benson had changed over the years. Though he loathed their arrangement early on, spending his life at Benson's side became something he grew to accept, as it afforded him the opportunity to witness the gradual decline of his rule. Nevertheless, he remained wary of the unhinged imperator's tireless pursuit of power. Benson's unhealthy obsession with Navaryn, and what integrating her power into his family could mean for the future of Celestine and the neighboring realms, was always a concerning subject to ponder.

·)☾(·

Successfully transmitted into the subterranean oubliette, Kumiko stumbled away from his father and collapsed to his knees in a disorienting fit of nausea. The residual transmission energy spiraled inside the dank room and kissed the wicks of the bordering pillar candles before dissipating into the darkness. Kumiko reached for the nearest receptacle and retched into it.

"I suppose it has been a while since you've been down here," said Benson as he hovered over his nauseated son. "Don't worry. It'll pass."

As the contents of his stomach pooled in front of his knees, Kumiko realized that the wicker basket wasn't the best choice.

Benson stood at his son's side with his hand extended and patiently waited for him to accept his gesture.

After wiping his mouth with his sleeve, Kumiko asked, "What are you hiding down here?"

"The keys to change," Benson answered vaguely. He opened a compartment in the wall shelf, removed the fitted velvet covers, and pulled out two small transparent cases, each containing a single orb of crystalline energy suspended within a peculiar apparatus.

Kumiko touched his fingertips to one of the cases and immediately felt the orb's powerful reverberation. "What are these?" he asked.

"The answer to our problems," Benson replied as he set the cases atop the dusty shelf. "This is how we'll bring Navaryn back to us. For good."

"*For good?* What does that even mean?"

"Not only will this orb undo the horrible sorcery that has trapped Navaryn inside of that human girl you've been chasing after, but it will bring her back to us with an unadulterated mind. All of her impurities will be gone, and she'll finally be rid of her infatuation with that Daeva. She will swear her heart to you, and her soul to Celestine."

For a moment, Kumiko stopped breathing. There was nothing more important than to have Navaryn back at his side, but the thought of it being a farce wasn't something he felt he could live with. "Father, the power I feel from these is not of Celestine origin," he said suspiciously. "Where did you get these?"

"That is not important. But what I will say is this," said Benson as he pushed away from the counter's edge. "I understand you've disapproved of my interference in the past. Say what you will of my unorthodox efforts to enrich your power throughout your life. Right or wrong, I've merely done what I deemed was necessary for your ascension."

Kumiko parted his lips, intending to interrupt his father, but not a word left his mouth.

"But *this*," Benson continued as he circled behind Kumiko. "This orb will put Navaryn back by your side, where she belongs. Your union with her will ensure the preservation of our realm. With your shared powers, your rule will be unchallengeable, and Daeva, nor any other realm, would never dare invade Celestine again."

Benson retrieved the orb meant for Navaryn and placed it into Kumiko's hands. The serene glow of crystalline energy accentuated the amethyst hue of his eyes as he marveled at it. Within the otherworldly power lay the gateway to the future his father had envisioned. He then curiously moved his warm gaze to the second orb on the shelf.

"Why are there two of them?"

"The other is meant for Lowenna," Benson replied nonchalantly.

"Lowenna?"

"She is not without her own deviances. They must be flushed away just the same," he said as he tapped against the second case. "She's back in Celestine, if you weren't already aware."

"Lowenna managed to break free?"

"Are you surprised? She's a Shahiri, after all. Navaryn, on the other hand—I may have a theory for why she hasn't done the same."

"What might that be?"

"As you well know, she sacrificed herself to protect Iæalprt. She may be intending to stay hidden away in that human girl to protect the secret of its location."

"You're saying you think she would sooner let the secret of the Order die with her than return home?"

Benson nodded. "As unruly as her behavior is, her discipline and commitment to the Order surely know no bounds. Nevertheless, I will not allow her to remain in that wretched imprisonment. We need her back in Celestine. *Immediately*."

Kumiko paced the room as he unexpectedly gave credence to his father's theory.

"Tell me, Kumiko. What happened last night?" Benson asked.

"While I was in Human?"

Kumiko watched as his father's inquisition tightened his face, then chose to divulge all the details of what he had experienced. He confessed to his use of Kaimaharaa, revealed the strange unfolding of Navaryn's metamorphosis, and made mention of the powerful being who tactfully blindsided him.

"I'm certain it was Joro who ambushed me. The stink of his energy is unmistakable," he concluded.

Benson clenched his teeth as he paced about the cubliette. "I expected him and Merisek to be on the hunt, but not for them to be this close."

Despite his deep resentment toward his father, Kumiko felt the burden lift from his shoulders after his reveal. For once, he felt his father had finally taken an interest in nurturing his fulfillment, and he couldn't help but entertain the thought of how everything would have played out had he only put more trust in him.

"Son, we must act quickly," said Benson as he approached

Kumiko. "Navaryn *will* be brought home with this orb. But I'm giving you the opportunity, here and now, to be the one to do it. What do you decide?"

Faced with yet another choice before him, Kumiko pivoted back to the strange orbs that danced inside their respective receptacles, then exhaled anxiously. His father's eyes were piercing yet full of eager determination. Though he fought the urge to put his faith in such diablerie, the temptation was impossible to resist.

"I choose Celestine. I choose *Navaryn*," he reluctantly conceded.

26

THE REUNION

Although Von and Claymar's return to the familiarity of Daeva was somewhat of a relief, the environment felt far different than it had several months prior. Their usual selection of hideouts to lay low was booming with patrolling soldiers throughout the cities, conducting random stops in search of Merisek's abandoned defectors. With the whole of Daeva's militant forces perpetually on high alert, Von and Claymar didn't want to risk being found on account of their previous history with Merisek. Their most viable option was to make their way to the vast forests of western Daeva, where they could formulate a new plan in the safety of obscurity.

Located among some of the highest-elevated landscapes, the western forest was far too remote for most to venture into. It was, however, some of the most serene, verdant land within the realm. Von had taken an interest in the region after discovering its splendor during his travels and had come to know the woods intimately. Nestled deep within a thicket of trees stood a spacious cabin where Von would retreat for bouts of solitude. However, it had since been abandoned when bounty hunters tracked him there. Considering the potential for danger, it was still the safest place amid the heightened military presence.

After stealthily gathering supplies and a few weapons from Von's hidden stashes, they Paralleled to a towering cliffside at the edge of the forest overlooking a deep valley below, as the dense canopy above prevented a direct Parallel deep into the trees. After a swift jaunt through the woods, they discovered winding vines and clusters of ferns had overtaken the cabin, yet it remained in one piece. Heavy rainfall had descended on the forest, prompting Von to task Claymar with fixing a leak in the cabin's roof while he cleared a space to operate the Delavine Crystal.

While Von resumed his search for Navaryn, Claymar retrieved a sturdy, well-crafted broadsword from their supplies. After unsheathing it, he breathed a sigh of relief with a subdued astonishment in his eyes. Erteskka, a five-hundred-year-old, magically imbued sword, felt gratifyingly weighty in his hand. Although the blade was worn and spotted with rust, Claymar was nonetheless thrilled to hold his most treasured weapon once again.

"I can't believe you found this. You went to the dunes looking for me," he said to Von.

"I did," Von replied with a nod. "There was a scorched clearing in the sand, and I found it buried halfway in the ground."

"Yup, that'd be where Merisek and Joro ambushed me."

"Sorry I wasn't there for you. By the looks of things, you must've put up quite a fight."

"No apologies necessary, my friend. It's thanks to you that I am reunited with Erteskka here," said Claymar as he moved to exit the cabin. "I'll be right back."

After a short while, he returned with a slab of stone cleaved from the cliffside, then quickly rummaged through the cabin in search of a bottle of mineral oil. Wasting no time, he proceeded to carefully, yet noisily, run the blade along the stone to remove the rust and sharpen its edges.

"Think you could be a little quieter?" said Von. "I'm trying to concentrate."

Blue sparks continued to jump from the blade as Claymar replied, "C'mon, Von. This sword has to be maintained if it's going to last. A swordsman like yourself should understand that."

"No need," he replied. "I'm well beyond using simple swords."

"You know well and good that this is not some simple sword," said Claymar as he shuddered. Von rolled his eyes and ignored the abrasive scraping coming from the opposite end of the room. "Just relax. This won't take long."

Dusk turned to nightfall as Claymar stood by with his freshly honed and oiled blade while Von continued his search late into the night to no avail. Exhaustion had set in and intensified as his frustration grew. Claymar then took it upon himself to break Von away from the Delavine Crystal to rest and regain his strength. He dug through their provisions and prepared a spread of various fruits and nuts along with a few fish they had procured from their beloved seaside town. Naturally, Von remembered he kept a stash of his wine at the cabin and retrieved a bottle from a hidden compartment beside the far wall.

"Trust there always to be a bottle or two hiding somewhere when you need it," said Claymar.

"How else would we tolerate each other for extended periods when we have to lay low?"

Chuckling, Claymar simply shrugged.

As they sat and dined upon their fare, Von humored Claymar with inquiries about Erteskka and its abilities, to which he excitedly responded with a few tales. It was said that despite its unsuspecting appearance, it held the strength of a massive battering ram fit for giants. Should the wielder be able to harness its full potential, they could devastate an entire castle tower with one slash. Although as enticing as Claymar's tales of the blade sounded, Von remained affixed to the Delavine Crystal at the other end of the room.

"That thing's not cooperating, is it?" Claymar asked as he balanced his overfilled wine glass while they sauntered to the dusty fabric couch.

"No. I don't know what's wrong," Von replied as he sipped his wine. "If I didn't like Fallon so much, I'd have smashed that thing by now."

Claymar snickered as he crunched on a handful of nuts, warm from his clutch. "Can't think you like him that much." After waiting a few moments for a laugh from Von that never came, he inquired,

"Think it has to do with us being in Daeva?"

Von shook his head. "No. The connection somehow feels stronger being in the forest. It's just—I've searched nearly the whole town, and I can't locate her. If it's not my fatigue ruining my concentration, then …."

"Then, what?"

"I can't help but fear something's wrong. I've checked each place the human girl should be. She's missing. If I didn't break for as long as I did—"

"Don't go blamin' yourself because you know as well as I that it won't fix anything." Claymar waited a few moments for his exhausted comrade to reply, then asked, "So what do we do?"

Von dipped his head backward and listened to the rain pattering on the roof as he searched his mind for ideas. Though he knew every minute that passed meant another minute they fell behind, he conceded to his tired mind and closed his eyes. "My instincts tell me we need to jump ship and go to Human. But without a plan, it's useless. Not to mention, we've got to be careful of Benson now. If we leave ourselves like sitting ducks, I'm sure he'll find a way to ruin it all. All my progress. Everything."

Claymar looked upon his exhausted comrade with a light smile. He knew Von needed rest, but declaring it outright would only lead to denial and a stubborn refusal to accept the notion. Opting out of his typical quirky, roundabout way to get his point across, he affirmed, "We'll figure it out. Don't worry. Nothing stays in our way for long when we work together as a team, you and me."

Von's breath didn't take long to deepen into a slow and steady pace. Deciding it was in his best interest to sneak in a nap, too, Claymar pushed himself into a comfy nook between a few pillows and closed his eyes. However, neither of them could escape to the blissful release of slumber. Through the sound of the rain hitting the ferns outside, their ears detected the subtle sound of careful footsteps approaching the cabin. Moments later, a knock at the door pulled their eyes open.

"You know, if you had told me you were expecting company, I would've bought more food," Claymar said sarcastically. He hoisted his sword and held it at the ready. "Search party?"

"You think they'd knock?" replied Von as he rose from the table and reached for one of his gauntlets. Just as he fastened it to his hand, a gentle voice called from outside the door.

"A woman?" whispered Claymar with scrunched eyebrows.

"Don't fall for it."

Claymar's gaze remained affixed to the door as if he tried desperately to see through it. "*That voice*," he muttered.

"I'll handle this," said Von as he approached the door with a smoky amethyst-colored energy blast ready to fire.

"Wait, Von. *Don't!*"

The haunting green light of a sparking energy field filled the cabin as Von threw the door open. Claymar quickly snatched his wrist before he could hurl the blast.

"Let go of me, damn it!"

"Calm down!" Claymar urged as he squeezed Von's wrist and turned toward the door. "*Look.*"

The electric green energy was an outright declaration that whoever was waiting on the other side of the door was not from Daeva, but from Celestine. Von feared it may have been the Halryn army or perhaps Benson himself. Clenching his teeth, he peered outside the doorway where a cloaked silhouette stood, clutching an ornate staff sparking with pulsing energy. Ever so slowly, she eased out of her defensive posture and dispelled the energy. As she locked eyes with Claymar, she removed the hood of her cloak. Von's grimace dissipated into awe.

"Clay," said Lowenna in a quivering voice, "you're really here."

Thin tears descended Claymar's cheeks as he stared into Lowenna's ocean-blue eyes in disbelief. "Dragonfly," he said, then released Von's wrist. "You're back!"

The two dashed toward each other and locked themselves into an embrace teeming with joyous longing. Lowenna eagerly pressed her tender lips to Claymar's as she clutched his face. Von stood by patiently, gratified to see Lowenna restored to her physical form and the jubilation in Claymar's entire being. Several moments passed before Von dispelled the glowing purple energy from his palm, pulling the couple's attention to him.

"Hi, Lowenna," said Von with a nervous chuckle as he slid off his gauntlet.

She separated herself from Claymar and approached him with a gleeful smile.

Von continued, "Guess I'm a little on edge. I'm—"

Shaking her head, Lowenna interrupted Von's apology with a tight embrace. "*Thank you*," she lightly sobbed into his shoulder. "Thank you for bringing him back to me."

Von gently reciprocated her hug as he looked up to catch Claymar flicking a tear off his cheek. The moment felt like a dream, but the three reveled in the reality of their blissful, albeit incomplete, reunion.

"How did you know where to find us?"

"Navaryn told me about this place when she came here with you. She described the forest and the mountains. Said it reminded her of home," said Lowenna with a smile. "So, when Aalrija told me you and Clay fled to Daeva, I figured this would be the best place to start my search. With your energy cloaked as tightly as it is, I couldn't lock onto either one of you."

A bittersweet smile found Von as he recalled his venture with Navaryn to the cabin, and Lowenna saw the longing in his eyes.

"Come. Let's get inside before the better part of the storm finds its way through the canopy," said Von lightly.

Von and Claymar ushered Lowenna inside, then prepared a soothing tonic to share beside the crackling fireplace. Emotions simmered as they settled into each other's company and relished in Claymar's mildly comical retelling of his rescue from Merisek's fortress, among other more upsetting recaps. Lowenna soon took the reins of the conversation and divulged the disturbing news of Navaryn's emergence in the realm of Human and how her energy signal, along with Kumiko's, had mysteriously vanished. Though she reported Kumiko's unexpected ejection into Celestine, it failed to provide a modicum of relief to the collective, considering Navaryn's whereabouts were still unknown. Floored by her remarkable yet foolish feat, Von pondered whether Kumiko's ejection was due to an altercation with her white-eyed counterpart or perhaps something far worse.

"The last thing I remember was seeing the charmed necklace upon Navaryn through the human girl's eyes. Yet, if she became wise to what it really was, I'm certain she would have trashed it." Dreading how she knew Von's eyes would harden, she opted against affirming Navaryn's vulnerability. "What are we going to do?"

"I've tried tracking her down with the Delavine Crystal before you got here."

Lowenna nodded as she thought back to Von's confession of how it happened in his possession. "I'm assuming that means you haven't had any luck, then?"

"Not since back in Celestine. Clay wasn't exactly helping my concentration by playing with his sword."

"Mind if I give it a try?" she asked.

"Be my guest," Von replied and gestured in its direction.

Lowenna settled herself on the floor in front of the Delavine Crystal. After a deep breath, she made an instant connection, evidenced by the glowing gold in her eyes.

Impressed by Lowenna's effortless tether, Von chimed, "I had to work myself into a trance, and here you are doing it with open eyes."

"This is my expertise, after all," Lowenna replied with a smirk.

Von impatiently paced about the cabin as Lowenna worked to triangulate Navaryn's location. Claymar kept himself occupied with repairing the sword's sheath but attentively watched Lowenna's glowing golden eyes use the crystal's sight to continue her search. Her efforts echoed Von's empty-handed results until a long stretch of rural landscape far from Rayshell's home came into view. A vast, remote area with scattered houses, barns, and abandoned structures resonated faintly with Navaryn's presence, but Lowenna could not look any closer.

"I think I've got something. It's faint, but it's there," she said.

"What do you see?"

Lowenna extended her hand to Von and replied, "Let me show you."

Puzzled, anxious, but intuitive enough to know Lowenna meant for him to take her hand, Von interlaced his icy fingers between hers.

In an instant, his eyes veiled over in a golden hue, and his vision linked with what Lowenna saw through the crystal's projection.

"Inside the barn?"

"This explains why you were having trouble. There are concealment charms in place here," Lowenna warily revealed.

"What? How can you tell?"

"Charms carry the signature of the caster, and I've learned to see them. In the realm of Human, it's an obvious phenomenon."

Von stewed for a moment in his incompetence. "Wait. That means you know who placed them, don't you?"

Lowenna was hesitant to answer. "Yes. But that's not what's important now."

Keen that Lowenna's sidestep meant Joro was behind the debacle, he attempted to steady his fiery nerves. "Can you get around them?" he asked.

"There's no getting around concealment charms," said Lowenna as she sharpened her focus. "But lucky for us, one of the links seems to be failing."

Claymar watched his comrades in suspense and didn't realize that he had been holding his breath.

"She's there!" Lowenna yelped as Rayshell came into focus. "Her vessel is inside the barn!"

From under a muddled, distorted blur, Von watched Rayshell frantically scratch away at one of the sigils.

"I see her," Von said in disbelief. "She's trying to disable the charm. Smart girl."

"Let me see!" clamored Claymar like a fussy adolescent, to which Lowenna offered her other hand to him. As he took it, his eyes glazed over with a vibrant golden glow. "*Whoa.*"

Seeing Rayshell's efforts gave the group encouragement. Together, they watched the image sharpen as she scratched away at the sigil. However, their relief was short-lived once they saw Joro enter the stall. Since the other sigils remained intact, they heard only a distorted, echoey sound as Joro spoke. Von's blood began to boil as he encroached upon Rayshell. The last instance they saw before the image faded was his smug countenance as he restored the sigil.

"We have to go. *Now*," Lowenna urged as she broke away from the Delavine Crystal.

"Hold it," Claymar interrupted. "You're crazy if you think you're coming with us."

"Excuse me?"

"You're staying here. We can handle this," he proclaimed, patting his chest.

"Clay, don't do this now," Lowenna fervently replied. "That girl needs our help, and saving Navaryn will take all of us together. There's no time to waste."

"Please, Lowenna. If Joro's there, then Merisek is bound to be too," Claymar cautioned. "You *think* you know how dangerous he is. But I've been with him, and let me tell you, Dragonfly, he's gotten *worse*."

"That didn't stop Von and Kumiko from getting you out of his fortress, *did it*?" Lowenna answered back. "Navaryn is my best friend, Clay. My *sister*. She needs all of us. We're a *team*!"

The sound of Von fastening the clasps of his gauntlets caught Claymar and Lowenna's attention. "You should stay, Lowenna. You'll be safe here," he concurred.

"Don't you do this, too," she griped as she approached him. "We're so close. Together, the three of us could end it all today."

"No," interjected Claymar.

"What do you mean, *no*?!" Lowenna folded her arms as he paced about the room. "If you don't think I have the strength to help, then tell me, Clay. Tell me how inept you think I am!"

"Calm down, already. You're acting just like Navaryn. This has nothing to do with your abilities."

"Then *what*?!"

In an instant, Claymar rushed over and took her by the shoulders. "I *can't* lose you again. Don't you see?"

"Damn it, Clay. You can't make my decisions for me. We've been over this before!"

"We need a backup plan in case this fails," proposed Von. "With

Kumiko back in Celestine and Benson privy to his hand in our efforts, we may no longer be able to count on him for support."

"If you take me out of the equation now, you're asking for things to go wrong."

"We can't all just charge down there," stressed Von. "The goal right now is getting the girl out of there, quick and smooth. The smaller our presence, the better our chances. With any luck, Joro might not even know we're there. Once she's safe, we'll all work as a team to free Navaryn."

Lowenna tsked and pulled away from her beloved Claymar. "I know what you're trying to do," she griped, "and I disagree. We are stronger as a team."

"Once we have Navaryn back, then we can put an end to everything. Joro. Merisek. *All of it*," emphasized Von.

Claymar sheathed Erteskka and strapped it over his shoulder. "Back us up, Lowenna. Just in case."

Reluctant to agree, Lowenna sighed, then replied, "I'll keep watch over you with the Delavine Crystal. You'd better not fail."

Von nodded as he grasped her hands. "Thank you," he said earnestly.

After a quick yet heartfelt embrace with Lowenna, Claymar departed the room beside Von and headed for the cliffside. Dawn was moments from breaking the horizon as they reached the edge of the forest.

"Thank you for that back there. I won't chance losing her."

"I know you want Lowenna safe. But I did mean what I said. Without a backup plan, this could all be for nothing," Von replied with his eyes arrowed ahead. "That being said, I still wouldn't count on her staying put. Especially if things get dicey."

Claymar sighed in agreement. "So what's the plan?"

"We get the drop on Joro, then get the human girl to safety."

"And just *where* is safety?"

Von took a moment to answer. "Here."

"To *Daeva?* Bringing her *here* is what you'd call safe?" said Claymar with a puzzled look, then chuckled deliriously at such a notion. "If you thought bringing the human girl out of her realm was safe, you or Kumiko would have already done it, right?"

Von's eyebrows creased as he feverishly recalled the handful of instances where he and the human girl connected. "Look—"

"Remember what Fallon told us. Those beings are no longer tethered to their mystical spirit. You can't simply Parallel a human from their realm and expect they'd survive."

"But this girl might be able to," Von replied. "Call it a gut feeling, but just know that's a decision we may be forced to make."

Shaking his head, Claymar responded, "If we lose that human girl, we'll lose Navaryn in the process. I need you to keep that in mind."

"We just have to act fast. That's what I did to get Lowenna to stay behind." Von looked to his comrade, whose tense eyes locked on the horizon. "I'm counting on us claiming the upper hand."

The pair arrived at the cliffside beyond the forest's protective canopy. They quieted their minds and mouths, then took in the view as the haze of sunrise erupted across the sky. With cautious optimism, they peered into the brimming rays of sunlight as though it signified the coming of a new era, free of restraints and full of possibilities.

Claymar took a hefty breath as he turned to Von, then placed his hand on his shoulder. "You ready?"

"Lead the way, friend."

Under a wisp of dark green smoke, the pair disappeared like a calling breath on a cold night.

·)(·

The barn steadily grew dark and cold as the cloudy afternoon gave way to evening. Rayshell's lips were pale as she shivered in the corner of the stable with only the matted, thin blanket and deflated, prickly straw to keep warm. The reinforced charms shielding her presence taunted her, though their deep luminous glow was no less enticing to her eyes. Joro impatiently paced about the barn, occasionally glancing at Rayshell in the stable as he awaited Merisek's arrival. He had brought the news of Navaryn's powerful emergence to him, to which he had elected to try his hand at drawing her out of Rayshell himself.

In the middle of Joro's gait, there came a pound at the barn doors. "Joro, it's me," a deep and scratchy voice called out.

"What took you so long, old man?"

Joro unchained the latch and opened the barn door to let Merisek in, but saw no one on the other side. Puzzled, he stepped out and peered side-to-side under the hazy sunset. His growing suspicion put him on high alert. Just as Joro stepped back toward the door, he heard the ringing sound of metal cutting through the air above him. Clutched high in Claymar's gripping hands was Erteskka, gleaming in the golden rays of sunlight. As he leapt from the barn's roof, he fiercely slashed the broadsword downwards. In a showy display of energetic red shimmer, the imbued energy scored the ground deeply and blasted through the far corner of the barn. Despite the power of his attack, Joro sidestepped the advance effortlessly. Wasting no time, Claymar drew him away from the barn with a parade of slapdash yet effective offensive strikes. After a few tense moments, Von slipped out of the shadows and dashed inside in search of Rayshell.

A haunting glow emanating from the nearest set of stalls immediately caught Von's eyes. He dashed before the stable door, pried it off its hinges, then ran to Rayshell's side. She was weak yet coherent enough to recognize the vibrant red eyes that looked upon her.

"Von?" she whispered through her chattering teeth.

Nodding, he replied, "I'm going to get you out of here."

Von quickly wrapped Rayshell in the tattered blanket and hoisted her into his arms. Within a second's glance over his shoulder, she saw Joro dash into the barn behind them like a feverish blur. Unable to word a warning in time, she clutched Von's shirt and braced herself for the collision. Once Joro had Von by his throat, he instinctively surrendered her from his grasp. As the pair blew past, she toppled over the rugged ground until one of the support beams in the center of the room broke her momentum. With her stamina depleted, her eyes went dark.

Joro unleashed blast after blast into Von's chest in a smooth, steady string of movements. The culminating force sent him soaring through the far end of the barn. He tumbled over the dewy grass and landed a few paces from Claymar, who was on his knees catching his breath.

A dapple of red glimmered from the corner of his lip as he barked, "You couldn't keep him occupied for just *ten more seconds?!*"

"Well, he's a lot faster than I remember," Claymar claimed breathlessly. "And in case you haven't noticed, I'm a bit out of practice."

Joro dashed toward the pair like a cyclone and zeroed in on Von. They each traded blows for blocks, but a wretched cheap shot landed Joro the upper hand. While Von buckled over, Joro called forth a black crystalline swirl of Daeva energy over his fist and sought out his opponent's chin. The light behind Von's eyes departed while suspended in the air.

Claymar winced as Von hit the ground back-first. Though it was a powerful blow, he knew his friend would likely wake from his daze in a matter of moments if left uninterrupted.

"Hey, old friend," taunted Claymar in a cheerful voice. "Long time no see. Why don't we catch up for a while?"

"Friend?" Joro shifted his emerald gaze to his former comrade and smirked. "Is that what you'd call the person at the end of your sword?"

"If memory serves me well, I remember us being at the end of each other's swords quite often," replied Claymar as he pushed himself off the ground. "Not like *that*, of course."

Joro, successfully lured away from Von, called out, "Still quite the comedian, aren't you?" He snatched Claymar by the collar of his shirt once he prepared to stand upright. "I'll give you credit. Your 'Merisek' voice was pretty convincing."

With a wink, he replied, "Thanks, Sugar. I've missed you."

"Can't say the same about either of you two bastards," griped Joro as he reeled him in close enough to detect Claymar's familiar tart redolence.

"You say that, but I know your heart is in another place," added Claymar while Von coughed himself awake.

Joro snorted, then shoved Claymar back, releasing his collar. "You'd both be dead by now if it were up to me. Merisek's the one who wants you alive."

"And a servant always obeys his Master," called Von as he rose to his feet. "As for myself, I don't have anything keeping me from tearing you apart right now."

As Joro's emerald-green eyes pulsed, Clay attempted to intervene. "Hey. Cool it, Von, will ya? You're ruining the pleasantries."

Von ignored Claymar's antics and stated, "Just give us the girl, Joro. And we'll let you walk away."

"You'll let *me* walk away?" Joro guffawed, then just as quickly as his reaction came, it departed. With an intense countenance, he proclaimed, "You're no threat to me."

"Give us the girl," Von pressed.

"Not a chance."

The pair closed their gap until they felt each other's hot breath whip past their faces. Fuming from Von's quip at his loyal obedience, Joro was ready to disregard consequence and quench his thirst for blood.

"Merisek's a fool for wasting his time with something like *you*."

Von stared Joro down and pondered the truth behind the insult he had heard time and time again. They were far from comrades when they had served under Merisek together, but the hostility had always been one-sided. Although Von never truly understood the reason for Joro's bitter temperament, he suspected it stemmed from his Dhimara bloodline.

Moments away from calling forth their radical Daeva energy, a tremor jolted Joro and Von, and in the next moment, a wondrous wispy green glow ignited under the blanket of night. Merisek stepped out from the center of his radiant Parallel with an unsurprised expression. He removed his hood and looked upon the trio of feisty Daeva, who were put to a halt by his arrival.

"Well, well. Von and Claymar," called Merisek with a smile. "What a fun little reunion this is shaping up to be."

A few straggling shimmers of Merisek's Parafall fizzled away, leaving the trio under a screen of thick clouds. Out from the shadows that veiled his monstrous countenance, he looked upon his band of former pupils. Von could hardly hide how appalled he was, even though Claymar had explicitly illustrated his condition.

"I'm ever impressed by your perseverance, Von. Just how did you manage to jailbreak Claymar?"

Von was more than privy to Merisek's manner of speaking and had come to expect the usual appeasements from him. However, he only met him with silence and a furious glare.

"Never mind. I can surmise as much on my own. It's clear your connections within Celestine are impressive, especially for you being as despised as you are." Merisek took a few steps forward and addressed his other former pupil. "And Claymar, you're looking rather well," he said through thinly veiled sarcasm.

"Sorry I can't say the same about you," Claymar fired back, wiping a trickle of blood from his mouth.

Merisek chuckled to himself. "Looks are *always* deceiving. Remember that."

"It's over, Merisek. We're leaving here with the girl," declared Von.

"I'm afraid not. Not while I still have unfinished business with the Guardian."

"Navaryn would sooner die than give Iaelprt to you!"

"That remains to be seen," he replied ominously, then moved to reason. "Why are you and Claymar so convinced I intend to cause harm with the Order?"

"We all know what it can do," chimed Claymar in Von's place. "The last thing existence needs is for you to be its author."

"Understand something, gentlemen," Merisek replied. "I want peace just as you do."

"Peace? You expect us to believe that after everything you pulled? How many things will you rewrite in order to achieve it, huh?"

Merisek disregarded Claymar's overly animated inquisition. "I aim to create a new world. A new existence, rid of this hostility between the realms. It is possible with the Order."

"By wiping out those who would oppose you, right? You think the murder of entire realms would lead to peace?" said Von.

"Murder? I speak not of murder. That is what you fail to grasp," Merisek pointed out. "One's existence is meaningless if it is simply undone. Considering everything I know, I understand that better than either of you. I simply wish to restore a manner of things to their rightful place."

"That is no one's decision to make, least of all yours, madman," griped Von.

"We'll tell you once more. Both of you go back to your frosty shithole in the mountains. We're leaving here with the girl," added Claymar.

"You won't be leaving here at all," growled Joro.

Merisek grew increasingly perturbed as the trio persisted with their senseless argument. Von and Claymar's repeated interruptions and their refusals to listen thinned his patience to a fine line.

"I haven't time for games, gentleman. I've attempted to reason with you, yet you refuse to listen. Though this may surprise you, I am not wholly without mercy. We can settle this without a fight." Merisek extended his hand toward both Von and Claymar. "With that, I'm giving you one last chance. Join us in the new beginning, or be left behind."

A frantic zephyr sailed between the equally divided quartet, and neither Von nor Claymar gave a response. Merisek shook his head and slowly exhaled as he relinquished the last of his hope.

"Can't say I didn't try," he muttered, then signaled to Joro unenthusiastically.

Joro closed his eyes and took a focused, meditative stance beside Merisek. Pulses of energy surrounded him as he filled his core with concentrated power. Once his conjuring peaked, his eyes sprang open to reveal a green glow emanating from within. His oily, bronze skin darkened to a tone deeper than a crow's feather. Crooked, spined horns emerged from his skull and curled toward the back of his head. His mouth bared a set of razor-sharp teeth in his signature devilish grin.

"Bet you wish Lowenna were here right about now, eh?" Von discreetly uttered.

Claymar snickered. "Funny."

They observed Joro's oddly tranquil demeanor as he stood before them with locked eyes.

"Well, looks like we're doing this," said Von. "I know it's been a while, but are you ready to let it out?"

Claymar gave Von a grin. "Never been more ready."

As though they were on cue, Von and Claymar simultaneously underwent powerful transformations of their own. In contrast to Joro's calm, frightening process, theirs was far more expressive and energetic. An electric aura engulfed Claymar's body as his power steadily rose to a new height. Meanwhile, red and gold energy surrounded Von as spiked bio-armor materialized beneath the skin on the back of his neck and shoulders. Finally, each of them gained a set of rear-angled horns that violently erupted from just above their temples; Claymar's being sleek and pointed, while Von's were more wavy and rugged. Both saw substantial increases in their muscle mass as their transformations concluded in a wondrous display.

Claymar took a deep, refreshing breath and drew Erteskka from behind his shoulder. Concurrently, Von engaged his gauntlets and slowly formed a pair of menacing blades from his palms. Despite Claymar's increased fortitude and power, he felt uneasy as he watched the flow of blood from Von's arms.

"In case either of us die, I just thought you should know, I really hate when you do that," Claymar said squeamishly.

Von's attention was too fixated on Joro drawing his blade alongside Merisek for him to hear Claymar's quirky remark.

"Ready when you are," Claymar continued. "Which one do you want?"

"I'll let you choose this time."

Claymar chuckled as he channeled energy into his sword. "You take pretty boy. I'll take the fossil."

"Thank you," whispered Von as a red shimmer ran across his eyes.

Simultaneously, Von and Claymar dashed toward their targets in a haunting blur. Joro darted forward with blistering speed and tackled Von to the ground while Claymar charged Merisek with Erteskka. Paired off in their respective battles, the four Daeva squared off in furious combat, each with their individual thoughts and motivations that drove them.

The searing burn of vengeance fueled Claymar's advance upon Merisek for the pain and torment he had inflicted upon him. He kept on the offensive as he furiously swung his blade, but Merisek effortlessly matched his strikes with psychic blades equipped on his frail-looking hands.

Meanwhile, Joro and Von edged closer to the forest line with each unheeding strike and energy blast. They each managed to land a few mighty blows, but with how effortlessly Joro continued to recover, Von was afraid he was holding back. After slashing in Joro's direction, banking on his sanguine blades ripping through flesh, he came up empty-handed. Frustrated, Von shouted and pummeled him with a barrage of sparking energy blasts. Their eerie purple haze lit the ravaged landscape and Joro's stalky form as they combusted. Joro waited within the billowing smoke for Von to give up the onslaught, then dashed his way at an undetectable speed. With a sharp-toothed grin, he slammed Von through the elm tree in front of him. Though the broken wood tore through their bodies in the same manner, Joro appeared utterly unfazed. Wincing, Von was driven deep into the ground by his throat.

As the debris settled, Joro taunted, "Give it up, Von. You won't even matter once we have the Order."

Von groaned and squirmed as Joro's grip tightened.

"Don't worry. I'll keep you around long enough so you can see what I have planned for Navaryn."

"I won't let you lay a finger on her," squawked Von.

"Too late for that."

During their eerie pause, the casting glow of Joro's eyes revealed the fury written upon Von's face. The shifter's succinct remark made it easy to surmise what he meant. Although Navaryn had never confessed the foul play Von had suspected, he never imagined such a dastardly act to be the cause of her abhorrence.

"I'll kill you, you faceless scum!" threatened Von as his soul lit aflame.

Quicker than Joro could detect, Von plunged his Sanguine blade deep into his abdomen. He was confident the blade sliced through a critical area, yet Joro reacted only with laughter.

"You fool. Do you think your faltered blood can affect me?"

Confused, Von looked at his fist. Joro's wriggling charcoal-toned flesh ignited and shattered Von's blade as the wound closed. The dreadfully incredible display illustrated the new level of power Joro had attained. Leering as if he intentionally allowed Von a few uninterrupted moments to come to his determination, Joro soon retracted his hand. From forearm to fingertip, his skin morphed into fearsome, sharp extensions intent on claiming his head. Von burst out from under Joro's guard and dodged the fatal strike, escaping with only a superficial nick to his armored neck.

As the fray carried on, Lowenna emerged from within a small grove of trees in the distance with her staff in hand. Under the waving shadows, she snuck to the rear end of the barn where Von and Joro had bulleted through earlier. She glanced over to the dashing flashes to ensure no one sensed her presence, then took a moment to tighten her energy suppression. Holding her breath, she peered inside the barn through a set of loose boards. Rayshell was unconscious, lying on her back halfway under the evening's murky light.

Intent on rescuing Rayshell, Lowenna slipped inside the barn but retreated to the shadowy nook behind her once she sensed a faint energy signal coming her way. A wispy green Parafall quickly flashed, revealing the arrival of Kumiko. He carried a peculiar satchel brimming with light and walked to Rayshell's side. His tense demeanor was resolute as he paid no mind to the ongoing battle outside the barn doors. Though Lowenna hoped to feel relief upon seeing him, she was more suspicious than anything else. Locked in her budding uncertainty, she chose to observe him cautiously.

Kumiko knelt beside Rayshell and pulled at the tattered blanket. The gritty sensation prompted her to stir gently, then slowly open her eyes. She rose to a seat atop the filthy floor, propped up by Kumiko's arm. In her weakened, confused state, she could hardly recognize the man before her, but his content lavender eyes conveyed that he meant her no harm. After a few short moments, he reached into his satchel, unlatched the acrylic case, and then pulled out the gleaming orb crafted by the mystics of Utsirri. Lowenna studied him as he intently looked upon Rayshell. The orb's glow was unexpectedly calming and gave no cause for alarm. Kumiko then whispered into her ear. As he lowered the apparatus between her breasts, Lowenna's nervous gait forced him to pause.

"*Kumiko?*"

Shocked, he answered, "Lowenna? You are back! I-I figured you'd be in Celestine. What are you doing *here?*"

Lowenna folded her arms. "I was about to ask you the same thing. What's going on? What are you doing to Rayshell?"

Kumiko nervously dismissed her inquiries and turned his attention back to Rayshell, who had moved her disoriented eyes to Lowenna. She recognized her beautiful countenance from the night she saw her apparition through her Elemental Parallel. With a short-lived smile, she slowly surrendered to her lethargy.

Lowenna locked her eyes on the glowing orb as she drew closer. Despite being the experienced Shahiri she was, she could not identify the nature of its power. "What is that thing?"

"Something that will free Navaryn."

"*How?*"

"I don't have time to explain, but Benson gave it to me."

"*Benson?!* What makes you so sure we can trust this? The power I sense from that thing is beyond my scope."

"My father has assured me of its potential. That's good enough for me."

"Let's just get Rayshell to safety and figure this out. I was able to separate myself without something like this. I *know* Navaryn can do the same."

As Lowenna's pleas grated in Kumiko's ears, he remembered Benson's words from their time in the oubliette. He set the orb back into the receptacle in his satchel and gently laid Rayshell's limp body on the ground. Exhaling, he rose to his feet to face her. "And what if she won't?" he said with a stern glare.

"*Won't?* What are you talking about?"

"I'm talking about Navaryn actively staying inside this girl to guard her knowledge of Iaalprt."

"That's absurd!"

"You said so yourself. You're confident that Navaryn could free herself if she wanted to. Don't you think she would have by now?"

"She's just confused, Kumiko. There's no way she would—"

"She watched as Merisek cast you out of Celestine. He was set to do the same to my father. Navaryn threw herself in front of the spell to protect Iaalprt. That alone tells you she was prepared to let the secret die with her."

"She ... did that?"

Kumiko nodded. "Being confined to this human in this listless realm is no fate meant for Navaryn. Celestine needs her. And this will bring her back."

Lowenna rested her head against her staff as she looked at Rayshell lying on the ground in her weakened and disheveled state. Not only would forcefully freeing Navaryn end the ongoing violence and lunacy immediately, but it would also spare the human girl from further pain, torment, and endangerment. The urgency in Kumiko's words had managed to hold true in Lowenna's heart.

"You can trust me on this, Lowenna," Kumiko urged. "This will bring her home."

Though his past tarnished their camaraderie, Lowenna saw the earnestness behind his eyes as he reaffirmed his pact with Von and Claymar, and his desire to right the wrong that Merisek had done. She acknowledged that he was, for once, fighting on the same side as her, just as Aalrija and Fallon were.

"Just ... tell me what I can do to help."

Kumiko's eyes shifted for a few seconds. "Go to Celestine and wait for Navaryn to arrive. She may need your aid. I'll give Claymar and Von a hand when I'm done here."

"And what about Rayshell?"

Kumiko looked deep into her blue eyes. "I'll get her home safe. I promise."

With mild reluctance, Lowenna agreed. Kumiko gave her an affirmative nod as she took a few steps backward to ready her Parallel to Celestine.

"Hey, Lowenna," Kumiko called to her. "I'm pleased to see you're safe."

In a gleaming white flash, Lowenna vanished from the barn and left Kumiko to proceed with his plan. Amazed that he successfully deterred her from interfering, he returned to Rayshell's side and retrieved the orb. Full of yearning and with nothing further standing in his way, he prepared himself to fulfill his eager desire.

The battle outside raged on between the Daeva. As confident as Joro was in his abilities against Von, the strain of his transformation depleted his stamina far quicker than anticipated. His fatigue steadily increased, as did his fear of Von's seemingly endless barrage of attacks. With every strike of his sanguine blades, he inflicted a haunting cry that reverberated within Joro's sword and chipped away at the imbued steel. Once Von found an opening in Joro's defenses, he viciously thrust his blade into his side. His sanguine blades remained intact as if smithed from the purest ore. Writhing in pain, Joro reactively grabbed Von's throat and squeezed with all the strength he could muster. Leaving the blade in Joro's side, Von torqued his arm, slammed him head-first into the ground, then broke off one of his jagged horns. The sound of crunching bone and gushing blood sang like sweet music as he repeatedly pounded his fist into Joro's face.

Von gnashed his teeth as he knelt above Joro, lying bloodied and broken on the ground. While relishing in Joro's defeated state, the glint of his broken horn beside him beckoned his attention. His gleaming red eyes glazed over the sharp edges as he held it in his hand. He clutched the base of the horn and plunged it into Joro's neck, prompting a bloody gurgle from his mouth.

As Von readied his grip with the intent to cleave Joro's head clean off, an eruption of white arcing light burst in an energetic rumble from inside the barn, bringing the battle to a halt. The disembodied voice of Navaryn wailed amidst Rayshell's anguished screams. Von glared at the barn in disbelief and paid no further mind to Joro, writhing with his horn stuck in his throat. Intense white light soon engulfed the entire mountainside, leaving everyone momentarily purblind.

The spectacle lasted only a moment before a foreboding calm

descended upon them. Von looked upon the nearly obliterated barn with eager anticipation, though he could no longer detect Navaryn's presence. His trepidation grew as he traded confused glances with Claymar. Out of the darkness, Kumiko walked up carrying Rayshell's limp body wrapped in the tattered blanket.

"Kumiko?" called Von as he approached with Claymar in tow. "What's going on?"

"It's over," he stated with a blank expression.

"What do you mean 'it's over'? What happened in there?" questioned Claymar.

Kumiko ignored the Daeva and gently set Rayshell on the ground. He then reached into his satchel and removed a glass orb of thick, silvery liquid. Claymar's eyes widened as he beheld the familiar glistening shimmer.

"Oh, shit," Claymar uttered.

Swiftly, Kumiko tossed the orb into the air and shattered it with a blast of energy, triggering the rapid spread of a toxic cloud of vapor. Within seconds, the Daeva were brought to their knees, painfully gasping for air. Merisek, however, remained unaffected as he watched the others become helplessly overtaken.

Claymar mustered enough strength to stumble his way over to Von. "It's C-Poison," he said in a strained voice. "We've gotta get out of here."

"No!" roared Von with blood spewing from his mouth and his eyes locked onto Kumiko's sickeningly smug countenance. "I'm gonna *gut* that *little* shit!"

"Now's not the time for that!" yelled Claymar as he placed his hands on his back. "*We're leaving!*"

Von and Claymar vanished together in a fiery red flash just before a thickened plume of vapor fell on top of them. With a menacingly tense countenance, Merisek tried to regain his footing as he angrily limped in Kumiko's direction. After a few sluggish paces, he turned to his side to find Joro frantically crawling to his feet, begging to be expelled from the realm. His body shook with pain, and his dimming eyes oozed dark green liquid as they looked at him in fear. Without a word, yet with a look of disgust, Merisek laid his hand on Joro's shoulder and Paralleled him back to Daeva.

Left with Kumiko amidst the lingering silvery smoke engulfing the mountainside like a dense fog, Merisek called out, "I certainly wasn't expecting to see you here."

"You can spare the pleasantries, Merisek," Kumiko jutted.

"Come now. Why this hostility? You know, we could have avoided a lot of trouble here had I known you'd planned a ruse."

"This is no ruse. And not at all something you'd benefit from," Kumiko replied. "Navaryn has been freed, and you have failed. Abandon this endeavor of yours."

Merisek felt a lump form in his throat. "You're saying Navaryn is back in Celestine?"

"Lowenna as well," Kumiko confirmed. "And if you ever show your face in Celestine again, rest assured it will be your last."

"How could you say that? If anyone could ever understand why I need the Order, I thought it'd be you."

"You banished our guardians and endangered their lives. I've warned you before that Navaryn would sooner die than surrender Iaalprt to you. You didn't listen." While Merisek tried to interject, Kumiko spoke over him. "*And because of that*, countless innocent Celestines, including many of my close friends, needlessly perished."

"Kumiko, please. Joro acted alone in the havoc wreaked on Celestine. I had only sought Iaalprt. I've told you this time and time again."

"You are just as accountable as he is in all of this. No matter *who* you are."

"I've made my regrets known to you. And these wrongs are exactly what I aim to correct once I possess the Order, in all its parts."

"You are not to be trusted. The power of the Order is not yours, nor *anyone* else's, to wield. Do what you will with Ananael and Zin, but all shall consider the Order lost from this point forward."

Merisek's heart pounded harder as his desperation grew. "But, what about Athelisa?" he pleaded. "I can bring her back. With the power of the Order, she can return to us."

"*Do not* speak her name!"

"You must listen to me. Your fath—"

"No, Merisek," Kumiko interrupted. "My mother is gone. And that is how she must remain. Make no further mention of her."

"But if it were Navaryn—"

"Enough! I have no desire to discuss hypotheticals with you. I have Navaryn now. The only thing left for you to do is return to Daeva. For good. No more bloodshed. No more futile quests. That is as much peace Celestine will ever afford you."

"Please, Kumiko," Merisek uttered in desperation as Kumiko turned away, "you must help me!"

"It's *over*! Return to Daeva and do your best to live among your failures. Be thankful I have not told my father where to find you."

Without another word, Kumiko plucked Rayshell from the dewy grass and then set out to right the final wrong of Merisek's failed endeavor. Following the burst of electric green mist, he left Merisek beside the barn in damning solitude.

Sirens wailed in the distance as Merisek stared through the haunting screen of C-Poison wafting through the landscape. Despite all that he demonstrated to his benefactors, allies, and enemies throughout his rise to power and disgraceful fall, his abilities were frequently underestimated, and his intentions misunderstood. Time was of the essence as the ailments that polluted his body drew closer to overtaking him. He sighed regretfully, then looked upon his wrinkled, frail hands. With the impending approach of his complete degeneration looming on the horizon, he dreaded the inevitability of his only ally leaving his side.

27

THE BETRAYAL

Lowenna tracked Navaryn's faint energy signal to a shoreline just north of the Halryn border. Once her gleaming Parafall vanished, she cautiously emerged from behind a tight cluster of palms and peered toward the rolling midnight waves ahead. One of Celestine's satellites crowned the rippling horizon, but it was still too dark to see through clear and confident eyes. Her rugged tan boots crunched over the carpet of opalescent ice plants as she approached a dark mass sitting close to the shore. With each step, the moonlight unveiled the figure's steady curves from mystery. Lowenna called after Navaryn and dashed to her side, nearly losing her footing in the lofty sand, but she paid no mind to her approach.

"Sister, I'm so happy you're safe," Lowenna earnestly whispered as she knelt beside her. After a tight, unreciprocated embrace, she pulled away, genuinely puzzled by her friend's vacant stare. A gust of frigid air spiraled between them, prompting her to fetch and unfurl a woven blanket from her satchel. "I had a feeling you'd be needing this. Ask me how I know." She chuckled as she draped it over Navaryn, hoping to rouse a reaction, but she couldn't break her eyes away from the waxing moon. "Nav? Can you hear me?"

Navaryn slowly dug her toes into the sand. "Is it really over?"

"It sure better be," Lowenna answered back with teary eyes. "We're gonna make Merisek pay for all of this." During a bout of silence, she considered the possibility that something was wrong, and her suspicions surrounding Kumiko's intervention began to return. Once she could no longer bear her unsettling thoughts, she said, "Nav, talk to me. What are you feeling?"

"I don't know," she eventually answered. "I-I don't know how I'm supposed to feel."

"What do you mean? What's the last thing you remember?"

Navaryn took a moment to answer. "Merisek. He expelled you. And all I could think about was protecting Iaalprt. I ... jumped in front of Benson. After that, there's nothing. Like I've been stuck inside of an empty dream." She finally turned to face her friend. "How long have we been gone?"

"Two seasons, just about."

Lost in confusion, Navaryn stared at Lowenna with vacant eyes for a moment before trailing off into the distance. As she put her attention back to the moon, a bright Parafall flashed beside them.

"Kumiko," Lowenna warily called as he trotted up.

"Sorry, I came as quickly as I could. How's Nav?"

"She's acting strange," she affirmed discreetly. "The tide's coming in, too." She pointed to a gentle foamy wave that kissed Navaryn's toes. "Nav. Come on, let's get you some clothes. You must be freezing."

Kumiko and Lowenna silently waited for her reply, but the moon held her unyielding gaze.

"*See?*" hissed Lowenna under her breath. "I told you she's acting strange."

"I'm sure she's fine. Probably just recalibrating after her transmission," assured Kumiko. "Come on. Help me get her onto her feet."

Holding the blanket in place, Lowenna cooed, "Easy does it," as she and Kumiko guided Navaryn off the sand.

Navaryn was compliant with each of the directives that followed, but her demeanor suddenly flipped the moment she broke her gaze from the moon. With a ferocious grimace, she roared and wrestled out of her comrades' grasp. Her blanket dropped to her feet as she took an offensive stance in the firm, wet sand.

"Nav, calm down," pleaded Lowenna with open hands. "Everything's fine. You're home. Let us help you."

Navaryn dashed her flickering white eyes to Kumiko as he stepped toward her. A menacing smile cut across her face when he timidly reached for her.

"Nav! Can you hear me?!" shouted Lowenna as Navaryn crossed her arms over her head. "What the fuck has gotten into you?!"

Navaryn slowly pulled her arms down through a rippling cuff of sparking green energy and unsheathed a pair of blades forged from her Celestine energy.

"Damn it. Not this again! Have you lost your fuckin' mind?!"

"Don't engage her, Lowenna," cautioned Kumiko as she prepared herself for the imminent confrontation. "Just relax."

"*Relax*?! How'm I supposed to relax when we're about to get blitzed by Ms. White-Eyes over there? You know how dangerous she is when she's like this! And I am not at full power."

As quickly as Navaryn's rabid disposition swelled, it suddenly ebbed. She staggered and released the conjured blades, then feverishly tried to shake the cuffs of energy from her hands. The energy around her wrists swelled, distended, and phased to a crystalline hue, mimicking a seemingly parasitic behavior. As Navaryn fearfully looked at Lowenna, she cried her name.

Lowenna quickly dashed to her side as the polychromatic energy burst apart like shattering glass. After the grating sound and blinding light dissipated, Navaryn fell backward onto the sand. Kumiko snatched up the blanket while Lowenna inspected her unconscious friend.

"What the fuck did you do to her, Kumiko?!" shouted Lowenna.

Kumiko covered Navaryn's naked body in the sandy blanket and then scooped her into his arms.

"Are you going to answer me, or what?"

"She's fine."

"*Dragonshit*, she's fine!"

"She just needs rest," Kumiko firmly declared. "I'll take care of her."

Far from trusting Kumiko's words, let alone his actions, Lowenna fired back, "You're not going anywhere with her!"

"I'm taking her somewhere safe. I'm taking her to her castle. Got it?"

"Don't be foolish, Kumiko. If you really want to bring her somewhere safe, then at least take her to Benson's infirmary."

"Would you just stop fighting me? I'm taking her home."

"*Then* what?"

"Then, I'm staying with her until she awakes."

"You know she's not yours," Lowenna uttered with folded arms. "I don't know what you're trying to pull here, but I'm coming with you."

Kumiko's expression hardened. "Fine! And while you're at it, summon Demelza. Summon Aalrija. Summon *everyone* for all I care!"

Before Lowenna could utter another word, Kumiko departed with Navaryn under bright arcing lights. Alone and frustrated beyond measure, she shouted into the night sky, then quickly followed after him.

·)(·

Accompanied by the Tiers, Fallon, Teagan, and a group of close friends gathered within Navaryn's bedchamber, Kumiko recapitulated most of what led to Navaryn's return to Celestine. Leaning against the wall amidst the summoned entourage, Lowenna stood with her diadem tied around her forehead and a grimace affixed to her face. She kept her suspicious eyes on Kumiko while a team of bustling attendants and medics tended to Navaryn as she lay unconscious in her bed. As anticipated, Kumiko neglected to mention any crucial details about the curious remedy he had administered. Lowenna required every shred of self-control to refrain from demanding a response to her catalog of audacious inquisitions.

Under peaceful candlelight, the lead medic conferred with her staff's findings and then walked to Benson and Kumiko's side. "I'm happy to report Navaryn hasn't suffered any critical injuries," she confirmed as her team closed in behind. "We've measured the healing rate of the gashes around her wrists. By sunrise, they should be fully healed.”

"That's only a few hours from now," said Benson with his fingers to his chin. "Excellent news."

"But I'm sure she'll require more rest than that to fully recover from her ordeal. Don't be surprised if she doesn't rise for a full day."

"I'm confident she'll rise before then," Benson asserted, then put his arm around his son. "We both are."

The lead medic quickly flipped through her handwritten notes. "There is one anomaly," she continued as she plucked out a single parchment from the stack, scribbled with illegible jargon. "The readings of her Celestine energy appear to be ... different."

Benson raised an eyebrow. "Different? How?"

"Well," the lead medic began, then walked to Navaryn's bedside with Benson and Kumiko in tow. "I'm quite familiar with our esteemed Celestine. Navaryn's been in my care for many years, and admittedly, she's much easier to evaluate when she's unconscious." She chuckled as she reviewed her notes, then cleared her throat. "In short, I've grown familiar with the jarring frequency of energy that courses within her. Now, this could just be the residual effects of her initial ejection, but I've detected some kind of pulse that has disrupted her typical frequency."

"Interesting," answered Benson as genuinely as he could. "Is this something that should be of concern?"

"I'd like to think not, but I suppose we won't know for sure until she's up and about. Just keep an eye out for anything out of the ordinary, such as low power, unexplained fatigue, or any other strange behavior."

Kumiko could feel Lowenna's penetrating, raking gaze from behind him, though he kept himself engaged with the lead medic's warning.

"I'd like to see her again if she doesn't wake by tomorrow evening. I can reevaluate the disruption and see if it has changed."

"Certainly," Benson agreed. "But as I said, I'm sure she'll rise before then."

"I do hope so," the lead medic concluded as she filed the stack of paperwork into a folder. "Do let me know if her condition worsens.

Will you have attendants on standby?"

"I will have my son stay by her side until she wakes."

"Very well," she said. "My staff and I will take our leave."

After the lead medic bid a brief farewell to Benson, Kumiko, and the other occupants, she and her team promptly filed out of Navaryn's bedchamber. Following Benson's request, the attendants stopped mid-task, collected their belongings, and took their leave. Lowenna stood amongst the entourage gathered at Navaryn's bedside.

Mila leaned in and moved some of her damp, gritty locks away from her browline while her husband, Mathias, chimed, "Glad you're back, Navaryn. We've all been eagerly awaiting your return. Especially me, because if I remember correctly, you were the next one up to cover rounds at Teagan's."

Mila rolled her eyes as Mathias guffawed. "Yeah, and we all know how well you pack 'em away," she said, patting his round belly.

"Well, if I were as tall as you, I'm sure some of this would even out," he said with animated hands circling his stomach.

Mila smiled with her eyes upon Navaryn's mellow countenance. "Sleep comfortably, friend."

"Rest well," called Abyl from behind Mila and Mathias.

The trio departed as Fallon dug through his satchel for an object carefully wrapped in layers of thick cloth. "I've kept this safe for you while you've been gone," he confessed as he set her ruby-hilted dagger atop her bedside table. "I know you never like to leave without it."

One by one, the occupants departed, leaving only Benson, Kumiko, and Lowenna.

"Finally, things are as they should be," said Benson as he led Lowenna toward the bedchamber door. "Are you prepared for tomorrow evening's festivities?"

"Festivities? No, sir."

"Come then. Let's join the Tiers for some wine. We'll toast to the return of you and Navaryn, and I'll fill you in on tomorrow's schedule."

"With all due respect, I'd like to stay."

"I'm sure you trust my son to watch over Navaryn."

"It's not a matter of trust. I'd just—"

"Then certainly you wouldn't reject your imperator's request," he interrupted.

Lowenna's eyes trailed to Kumiko standing at Navaryn's bedside and opted to remain silent.

"I've tasked Kumiko with a few key things, including summoning us the very moment Navaryn regains consciousness," added Benson as he gestured toward the bedchamber door. "Shall we?"

Reluctantly, Lowenna obliged his request and led the way out of the room. Following a discreet glance at his son, Benson followed behind her furious gait.

Kumiko held his breath until their heavy footsteps soon echoed off into silence. Dizzy from the palpable tension and his racing heart, he finally released his tense breath. Lowenna clearly hadn't let go of her suspicions, and there was only so much Benson could do to stall an inevitable confrontation.

Through it all, considering the ominous fallout looming on the horizon, Kumiko managed to find a moment of reprieve inside the warm, candlelit room. It was quiet enough to hear Navaryn's deep and steady breath. His gentle smile faded as he realized how much time had passed since they had last shared a peaceful moment in her bedchamber together. No matter how far she strayed, he remained hopeful she would return to his side one way or another.

Kumiko tucked the lofty navy blue comforter around Navaryn, then removed his boots. His intention of settling into one of the tufted accent chairs across the room for the night had nullified once he beheld her sleeping face. While fighting away a swell of hesitation, he carefully climbed into the bed beside her. He settled into a pair of pillows close enough to detect the briny scent of ocean sand still stuck in her hair but far enough away to mind her personal space. With a light smile tugging his cheeks, he studied her with his lavender eyes until he finally drifted into slumber.

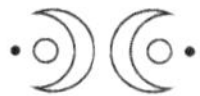

Breathing anxiously, Navaryn clomped atop a patterned runner carpet in her dirty boots. The gilded elements within the maroon corridor flashed as she passed under the waving candlelight of each chandelier. Though she tried her hardest to refrain, her eyes wandered back to the series of haunting paintings hanging on the walls. From treasured times with Von, Lowenna, and Claymar to bouts of training and battles in Opiri and Celestine, each painting depicted a memory from Navaryn's past, seen through her eyes. Brimming with tears, she continued down the damned corridor with no end in sight and no way to turn back. Behind her, a cloud of darkness kept a close pace and consumed all that she passed.

Navaryn's heart fell to her toes as the next painting came into view. Captured inside the ornate golden frame was Von lying shirtless on his back, in a moment of ecstasy. His lips, delicately parted, wore the glossy sheen of her passionate kiss, and his tense red eyes were rolled toward the headboard behind him. The very memory was etched within her mind so profoundly that looking upon it in such an outright fashion set her heart ablaze. Confused, distraught, and with no other choice but to press forward, Navaryn sprinted ahead unheedingly.

The corridor eventually ended at a remarkably ornate, dark wooden door. With the cloud of looming darkness twisting behind her, Navaryn wiped away her tears and steadied her breathing as she pushed it open. Amidst the scant candlelight, the gilded elements within the capacious room twinkled like gems inside a cave. She carefully scanned the room until she happened upon a curvy figure cloaked in elegant red and golden brocade standing by the far wall.

"Hello?" she called, but no answer came.

Navaryn turned back to the door and found a wall in its place. Apprehensively, she placed her fingertips where she remembered the doorjamb to be only moments before. As she motioned to approach her obscured, gilded companion, her gaze fell upon an immense painting hanging in the middle of the joining wall. One after another, the candles around the room caught fire.

With a racing heart, Navaryn muttered, *"What is this?"*

Standing arm in arm in garish, clinquant garb, Navaryn saw herself beside Kumiko as they gestured proudly to a Celestine crowd below. The false instance and her disturbing, unfamiliar expression, painted as if captured through a spectator's eyes, sent chills down her spine.

Navaryn turned away but found the very same toothy, prideful smile mocking her from within the other paintings hanging on the walls. Her face soured in disbelief as she skimmed over them. She was depicted prominently, boasting her pristine Celestine wings beside Benson and Kumiko, sitting tall above the Halryn council. Just as well, she found herself pictured beside Kumiko in a catalog of moments when they had started a family. Yet, not a single painting in the cursed room housed her beloved friends Lowenna and Claymar, her dearest Von, Aalrija, Fallon, or the number of others who held a special place in her heart.

Dizzy from a fit of rapid respiration, Navaryn struggled to maintain her composure. When her eyes fell back upon the painting of her pregnant belly, draped in fine silvery velvet and lace, she frantically ran toward the embellished figure. Through teary eyes, her vision quaked with a white blur, and she lost her balance under her clumsy feet.

"What is this place?!" shouted Navaryn as she gripped the shimmery train of the woman's dress.

The sound of Navaryn's incessant crying filled the silent room. Lost in her despair, she felt the fabric slip from her hands as the woman turned around, gently hushing her. Her eyes jolted open once the delicate coos caught her ear. Fearful for what she knew she would see, she slowly raised her face to the woman.

"Everything that surrounds you here in this room will now be set into motion," said the woman, placing her decorated hands upon Navaryn's cheeks. "For our imperator commands it."

The gentle voice and placid countenance, framed in a headdress of gemstones and twinkling gold, was undeniably her own.

Navaryn recoiled in disbelief. "Our *imperator*? Benson?"

She watched the sparkling ruby-painted lips of her doppelganger curl into a smile. "Look around you. Your imperator is no longer Benson."

The ominous statement immediately coaxed heavy tears to her eyes. "I want nothing to do with anything here!" she roared with flashing white eyes. "This is not my life!"

Navaryn's decorated doppelganger gestured toward a multitude of paintings that suddenly materialized from the shadows. Following a light chuckle, she replied, "You've never had a choice in the matter. It's a shame you didn't realize it sooner."

One by one, the paintings morphed perspective, appearing as though they were moments Navaryn had experienced firsthand, like the ones that hung in the corridor.

"What's happening?!" Navaryn shouted, then jumped to her feet.

One haunting image in the distance immediately grabbed her attention. While she approached the painting in disbelief, her doppelganger strolled to the far wall, placed her hand against a door concealed by darkness, then saw herself out of the room without another word.

Navaryn rubbed away the blurry pools of tears from her eyes, only to be thwarted by more. The feverish memory of Von's ecstasy, a moment so sacred to her heart, was replaced by Kumiko's frame, mimicking his exact position and expression. With her gut twisting tightly, Navaryn touched her fingertips to the painting.

"No, no, *no!*" she frantically repeated, denouncing the instance until her mind could take no more. Roaring wildly, she ripped the painting off the wall. With glowing white eyes, she peered into the empty room and called, "Where are you?! Let me out of here!"

Amidst Navaryn's rage, the scent of smoking candlewick caught her nose, though she paid it little mind. She tore everything within her arm's reach from the walls in search of a way out. While she continued to thrash about in the darkening room, the unrelenting twirling void that chased her down the corridor reappeared, stretching out from the far corners of the room. Unable to call forth her Celestine wings writhing beneath her shoulder blades, and with nowhere to run, she threw what she could at the twisting, smoky apparition, attempting to ward it off. As the looming cloud dove around her body like a falling wave, she unleashed a final shriek that fell silent as the darkness claimed both her body and mind.

28

THE DELUSION

Clamoring blackbirds sailed past Navaryn's bedchamber window through the warm, early morning sun. Kumiko felt the light behind his eyes and slowly stirred awake. His blurry vision gradually focused on the opposite side of the bed, where he found only wrinkled blankets studded with sandy depressions. Confused, he jolted out of bed and quickly surveyed his surroundings.

Yet again, the presence of Tobias' thoughts and emotions conflicted with his own. Candelabras among carved alabaster decor adorned the walls, where he hoped to find the familiar scatterings of colorful posters and bookshelves. He ran to the window, expecting to see his motorcycle parked in the driveway below, but instead beheld a vast, verdant landscape before him. Though the air in Celestine smelled sweet, it was unrecognizable. Kumiko frantically paced the bedchamber as the door creaked open.

Navaryn slowly entered the room, tightening the sash to her olive-colored satin robe. When their eyes met, she paused momentarily with a vacant stare. Bound to the clutches of trepidation, Kumiko slowly raised an outstretched hand.

"I didn't mean to leave you behind," she said, resuming her pace. "I had something I needed to take care of."

He blinked his lavender eyes hard as she walked to him with a smile.

Following a gentle kiss, she asked, "Did you sleep well?"

From one moment to the next, Kumiko's consciousness resurfaced, yet he still felt as though he was trapped in a dream within a dream. The familiarity of his surroundings nestled back into his mind, yet he was no less shocked to have Navaryn's arms wrapped around him. He stood in disbelief as the fantasy that only existed in his dreams suddenly took hold in reality.

"Hey, what's wrong?" she said softly. "You seem a little tense."

"I-I'm fine," he bluffed. "Um. Where did you go?"

"Well, if you must know, I took a moment to reconfigure the sigils in the safe room."

Kumiko suspected she revoked the set of permissions that allowed passage for Von and Claymar.

"And," she continued as she headed for her closet, "I've relocated Iaalprt for safe measure. We should inform the Tiers that it's safe. I'm sure that'll lift some weight from their shoulders." She paused before setting an armful of garments atop the sandy bed and groaned, "Why is there all this sand in my bed?"

"Sorry about that. Bringing you back here right away was my call. I just wanted to get you home."

"Home ...." uttered Navaryn as her eyes trailed off to the wall behind him.

While Kumiko briefly summarized her entry back into Celestine, Navaryn searched her cloudy mind for the memories before her banishment. She hadn't considered Celestine much of a home for many years, but such a notion had been absolved, like every other thought and feeling that tarnished her rank. Navaryn focused back on Kumiko's lavender eyes. Due to the effects of the mysterious orb, the Halryn elite standing before her was someone she believed to be both her lover and equal.

Kumiko started to pull off the bedding and chimed, "Let me take care of it for you while you clean up."

With a smirk, Navaryn replied, "Why don't you join me instead?"

Kumiko stopped and slowly turned to Navaryn. "What?"

Navaryn shook her head as she slipped out of her robe. "What's the big deal? You're about as dirty as I am."

Kumiko averted his nervous eyes as Navaryn approached.

"Why are you acting so weird?"

"I'm not. I'm just, I thought—"

Navaryn took him by the chin and asked, "*What* did you think?" while she guided his eyes back to her.

"That, um, maybe you would want some privacy."

"You're acting as if you've never seen me naked before," she teased. "Come on. I'll start the shower."

While Navaryn walked into the bathroom, Kumiko rolled the bedding into a pile. His uneasy pulse thumped with a quickening rhythm behind his eyes. Though the closeness with Navaryn was precisely what he had yearned for, he found himself incredibly hesitant to embrace it. He paced the room to stall himself, then dropped the sandy linen off in the laundry room. After he had remade the bed and swept the floor of sand, he meandered into the bathroom while recalling Navaryn's earlier comment. Bathing together was not uncommon; they had become accustomed to it among friends as a relaxing pastime. However, such settings lacked intimacy.

While Kumiko disrobed, Navaryn admired his athletic physique from the other side of the steamy shower door. As he walked toward her, an opalescent glimmer quickly cascaded over her eyes. Curtaining black hair unexpectedly swayed over Kumiko's blurry outline. While she intently observed the phenomenon, he slowly slid the shower door open. The mirage simply vanished once she beheld him in the flesh.

It wasn't often that Kumiko caught Navaryn amidst such an intimate moment of awe, aside from the view of Hirunae in the sky. He waved away the plumes of steam and stepped inside the spacious shower just as Navaryn dashed her eyes away from his waistline. While she fumbled through the jars standing inside the tile nooks for the lavender and chamomile hair soap, Kumiko couldn't help but chuckle.

"What?" she asked after turning a discreet eye to him.

"I thought you said it would be no big deal if we showered together," he teased as he plucked a moistened loofa from the tree rack beside one of the shower heads.

"It isn't a big deal."

Kumiko's smile grew. "Fine then. Care to pass me some soap?"

Navaryn set the jar of hair soap on an empty nook, then quickly plopped a gooey mass atop her head. "Oops. I'm busy now, so you'll have to get it yourself."

Kumiko smirked while Navaryn quickly worked the soap into a luxurious foam with a prominent counterfeit pout. They continued to stare each other down until they lost themselves to laughter. He promptly lunged for her and took her by the waist before she moved out of arm's reach.

"Don't you do it!" she playfully shouted as he brought her beneath the center waterfall shower head.

"It doesn't look like you're busy anymore," he teased as the luxurious lather ran down her skin and swirled around her feet.

The velvety suds made Navaryn's skin slick, and she effortlessly slipped away. "What's that, Kumiko? The water's too *cold?*" she jeered. "I'll fix that for you."

"No, Nav. *No!*" he clamored as she fiddled with the temperature handles. "Ugh, you are the *worst!*"

Navaryn nearly buckled over when she saw the awkward pose Kumiko held to avoid the various streams of steaming water. "Okay, okay. I'll turn it down," she said after she collected herself. "But now you have to wash my hair."

"Seriously, I'll do anything you want. Just please turn it down before my skin starts to peel."

Smiling, she returned the temperature to something barely tolerable for both of them, then handed him the jar of soap. She hummed an offbeat tune while Kumiko worked a velvety lather through her hair from behind. His attentive fingers frisked her scalp free of sandy debris while he watched the foam slide down her skin.

"One more pass and I think we should be good," said Kumiko as he guided her to one of the nearby shower heads. "I think there's just enough left, too."

"I'll have to bug Lowenna for more."

Kumiko inhaled a deep breath as he worked the silky soap into a lather once more. He paid silent thanks to the formula's relaxing scent, which he believed was why his mind remained at ease. But Navaryn challenged his theory when she turned around to face him. At a complete loss for words, Kumiko continued to stare into her sultry hazel eyes while he massaged her scalp. With her signature smirk in place, Navaryn pressed against his dusty pink chest, directing him toward the tile bench extension. After he took a seat, Navaryn climbed atop his lap.

"Nav, I don't think this is a—" he managed before she dove into his mouth.

Defenseless against her eagerness, Kumiko embraced her until guilt conquered his lovesick angst. He gently took her by the shoulders and slowly pulled away.

"What's wrong?"

Before he could reply with a half-baked answer, the bathroom door swung open.

"Nav!" Lowenna's frantic voice called. "Kumiko was supposed to tell me when you woke up." Intent on verifying Navaryn's condition, she slid the shower door open. "What the *fuck* is going on here?!"

"Thanks for knocking," hissed Navaryn.

"I don't have to! I never had to. I-I—"

"We'll be out in a minute," she groaned as she slumped over Kumiko's shoulder.

Lowenna's piercing eyes were arrowed straight at Kumiko, wordlessly demanding an answer for Navaryn's unprecedented behavior, yet all he could do was look at the shower floor.

"I'll be waiting for you downstairs, Nav," said Lowenna, then shook her head.

"I hope you've come to help with breakfast because I'm starving!" she shouted.

Navaryn waited for the sound of her dear friend's groan that arrived right on cue at the moment before she exited the bedchamber.

·)(·

Not more than ten minutes later, she and Kumiko met up with Lowenna in the barren kitchen. Dressed leisurely and patting her thick hair dry with a gold-tasseled towel, Navaryn inspected the space. Aside from an old jar of pickled onions and a desiccated garland of garlic bulbs, nothing was remotely edible.

"Looks like we're gonna have to literally dig up breakfast," uttered Navaryn.

"I did bring some bread and preserves in case you weren't feeling well," said Lowenna, then placed her satchel atop the counter. "If this will suffice."

"I wouldn't mind taking a look around the garden if that's okay. I haven't seen it in ages, it feels. Kinda nervous it will be nothing but weeds."

"You may find yourself surprised," said Kumiko with a wink.

Navaryn's dispirited eyes suddenly glimmered with excitement. She took him by the hand and dashed through the back door while Lowenna trailed behind with folded arms. Once her bare feet touched the first patch of clover, a gust of fresh aromatics energized her senses. She curiously scanned the immaculate plots and beds.

"Kumiko, this is amazing. Did you do this?"

"You know the only things I can grow well are potatoes and alliums," he chafed. "From what I understand, you have Aalrija to thank for this."

Navaryn ran to her plot of peas and nabbed a few tender pods for a quick snack as she surveyed the copious produce, most of it ready for harvest.

"Demelza obliged me with the same," confessed Lowenna in a tone more serious than intended. "I guess it was their way of showing us that they never gave up hope."

Navaryn's eyes teared as she walked to Lowenna for an embrace.

"It's all over, Nav," she said, though her affirmation was insincere.

After wiping the tears from her eyes, Navaryn smiled and asked, "Well, what should we eat?"

"I have an idea," voiced Lowenna with her index finger pointed skyward. "Why don't you dig up some potatoes and garlic while Kumiko and I grab fruit from the orchard?"

Kumiko jumped when Lowenna firmly patted his shoulder following her suggestion.

"But I just took a shower," she griped.

"Since when has that ever bothered you?" Lowenna replied as she grabbed a couple of wicker baskets that hung next to the wall of sleeping moonflowers. "We'll be right back, okay?"

Navaryn grumbled, "Fine," then snatched a nearby garden fork. "Can you grab some lemons and apples if they're ripe?"

As soon as Navaryn stepped behind the vigorous vines of cucumbers, Lowenna's counterfeit smile dissolved. "You've got a lot of explaining to do, Kumiko," she hissed, then pushed him ahead of her with a stiff arm. "Wait until we're in the orchards. I don't want to take the chance of Nav hearing us."

During the silent and uneasy trek, Kumiko failed to concoct a believable explanation. He knew he had the gall to continue his lie; however, he felt justified to play along with the charade. Navaryn, free from her wanderlust and recharged with Halryn pride, guaranteed Celestine a venerable future.

Once they cut into the cluster of almond trees, Lowenna spun Kumiko around, took him by the breast of his shirt, and then pinned him against a sturdy trunk.

"Hey, take it easy, Low—"

Her swift fist flew into his cheek, throwing his face sideways. "You *worm*. You're going to tell me what the fuck is going on right now! What did that orb do to Navaryn?!" As Kumiko opened his mouth to reply, she added, "You lie to me one more time, and it will be your last."

Lowenna had her ways of coaxing the truth from the many people she encountered. For some, merely the look in her piercing blue eyes was enough for them to buckle under pressure, and she knew Kumiko's vulnerabilities well enough. The conflict within him pulled at his urges to dismiss her prods, though the enticing decision to come clean tugged him in the other direction.

Kumiko shook off his daze and let out a tense breath. "As I told you, the orb was meant to extinguish the diablerie that bound Navaryn to the human girl." After a few silent moments, he added, "And to realign her mind."

"Realign her mind?" Lowenna cringed. "What are you saying? That you *brainwashed* her?!"

"I'm saying that now she's the Navaryn she's supposed to be. She's free from all of the deviances that jeopardized Celestine," Kumiko said snidely. "You'll come to understand this is for the greater good."

Lowenna released Kumiko's shirt and furiously paced while digging her fingers through her scalp. After his cold affirmation, she rolled her firm tongue around her mouth and pondered the looming possibility that a similar fate awaited her. "Are you even listening to yourself right now?! I-I can't believe you would ever take part in something so heinous! Whose idea was this?"

Kumiko avoided her eyes until she took him by his shirt again.

"*Whose was it, Kumiko?!*"

"Benson's."

"And you agreed to it? You agreed to betray the trust of your friends who have shed *blood*! For *you*! This makes you no better than Merisek!"

"He didn't give me much of a choice!" Kumiko barked. "Look, you don't know the kind of pressure my father puts on me, okay? You just wouldn't understand."

"Oh, believe me. I understand enough. And I suppose all that talk of Navaryn wanting to stay hidden away in that human girl was Benson in your ear, wasn't it?"

Kumiko fell silent, stewing in the possibility that he had fallen victim to his father's deceitful influence. Whether the theory was grounded or not, he didn't know what to believe.

"You and I, we're gonna fix this," Lowenna stressed.

"What's done is done, Lowenna. There's no undoing this."

"So help me, Kumiko. We are going to find a way to reverse this diablerie, or you're going to have a lot of trouble on your hands," she threatened with her finger pointed dead between his eyes. "Meet me at my castle after this delusional celebration tonight."

Desperate to break free of the tense situation, Kumiko conceded. "Fine. I'll meet you."

"Remember what I told you."

Thoroughly embarrassed and ashamed, Kumiko watched Lowenna disappear under the red flames of her Parallel. Her bold move signaled an unsanctioned venture to Daeva, one she would later have to explain to the Halryn Tiers, who monitored inter-realm transmissions. Though the fervent exchange with Lowenna left Kumiko shaken, he remained hopeful that the tension would soon settle, for he envisioned himself as the one to operate the second Alignment Orb that awaited her.

Kumiko returned to the kitchen with both baskets half-full of the fruit Navaryn had requested. When he set them atop the counter, she turned to him from the stove while he pressed his fingertips over the welt on his cheek.

"Are you okay?"

Kumiko nodded, then fibbed, "Just a renegade apple that fell from the tree while I was harvesting. Classic perfect timing."

Navaryn chuckled as she stirred the colorful diced potatoes, sizzling in the pan. "Where'd Lowenna go?"

"Something came up, and she had to take a rather precipitous leave."

"Was she called to duty? I could have sworn I felt her energy depart from the plane."

"I'm not sure. But she said she's looking forward to seeing us this evening."

Navaryn plucked a gem from the pan and tossed it into her mouth after a quick blow. "What's going on this evening?"

Kumiko took the basket of fruit to the sink to rinse everything off. "A gracious gesture from my father. A celebration for the safe return of both you and Lowenna."

"For us?" she whispered as her eyes lit with excitement. "This is such an honor."

Kumiko's awkward smile twitched after her statement. He knew very well that Navaryn dreaded formal gatherings, and he was ready to endure a list of outlandish ideas on how she could weasel her way out of attending the event. Having finally experienced such a cooperative response, as opposed to her typical bouts of groaning and complaining, he wasn't sure how to feel.

Having finished plating their fare, Navaryn and Kumiko situated themselves at the table with a carafe of hot, steeping tea. While she reveled in the soft, warm texture beneath the crispy exterior of the potatoes, Kumiko unknowingly stared blankly at his plate.

"What's on your mind?" said Navaryn as she swatted Kumiko's shoulder with the back of her hand. "For someone talking about a party, you don't look very excited."

"Tell me something, Nav," he began as he set his fork down. "What do you remember from being trapped in the realm of Human?"

"Do we have to talk about that right now?"

"Just tell me," he persisted. "Do you remember anything at all?"

"No. Nothing. Why are you asking me this?"

"It's just," he continued, "you were away for so long, and it took a while to find you. I can't help but wonder if you tried to stay hidden so that Merisek couldn't find Iaalprt."

Navaryn glanced at Kumiko as she poured tea into her cup over a layer of honey. "That sounds pretty extreme."

"But could it be true?"

The gentle steam from Navaryn's teacup wisped past her face. Just like earlier, Kumiko caught the opalescent glimmer in her eyes as she delved into thought. She slowly twirled her spoon around her tea to unsettle the honey, then took the cup into her hands.

"I cannot say for certain," she began. "The Order is everything. It is knowledge beyond knowledge. I respect it, just as it should be by all. Though, I fear it even more."

Kumiko grew uneasy by the sudden change in Navaryn's demeanor. She spoke softly yet with steady enunciation and a hardened tone.

"I will admit," she continued, "perhaps a part of me would have gone that far to protect the Order."

"And ... what part *is* that?"

"I haven't a name for it. I can only describe it as a seed within myself. One that sprouts my fervor, feeds my devotion, and opens my eyes to what is real."

"Nav?" Kumiko uttered to break her out of her thoughts, though she carried on uninterrupted.

"It is the center of all the things that I am hopelessly tied to, and to which I battle with constantly."

"Navaryn, can you hear me?"

"If sealing myself away meant I could ensure the lives of the people I love and care for, to preserve who they are, and what they built with their hearts as well as their own two hands, then I ask ... why *wouldn't* I do something like that?"

Ever so slowly, Navaryn raised her cup and let the velvety sweetness of the tea wash over her tongue. Then, just as she set her cup back onto the table, the cascade of the opalescent glimmer in her eyes dissipated. Her senses seemed to return to her, though Kumiko could only look on in confusion.

"Besides, what does any of that matter now, right?." Navaryn beamed. "After all, I'm back home now. With you."

Navaryn reached for Kumiko's hand and gripped it tightly. To him, feeling her warmth and the abrasive pads of her fingers against his skin was all he needed to make her real. Despite being left with no definitive answer to his burning question, he opted to abandon the senselessness of pressing any further.

"You're right," he said, cracking a grin. "None of that matters now."

The pair inhaled their breakfast in a matter of moments. After a few cups of tea and some of the bread and preserves Lowenna had left behind, Kumiko opted to rest in the sunroom. At the same time, Navaryn went upstairs to sift through her closet for an outfit suitable for the evening's festivities. Sprawled comfortably over his favorite piece of furniture, Kumiko studied the room with a cold towel pressed over his cheek. Much hadn't changed since the last time he visited, and he was rather amazed at the amount of care Aalrija showed the estate while Navaryn was gone. In a room notorious for dust and cloudy windows, even when Navaryn did the cleaning, everything therein was pristine and orderly.

Kumiko sipped on the glass of water he brought and indulged in a couple of sections of poetry from the obscure collection tucked inside one of the side tables. The blissful sensation radiating within his core coaxed his heavy eyes closed. As his steady, lulling breaths pulled him into the clutches of a fervid dream, the floorboards in the front of the room creaked. His hazy eyes shot to the doorway, where he discovered Navaryn dressed in panels of revealing lace and a black satin robe at her feet.

After clearing his throat, Kumiko scrambled to situate himself upright on the chaise. "Um, Nav," he muttered nervously. "What are you doing?"

The gentle smirk Navaryn wore as she sauntered over made Kumiko even more anxious. "Do you like it? I came across it when I was digging through my closet."

"It's, ah, very nice."

"I must have bought it years ago, then forgotten about it. It still had the maker's tag pinned to it. I'm surprised it still fits." She ran her fingers over the parts where her breasts spilled over the seams. "Well, mostly, I suppose."

Navaryn carefully climbed atop Kumiko's lap and then pulled off his simple earth-toned shirt. As she ran her fingertips down the scape of his tight chest, the rapid pulse behind his eyes returned even more feverish than before.

Shallow and anxious breaths left their open mouths as the space between their lustful visages closed. Once their lips met, the warm swell inside Kumiko's stomach surged through his limbs with such force that it made him nauseous. The taste of her mouth was just as sweet and addictive as he remembered. Hypnotized by the overwhelming febrile sensations he had waited so long to experience, he disregarded every nagging, prodding thought that beckoned his better judgment and followed her lead.

While Navaryn fed him her warm, delicate tongue, Kumiko firmly gripped her hips and pulled her close. The sudden, assertive motion made Navaryn disconnect with a wide-eyed gasp. Contentedly, she watched his hands journey the voluptuous curves of her firm bodyscape. He slipped underneath the panels of black lace and filled his palms with her soft breasts. As Navaryn's cheeks caught fire, a torrent of guilt ripped Kumiko away from his sensual desire.

Navaryn immediately recognized the strange shift in his energy. "What's wrong?" she asked as he pulled his hands away.

"I don't think I'm ready for this," confessed Kumiko. "Not yet."

It took Navaryn a moment to answer, "After all this time, I'm surprised to hear you say that."

"I-I'm sorry. I just—"

Navaryn put a finger to his lips and gently hushed him. "It's fine. I mean, it has to be, right?"

"This has nothing to do with you," he assured as she slipped to his side.

"Obviously," she said and poked the outline of his bloated cock tented beneath the crotch of his pants.

Kumiko yipped, "Geez, Nav," then snatched a small bead-fringed pillow at his side to hide himself with.

Navaryn rested her chin atop her fist, then scanned the other side of the room through frustrated eyes. "So, what now?" she muttered.

"I'm gonna go and check in with my, ah, Benson," fumbled Kumiko as he rose to his feet, holding the pillow to his crotch. He shook his head and took a moment to gather his thoughts. "My father. And, the Tiers. I'll inform them that Iaalprt is safe and return before sunset. Then we can get ready for the event together. How's that sound?"

"*Splendid*," Navaryn replied with a brush of sarcasm.

Kumiko sighed. Following a passionless kiss to Navaryn's cheek, he took his prompt leave.

With a devious grin, she shouted after him, "I'll be wanting my pillow back when you return!"

29

THE HOMECOMING

Benson's estate was bustling with esteemed guests who resided within the Halryn border. The elegantly dressed gathering conversed among themselves amid the drone of fine music and a lavish spread of refreshments, patiently awaiting the guests of honor. In desperate need of a break from the insufferable excitement, Lowenna and Aalrija stood with wine in hand on the outdoor staircase adjacent to the back room where Ciaran and the Tiers anticipated Kumiko and Navaryn's arrival. The weary pair looked ahead to the intermittent Parafalls that flashed ahead, hoping to spot Navaryn's approach within the crowd.

Lowenna sloshed the last sip of wine around in her glass, then slugged it back, hoping it would finally be enough to quell the frustration churning within her gut. Before they joined the others, she brought Aalrija up to speed on Navaryn's peculiar state and the role Benson and Kumiko had to play in it.

"This is *inconceivable*," said Aalrija. "How could this have possibly turned into an even worse mess than before?"

"I should have stopped him. I *knew* I should have."

"You mustn't blame yourself," urged Aalrija. "What of Von?"

"He knows. Suffice it to say, he's beyond furious."

"Does Navaryn hold *any* memory of him?"

"I don't know. She hasn't mentioned him at all."

"I must speak with Fallon about this. Ailbhis, too, seeing as we're going to need to utilize both of their expertise. We'll get this sorted out. Trust me," said Aalrija as she patted Lowenna's shoulder over her shimmery shawl.

"I hope so," said Lowenna with a tense exhale. "I just can't find the energy needed to play along with this anymore. I'm tired, Aalrija."

With a discouraged look, Aalrija smoothed down the glistening emerald fabric at her hips. "I am too, my child. But if I've managed to teach you anything over the years, it's not to give up. Especially when the greater good is at stake. But we have to be careful. Benson has eyes on me."

Though they were out of earshot, Lowenna refrained from expressing the better part of her grievances against Benson and Kumiko. She leaned against the stone baluster and puttered her lips.

"Get it all out of your system while you can," Aalrija uttered. "I think I see Navaryn ahead."

Lowenna's blue eyes widened as she gazed upon Navaryn in her favored gown. As expected, her ruby-hilted dagger was visible through the high slit on her thigh. Although Benson never allowed his guests to carry their weapons inside his estate, Navaryn's dagger was his only exception. The familiarity within her gait settled Lowenna's anxious heartbeat until the moment she clutched onto Kumiko's arm.

"I think I'm gonna be sick," blurted Lowenna with an incredibly jaded expression.

Aalrija put her fingertips to her chin and observed Navaryn's strange behavior. "It's just as you said. It reminds me of when their romance was young."

Lowenna shuddered, then affirmed, "It's more than that," as she recalled when she interrupted them in the shower.

Kumiko gestured toward the far end of the castle where the others were waiting, prompting Lowenna to straighten her posture.

"At this point, we must assume that Kumiko knows you've told me everything," said Aalrija. "Let's just try to get through the evening."

Lowenna's expression continued to unravel the closer the pair advanced. "I'm gonna need a whole lot of help with that."

Aalrija sighed, then handed Lowenna her wine glass, which she promptly guzzled. "You can do this," she encouraged.

Navaryn's cheerful chatter abruptly paused once her eyes fell upon her former caretaker. "Aalrija!" she cried, then dashed up the stairs to greet her while Kumiko stepped inside to inform the others of their arrival.

"My child," said Aalrija with a warm smile as they embraced each other. "I've missed your beautiful face dearly."

"I've missed you more," Navaryn whispered with teary eyes.

Lowenna slipped the two empty wine glasses onto the steps behind her, then took a moment to compose herself before descending behind Aalrija. Her uneasy expression fell flat when Navaryn's eyes fell upon her.

"You look great this evening," Navaryn said as she finally pulled away. "Both of you."

Aalrija took charge of the next round of playful banter until Benson's hearty voice interrupted them. "Could that be our guest of honor, I hear?" he sounded as he passed through the threshold with his son in tow. "What a pleasant sight to behold."

Navaryn descended the stairs and took a firm stand before him. "My Lord," she said with a bow.

Aalrija was quick to give Lowenna a firm nudge with her elbow in hopes it would prompt her to correct her twisted grimace.

"It is such a relief to have you and Lowenna back home safe," said Benson. "I am indebted to you for your sacrifice."

Demelza, Labraid, and Ailbhis split themselves around Navaryn to personally welcome her back, while Aalrija gestured to Lowenna that they join them.

"This evening means more to me than you will ever know," said Navaryn as she put her arm around the small of Kumiko's back.

The trio of Tiers was shocked by Navaryn's abnormal behavior, especially her apparent rekindled romance with Kumiko. They knew their relationship had ended several years earlier, but Benson had a plan to quell their reservations.

"Come. While Ciaran and the attendants work to corral the guests, let's take our places."

"Places? For what?" asked Navaryn curiously as she followed Benson's lead.

"Why, for our grand entry, of course," he replied.

Kumiko trotted close to her side, expecting her typical nervous rejection. "Don't worry. The speech will be short and straight to the point."

"Me? Worry? *Nonsense.*"

Lowenna rolled her eyes over to Aalrija, who was busy trying to listen to what her comrades were mumbling just ahead of her. "Ugh, is there any more wine in here?" she muttered.

Aalrija whispered, "Pace yourself, my child. You'll need to keep your wits about you if—" She stopped mid-sentence as Lowenna snatched a full glass someone left atop an ebony table. "Are you even listening to me? Put it down."

As Lowenna moved the glass to her lips, Aalrija tried to wrangle it away. One by one, the others in their party turned to their bickering.

"Is there a problem?" called Benson as Ciaran stepped into the room.

Lowenna successfully claimed the wine for herself while Aalrija reset her posture with a disappointed sigh.

"We're ready, sir," said Ciaran while trying to keep his green eyes from wandering. "The Halryn guards are lined up at the hall threshold, and musicians are awaiting their cue."

While Benson shook out his arms, trimmed in braids of gold, Lowenna took her place on the other side of Kumiko with her glass in hand. She peered at him as she sipped at the pungent crimson liquid. The warmth that grew in her belly made her face flush, but it wasn't enough to dampen the sensation of her fringed nerves. Benson then boastfully reminded everyone of their formation while Ciaran cued the band of musicians stationed beside the ballroom staircase to begin.

A sudden upbeat harmony of strings and percussion lit up the air as Ciaran took his place beside the first staggered group of guardsmen. Benson entered the dazzling, jovial ballroom with a proud visage, followed by Kumiko, then by his four seasoned Tiers. Once they split themselves evenly between the father and son pair, the guests of honor made their entrance. Lowenna messily gulped down what was left of her wine, then tossed the glass behind her.

"Are you okay?" whispered Navaryn, taking her by the hand.

After wiping away the drips of wine from her chin and neck, she replied, "Never better," and then walked into the dizzyingly bright ballroom.

Although the two guardians were met with acclamation from the crowd upon their entrance, not every attendee was thrilled to lay their eyes upon the esteemed guests Benson so cherished. Navaryn's known recklessness earned her a subpar reputation that superseded all her efforts to atone for her misdeeds. Many still blamed her for Daeva's devastating invasion that claimed the lives of thousands of Celestines, regardless of Benson's efforts that proved otherwise. Lowenna was more than receptive to the pressure from those in the audience who were displeased with their grandstand reveal. For such an occasion supposedly marked for celebration, Lowenna felt that she was no more than a token to place upon display for the sake of mere optics and to embolden the doe-eyed congregation standing before them.

The sheer flounces of Lowenna's ethereal beige and teal gown trailed behind her as she kept a steady pace beside her comrade, who embraced the celebrity treatment. Navaryn walked tall and proud, waving at the guests with her thumb, index, and middle fingers pronged, a gesture identical to both Benson and Kumiko. The recognition of the symbolic cohesion sickened Lowenna, making it harder to ease her tense expression.

"Friends. Delegates. My esteemed colleagues. I welcome you all here tonight," announced Benson in a hearty voice as the young Tiers took their places beside him. "After nearly two seasons of boundless effort that will not go unrecognized, it is with a jubilant heart that I welcome back our Halryn guardians, Lowenna and *Navaryn*."

With cheeks flushed with embarrassment, Lowenna simply bowed modestly while Navaryn waved and blew kisses to the cheering crowd.

"Now that Celestine is whole again, we will rebuild and fortify our defenses. We shall become impervious! Never again will we suffer at the hands of Daeva's treacherous forces, nor any other threat that may be so bold as to loom on *our* horizon."

The crowd cheered as Benson gestured for Kumiko, who then took Navaryn by the hand.

"Together with my son, and a partnership reforged, these three will carve the path for our future. A toast!" Once the attendants delivered flutes of bubbling gold to the Tiers, he continued, "To a brighter future. For all of Celestine."

As the collective repeated the exultant utterance with their glasses held high, Ciaran signaled the musicians to step away from their formal tune and return to their earlier, pleasant ambiance. For better or worse, Benson's grandiose speech, coupled with the promising display of Kumiko and Navaryn, managed to clear away the hints of dissent within the crowd.

"Now, let us enjoy every pleasure of this evening." Benson lifted his flute to his guests, then clinked the rim with his circle of Tiers.

Lowenna was the first to break away from the suffocating collective and paced straight for the banquet table. She slipped in for a plate and quickly piled it with slices of vegetables, cheese, and delicately stacked finger food that toppled over one another.

"Get a hold of yourself, Lowenna. You've had too much wine," griped Aalrija from the side. "I'd grab some bread or some of those potatoes if I were you."

With creased brows, she obliged by stealing a fistful of bread and crackers. "Happy?" she hissed as she dropped them on top of her plate as though she were garnishing an entrée with chives, then stormed away from the curious eyes surrounding her.

"Ecstatic," muttered Aalrija as she followed behind.

The rousing noise of insufferable mingling throughout the ballroom intensified, and Lowenna grew desperate for an escape. Before she could hide away in the secondary conversation room that was usually vacant, she was stopped mid-path by a jovial Navaryn.

"There you are!"

Caught off guard by her abrupt appearance, Lowenna jumped

backward and dropped some of the contents of her plate to the ground.

"I'm sorry. I didn't mean to—"

"Don't worry about it."

Navaryn sighed, then spoke with a grandiose smile, "Isn't this celebration remarkable? What a lovely gesture from Benson."

"Yeah. It sure is great," answered Lowenna passively as Kumiko paced over from behind. She kept her fierce blue eyes upon him as he handed Navaryn a glass of wine.

She thanked him with a kiss, which yet again caused Lowenna's face to contort. "Is that a crostini I spy under those carrots? May I?"

"Help yourself," she uttered and held the plate to her brainwashed comrade.

After Navaryn popped the herb-crusted treat into her mouth, she heard a familiar voice call to her.

"Well, well. Look who we have here."

"Fallon!" cheered Navaryn as she ran to him. "I'm so happy to see you!"

They tightly embraced each other as Aalrija walked up with a neatly stacked plate of dainty snacks. "If anyone has been waiting for this day, it's certainly this man here," she claimed as the collective chuckled cheerfully.

"I see you've found your dagger," observed Fallon. "I could only imagine how you must have felt without it."

Navaryn tilted her hip to better inspect the ruby-hilted dagger affixed to her thigh with lavender ribbon. "I can't recall anything from when I was gone. I guess I'm thankful for that, at least."

"Forget I even mentioned it," he replied earnestly with a wave of his hand.

As Fallon reveled in his long-awaited reunion with Navaryn, searching through the multitude of questions in his mind, his eyes caught the attention of Kumiko as he walked up behind her. The moment Navaryn took his hand with a gleaming smile, Fallon tilted his head in confusion.

"You okay, Fallon?" Navaryn innocently inquired with a slight giggle.

He discreetly turned to Aalrija, who responded with a firm look, though not nearly as severe as the one Lowenna wore. She could hardly breathe under the tension in her chest. While her party's conversation carried on, Lowenna's eyes grew distant. The crowd's indiscernible prattle, along with the musicians' upbeat melody, racketed inside her eardrums and slowly accumulated into jarring dissonance.

"I'll be right back," she groaned as she passed off her plate to Aalrija.

Lowenna trailed off toward one of the refreshment stations, where an attendant opened a row of wine bottles. Without a word, she casually swiped a freshly uncorked bottle and walked straight ahead for the side exit. She continued through the terrace and traipsed forth until the ambiance finally dissipated. As soon as she made her way to a clearing, she slugged straight from the bottle, unpinned her curly updo, then ditched her heeled shoes midway through a long patch of clover. Once she stepped onto the gravel walkway bordering Benson's neatly pruned hedge maze, the sound of familiar hushed voices stood her hair on end.

Von emerged from behind the maze entrance, equipped with his gauntlets and a fit of light armor.

"Von?" Lowenna hissed in disbelief. "What do you think you're doing here?!" Following her panicked question, Claymar stepped out from behind him. "Oh, no. Not *you*, too?!"

"Now, now. Calm down, my little Dragonfly," Claymar said gingerly with open arms. "I tried to get him to stay."

"Cut it, Claymar. It was your suggestion to come here," groaned Von as he folded his arms.

"I can't believe you both would be *this stupid* to venture here," Lowenna fumed. "Don't you realize who's here?"

"Yeah, everyone who wants our heads. What else is new?" Von uttered nonchalantly as he approached.

While Claymar ran his thick fingers through Lowenna's hot, damp locks, she looked ahead with a straight face, put the wine bottle to her lips, and began to guzzle. "*Whoa, whoa.* Take it easy there," he griped.

As they tussled over the wine bottle, Von firmly interjected, "That's *enough*," causing Claymar to cease vying for control. He then gently took Lowenna by the shoulders. "Take a moment to breathe."

The intensity and warmth in Von's voice helped calm her heartbeat. Reluctantly, she handed the wine bottle to Claymar, to which he then helped himself to a large gulp.

"Let's *please* get out of sight," she said, then led them around the far corner of the maze.

Under the gleaming moonlight, the trio stuck to the shadows as they rounded the tall hedges and halted at a discreet resting area. Lowenna sighed and plopped down onto a large stone bench. Von knelt to her level as she massaged her temples with her fingers.

"Von, why'd you come here? I told you both I would take care of this."

"I know that. But clearly, you're not handling things well. And I get it," he said bluntly. "I'm going to get Navaryn out of here."

"You can't be serious. All the Tiers are here, and both the Shahiri and the Meridians are standing guard. Taking them on would be suicide. Besides," Lowenna continued, "I'm sure Navaryn would fight you every step of the way. She's *not* herself."

Von peered toward the castle in frustration. "So what do you suggest then?"

"I'm meeting with Kumiko to talk about this later on."

The mere mention of the deceitful Celestine made Von clench his fists. "You can't possibly still trust him after what he pulled."

"Benson swayed him to do what he did. I have to make him see that."

"Don't give him any credit, Lowenna. He lied to you. He lied to all of us. I'm done believing *anything* that piece of shit has to say."

"Von, please," pleaded Lowenna as her voice began to crack.

"It's my fault for involving him in the first place. We'll find a way to help her. We *have* to."

Lowenna hoped Von's optimism and confidence would give her the fortitude she needed, but his understanding of the grave situation differed significantly from hers. She could no longer withhold the anguish that grew within her and broke down into a sob fit for grieving a loss.

"I just don't know if we can anymore, Von," she said with teary eyes. "When I felt her energy tonight—it's just not her. I can't explain it. She's just not the Navaryn we knew. She's someone else now."

Claymar sat next to Lowenna, pulling her in for a consoling embrace. The distraught sobbing he seldom heard from her left him unable to find a cheerful quip. "I think what we're dealing with here is more serious than we thought," he claimed. "Got any ideas?"

Von began to pace in thought. "I just need to see her. I have to try something. *Anything.*"

As an ominous breeze zipped past the three friends, a swell of upbeat music sounded from the ballroom. Lowenna dried her eyes and rubbed her arms to shake the shivers from her body.

"I need to get back before they come looking for me. We can discuss this later. Can you both please just get out of here?"

"Not without Nav," Von persisted.

"*Damn it!* I need to keep my cool in there, and I'm *this close* to losing it completely," confessed Lowenna with her thumb and index finger a hair away from touching. "Any more tension, and I'm likely to have the better part of my life pulled out from underneath me."

Before Von could angrily retort, his ears caught the sound of approaching footsteps trouncing on gravel. He engaged his gauntlets and looked to the rustling corner of the hedges in cautious anticipation, followed by Lowenna and Claymar, who did the same.

"Hey! I thought I might find you over here," called Navaryn as soon as she finished rounding the corner.

Her cheerful attitude quickly switched to one of indignation when she took notice of Lowenna's peculiar company. As beautifully adorned as she was, Von's heart sank with confusion as he beheld Navaryn in her showy gown and clinquant baubles. She stopped in her tracks and unsheathed her dagger.

"What's going on here, Lowenna?" she uttered sternly.

Drained, intoxicated, and unprepared to explain herself, Lowenna answered back while thrusting her hand in the air, "That's exactly what *we're* trying to figure out."

Navaryn scrunched her dolled-up face as she looked at her friend.

"What are you talking about?"

"Nav," began Lowenna as she rose to her feet, "you're not in your right mind."

"You've got some nerve saying that to me. Especially when I find *you* in the company of Daeva."

After taking another hearty swig from the wine bottle, Lowenna replied calmly, "Listen to me, Nav. Something has happened to you. You're not the same person I remember."

"And just who am I supposed to be, huh? A conspiring traitor like yourself?!"

Lowenna exhaled defeatedly as Navaryn's derisive comment cut the last thread of patience she had. "*I've had enough of this,*" she seethed as she closed her eyes.

"Easy now, Dragonfly," cooed Claymar from behind as she passed him the bottle of wine.

With conviction, Lowenna reached to her side and untied her diadem tethered to her gown. "I'll tell you who you're supposed to be. You're supposed to be Navaryn—my friend. My *sister!*" she yelled while affixing the diadem in place. "You've forgotten who you are and what *we* were. It's Benson and Kumiko who have blinded you from the truth."

"How could you even think that?!" Navaryn said confoundedly.

"Look, would you both just calm down before you draw attention?" called Von with hands that beckoned cooperation.

Navaryn glared at Von. "*You!*" she snapped as she pointed her dagger at him. "You and I have a score to settle."

He shook his head. "There is no score to settle. We've closed that chapter of our lives, and I refuse to believe that all of our memories together have vanished from your mind."

With a heavy heart, Von slowly closed the gap between them in a gentle stride. Navaryn's furious gaze softened as the moonlight revealed his brilliant red irises from the shadows as he approached.

"I mean no harm, Nav," affirmed Von as he reached behind his neck. "Please, let me just show something to you."

Von tugged at a silver chain, revealing the concealment medallion beneath his shirt. Without a moment's thought, he removed it from around his neck and slowly continued his approach.

"Uh, you sure you wanna take that off right now?" warned Claymar.

With an earnest gaze, Von held the medallion up for Navaryn to see. Almost immediately, she lowered her dagger while she curiously looked at the soft moonlit gleam reflecting off the engraved pattern.

"Take it," said Von as he carefully placed it into her unsteady hand. "You wore this. Back in Daeva, where we met. Tell me you remember."

Although the veil of darkness made it difficult to notice, the subtle opalescent glimmer flashed again over Navaryn's eyes. "It's been so long since I've seen this," she said as she thumbed over the textures. "How is it that *you* have it?"

"Fallon. He gave it to me."

Clutching to his sincerest of hopes, Von believed he had breached the diablerie that overshadowed Navaryn. Her wide eyes grew glassy, and she looked at him in the same wondrous way she looked at the full moon. With less than a few steps separating them, he reached for her hands, but quicker than his next breath left his lips, all familiarity within her mind-swept gaze vanished. She gripped her dagger and viciously slashed across Von's face in a blinding swipe.

"Thief!" Navaryn shouted. "You *stole* this from Fallon!"

"Stop it!" Lowenna chimed. "He *didn't* steal it! Fallon trusts him!"

"You're insane, Lowenna. He would do no such thing. This Daeva scum is playing you for a fool!"

"You're being lied to, Nav!" Von declared as he clutched the gash on his cheek. "We love each other! We pledged ourselves to one another!"

"Shut up! I've had enough of your blubbering!" she barked. "You're nothing but a disgusting monster! A murderous freak, unworthy of love!"

Blood streamed from Von's face onto the ground and hardened into a rigid slab of translucent stone. A pain like no other radiated through his body as Navaryn's scornful stare tore his heart wide open. Lowenna's proclamation from their earlier discussion began to ring true, as he could no longer sense the spirit of the woman he cherished so deeply. As her string of stinging insults drove their way into his core, he involuntarily succumbed to his urge to form a blade out of his palm.

"I will personally see to it that *all* of your kind are dead. Starting with you!" Navaryn shouted, then lunged forth with a tight grip on her dagger.

Von quickly stepped out of the blade's path, gripped his spire of blood, then promptly deflected her onslaught of offensive strikes. The furious outcries that Navaryn belted garnered the attention of the guests gathered upon the terrace. Claymar moved in and restrained Navaryn, but their tussle halted when she broke free and thrust her dagger through his forearm. With a tense grimace that conveyed apathy to Von's tragic circumstance, Lowenna found an opening to stand between them.

Navaryn barked, "Get out of my way, Lowenna, or else," while keeping her eyes on Von.

"Or else, what? You'll run me through?"

Glowering, Navaryn then focused on Lowenna as she encroached. "I said step aside!" she demanded.

The clamor of a distant, hysterical collective grew louder as the castle terrace filled with onlookers. From within the castle's inner corridors, the Halryn guard assembled. Lowenna unfurled the last of her inhibitions and engaged the diadem upon her brow. While Navaryn was momentarily distracted by the wave of guests spilling onto the terrace, Lowenna quickly advanced in her direction. She grappled against Navaryn's immense strength and deftly disarmed her. Just as Lowenna chucked the dagger, the Halryn guardsmen charged around the far corner of the castle.

"I'd hate to ruin this charming reunion, Von," muttered Claymar in a playful but nervous manner as he clutched his wound, "but, uh, I think it's in our best interest to get out of here. We've got *a lot* of eyes on us right now."

At the head of the charge was Kumiko, leading them into the courtyard towards the quartet.

"Oh, look, and here comes the prince now," Claymar scoffed as he rolled up the sleeves of his thick gray shirt. "If we ain't leaving, it might be time for this to get real ugly."

"Claymar, don't you dare!" shouted Lowenna.

In the midst of the fray, a wispy fog trailed into the maze from the distant trees and floated over the hedges. Von stood with a shaky grasp on his blade as the echo of Navaryn's words filled his ears with hopelessness. He felt himself sink into despair as he watched the Celestine guardians, who had once regarded each other as sisters, battle one another with fury in their eyes.

"Come on, Von. We'll figure this out later, alright? We're dead if we stay here," warned Claymar as a cavalcade of Halryn guardsmen shoved their way through the side doors.

Left with no other choice, Lowenna stunned Navaryn with a concussive blast and began to conjure energy into her arms. "Get out of here now!" she belted as violet crystalline discs formed over the palms of her hands. "I'll hold them off until you get outside the castle's barrier!"

Kumiko closed in ahead of the guards but hesitated when Von's eyes locked onto him and erupted into a deadly crimson glow.

"Let's *go*," urged Claymar. "Lowenna will Snare us herself if we don't get a move on!"

Through a break in his seething chagrin, Von finally regained his sense and conceded to his friend's directive. As the two set off toward the distant forest line, the approaching Halryn guardsmen clamored. Once in formation, they prepared to pelt them with a violent barrage of energy blasts.

"Everyone, stand down! Listen to me!" shouted Lowenna, though her request went unheeded.

She threw up her violet crystalline barrier and thwarted their assault of flashing energy blasts. As the flanking battalion from the far end of the courtyard continued to give chase, she encapsulated Von and Claymar inside a barrier dome. She sustained the protective shields until they Paralleled to safety. The crystalline energy dissipated, and a collective murmur rose among the guards as she shook the residual sensation from her hands.

As the guards moved to reconvene with the approaching Tiers,

Navaryn slowly regained her footing. She reclaimed the concealment medallion nestled in the grass by her feet and glared at Lowenna. "You know," she began as she carelessly wadded the article into her hand, "as impressive as all of that was, word of your treason will resonate throughout Celestine."

Unfazed by Navaryn's remark, Lowenna stood tall with a straight spine and an angered brow beneath the pulsing glow of her diadem.

"As the Tier that you still are, admit your wrongdoing here and now," Navaryn demanded, "and I will make you my only offer to defend you as well as I can."

"I decline. I stand by my actions."

"The council will reprimand you for what you did, and you will be branded as a traitor," Navaryn continued as she raised the medallion gripped in her hand. "The Daeva managed to trick you with this and turned us against each other."

Lowenna shook her head. "If you trust Fallon as much as you say, then ask him about the medallion yourself."

Navaryn's brows furrowed at the idea as she continued to inspect the intricate silvery medallion. "There's no need. This is clearly no more than a fake."

"What are you afraid of, Navaryn?" Lowenna asked sternly. "*The truth?*"

Suddenly, Kumiko approached from behind, though he could not gain the attention of either Navaryn or Lowenna as they stared intently at each other.

"Understand what it is that I see, Lowenna. You, hiding in the shadows, conspiring with two of Daeva's most dangerous criminals—"

"I love Claymar," Lowenna interrupted, bringing Navaryn to silence, "and that is all you need to understand. I love him, just as you loved Von. And *that* is the truth."

Lowenna's words regrettably failed to reach any semblance of her old friend. Only the fraudulent conveyance of betrayal was all that she could interpret in her mind. Without another thought, she threw the medallion deep into the hedge maze.

"So you *are* afraid," uttered Lowenna before she turned toward

Kumiko, holding his breath. "And as for you, you disgraceful, disgusting coward. You deserve nothing less than death for what you've done."

Lowenna arrowed her icy blue eyes through Kumiko as she waited impatiently for a retort that never came. Surrounded by the collective Halryn elite and distinguished guests, the last of her reserve fell apart. "Hear me now! All of you!" she shouted.

Determined to prevent Lowenna from further tarnishing her reputation, Aalrija wailed for her attention from behind the chain of soldiers. To her great disappointment, she ignored her cries.

"I will not tolerate the falsehoods brought to you all that you so willingly follow, for they only seek to fuel misguided hate and intolerance toward our neighboring realms! War has waged for far too long under such pretenses. It is time to do away with them and rethink our position amongst the stars!" The crowd's clamor of gasps and murmuring made Lowenna's heart flutter uneasily. She then pointed toward the castle terrace and continued, "This so-called leader of ours has stained Celestine and has bewitched Navaryn! And in the wake of this profound anomaly before you, I beg of you to join me and hold him accountable!"

With fiery eyes, Navaryn sauntered to Lowenna until they stood eye to eye. "I've had enough of this dissent!" she screamed. "You dare to lie to your people and defend the honor of a realm of foes who work to see us dead!"

"Why not work toward peace?!" Lowenna fired back. "There is something greater to consider beyond such meager squabbling. A truth which has eluded you all."

"Meager squabbling?! Is that what you have to say of the unspeakable acts of war waged upon our land!"

"Celestine is guilty of the same! If you would just listen—"

"To the words of a traitor?" interrupted Navaryn. "*Never.*"

Lowenna shook her head. Though she knew that Navaryn's demeanor was a farce, it was challenging to maintain composure. She spoke softly, "My only wish is to rid you of this bewitched existence bestowed upon you. To restore your mind so that you may remember what you held so dear. If that makes me a traitor, then so be it."

Navaryn sneered with condescension. "You're a disgrace. And undeserving to be a Celestine Tier."

Tears welled in Lowenna's eyes. Unable to detach herself from the perpetual frustration she had felt since she returned to Celestine, she threw her open palm across Navaryn's face. The crowd sucked back their breath in disbelief. In a state of shock, Navaryn rubbed away the superficial sting with a slack jaw while Lowenna turned and walked away. Anticipating that the incident would escalate, Kumiko took Navaryn by the wrist once she made the slightest movement to give chase.

"Just let her go," Kumiko urged.

"*What?! Why?!*"

He then focused on the guardsmen who readied themselves to pursue her just the same. "Do not engage her!" he demanded. "She is free to exit the barrier."

The confused guardsmen whispered amongst themselves as Navaryn turned with a perplexed look. "But, she must be detained! We can't just let her leave!"

"I'd prefer to address this properly in the morning. There's no need for further incident."

Regrettably, the members of the Hairyn council and the guardsmen regarded Lowenna's expressed discussions as nothing more than deranged rantings. Nevertheless, Kumiko opted to hinder the reveal of further details behind Navaryn's strange behavior by letting her leave. Avoiding the situation, so it seemed to Kumiko, was the best course of action to keep her from continuing to speak candidly amidst the gathering.

"This isn't right. Conspiring with Daeva is an egregious offense."

Kumiko pinched the bridge of his nose to quell the pressure behind his eyes. He wasn't keen to debate the formalities, given Navaryn's newfound Celestine pride, and he dreaded the possibility that she would continue to challenge his request. "I'm aware of that," he admitted, then gestured toward the crowd around him. "But given the current circumstances, it is safer to simply let her go. We will give her the opportunity to speak before the Tiers tomorrow."

Navaryn huffed. "And if she flees? You can't expect her to remain here after tonight."

"Then we will confer with the council." Kumiko looked at Navaryn's displeased face. "Look, I've already made up my mind. Forget about Lowenna, and let's see what we can salvage from this gathering. I need a drink."

Benson stood atop the terrace overlooking the courtyard, alongside Ciaran and Labraid. The trio stood in silence, patiently observing the conflict unfold before them. As Benson watched his son direct Navaryn back into the castle, he chuckled lightly and patted Labraid on the shoulder.

"Now, what did I tell you, my dear friend?" said Benson. "Now, she *can* be controlled. And she'll obey Kumiko's every word. Soon, we'll tear Daeva apart and recover the remainder of the Order."

Labraid slowly nodded his head with an arched brow. "I wouldn't have believed it if I hadn't seen it with my own eyes. I'm certainly impressed, but I must say this came at a hefty price. If we've lost Lowenna—"

"We have not lost her," he interrupted as he moved his sly, steely blue eyes to Labraid. "We'll hunt her down wherever she goes. It won't be long before she, too, is cleansed of wanderlust. Just you wait."

Benson promptly cleared his throat as the nearest group of confused and uneasy guests looked his way. In a typical prideful and boisterous fashion, he assured there was no reason for anyone to worry, falsified some vague theories behind Lowenna's outburst, and insisted the evening's festivities proceed as planned.

Labraid, the Tiers' Master Trainer, remained at the threshold of the terrace as both Benson and Ciaran marched back indoors. He affixed his potent, minty-gray eyes on Navaryn as she approached hand in hand with Kumiko. For many years, he had voiced his concerns to Benson about the instability of Navaryn's power and her rebellious nature toward authority. Benson's adamance and apathy toward her affliction nearly drove Labraid to relinquish his role when he was teaching her to control her white-eyed counterpart. With the potential monumental loss hovering over Benson, he chose to divulge enough of the devious solution to Labraid to appease him. Though Labraid recognized the implications of using the Alignment Orb, he was ultimately more concerned with the bigger picture. Having found a way to safely contain Navaryn's volatile counterpart assured far more than the ease in his occupation; it assured the safety of the realm of Celestine itself.

30

THE TRAVELER

Several bleak months passed since the dramatic events in the realm of Human and the return of Celestine's guardians. Although Merisek remained at large, the turmoil within the realm of Daeva had simmered as most of his former militant forces had been apprehended and brought to justice. Over time, much of the populace concluded that Merisek had died, though some had yet to accept it. Lowenna abandoned Celestine and joined Claymar to build a peaceful revolution within Daeva. Their efforts to usher in a new era of unity among the realms had caught the attention of the notable leaders of Western Daeva, who dared to welcome a Celestine into the fold. Although their combined voices had managed to reach the hearts and minds of many in the West, their scattered opposition throughout the realm remained unyielding. A long and hard-fought campaign lay ahead of them, yet they were committed to their ultimate goal.

Meanwhile, fervent hostility had surfaced in Celestine following Lowenna's departure. In a trial overseen by Navaryn, Benson unilaterally stripped Aalrija of her privileges and standing as punishment for her insubordination. The decision angered the Halyrn council, prompting Benson to declare the removal of any other dissenters from their positions as well. Ailbhis and Demelza, being the ever-faithful friends that they were, voluntarily relinquished their noble positions and accompanied Aalrija in exile. Although Benson's actions jarred the remainder of the council, they were too afraid to follow suit and abandon the security of his good graces.

Kumiko refrained from exposing Fallon's involvement in Aalrija's plan. His leverage over Fallon was enough to keep him in line with providing the Halryn army the support they demanded, affording him the opportunity to continue the work he inherently valued so dearly. As troubled as Fallon was by the shift in Navaryn's behavior, he aimed to remain in service to the Halryn so that he could stay close to her, even if it meant their close-knit relationship would continue in disillusionment.

Suspicions of Navaryn's unshakable militant behavior took root within the Halryn council and grew. Because of the unsettling shift in her personality, they once again questioned her standing among them. Navaryn's icy demeanor only deepened their concern and distrust until, one day, they made their voices heard. Mirroring Navaryn's coldness, Benson eventually dismantled the council and left authority solely to her and Kumiko. Labraid was appointed their Prime General and tasked with overseeing the Halryn army, which became a well-disciplined yet brutal force under his command. The seeds of a merciless rule were, therefore, sewn.

Through it all, Navaryn's affinity for Kumiko was unwavering and absolute. They officiated their union in accordance with Celestine's longstanding tradition, and grew into a powerful, unprecedented force within the realm. Benson relieved himself as imperator and operated as a figurehead, while Kumiko assumed primary rule over Celestine with Navaryn at his side. Although as disingenuous as Kumiko's affection for Navaryn was, the taste of his newfound power became overwhelmingly intoxicating. However, as time went on, he spiraled deeper into madness as the effects of Kaimaharaa took a stranglehold on his consciousness and fragmented his mind. In more ways than one, he no longer saw himself as the man he used to be.

Full-blown chaos and disarray in Celestine were narrowly avoided, yet the realm had become completely unrecognizable. If there had ever been a chance for Lowenna and Claymar to create a unifying force within Daeva, the prospect of finding peace with Celestine had become virtually impossible. A violent clash between the realms was more than an inevitability; it had become imminent.

Von, however, clung to his desperation to reach Navaryn and dissuade her from the apparent mysticism surrounding her mind. His efforts to contact Aalrija and Fallon often faltered, and his pleas were ultimately left unanswered. Regardless of how strong his yearning for resolve seemed, his rage managed to get the best of him with each treacherous, single-handed venture into Celestine. His repeated bouts with the Halryn guard led to many brutal encounters that yielded several bloodied and slain Meridians and Shahiri by his hand. In Navaryn's eyes, Von seemed tortured by his numerous failed intrusions, but such a notion held no bearing in her heart. Thus, she pressed the Halryn to pursue him further every time he was forced to retreat.

Given the dire state of affairs and the futility of his efforts, Von decided to withdraw from the chaos and isolate himself at a place where he always found comfort. Kael and his wife, Lavena, the couple who had raised him since he was a small boy, operated a sizable tavern in the foothills of Western Daeva. They lived simple and comfortable lives and did well to offer their services and care to travelers from all reaches of the realm. Von kept himself occupied by tending to the farmland and lush vineyards, though hardly a day went by that he didn't think back to the longest night of his life. He took each day at a time, yet the pain he bore from his severed bond with Navaryn, exacerbated by the feel of the tight scar on his cheek, was inescapable.

One morning, Von woke to Kael handing him a letter from Claymar. Although the weekly occurrence always went unreciprocated, Claymar nonetheless faithfully kept him apprised of his and Lowenna's whereabouts and accomplishments. And while his correspondence often contained his typical lighthearted quips, encouragements, and well-wishes, his latest one had brought the regrettable news of Navaryn's conception with Kumiko. From that moment forward, Von opted for complete solitude and asked that Kael destroy any further letters that arrived for him.

·)(·

The first warm night after a relentless winter came upon Daeva. After a productive day of harvesting winter crops and restocking the cellar with his house wine, Von rested himself at his usual seat at the bar with a fresh bottle and glass. The bouquet of dried pine wreaths studded with cloves hovered over the earthy aroma of simmering stew, which became one of Von's treasured comforts. Oddly enough, the scent reminded him of Onyx's shed skin that he burned while in Celestine. He thought fondly of the rambunctious reptile that gave him company and often wondered what, if anything, had become of him.

Von took some pleasure in eavesdropping on conversations throughout the tavern if they piqued his interest. However, since only a meager collective of destitute yet unsavory explorers occupied the tables, the evening proved to be a mostly quiet one. Nevertheless, the tavern was not without the occasional heated argument that often escalated to a drunken brawl, so Von kept at least one of his gauntlets equipped at all times should the need to subdue arise.

As he raised his glass to sip his wine, a man wearing a hooded cloak walked in through the doors. Von kept his attention on Kael, preparing a flight of brews, but listened to the man's lumbering footsteps grow closer until he situated himself on the barstool beside him. He sat quietly for a moment as he steadied his labored breathing, but then spoke up to order a drink once Lavena approached. His request was unavoidably distinctive: a double of whiskey garnished with a sprig of rosemary and a wedge of citrus. Upon hearing the gruff voice uttering the signature libation, Von realized who was sitting next to him.

"This feels a bit familiar, doesn't it?" said Merisek quietly.

Von felt his blood begin to rush. "What are you doing here?"

"Just stopping in for a drink. And to have a word with my old friend."

"You're in the wrong place for that." Refraining from making eye contact, Von engaged his gauntlet with a subtle movement.

"You needn't be alarmed, Von. I mean no harm in coming here. Please, let's talk."

Lavena returned with a tray in her hand, carrying Merisek's order. As she placed the glass in front of him, she flinched when she caught a glimpse of his deformed hand resting on the bar. She quickly returned to the kitchen after he paid and thanked her. While hesitant at first, Von turned toward Merisek with an unintentional glare. The hood of his cloak hid much of his face, yet it did little to conceal his progressive hideousness.

"It's my punishment, you see," Merisek uttered, referring to his horrific condition. "The price I pay for tinkering with that cursed poison."

Von felt a lump in his throat as he swallowed. Merisek had become utterly unrecognizable due to the degeneration of his body and facial features, which he had tried so earnestly to hide. However, the distinctive, albeit weakened, yellow glow in his eyes remained. The skin of his sunken face had grown grayer, and his blackened veins more pronounced.

"How are you faring, Von?"

"About as well as you'd expect. And you?"

"Much the same," Merisek replied.

"I don't suppose your little pet is here, hiding somewhere in the shadows like a coward."

"Joro? *Hmph.* I wouldn't know. He disappeared a while ago."

"Disappeared?"

"Yes. The rift between us grew far too great as our motivations deviated," said Merisek. "I awoke one morning to the sound of him destroying a section of the fortress where his quarters were. Blasted away a large section of the façade. He left behind everything he had and left no trace of where he went."

Von smirked. "Funny. At least I had the decency to tell you goodbye when I left."

"True." Merisek nodded with a slight grin. "Even his own mother and father grew frightened of him. I've since, shall I say, inherited them."

"Too bad. I'd hoped he'd be here so I could stick his head on a pig pole."

"Forget about him. The humiliation you put him through that night at the farm undoubtedly took him over."

An awkward silence followed as Von slowly sipped his wine. Merisek took note of the gauntlet on Von's hand, gently pulsing with energy as he gripped his glass. Tension was high, and his assurances were insufficient to quell Von's broiling hate. With every passing minute sitting idly in each other's presence, it became clear to Merisek that Von's cordiality was purely superficial.

"Look, Von. You may imagine I've had some time to reflect upon our last encounter months ago," Merisek continued. "I know it may not account for much right now, but I want you to know that I am sorry for everything that happened."

In a near instant, Von sprang out of his stool and snatched him by the throat. "Pathetic bastard! After everything you did to turn our lives upside-down, *now* you're sorry?!" he growled as he pulled him closer.

Merisek winced as he felt the pointed claws of Von's gauntlet begin to pierce his skin. The glow in his near-lifeless yellow eyes grew dim as he struggled for breath. "P-please, Von. If you kill me, then I c-cannot help y-you."

"Killing you is the only thing that can help me now!"

"And you'd be right in doing so. I deserve death. But first, I only ask that you hear what I have to say."

"I don't need to hear anything more from you! Claymar gave so much of himself to you, and you nearly tortured him to *death*. And because of you, Navaryn, the *only* thing that gave meaning to my life, is lost to me!"

Merisek widened his eyes and strained his voice through Von's grasp as he uttered, "What if I could give her back to you?"

Von's grimace relaxed slightly as Merisek's words resonated within his ears. He loosened his grip on his neck but stopped far short of releasing him. "What do you mean 'give her back'?"

"I know what happened to Navaryn. I understand the pain you are feeling. But you don't have to live with it. We have a chance, Von," Merisek continued through labored breath. "One final chance to set things right."

A few alerted patrons took up weapons as they watched the scene unfold, but halted once they heard Kael's heavy footsteps coming from the kitchen. He came into view wearing a soiled apron covered in red splotches and wielding a gnarled club. His visage alone was enough to make the patrons stand down and lower their weapons.

"What's going on, Von? Do we have a troublemaker here?" Kael boomed.

Von was unmoved by Kael's burly figure looming over him as he held Merisek's throat in his hand. All he could envision in the immediate moment was exacting cold-blooded vengeance by tearing Merisek's head from his body, but the last words from his mouth kept him from following through. He glared into the deep sadness in Merisek's weak eyes and saw the absolute shame and regret that filled them. For the very first time, he sensed an earnest, deathly fear in Merisek.

"It's nothing, Kael," Von replied, releasing Merisek.

"This doesn't look like nothing. Who is this, and what is he doing here?"

"Don't worry about it. Just a misunderstanding, is all."

Kael sighed, rested his club on his shoulder, and said, "Son, you should know I'm not buying that. Take this elsewhere if you plan on making a mess. Again."

Kael slowly ambled away after his stern warning. Tension between Von and Merisek calmed as they awkwardly reseated themselves and turned their attention back to their drinks. The patron's alarmed eyes remained on them, yet they cautiously refrained from eavesdropping.

"Interesting that no one recognized me. Not even Kael," uttered Merisek as he cleared his strained throat.

"Have you seen yourself lately?" Von quipped, to which Merisek responded simply with a disparaging look. "Alright then. You wanted me to listen, then get to talking before I cut you in half."

Merisek rose from his seat, then suggested, "Let's honor Kael's wish and go outside. What I have to tell you is of vital importance and requires complete discretion."

Von pensively remained seated while he watched Merisek hobble away from the bar with his drink.

"Please," he pleaded.

After Von slowly swallowed the wine nestled in his cheeks, he set his glass down, then took the half-empty bottle into his hand. Reluctantly, he started toward the tavern door behind Merisek. Prying eyes of the patrons looked their way as they passed the scattered tables. Von glanced over his shoulder and saw Kael and Lavena behind the bar, looking curious and somewhat concerned. Though he had made numerous unannounced departures from the tavern in the past, he made a point to give them a nod of confidence to ease their minds before closing the heavy wooden door behind himself.

Atop a small hill outside the tavern was a group of scattered, unoccupied wooden tables. A perimeter of torches coated the seating area in soft golden light. Together, they walked to the furthest table and took their seats across from each other.

"Get on with it," Von clamored, taking a swig from his bottle.

Merisek set his glass down and folded his shaky hands. "Someone close to me said to live out the rest of my life amidst all my failures. That has echoed incessantly in my ears ever since. I've caused so much disorder and upheaval in countless lives. I've lied. I've killed. I've betrayed—"

"This had better be going somewhere, Merisek," Von interjected, tapping the claw of his gauntlet on the table.

Merisek lowered his head. The glow in his eyes hardened as he continued, "I've become something I was never meant to be ... a monster. No better than my damned brother."

Von arrowed his gaze with rousing curiosity. "Brother? You have a brother?"

"Indeed, I do," Merisek affirmed. He looked up at Von with glassy eyes. "Benson."

Dumbfounded by the candid reveal, Von leaned forward. "You and Benson are *brothers*?! But how? You're a Daeva."

"We share a father, but have different mothers. His, born of Celestine. And mine of Daeva. Thus, I am only half."

Von's eyes widened. "Wait. Then, that'd make Kumiko—"

"My nephew. Yes," Merisek confirmed, swirling his glass of whiskey. "I believed I had an ally in him. But sadly, he's nonetheless become a distraught man. So afraid of becoming like his father, yet unaware of the ways he already has."

Von shook his head in disappointment, having been so dismissive of Kumiko's unmistakable motives, deftly played by the crude actions of the foremost echelon of Celestine. The revelation lent credence to the way Kumiko had conducted himself throughout their partnership.

"So. All this time, you've been in between worlds."

"*Hmph.* I wish it were that simple. The truth is this. What I am makes me neither Celestine nor Daeva. I'm known by some as a Chimera." Merisek paused to sip his drink, then proceeded, "Just as you are."

"Me? A Chimera?" Von sat in intensifying confusion. "I don't understand. Where are you getting this?"

"There is a truth that you can't remember, buried within the veiled memories in your mind. And Benson is behind all of it."

"What *truth?*"

Merisek fidgeted nervously. "One that I've kept from you, fearing it would undo you."

"Then tell me now," Von commanded. "If I am not a Daeva, then what am I?"

A slow breath crept into Merisek's chest with a yearning to divulge everything he knew, from the secret of his origin to the tumultuous nature of his past. Yet, despite his rediscovered humility and compassion, he begrudgingly refrained.

"*Why?*" Von asked frustratingly. "Even now, why can't you tell me *who I fucking am?!*"

"Because I'm afraid of what you will do. I know your tendencies, Von. And to have you bear the truth in this time, in this ... reality, I fear you will be doomed to live in it forever."

Von gnashed his teeth and then angrily rose from his seat. He began to pace with clenched fists, then shouted, "You're not making any sense! What *reality?!* And what does any of this have to do with Navaryn?!"

"Everything! She holds the key to setting things back to the way they should be."

Slowly, Von turned to Merisek and said, "You're talking about the Order."

"Yes. Precisely."

Von groaned in disgust. He opened his fist and slowly called his blood forth into his gauntlet. "Again, with those *stupid* books. That's *all* you're after. I should have known talking to you was a waste of time."

"What I am after is the same thing you want. You must listen—"

"You know *nothing* of what I want."

"You're wrong, Von." Merisek's voice started to break, working to conceal the excruciating pain radiating throughout his body. After taking a moment to regain his composure, he rose from the table, then declared, "I have nothing. I am alone. I belong nowhere. But I *accept* that I am to blame for everything that has happened—"

"Save it," Von interrupted. "Spouting off as though you're on your deathbed won't save you."

"I might as well be. I'm dying," Merisek confessed. "I cannot defend myself, even if I wanted to."

Von fell silent with indifference upon Merisek's morbid confession. Beyond the severe and apparent disfigurement of his features caused by the C-Poison, his body had undergone an even greater degeneration unseen to the plain eye.

"So what of my death, for it will only brighten Daeva's days. If you wish to kill me now, then get on with it ..."

A long, deathly sharp, sickled blade formed out of Von's palm. With his mind fixated on how simple it would be to slice through Merisek's frail neck, he then gripped it firmly and brought the point to his throat.

"... But know full and well that if you do, you will have destroyed every hope of saving Navaryn, as well as your friends. And you will remain in this existence for the little time you have left."

Merisek's pulse resonated through the sanguine blade resting against his neck. It was oddly calm, carrying with it the acceptance of responsibility and blame for everything he had done. Von sensed his unexpected peace and resolve coursing through his bloodspeak, and fought the urge to bestow mercy on a surrendered enemy.

"Calm yourself and lower your weapon, Von," Merisek pleaded. "I will explain how I can lead you back to Navaryn and give you the answers to *everything* you seek."

The fury coursing through Von's body reached an intoxicating height, but the enticement of Merisek's plea grew too great for him to dismiss. Reluctantly, with a calm breath, he softened his grip on the blade and dissolved it back into his hand. After they both retook their seats, Merisek then went on to illustrate a series of experiences, which he had kept to himself, that began before Joro's expulsion from the realm of Human.

One day, while in his study, Merisek felt a pull emanating from Ananael that compelled him to open it. Upon turning a few of its blank pages, the book revealed what could be described as endless nothingness, a void that brought visions of various pathways of time and space to his mind. He then realized he was viewing instances of the past, seemingly random at first, then more relevant to himself as they persisted. Frightened, he quickly closed the book to halt the flow of energy to his mind.

"These visions weren't simply happenstance. Ananael beckoned me, forced me, to look into that void and reflect upon the course of actions I have taken throughout my life. And it would not be satisfied until I saw everything it wanted to show me."

Months later, what began as a bizarre set of occurrences that defied explanation ultimately led to an incredible discovery. In a behavior similar to what Merisek had previously witnessed with Zin, Ananael began emitting orbs of gentle luminance from its binding, creating peculiar illusions on everything it touched. The specks of light then drifted toward him and poured into the Augo Mundus around his neck.

"I didn't understand what it had meant at first. But then I realized that Ananael, seemingly out of necessity, had entrusted me with the knowledge of a new power. One that I couldn't fathom until recently—the power to see, and *move through*, time itself."

Merisek explained to Von that such a feat revolved around the concept of Paralleling, which simply involved traveling distances through small rifts within the same dimensional space. However, the reach of Ananael's power was virtually limitless. Not only could its power transmit a being to another location, but to another point in time or into an alternate dimension if desired. Merisek then revealed his ludicrous yet ultimately straightforward plan. Using Ananael's power, he sought to send Von back to a time before the fateful day of Navaryn and Lowenna's banishment to the realm of Human. His mission, so to speak, would be to obtain Iaalprt and bring it directly to him. With his past self in full possession of the Order, Merisek would then, in theory, be in the position to fulfill his goal of altering the course of their existence and create a more fruitful and promising future.

"At first, I couldn't make sense of this connection with Ananael and thought I was imagining everything before me. But this is no delusion, Von. This is real power. A true promise of peace. And with it, a chance for you and Navaryn to be as you were once again."

Von listened as Merisek spoke with undeniable clarity and integrity, though his instincts urged him to doubt the sincerity in his words. "All this talk of Ananael *speaking* to you. And this idea of yours, about Navaryn. You seem to have put all this together quite conveniently. How do you expect me to buy any of it?"

Merisek's face sank as he sat back in his seat. "Because, frankly, there isn't much of a choice. I believe Ananael revealed this power to me because it is asking for help."

Von furrowed his brow slightly. "Help? With *what?*"

Merisek finished the last of his whisky, then slowly rose from his seat. "Come with me, and I'll show you."

The moons of Daeva hovering over the distant mountain range came into view as the wispy cloud cover gave way. As Von sat in thought, he turned his gaze toward a field of orchids adorning the mountainside, deep magenta and wondrously illuminated by moonlight as they entered their first bloom of spring. An unexplainable calling urged him to respect his instincts, yet also to be willing to see beyond them.

"Fine," Von replied, then gulped down the remaining wine in his bottle.

Gratified, Merisek led the way down the mountainside to move clear of the protective barrier preventing Paralleling close to the tavern.

Amidst the clear starlit sky, Von felt a soft crisp breeze as he ambled along the vibrant pathway behind Merisek. He glanced at the vineyard atop the hill and watched his workhorse stroll through the barren isles, nibbling on stray blades of grass poking out through the soil. The light smile that found his face was fleeting. Immediately after he fixed his eyes on Merisek's lumbering frame, he began to ruminate upon their dubious discussion at the tavern. Humoring Merisek by accompanying him seemed harmless enough, yet Von couldn't help but imagine what could change if Ananael truly had the power to transmit him back in time. And all it would cost was leaving behind the present state of his tattered life.

Once clear of the tavern's barrier, Von and Merisek halted at a sizable clearing beyond the pathway.

"Are you ready?" asked Merisek as he turned to Von.

"Where are we going?"

Merisek placed his hand on Von's shoulder. "Perhaps one of the last places you'd ever think to see again."

In a fiery red flash, Von and Merisek Paralleled away, then arrived at a cliffside overlooking the desolate lowlands of Daeva. The majestic peak of Mount Korviniah stood in the distance behind them, its towering summit still capped with snow. Von surveyed the arid region and quickly recognized it as part of his former training grounds, though it looked nothing like he remembered. The lowlands were typically known for their environmental hazards, ranging from extreme climate and unforgiving landscapes, though something far more terrifying had struck the area. He looked over the cliffside into a familiar-looking canyon and could hardly believe what he saw.

Since Von's last visit to the lowlands, the canyon had grown tenfold in depth and area. Riddled with perpetual tremoring, deep cracks spewing ribbons of sickly fire cut the lifeless ground below. Most disturbing was the massive crevice in the center of the canyon. Plumes of noxious, rust-colored fumes ascended from the swirling pit and into the clouds above. Not a speck of sky was visible through the thick, virulent smoke. Fraught with dread, Von stood stoically as the palpable essence of death surrounded him and recalled the toll that the lowlands had taken on his mind as a younger man.

"We've been here before. Do you remember?" asked Merisek.

"I've tried to forget, though it's far worse than I remember," Von replied, overcome with disbelief. "What's happening here?"

"I've discovered the true nature behind the lowlands," Merisek revealed in a concerned tone. "Daeva is dying, Von,"

"Dying?! What do you mean? What's causing this?"

"If I were to give it a name, I would call it a Spectral Blight. I've since located several other sites throughout Daeva, such as this," Merisek explained. "This has been an ongoing problem in Opiri for some time now, and I have no reason to doubt the same is happening in Celestine. To put it simply, death is bleeding out into our world. Into our dimension."

There was much for Merisek to theorize about the strange phenomenon slowly swallowing the land. Despite his research, expertise, and available tools, he could not arrive at a definitive explanation. The only clear determination was that Daeva and the surrounding realms would vanish into nothingness without intervention, only possible with the Order.

"How much time does Daeva have?" asked Von.

Merisek scrunched his eyebrows in thought. "Difficult to say. Judging by how much the land has deteriorated, I'd wager no more than five years. The situation in Opiri, however, is far worse."

The state of the lowlands was a sobering realization for Von, and the prospect of an imminent collapse of everything and everyone he knew gave the situation dire urgency. Beyond saving the realms from destruction, Merisek revealed more of what he envisioned by using the Order. His prospects included helping the realm of Opiri flourish into the peaceful utopia it once was, and bringing an end to the corrupt and tyrannical rule in Celestine. However, he stopped short of revealing his more personal motivations, rooted in his love for his departed Athelisa.

It was when the future of Daeva came up in discussion that Von interjected. While he acknowledged that the Order could correct many things, he argued against overstepping people's ambitions. In his eyes, the preservation of free will carried just as much gravity as salvation. He explained Claymar and Lowenna's vision to broker peace between Daeva and Celestine. Their will was something Von truly wanted to see carried out of their own accord, even though he neglected to share it with his dearest friend. He then made it clear that he would present Iaalprt to Merisek's past self on that condition, which he had surprisingly agreed to. Yet, before Merisek would proceed any further, there was one final pertinent point he felt compelled to reveal.

"You should know that this kind of power does not come without a toll. Sending you back in time will drain me of any energy I have left, and I will die. Ananael has made that clear to me," Merisek explained. "If my death is something that you still desire, then, in a way, you shall have it."

"You're really willing to die for this?"

"I'm dying as it is, remember?" Merisek replied nonchalantly. "The Order is all that matters now, and I am willing to trust that we can succeed in this."

Putting his confidence in Merisek for a second time wasn't something Von anticipated ever doing. However, he could no longer fool himself into believing his isolation could spare him from the effects of his shattered life. Hope alone wasn't enough to restore an inkling of what he held dear; it was time for action. Therefore, his decision came far more easily than he imagined.

·)(·

Ominously situated on the stone table in Merisek's study, flanked by taper candles, were Ananael and Zin. It was evident that Merisek revered the tomes as if they were holy relics. Von approached the lavish yet unsuspecting books as Merisek positioned himself at the opposite end of the table within his study.

"Be forewarned, Von. Ananael may show you things you might not want to see," said Merisek, slowly opening it to the tenth page.

Just as Merisek had cautioned, the blank paper morphed into

an open void. Confused, Von stared into the black nothingness until various images began to appear. Among them were moments he remembered well. He saw himself walking alongside Claymar through a seaside merchant town in Daeva, engaged in a sparring bout with Navaryn in Celestine, then tending to the stable animals at Kael and Lavena's tavern. However, there were some that puzzled him. Of those, he saw long stone corridors lined with torches, a frozen river amid a violent blizzard, and a sizable sea vessel at port wholly engulfed in flames.

"Do you see them?" Merisek asked. "The windows in time?"

"I see them. But ..."

"What is it?"

"This doesn't make any sense," Von continued. "In some of them, it's like I'm looking into my dreams."

"Your dreams?" said Merisek as he curiously stepped forward and peered into the book. Along the pages, the stream of equivocal images prompted a bygone recollection of Von's days as his pupil. "You're referring to your nightmares. You still have them?"

Von nodded. "I'd given up hope of ever being free of them."

At that moment, Merisek made a startling revelation. "This can only mean one thing," he began. "These dreams are, in fact, your memories."

Von's eyes widened. "My memories? You don't mean—"

"Yes, Von," Merisek affirmed. "The memories hidden away in your mind. The very pieces of your childhood that remain shielded from you. Ananael can *see* them."

Ananael's latest display of power left Von astonished. Ever since he was a boy, he had toiled with haunting nightmares that tormented him nearly every night. To his amazement, Ananael reflected those same nightmares within its pages. Images of his veiled past came into view, and he reached an even deeper realization with each one.

One of the most striking sequences matched a recurring nightmare of looming silhouettes of sickly people slowly approaching within a cold, dim room. The figures were tall and moved in a jarring, stumbling manner, their gazes fixed downward. They had encroached upon Von as he backed into a corner, close enough for him to see the whites of their eyes. Instead of ending abruptly, as it usually did in his dream, the sequence continued further. In an unexpected turn, the figures became stricken with fear and retreated to the far end of the room. It was an empowering moment for Von, one that revealed a potential trove of answers about his past awaiting him.

Merisek placed his hand on Von's shoulder, "I'm sorry I couldn't do more to unlock your memories so long ago. But with the Order, they can be restored. We can end your nightmares once and for all, and you will discover everything. Who you really are."

Von was ever more enticed by the path laid before him. There was no mistaking the link between his perpetual subconscious torture and his distant, obscured past. Discovering the meaning behind it all finally felt within reach. Their discussion sparked a yearning that he hadn't felt in a long time. It was the closest he had ever come to understanding the bewitchment that had befallen him as a boy, and for once, the memories of his early life felt more present than ever before.

With a newfound determination, Von turned to Merisek and urged, "Let's get started."

Merisek's glowing yellow eyes gleamed in the candlelight following a cathartic exhale. He repositioned himself alongside Von and stood facing Ananael in preparation for his final feat. "Now, place your focus on the time when you first saw Iaalprt. This is where you must go."

"I had access to Iaalprt just a matter of months ago. Why not send me back there?" asked Von.

"Unfortunately, it's not that simple," said Merisek. "Ever since you first saw Iaalprt, countless alternate timelines stem from that moment. Different dimensions, if you will. Essentially, they are all in flux, happening at the same time. The only way to ensure that you land in our dimension, and not fall into a limbo between timelines, is to send you to the point in time when you first saw Iaalprt with your own eyes. The very moment when the Order became true to you."

Von thought back to the memorable day and immediately saw it reflected in Ananael's pages. He beheld himself standing alongside Navaryn in the forests of Celestine, where they would meet covertly.

As he ruminated on his oath to Navaryn, his expression had changed.

"Is something the matter?" asked Merisek.

"What if I didn't have to steal Iaalprt? When I go back, I can just explain all of this to Navaryn."

"May I ask what gave you this idea?"

"I gave her my word that I'd protect Iaalprt. And the thought of betraying her trust is not sitting well with me."

"Von, remember why we are doing this," Merisek replied sincerely. "This goes far beyond simply protecting the Order. We aim to restore it and prevent the death of the realms."

"But if she understood the truth, and this so-called Spectral Blight, she could help us."

"And what if she then grows suspicious of you? What if she then refuses to help?" Merisek warned. "Consider the state of mind she will be in. She may relocate Iaalprt, then all hope would be lost. It's best not to complicate the matter."

"And considering your state of mind back then, there's no guarantee that your actions won't be hostile once the Order is in your hands."

Merisek acknowledged the validity of Von's point. The future of the alternate reality was not set, and it became clear that the task at hand would not be as straightforward as initially conceived. Many known and unknown factors needed to be carefully navigated to stay the course. Specific actions, and even words, could determine unanticipated outcomes, and a dangerous encounter with Merisek was still a likely possibility to consider.

"I cannot promise how welcoming I will be," he confessed. "But when you find me, open Ananael before me."

His proposal was puzzling initially, but Von quickly made sense of it. "I get it," he said. "You're thinking it may connect with you and show you what you need to see."

"Correct," Merisek replied. "With its trust, it will respond to the Augo Mundus. Then, and *only* then, should you bring Iaalprt to me."

Von understood the risk and agreed with Merisek's idea. Ensuring cooperation between them was crucial for their words to be believed and kept, and Ananael seemed to be the key in linking them across space and time.

"I truly commend your devotion to Navaryn, Von. I cannot stop you from involving her in this," said Merisek. "But before we can proceed, please tell me you understand why I came to you with this."

"I do understand," he replied. "I've seen for myself what's at stake. I've experienced what just one tome is capable of. It has chosen us to help restore it."

Merisek nodded and continued, "Navaryn and Lowenna know little of the Order other than to guard it. What these books mean for existence itself is far more than they could ever realize."

"Just let this be a fair warning. If you make me regret this decision in any way, I will not hesitate to take your head."

"I must trust that Ananael won't steer us wrong. If you won't believe in me, then believe in Ananael," said Merisek. "That being said, any betrayal on my part should not be tolerated. Kill me proudly if it comes to it."

As unexpected as it was, the unfazed manner of Merisek's response was precisely what Von needed to hear from him. Given his unique connection with Ananael, placing every confidence he had in it was not difficult. Von realized that, in his current position, offering the same kind of confidence was his only hope of being guided to the right path in time.

"Now," Merisek said calmly, "are you ready to do what's necessary?"

Von turned to Ananael on the table and looked at the image of Navaryn leaning against a tree in Celestine. There she stood with anticipation as she waited for Von to arrive so she could share the secret of the Order with him. He then concluded that, beyond bringing salvation to the realms, his longing to have her back, with the chance to save her from an abhorrent fate, was ultimately more than enough reason he needed to embark on this journey through time.

"I'm ready when you are," Von affirmed.

Merisek reached out and called forth Ananael's power. A silvery swirl of gentle, luminous vapor rose from the tome and encircled his arm. The energy emitted a warm, calming resonance as it danced delicately.

"So, what exactly will happen to me?" asked Von. "Will this be like a Parallel?"

"It's similar in concept, but it will differ greatly from a Parallel you are accustomed to. It will feel more like an awakening within yourself," Merisek explained. "In short, Ananael will transmit your present essence into your past self. Your body here will vanish from this physical plane, and you will begin a new existence within your former self."

"Seems simple enough," said Von nervously.

"As for myself, this room will become my tomb. But should you succeed on this journey, this reality will cease to exist, and all will be saved from this horrid fate. I, as will the realms, will forever be in your debt."

The mysterious energy weighed heavily on Merisek's frail arm as it grew in substance, but he managed to stabilize the conjuration well enough to bring it to completion. He then contentedly held a hypnotic, amorphous silvery mass ensconced in his palm. As a gesture of his most sincere goodwill, he extended his frail right hand.

"Take my hand, Von," said Merisek. "Leave this disastrous time behind and let it fade from existence."

Von glared at the inviting mass of energy in Merisek's hand, bewildered at the beauty of its tranquil vibrance. Within it, he saw an openness with every possibility he could conceive.

"Travel well, my friend. And remember, believe in Ananael."

Von slowly reached forward with his right hand. "Farewell, Merisek."

As their hands clasped together, the mass of opalescent currents shifted into vapor and slowly wrapped around Von. Suddenly, a vibrant cluster of energy bands emerged from Ananael's pages and tethered onto his body, tight like shackles he was powerless to break free from. Merisek tightened his grip as though the process would fail if interrupted. Von grew frantic as the mystical restraints intensified, though he directed his attention back to Merisek once he felt a tug on his arm.

"Do not fear. Let it take you," he uttered in a hushed tone.

Tighter and tighter, Merisek clutched his former apprentice's hand as he urged him to cease his struggling. His disembodied voice trailed through the mist, and his desperate grip conveyed a sentiment most profound.

"*Do not fear. Let it take you,*" Merisek repeated, creating an echo unto both himself and Von.

Von realized that what he spoke was a plea on his behalf to quell the growing fear of his deathly approach, which paled his own trepidation. He then placed his other hand, still encased within his gauntlet, upon Merisek's trembling limb. Ever so slightly, he felt his grip soften.

Time slowed to a crawl as Von and Merisek exchanged one final glimpse of each other. As gradually as the conjuration began, Von dematerialized into a flowing mist and was carried into the pages of Ananael. Merisek's weakened eyes followed the gentle flow of vapor as it disappeared into the void. Before long, the cloud vanished, and the tome closed itself upon the stone table.

Cold silence once again reclaimed the study. Merisek's body ceased trembling as he caught himself in his chair. At last, after what felt like a never-ending spell of agony that began with his experimentation with C-Poison, his body went numb. Unable to contract his muscles to hold his posture, he slipped from his chair and fell onto the stone floor. Alone in the dark and gazing at the ceiling as he lay on his back, he focused on the icy chill behind his head as it slowly faded. His final lingering thoughts were ones of tranquility and contentment. Having managed to taste a mere fraction of the Order's power and successfully wielding it to guide his former apprentice to the past, he had fulfilled his promise to himself in the end.

As much as Merisek had assured himself of the inevitable, no amount of preparation could ease the impending fate that awaited him. But it was his ever-faithful thoughts of Athelisa, coupled with Von's devotion to Navaryn, that fueled the core of fighting for what was right and just; to atone for the pain he instilled in such an existence filled with tragedy.

The candle flames floating in the dark atop the stone table were all Merisek could see from the floor. With every second that passed, his life force drifted further away. As he turned his head to the side, an immense flood of emotion overwhelmed him. Tears streamed down his face as he surrendered the restraint he had held within himself for so long. Among Von's textile remnants left behind, the fingers of his gauntlet remained wrapped around Merisek's hand. As he beheld his withered limb cradled within the gauntlet, he saw the fragile and unspoken bond he shared with Von. He sobbed gently with a longing so pure and distant, though he had hoped it would prove to be fruitful and indomitable on the other side. In a way, contradictory to what he had feared so greatly, he was not alone in death.

Merisek, lying in wait, strove to take solace in the candles' dwindling glow atop the table, for something more profound burned within the still flames. A glimpse of Athelisa's reaching hand came into view through a welcome illusion he hoped would manifest in another life. Her visage appeared with a gentle smile, capable of lending more comfort than candlelight ever could, and warmed his slowing heart. He parted his lips, compelled to finally confess what he lacked the courage to say before her passing. However, his light faded before the words came to surface.

EPILOGUE
THE WORD OF ANANAEL

It was a clear and frigid Friday afternoon, and Trish stood beside her glowing barbeque pit, waiting for Tobias and Rayshell to join her for an early dinner. Traditional winter holidays and New Year celebrations had come and gone, marking nearly two months since the Celestines broke free and departed their world. The incessant media coverage and other gossip that followed their emergence had waned, including Elizabeth's claim that Rayshell was brought home by an angel. Trish often pondered if it was Kumiko who had delivered her while neglecting to conceal his wings, but resolved to remain satisfied with the thought of it being nothing more than a perceived illusion.

Rayshell had no memory of the strange experiences they had shared, and Tobias appeared to have no ill effects from Kaimaharaa. Though it pained Trish to bear the burden alone, she knew it was for the best. Energetic flames danced atop the briquettes and stretched up like reaching hands. She embraced the pleasant warmth for a few silent moments, then finished tearing out the last stack of paper from the notebook in her arms. Aside from the final page, she tossed the sheets that chronicled her otherworldly experiences into the pit. Her gaze hardened as the ignited edges of paper curled into ash, then she took a moment to read over the last passage left by Lowenna.

Knowledge is powerful and can be equally dangerous
should it fall into the wrong hands.
Though it may seem scandalous,
some knowledge must be protected by secrecy.

Repercussions are not enough to deter misuse,
and the unsanctioned practice of secret knowledge
will undoubtedly lead to an irremediable disruption
throughout the realms.

This is something that took me many years to understand,
let alone accept, and now I am trusting you to make the right choice.

Ananael, or simply the 'secret knowledge,' is now yours to protect.

A momentary smile tightened Trish's cheeks as she reread the ominous note. Destroying the claims of Celestine, of Daeva, and the host of mystical abilities cataloged from Lowenna's memories was the only surefire way Trish felt she could safeguard the secret knowledge that came to her from beyond the stars. Just as she fed the note to the flame, the side gate scraped open.

"There you are!" clamored Rayshell while she pulled out the shopping bags crammed in her backpack. "We were knocking on the front door for, like, ever."

Trish turned with a smile as Tobias closed the gate behind them.

"And why do you insist on barbequing when it's practically snowing outside?" Rayshell asked playfully.

"Snowing?" Trish answered with her eyes asquint as she gestured to the clear, sunsetting sky. "It doesn't even snow here, stupid."

"It's so cold that it might as well be," griped Rayshell as she set the bags atop the outdoor table.

"There's never a bad time to barbeque."

Rayshell paused from taking the groceries out of the bags for a quick, playful stare-off.

"I'm gonna have to side with Trish on this one, Ray," chimed

Tobias with a grin. "Plus it's only, what, fifty-five?"

"You both are insane," hissed Rayshell as she pulled her black and silver scarf closer to her throat. "It's freezing."

"Well, stand next to the fire then. I got this," said Tobias as he took over emptying the various bags of vegetables, fruit, and chips.

Once Rayshell turned, a cold gust blew the billowing smoke into her face. She batted the pollutants away with a scowl, then barked, "Ugh, it stinks! What the hell are you burning out here, Trish? Your underwear?!"

Tobias and Trish doubled over in laughter.

Through her waning fit, Trish responded, "Just getting rid of a few old diaries I found," then set the grate back into place once the fire had calmed.

After a few fistfuls of potato chips, Rayshell finally forgot about the cold. Trish listened to her ramble on about a group of people that pissed her off at the grocery store, then her plans to visit Brian and his new girlfriend with Tobias. Her focus drifted away from the conversation, tuning out Rayshell's repeated recount of Jack and Laura's astronomical credit card bill the month prior, and their pledged abstinence from all meal delivery apps. Nibbling her clutch of grapes, Trish smiled and embraced the wholesome sensation that overcame her while she watched Rayshell's animated gestures. The fragments of their once-shattered lives had fallen back into their proper place. Liberated from any physical trace of her Celestine visitor yet still burdened by Ananael, Trish remained hopeful that time would chip away at her memories until they disappeared just the same, just as Lowenna would have wanted.